Hugh I

MW01674750

The Headship of Christ, and the Rights of the Christian People

SALZWASSER
VERLAG

Hugh Miller, Peter Bayne

The Headship of Christ, and the Rights of the Christian People

Reprint of the original, first published in 1865.

1st Edition 2022 | ISBN: 978-3-75259-014-2

Verlag (Publisher): Salzwasser Verlag GmbH, Zeilweg 44, 60439 Frankfurt, Deutschland
Vertretungsberechtigt (Authorized to represent): E. Roepke, Zeilweg 44, 60439 Frankfurt, Deutschland
Druck (Print): Books on Demand GmbH, In de Tarpen 42, 22848 Norderstedt, Deutschland

THE WITNESS PAPERS.

THE

HEADSHIP OF CHRIST,

AND THE

RIGHTS OF THE CHRISTIAN PEOPLE,

A COLLECTION OF

ESSAYS, HISTORICAL AND DESCRIPTIVE SKETCHES, AND PERSONAL PORTRAITURES.

WITH THE AUTHOR'S

Celebrated Letter to Lord Brougham.

BY

HUGH MILLER,

Edited, with a Preface,

BY PETER BAYNE, A.M.

BOSTON

1865.

ADVERTISEMENT

TO THE AMERICAN EDITION.

This volume, like the previous works of Hugh Miller, is issued by special arrangement with the author's family; while Mr. Bayne, the editor, in a note to his Preface to the English edition, presents in brief the historic facts that caused the division of the Scottish Church, and has thus rendered the entire discussion more intelligible to American readers, and at the same time developed the great importance of the principles involved.

Hitherto the author has been chiefly known for his writings on Geology, and in some other departments of secular literature, where he has won a distinguished name and achieved a prominent place among the lights of his age; in this work he is presented in a new character, as *the champion of the* Church in the exciting period of her history to which these articles refer. In this field of effort, no less than in those more quiet walks in which he delighted to range, he exhibits a fresh, vivid, and natural style, and that wonderful skill in description which Dr. Buckland said he would give his left hand to possess.

The celebrated letter to Lord Brougham, which first directed public attention to Mr. Miller as a powerful writer, and as the man best fitted to espouse and maintain the cause of the Church, will be found at the opening of the volume; and the papers, generally, prepared by Mr. Miller in this cause, which enlisted his warmest interest and engaged his best powers, are characterized by Mr. Bayne, in his Preface, as "noble in eloquence, keen in satire, powerful in invective, and masterly in argument."

Though written with primary reference to the Church of Scotland and the spiritual welfare of the Scottish people, the great principles advocated in the work lie at the foundation of all religious prosperity, while those against which it contends are inseparably associated with spiritual torpor and death; and the discussion is thus appropriate to all times and places.

The English edition of this work contains an Appendix on "the Cardross Case," embracing the address of Dr. Candlish before the Commission of the General Assembly in relation thereto. As the address is of considerable length, and its details of no special interest to American readers, instead of this Appendix will be found a brief outline of the more recent history of the controversy, including a statement of the Cardross case, and of the present aspect of the whole question.

The work will secure many readers on this side of the Atlantic, and add to the author's great popularity.

AMERICAN PUBLISHERS.

BOSTON, OCTOBER 1, 1863.

PREFACE.

To enter into the spirit of this book we must distinctly apprehend the conception formed by its author of the Presbyterian Church of Scotland.

Throughout her entire history the Scottish Church has been distinguished by two leading characteristics, seldom found in combination.

First: She has assumed a high and commanding ecclesiastical position, claiming a jurisdiction in spiritual concerns independent of and coördinate with the jurisdiction of the civil magistrate. She has declared Christ the Head of the Church, not in any abstract and inconsequential sense, but to the clear practical effect of having given his Church upon earth a code of law, — the Scriptures of the Old and New Testament, — and of empowering and requiring her to regulate her affairs by that code alone.

Secondly: She has been eminently a Church of the people. What she claimed, she claimed not as a hierarchy, not as a clerical corporation, but as a congregation of Christians. The minister had his place; the member had his place. The powers and rights of each were held equally from Christ the King.

By both these characteristics the Church of Scotland has been distinguished from the Church of England.

The southern Establishment was the work of kings and statesmen. The constitution of the Church grew gradually into shape and form as part of the civil constitution of the realm. Slight share in its construction was taken by divines; — no share at all by the people. It was Henry, it was Burleigh, it was Elizabeth, who were the nursing fathers and nursing mothers of the Church of England. Ecclesiastical personages aspired to nothing higher than being their recognized and rewarded functionaries. From their position as divines they derived no commanding or regulating authority. The mechanism of the Church of Rome occupied the land, and they complacently lent their aid while it was adapted to the circumstances of a civil popedom. The question of the original constitution of the Christian Church was not forced upon them by circumstances, and they were well content to evade it. The result was, that independent spiritual jurisdiction was conclusively withheld from the Church of England. The Act of Supremacy bound her to the state.

The part played by the people in the construction of the Church of England was still more insignificant than that played by divines. The Tudor sovereigns — able, energetic, imperious, proud by nature, proud in virtue of their prerogative — thought little of the feelings of the commonalty in promulgating their haughty decrees. The English — the most peaceable, long-suffering, and loyal of European nations — had not yet dreamed of asserting their dignity and rights against the majesty of monarchs. They did, indeed, at last awaken. When the sceptre was held by a race intellectually and morally inferior to the Tudors; when loyalty and reverence had been sapped by contempt; when nearly half a century of treacherous oppression had roused to irresistible fury the tremendous instincts of religion and natural justice, — the people of England showed themselves. The Puritans engaged in a struggle for two objects: civil liberty, and the reformation of religion. The civil constitution of England they vindicated in its ancient principles, and placed impregnably on its modern basis. But when the long and eventful conflict was at an end, the constitution of the Church of England remained essentially unchanged, and the Christian people were *not* recognized as one of its integral parts.

The history of Scotland presents an entirely different ecclesiastical prospect. The vehement and impetuous nation north of the Tweed embraced the Reformation with a decision and enthusiasm which brooked no half-measures. The Church of Rome was first of all overthrown from base to turret, and a platform found for a new construction. In rearing the new edifice, divines bore a chief, and statesmen a subordinate part. And these were divines who magnified their office! They had learned in the school of Calvin to see the glitter of earthly crowns pale in the light of the sanctuary, to exalt the Church as the city of God upon earth, to set small store by human authority against the voice which they believed they heard speaking direct from heaven. They invoked their Divine King to lay the foundation of His House. Ten centuries of prescription were less to them than one promise of Christ. They have been accused of narrowness, of fanaticism, of violence; but all the world has recognized them as men of intrepid courage, of iron will, of high devotion, who quailed not in the presence of kings. Knox, Melville, Henderson, were very different personages from those politic and temporizing prelates who showed a courtier-like subservience to Henry, or trembled lest Elizabeth should unfrock them. As churchmen, they would have no king but Christ. They practically vindicated the doctrine of Christ's Headship, by securing that no Act of Supremacy was inscribed in the statute-book of Scotland. And they had a nation at their back,—an earnestly, ardently believing nation,—"a nation," says Carlyle, "of heroes." The circumstances of their position were such that they could not, and their character and the doctrines of their Church were such that, under any circumstances, they assuredly would not have overlooked the people. The consent of the congregation—laid down by Calvin in the Institutes as an essential element in the appointment of ministers—was given effect to in the ecclesiastical constitution by means of the Call. And thus the Church of Scotland became known to history and to fame as having reconciled the seeming contradictions of an intensely ecclesiastical and a broadly popular character.

Under these auspices the General Assembly of the Kirk came into existence. Implicitly confided in by the people, and representing even the laity to a far larger extent than the Scottish Parliament, it exercised throughout the seventeenth century a commanding influence in all the affairs of the kingdom. The objects for which it contended were the same as those of the early English Puritans; but its victory was more complete than theirs. At the Revolution settlement, it appeared that both the civil and religious liberties of Scotland were vindicated. In the Treaty of Union, which speedily followed, the constitution of the Church of Scotland was carefully guarded. The Act of Supremacy was confined to the southern part of the island, and no provision was made for the introduction of patronage into Scotland. In possession of a spiritual independence never claimed by the sister Establishment, and with the rights of the Christian people intact, the Kirk of Knox and Melville, the Kirk of the Westminster Confession and the Solemn League and Covenant, — the old, indomitable Kirk of Scotland, — rested from her labors.

All this was to Hugh Miller a faith deliberately ratified by his intellect, and enshrined with dearest and most exalting associations in his heart of hearts. Patriotism and affectionate reverence — the feeling with which an Englishman regards the Long Parliament, and the feeling with which a Jew of old regarded the Temple on Mount Moriah — were combined in the emotions with which he contemplated his Church. To stand in spirit by the side of her great men; to follow her with compassionate or exulting sympathy from reverse to reverse, from triumph to triumph; to draw his breath deep in unutterable execration at thought of the apostate Lauderdale or the bloodhound Claverhouse; to know her for his country's Church, when her canopy was the mist of the hill, and the trampling of the troopers broke in upon the lifted psalm, as well and as proudly as when she bearded monarchs, and set her foot on the necks of her enemies, — this seemed involved in the fact of his being a Scotchman. That a fundamental principle of her constitution, such as the right of the Christian people to have no minister intruded upon them, after being preserved through the storms and treacheries of a century, should be set aside by a Patronage Act smuggled by Tories through the British Parliament in contravention of the Treaty of Union, was to him an absurd idea. He looked upon the Patronage Act as a galling fetter, which her creed and her history pledged the Church to cast off. He sympathized with the Seceders of the last century in their refusal to wear it. He assented to the petition against it sent up year by year to Parliament from the General Assembly, until Moderate ascendency culminated under Robertson, and the Church, for the first time in her history, winked at her own humiliation. In the evangelical minority of the eighteenth century, headed by Erskine, he recognized his beloved Church as cordially and as confidently as in the homeless hill-men who clung to Peden and to Cameron in the seventeenth. When that minority swelled into a majority, — when the ancestral principles of the Church of Scotland shone out once more broad and clear,— there was no man better fitted to understand the position of the Establishment — no man more ready to support and defend her — than Hugh Miller.

The struggle between the Church of Scotland and the civil authority, which ended in the Disruption, was inaugurated by the passing of the Veto Act by the Church. The conflict took shape and character throughout from that celebrated enactment. In daring to put into the hands of the people a veto on any minister presented to a charge, but not accepted by the congregation, the Church vindicated both her ancient and distinctive principles. She proclaimed that the rights of the Christian people were inalienably secured to them; and she asserted her power, in face of an existent act of Parliament, to give those rights effect. Non-intrusion and spiritual independence were thus linked together throughout the Ten Years' Conflict.

That Hugh Miller viewed the contest in this manner, we know from his own words. "The contendings of the Secession in the last century," he wrote, shortly before the Disruption, "involved mainly the Non-intrusion principle. The contendings of our Presbyterian fathers in the century previous involved mainly the great doctrine that Christ is the only Head of the Church, and that, in the things which pertain to his kingdom, she owns no other Lord but Him. And in our present struggle, *both these twin principles of strength are united.*"

The present volume consists of two celebrated pamphlets written by Hugh Miller in defence of the contending Church, and of a gleaning — a scanty and desultory gleaning — from his articles in the *Witness* newspaper on the Church question. These will assuredly convey no adequate idea of his part in the Disruption controversy. It was only here and there that an article could be selected. To have taken all that displayed high excellence, — all that were noble in eloquence, keen and brilliant in satire, powerful in invective, or masterly in argument, — would have been to fill many volumes. It is likely that articles which created a particularly wide and deep sensation at the time, and are still vividly remembered, will be missed. To revive the interest which made them effective, — to call from oblivion some speech, pamphlet, or party manœuvre, agitating all minds at the time, and now everlastingly forgotten, — was impossible. It has been carefully endeavored, also, to avoid inflicting pain upon any still alive who were engaged in the conflict, or upon the surviving relatives of those who have died. Controversy is controversy; and Hugh Miller fought for his Church with the earnestness and vehemence of his covenanting fathers at Marston Moor or Drumclog. But when the dust of the fight is laid, and its din is over, — when the grave has closed over so many of the combatants, — it would be useless, and it would be ungracious, to reawaken its animosities.

Of the influence exerted upon the public mind of Scotland by Hugh Miller's articles in the *Witness* on the Church question, there are thousands still living who can speak. A year or two before the Disruption, I passed a winter in a Highland manse. I was too young to form a distinct idea of the merits of the dispute. But there was a sound then in the air which I could not help hearing. It seems as if it were in my ears still. Never have I witnessed so steady, intense, enthralling an excitement. And I have no difficulty, even at this distance, in discriminating the name which rung loudest through the agitated land. It was that of Hugh Miller, — the people's friend, champion, hero. There are men, there are family circles, to whom certain of these articles will suggest pathetic recollections. A sentence, a word, will recall the olden time, with its hallowed, its tender, its stirring associations: the fireside of the manse, round which member after member of the family grew up; the garden, with its old fruit-trees and familiar walks; the broad, bright, placid landscape, stretching from the manse-door; the unadorned church close at hand, with the household graves around it; — and then the eye will see to read no more.

With all its defects, this volume will illustrate with some comprehensiveness the manner in which Hugh Miller took part in the Disruption Controversy. It will show to what a marvellous point of perfection he was equipped for the work he had to do: how familiar to him was the whole range of Scottish history, ecclesiastical and literary; how accurately he had appreciated Presbyterianism as an influence in all provinces of Scottish life; how perfectly he understood the relations of parties in the Church and kingdom of Scotland, at every stage of the national history. He is seen assailing patronage from every point, — exposing its unconstitutional introduction, its disgraceful history, its pernicious practical effects. The volume contains also his deliberate and emphatic testimony to the doctrine of the Headship of Christ. Though dead, he may still be heard speaking to the people of Scotland on that sacred and momentous theme. The following sentences, in which he described the impression made upon certain persons by attempts practically to insist upon the doctrine in question, read in the light of present occurrences and prevailing frames of mind, may seem almost prophetic:—"As a practical rule of conduct, that sets itself in opposition to secular interests, judicial interdicts, and the decisions of magistrates, they cannot and will not tolerate it. Their merely nominal belief in Christianity—held as so respectable and so praiseworthy at other times—always puts on, in such circumstances, its true character as simply no belief at all. Christ becomes to them a mere phantom King, unreal and invisible; and his kingly authority appears but as a mischievous and repulsive fiction, subversive of the principles of good government."

And are these questions of spiritual independence and of non-intrusion, after all, but lingering phantoms, paling gradually, and sure to pass away in the light of progress? Many think so,—many able, and not a few devout men. I think they err. That, in face of all the coercion which can possibly be brought to bear upon the subject, the genuine Presbyterians of Scotland will maintain both, need not be doubted. But may not England awake to a new interest in the rights of the Christian people, and in the independence of the Church? May not the liberal and thinking part of the community, scandalized and distressed by such scenes as have recently occurred in a London church, ask whether the just and rational remedy for such a state of things is not to give congregations a voice in choosing their own ministers? And may not those in the Church of England who hold most closely by the principles of the Puritans bethink themselves whether they have not unwisely lost sight of one doctrine professed by Cartwright in England, and by all the reformers in the northern part of the island, — the doctrine that Christ is King and Head of his Church, and that it is in the prince's province "to exercise no spiritual jurisdiction"?

It is hardly necessary to add a single word to the preceding, in order to render this volume intelligible to American readers. Stated in the simplest form, and apart from technical phraseology, the principles for which the Church of Scotland contended in the years preceding the Disruption of 1843 were these: — the right of congregations to choose their pastors, and the competence of a Church of Christ to manage her spiritual and distinctive concerns in her own courts. In 1834 the Church of Scotland decreed that the will of congregations should form an essential element in the settlement of pastors. In the same year Lord Kinnoul, patron of the parish of Auchterarder, in Perthshire, presented that living to Mr. Robert Young, preacher of the Gospel. The Call, or document signifying the assent of the congregation to the appointment of Mr. Young, was signed by three persons, only two of whom belonged to the parish. Dissatisfaction with the appointment was expressed by two hundred and eighty-seven out of three hundred and thirty, who, as being in full communion with the Church, were entitled to exercise the privilege. To install

Mr. Young, therefore, as minister of Auchterarder, would have been a clear case of *intrusion*, — exactly such a case as the Church had guarded against by her act of 1834. The Presbytery, in obedience to the law of the Church, refused to ordain him. Lord Kinnoul and Mr. Young had recourse to the Court of Session, to compel the Presbytery to proceed with the ordination. The court granted their request by a decision pronounced in 1838. The House of Lords confirmed this judgment in the following year. Between the decision of their Lordships and the occurrence of the Disruption no new principle emerged. A civil court had undertaken to force the Church of Scotland to ordain a minister, and to ordain him against the will of the people. Rather than submit, the Church cut her state moorings, and became free. To recount the incidents of the conflict would be neither interesting nor useful. For several years State and Church in Scotland were continually in collision. Many attempts at reconciliation were made. But to understand the position taken up by each we need only to understand the Auchterarder case.

PETER BAYNE.

LONDON, OCTOBER 2, 1863.

CONTENTS.

THE HEADSHIP OF CHRIST.

PAGE

Letter to Lord Brougham (June, 1839) 19

The Whiggism of the Old School (August, 1839) 40

The Literary Character of Knox (Mar. 4, 1840) 81

Dr. Thomas M'Crie (June, 1840) 93

The Debate on Missions (October, 1841) 144

THE RIGHTS OF THE CHRISTIAN PEOPLE.

The Two Parties in the Church of Scotland (Jan. 15, 1840) . 200

The Twin Presbyteries of Strathbogie (Feb. 5, 1840) . . 204

The Two Students (Feb. 8, 1840) 209

The Presentation to Daviot (Feb. 12, 1840) 215

The Communicants of the North Country (Feb. 22, 1840) . 220

Spiritual Independence the Distinctive Privilege of the Church of Scotland (March 7, 1840) 228

The "Grasping Ambition" of the Non-Intrusionists (Mar. 25, 1840) 230

Popular Estimate of the Two Parties (April 25, 1840) . . 235

The Earl of Aberdeen's Bill (May 9, 1840) 241

The Scotch People and the Presbyterian Church (May 20, 1840) 218

PAGE
Moderatism Popular, Where and Why (June 6, 1840) . . . 251
The Earl of Aberdeen v. the People of Scotland (June 17, 1840) 256
Debate in the Edinburgh Presbytery on Lord Aberdeen's Bill (July 4, 1840) 263
Revival in Alness (Sept. 2, 1840) 270
Conservatism on Revivals (Oct. 14, 1840) 279
The Outrage at Marnoch (Jan. 27, 1841) 285
Supplementary Notes of the Settlement at Marnoch (Feb. 3, 1841) 292
Sketches of the General Assembly of 1841 (May 21, 1841) . 298
Scottish Lawyers: their Two Classes (June 5, 1841) . . 335
The New Policy: Evangelical Moderates (Sept. 14, 1841) . 339
Moderatism: some of the Better Classes (Sept. 22, 1841) . 347
Prayer: the True and the Counterfeit (Dec. 29, 1841) . . 352
Mr. Isaac Taylor on the Independence of the Church (Jan. 1, 1842) 356
Defence Associations (Jan. 8, 1842) 359
Foreshadowings (February 2, 1842) 364
Translations into Fact (February, 1842) 368
The Two Conflicts (May 25, 1842) 391
Tendencies (December, 1842, to May, 1843) 402
Mr. Forsyth's "Remarks" (Jan. 14, 1843) 455
State-Carpentry (May 17, 1843) 465
The Disruption (May 20, 1843) 475
The Close (June 1, 1843) 482
Union and its Principles (June 10, 1843) 488

Appendix—An outline of the more recent history of the controversy, with a statement of the "Cardross Case."

THE

HEADSHIP OF CHRIST.

LETTER TO LORD BROUGHAM.

A VOLUME consisting of the principal contributions made by Hugh Miller to the literature of the Ten Years' Conflict cannot be more appropriately introduced than with the celebrated pamphlet in which he first stepped forward to take that lead in the lay and popular championship of the Church which he thenceforth continued to hold. Having, as he informs us in the "Schools and Schoolmasters," been deeply moved by the decision, adverse to the claims of the evangelical majority, delivered by the Court of Session in March, 1838, and by that of the House of Lords in 1839, he experienced an ardent aspiration to offer some aid to his Church in her hour of peril. The speech of Lord Brougham in the Upper House furnished the occasion required. "I tossed wakefully," says Mr. Miller, "throughout a long night, in which I formed my plan of taking up the purely popular side of the question; and in the morning I sat down to state my views to the people, in the form of a letter addressed to Lord Brougham." He was at the time occupied with the duties of a bank office, but in the fulness of his heart the words flowed apace: in about a week the composition was finished. Being transmitted to Edinburgh, and brought by Mr. Robert Paul under the notice of Dr. Candlish and other evangelical leaders, its immediate result was the appointment of Mr. Miller to the editorship of the then contemplated "Witness" newspaper. On being published, it ran rapidly through four editions, and was referred to in terms of high encomium by Mr. O'Connell on the one hand, and by Mr. Gladstone on the other. It is beyond doubt one of the most masterly performances of its illustrious author. The eloquence, at once impassioned in its earnestness and majestic in its calmness, and the comprehensiveness and clear depth, worthy of the statesman or the philosophic historian, by which it is characterized, impart to it an interest superior to all local or temporary circumstances. It is an essay, and one of high and permanent value, upon a question inextricably associated with what is noblest and most instructive in the history of Scotland. — Ed.

My Lord: —

I am a plain working man, in rather humble circumstances, a native of the north of Scotland, and a member of the Established Church. I am acquainted with no other language than the one in which I address your lordship; and the very limited knowledge which I possess has been won slowly and painfully from observation and reflection, with now and then the assistance of a stray volume, in the intervals of a laborious life. I am not too uninformed, however, to appreciate your lordship's extraordinary powers and acquirements; and as the cause of freedom is peculiarly the cause of the class to which I belong, and as my acquaintance with the evils of ignorance has been by much too close and too tangible to leave me indifferent to the blessings of education, I have been no careless or uninterested spectator of your lordship's public career. No, my lord, I have felt my heart swell as I pronounced the name of Henry Brougham.

With many thousands of my countrymen, I have waited in deep anxiety for your lordship's opinion on the Auchterarder case. Aware that what may seem clear as a matter of right may be yet exceedingly doubtful as a question of law, — aware, too, that your lordship had to decide in this matter, not as a legislator, but as a judge, — I was afraid that, though you yourself might be our friend, you might yet have to pronounce the law our enemy. And yet, the bare majority by which the case had been carried against us in the Court of Session, — the consideration, too, that the judges who had declared in our favor rank among the ablest lawyers and most accomplished men that our country has ever produced, — had inclined me to hope that the statute-book, as interpreted by your lordship, might not be found very decidedly against us. But of you yourself, my lord, I could entertain no doubt. You had exerted all your energies in sweeping away the Old Sarums and East Retfords of the constitution. Could I once harbor the suspicion that you had become tolerant of the Old Sarums and East Retfords of the Church? You had declared, whether wisely or otherwise, that men possessed of no property qualification, and as humble and as little taught as the individual who now addresses you, should be admitted, on the strength of their moral and intellectual qualities alone, to exercise a voice in the legislature of the country. Could I suppose for a moment that you deemed that portion of these very men which falls to the share of Scotland unfitted to exercise a voice in the election of a parish minister? or, rather, — for I understate the case, — that you held them unworthy of being emancipated from the thraldom of a degrading law, the remnant of a barbarous code, which conveys them over by thousands and miles square to the charge of patronage-courting clergymen, practically unacquainted with the religion they profess to teach? Surely the people of Scotland are not so changed but that they know at least as much of the doctrines of the New Testament as of the principles of civil government, and of the requisites of a gospel minister as of the qualifications of a member of Parliament!

You have decided against us, my lord. You have even

said that we had better rest contented with the existing statutes, as interpreted by your lordship, than involve ourselves in the dangers and difficulties of a new enactment. Nay, more wonderful still, all your sympathies on the occasion seem to have been reserved for the times and the memory of men who first imparted its practical efficiency to a law under which we and our fathers have groaned, and which we have ever regarded as not only subversive of our natural rights as men, but of our well-being as Christians. Highly as your lordship estimates our political wisdom, you have no opinion whatever of our religious taste and knowledge. Is it at all possible that you, my lord, a native of Scotland, and possessed of more general information than perhaps any other man living, can have yet to learn that we have thought long and deeply of our religion, whereas our political speculations began but yesterday; that our popular struggles have been struggles for the right of worshipping God according to the dictates of our conscience, and under the guidance of ministers of our own choice; and that, when anxiously employed in finding arguments by which rights so dear to us might be rationally defended, our discovery of the principles of civil liberty was merely a sort of chance-consequence of the search? Examine yourself, my lord. Is your mind free from all bias in this matter? Are you quite assured that your admiration of an illustrious relative, at a period when your judgment was comparatively uninformed, has not had the effect of rendering *his* opinions *your* prejudices? Principal Robertson was unquestionably a great man; but consider in what way: great as a leader, — not as a "father in the Church," — it is not to ministers such as the Principal that the excellent among my countrymen look up for spiritual guidance amid the temptations and difficulties of life, or for comfort at its close; great in literature, — not, like Timothy of old, great in his knowledge of the Scriptures, — aged men who sat under his ministry have assured me that, in hurrying over the New

Testament, he had missed the doctrine of the atonement; great as an author and a man of genius,—great in his enduring labors as a historian,—great in the sense in which Hume, and Gibbon, and Voltaire were great.[1] But who can regard the greatness of such men as a sufficient guarantee for the soundness of the opinions which they have held, or the justice or wisdom of the measures which they have recommended? The law of patronage is in no degree the less cruel or absurd from its having owed its reënactment to so great a statesman and so ingenious a writer as Bolingbroke; nor yet from its having received its full and practical efficiency from so masterly a historian and so thorough a judge of human affairs as Robertson; nor yet, my lord, from the new vigor which it has received from the decision of so profound a philosopher and so accomplished an orator as Brougham.

I am a plain, untaught man; but the opinions which I hold regarding the law of patronage are those entertained by the great bulk of my countrymen, and entitled on that account to some little respect. I shall state them as clearly and as simply as I can. You are doubtless acquainted with

1 Is the writer's estimate of Dr. Robertson's religious character too low? Take, then, the estimate of William Wilberforce—a name to which even the high eulogiums of Lord Brougham can add nothing. In the "Practical View," chapter VI., there occurs the following passage:

"It has also been a melancholy prognostic of the state to which we are progressive, that many of the most eminent *literati* of modern times have been professed unbelievers; and that others of them have discovered such lukewarmness in the cause of Christ as to treat with especial good-will, and attention, and respect, those men who, by their avowed publications, were openly assailing, or insidiously undermining, the very foundations of the Christian hope—considering themselves as more closely united to them by literature than severed from them by the widest religious differences. It is with pain that the author finds himself compelled to place so great a writer as Dr. Robertson in this class. But, to say nothing of his phlegmatic account of the Reformation (a subject which we should have thought likely to excite in any one who united the character of a Christian divine with that of a historian, some warmth of pious gratitude for the good providence of God),—to pass over, also, the ambiguity in which he leaves his readers as to his opinion of the authenticity of the Mosaic chronology, in his Disquisitions on the Trade of India,—his letters to Mr. Gibbon, lately published, cannot but excite emotions of regret and shame in every sincere Christian."—Page 304, fifth edition.

that beautiful little piece of antique simplicity, drawn up by Knox, on the election of elders and deacons. It forms an interesting record, by an eye-witness, of the earliest beginnings of reformation in Scotland. At first, pious individuals, "brought, through the wonderful grace of God, to a knowledge of the truth, began to exercise themselves by reading of the Scriptures secretly," and to call the members of their own households around them to join with them in prayer. In the next stage a few neighboring families of this character learned to assemble themselves together to pray and to exhort, sometimes under the cloud of night in houses, sometimes in lone and sequestered hollows in the fields. Their numbers gradually increased, and that diversity of talent so characteristic of the human family, and so nicely adapted to man's social nature, began to manifest itself in this first germ of the Reformed Church in Scotland. To assign to individuals among them by the general voice that place for which nature and the Holy Spirit had peculiarly fitted them, was but a giving of effect, through the agency of man, to the will of God, and essentially necessary for the maintenance of decency and good order. "And so began that small flock," says the reformer, "to put themselves in such order as if Christ Jesus had plainly triumphed in the midst of them by the power of the Evangel; and *they did elect* some to occupy the supreme place of exhortation and reading, and some to be elders and helpers to these for the oversight of the flock, and some to be deacons for the collection of alms to be distributed to the poor of their own body. And of this small beginning is that order that now God, of his mercy, hath given unto us publicly within this realm."

One stage more, and the history is complete. The devotions of the closet had passed into the family; the members of Christianized families had formed themselves into a church. But this process of germination and growth had not been confined to a single locality. The long winter was over; the vital principle was heaving under the clods of separate fields and widely distant valleys; the deep sleep of ages had been broken; the day-star had arisen; the Spirit of God had moved upon the face of the waters; many families had been enlightened — many churches had been formed. How was "the bond of unity" to be best preserved, and wise and equal laws established for the good of the whole? "Wisdom," saith the Saviour, "is justified of her children." The churches instructed their best and wisest to deliberate in council, — their learned and strong-minded, their tried and venerable men, whom they had chosen to be their guides and leaders, because God had chosen them first; and these met in assembly, each recognizing in each an equal and a brother, and in Christ the Head and Governor of the whole. The Scriptures were opened, that the "mind of God" might be known. They sought advice of the Reformed Churches abroad; conferred with princes and magistrates at home; enacted wise laws; drew up books of order and of discipline; framed Catechisms and Confessions of Faith. The God in whom they trusted breathed a spirit of wisdom into their counsels; and the inestimable blessings of a pure and scriptural religion were thus secured to our land. Is the picture faithfully drawn? Look at it, my lord. The Presbyterians of Scotland deem it a picture of their Church in her best estate; and believe that the one great object of her saints and martyrs in all their struggles with kings and patrons, priests and curates, leaders in the General Assembly and dragoons on the hill-side, has been to restore what of the original likeness had been lost, or to preserve what had been retained.

Now, with many thousands of my countrymen, I have been accustomed to ask, Where is the place which patronage occupies in this Church of the people and of Christ? I read in the First Book of Discipline (as drawn up by Knox and his brethren) that "no man should enter the ministry without a lawful vocation; and that a lawful vocation standeth in the *election of the people*, examination of the ministry, and admission by them both." I find in the Second Book, as sanctioned by our earlier Assemblies, and sworn to in our National Covenant, that as this liberty of election was observed and respected so long as the primitive Church maintained its purity, it should be also observed and respected by the Reformed Church of Scotland; and that neither by the king himself, nor by any inferior person, should ministers be intruded on congregations contrary to the will of the people. I find *patronage* mentioned in this Second Book for the first time, and mentioned only to be denounced as "an abuse flowing from the Pope and the corruption of the canon law," and as contrary to the liberty of election, the light of reformation, the word of God. Where is the flaw in our logic when we infer that the members of our Church constitute our Church, and that it is the part and right of these members in their collective capacity to elect their ministers? I, my lord, am an integral part of the Church of Scotland, and of such integral parts, and of nothing else, is the body of this Church composed; nor do we look to the high places of the earth when we address ourselves to its adorable Head. The Earl of Kinnoull is not the Church, nor any of the other patrons of Scotland. Why, then, are these men suffered to exercise, and that so exclusively, one of the Church's most sacred privileges? You tell us of "existing institutions, vested rights, positive interests." Do we not know that the slaveholders, who have so long and so stubbornly withstood your lordship's truly noble appeals in behalf of the African bondsmen, have been employing an exactly similar language for the last fifty years; and that the onward progress of man to the high place which God has willed him to occupy has been impeded at every step by "existing institutions, vested rights, positive interests"? My grandfather was a grown man at a period when the neighboring proprietor could have dragged him from his cottage, and hung him up on the gallows-hill of the barony. It is not yet a century since the colliers of our southern districts were serfs bound to the soil. The mischievous and intolerant law of patronage still presses its dead weight on our consciences. But what of all that, my lord? Is it not in accordance with the high destiny of the species that the fit and the right should triumph over the established?

It is impossible your lordship can hold, with men of a lower order, that there is any necessary connection between the law of patronage and our existence as an Establishment. The public money can only be legitimately employed in furthering the public good; and we recognize the improvement and conservation of the morals of the people as the sole condition on which our ministers receive the support of the state. Where is the inevitable connection between rights of patronage (which, as the law now exists, may be exercised by fools, debauchees, infidels) and principles such as these? Nay, what is there subversive of such principles in a Christian liberty of election as complete as that enjoyed of old by the first fathers of the Reformation, or exercised in the present day by our Protestant Dissenters? I may surely add, that what is good for the Dissenters in this matter cannot be very bad for us; that I can find none of the much-dreaded evils of popular election — the divisions, the heart-burnings, the endless lawsuits, the dominancy of the fanatical spirit — exemplified in them; and that there can surely be little to censure in a principle which could have secured to them the labors of such ministers as Baxter and Bunyan, Watts and Doddridge, Robert Hall, and Thomas M'Crie. Even you yourself, my lord, will hardly venture to assert that our Scottish patrons could have provided them with better or more useful clergymen than they have been enabled to choose for themselves.

But on these points we are not at issue with your lordship. You tell us, however, that we are protected against the abuses of patronage by the provision that patrons can present only qualified persons, — clergymen whose literature the Church has pronounced sufficient, and their morals not bad. And when, under the suspension of our higher privileges, we challenge for ourselves the *right of rejecting ministers thus selected without assigning our reasons*, you ungenerously insinuate that we are perhaps anxious to employ this liberty in the rejection of good men, too strict in morals, and too diligent in duty to please our vitiated tastes. "Have a care, my lord." You are a philosopher of the inductive school. Look well to your facts. Put our lives to the question. Ascertain whether we are immoral in the proportion in which we are zealous for this privilege; determine whether our clergymen are lax and time-serving in the degree in which they are popular; and see, I beseech your lordship, that the scrutiny be strict. We challenge, as our right, *liberty of rejection without statement of reasons.* What is there so absurd in this as to provoke ridicule? or what so unfair as to justify the imputation of sinister design? It is *positive*, not *negative*, character we expect in a clergyman. We are suspicious of the "*not proven;*" we are dissatisfied with even the "*not guilty:*" we look in him for qualities which we can love, powers which we can respect, graces which we can revere. It matters not that we should have no grounds on which to condemn: we are justified in our rejection if we cannot approve.

But we are aware, my lord, that there is a noiseless though powerful under-current of objection, which bears more heavily against us in this matter than all the thousand lesser tides that froth and bubble on the surface. We are opposed by the prejudices of a powerful party, who see an inevitable connection between the exercise of the popular voice and what I shall venture to define for them as *a fanaticism according to the standards of our Church.* We have but one Bible and one Confession of Faith in our Scottish Establishment; but we have two religions in it; and these, though they bear exactly the same name, and speak nearly the same language, are yet fundamentally and vitally different. They belong, in fact, to the two very opposite classes into which all religions naturally divide. The one is popular, and has ever contended for the infusion of the popular principle into the Church as a necessary element; the other is exclusive, and has as determinedly struggled against it. The Logans, Homes, Blairs, Robertsons, of the last age, may be regarded as constituting the fit representatives of the latter class. The other recognizes its master spirits — its beloved and much honored leaders — in our Thomsons and Chalmerses, our Knoxes and Melvilles, the fathers of the Secession, and the champions of the Covenant. The infusion of the popular principle, while it would mightily strengthen the one class, would assuredly diminish, if not altogether annihilate, the other; and while the thousands which form the one reckon on it as their friend, the hundreds which compose the other hate and oppose it as their enemy.

Now, there are important, though perhaps somewhat occult, principles couched in this circumstance, regarding which your lordship's opinion, as a philosopher, would be of great value, had you not already foreclosed the question in a very different character indeed. It will be found that all the false religions of past or of present times, which have abused the credulity or flattered the judgments of men, may be divided into two grand classes, — the natural and the artificial. The natural religions are wild and extravagant; and the enlightened reason, when unbiassed by the influence of early prejudice, rejects them as monstrous and profane. But they have unquestionably a strong hold on human nature, and exert a powerful control over its hopes and its fears. They are, like the oak or the chestnut, the slow growth of centuries; their first beginnings are lost in the uncertainty of the fabulous ages, and every addition they receive is fitted to the credulity of the popular mind ere it can assimilate itself to the mass. The grand cause of their popularity, however, seems to consist in the human character of their gods; for is it not according to the nature of man as a religious creature that he meet with an answering nature in Deity?

The artificial religions, on the other hand, are exclusively the work of the human reason, and the God with which they profess to acquaint us is a mere abstract idea, — an incomprehensible essence of goodness, power, and wisdom. The understanding cannot conceive of him except as a first great cause — as the mysterious source and originator of all things; and it is surely according to reason that he should be thus removed from that lower sphere of conception which even finite intelligences can occupy to the full. But in thus rendering him intangible to the understanding, he is rendered intangible to the affections also. Who ever loved an abstract idea, or what sympathy can exist between human minds and an intelligent essence infinitely diffused? And hence the cold and barren inefficiency of artificial religions. They want the vitality of life. They want the grand principle of *motive;* for they can lay no hold on those affections to which this prime mover in all human affairs can alone address itself. They may look well in a discourse or an essay; for, like all human inventions, they may be easily understood and plausibly defended; but they are totally unsuited to the nature and the wants of man.

Now, is it not according to reason and analogy that the true religion should be formed, if I may so express myself, on a popular principle? Is it not indispensable that the religion which God reveals should be suited to the human nature which God has made? Artificial religions, with all their minute rationalities, are not suited to it at all, and therefore take no hold on the popular mind; natural religions, with all their immense popularity, are not suited to improve it. It is Christianity alone which unites the popularity of the one class with the rationality and more than the purity of the other — that gives to Deity, as the man Christ Jesus, his strong hold on the human affections, and restores to him, in his abstract character as Father of all, the homage of the understanding.

Question the principle as you please, but look, I beseech you, to the fact. Who was that most popular of all preachers, whom the immense multitudes of Judea followed into waste and solitary places, and of whom it is so expressly told that the "common people heard him gladly"? And what the religion taught by the twelve unlettered men, whose labors revolutionized the morals of the world? Christianity, in its primitive integrity, is essentially a popular religion; and what we complain of in the Churchmen opposed to the popular voice is, that they have divested it of this vital principle. What God has done in the framing of it they undo in the preaching of it; they impart to it all the cold inefficacy of an artificial religion; they tell us well-nigh as much of the beauty of virtue as Plato could have done; of the incarnation or the atonement they tell us well-nigh as little, or tell as if they told it not; and what wonder if they should be left to exhibit their minute and feeble rationalities to bare walls and empty benches, and to dread in the popular principle the enemy which is eventually to cast them out of the Church? We are acquainted with our New Testaments, and demand that our ministers give that prominence and space to the peculiar doctrines of Christianity which we find assigned to them in the epistles of Paul and of Peter, of James and of John.

I have striven, my lord, to acquaint myself with the history of my Church. I have met with a few old books, and have found time to read them; and, as the histories of Knox, Calderwood, and Wodrow have been among the number, I do not find myself much at the mercy of any man on questions connected with our ecclesiastical institutions, or the spirit which animated them. Some of the institutions themselves are marked by the character of the age in which they were produced; for we must not forget that the principles of toleration are as much the discovery of a later time as those principles on which we construct our steam-engines. But the spirit which lived and breathed in them was essentially that "spirit with which Christ maketh his people free." Nay, the very intolerance of our Church was of a kind which delighted to arm its vassals with a power before which all tyranny, civil or ecclesiastical, must eventually be overthrown. It compelled them to quit the lower levels of our nature for the higher. It demanded of them that they should be no longer immoral or illiterate. It was the Reformed Church of Scotland that gave the first example of providing that the children of the *poor* should be educated at the expense of the state. Not Henry Brougham himself could have been more zealous in sending the schoolmaster abroad. But ignorance, superstition, immorality, above all, an intolerance of an entirely opposite character, jealous of the knowledge and indifferent to the good of its vassals, were by much too strong for it; and there were times when the Church could do little more than testify against the grinding tyranny which oppressed her, and to the truth and justice of her own principles; and not even this with impunity. I have perused, by the light of the evening fire, whole volumes filled with the death-testimonies of her martyrs. Point me out any one abuse, my lord, against which she has testified oftener or more strongly than that of patronage, or any one privilege for which she has contended with a more enduring zeal than that for which our General Assembly is contending at this day. Moulding her claims according to the form and pressure of the opposition from without, — casting them at one time into a positive, at another into a negative form, — asserting at one time *a free election*, at another a *non-intrusion principle*, — we find her, on this great question, perseveringly firm and invariably consistent; and we regard the abolition of patronage, and the recognition of the popular right, as entirely a consequence of that dominancy of just and generous principle which was in part a cause and in part an effect of the Revolution, as we do any of the other great liberties which the Revolution has secured to us; nor does the very opposite opinion expressed by your lordship weigh more with us in this matter than if it had proceeded from the puniest sophist that ever opposed himself to the spread of education or the emancipation of the slave.

Twenty-one years passed, during which the Church, in the undisputed possession of her hard-earned privileges, was slowly recovering from the state of weakness and exhaustion induced by her sufferings in the previous period. And well and wisely were these privileges employed. Differences inevitably occur wherever man enjoys the blessings of liberty, civil or ecclesiastical; but during these twenty-one years there were few heats or divisions, and no schisms, in the Scottish Church. Such, at least, is the view of the matter given us in that life of Wodrow affixed to the late edition of his history; and sure I am that it tenders its information in a better spirit than that of any of the acts of Parliament which disgraced the latter years of Queen Anne. But a time had arrived in which no privilege was to be respected for its justice, or spared for its popularity, and in which our governors were to pursue other and far different objects than the good of the people or the peace of the Church. The Union had sunk the Presbyterian representation of Scotland into a feeble and singularly inefficient minority. Toryism, in its worst form, acquired an overpowering ascendency in the councils of the nation; Bolingbroke engaged in his deep-laid conspiracy against the Protestant succession and our popular liberties; and the law of patronage was again established. But why established? On this important point your lordship's great historical knowledge seems to have deserted you at once; there was a total lapse of memory, and all that remained for your lordship, in the peculiar circumstances of the case, was just to take the law's own word for the goodness of the law's own character. Was it not sufficiently fortunate in its historians? Smollett, ere he composed his English History, had abandoned his whig principles; Burnet was an Episcopalian and a bishop; Sir Walter Scott a staunch tory, and full of the predilections and antipathies of his party. But all the three, my lord, were honest and honorable men. Smollett would have told your lordship of the peculiarly sinister spirit which animated the last Parliament of Anne; of feelings adverse to the cause of freedom which prevailed among the people when it was chosen; and that the act which reëstablished patronage was but one of a series, all bearing on an object which the honest Scotch member, who signified his willingness to acquiesce in one of these on condition that it should be designated by its right name, — *An Act for the Encouragement of Immorality and Jacobitism in Scotland*, — seems to have discovered. The worthy Bishop is still more decided. Instead of triumphing on the occasion, he solemnly assures us that the thing was done merely "to spite the Presbyterians, who from the beginning had set it up as a principle that parishes had, from warrants in Scripture, a right to choose their ministers," and "who saw, with great alarm, the success of a motion *made on design* to weaken and undermine their Establishment;" and the good Sir Walter, notwithstanding all his tory prejudices, is quite as candid. He tells us that Jacobitism prevailed in Scotland more among the upper than the lower classes; and that "the act which restored to patrons the right of presenting clergymen to vacant churches was designed to render the Churchmen more dependent on the aristocracy, and to separate them in some degree from their congregations, who could not be supposed to be equally attached to or influenced by a minister who held his living by the gift of a great man, as by one who was chosen by their own free voice." You see your lordship might have learned a little, even from writers such as these. Historical evidence is often of a vague and indeterminate character; there are disputed questions of fact which divide the probabilities in directions diametrically opposite; but on the question before us it is comparatively easy to decide. The law which reëstablished patronage in Scotland, which has rendered Christianity inefficient in well-nigh half her parishes, which has separated some of her better clergymen from her Church, and many of her better people from her clergymen — the law through which Robertson ruled in the General Assembly, and which Brougham has eulogized in the House of Lords, — that identical law formed, in its first enactment, no unessential portion of a deep and dangerous conspiracy against the liberties of our country.

There is, my lord, a statesman of the present day, quite as eminent as Bolingbroke, who is acting, it is said, a somewhat similar part. It is whispered that not only can he decide according to an unpopular and unjust law, which he secretly condemns, but that he can also praise it as good and wise, and stir up its friends (men of a much narrower range of vision than himself) to give it full force and efficacy; and all this with the direct view of destroying a venerable institution on which this law acts. Now, I cannot credit the insinuation, for I believe that the very able statesman alluded to is an honest man; but I think I can see how he *might act* such a part, and act it with very great effect. At no previous period were the popular energies so powerfully developed as in the present; at no former time was it so essentially necessary that institutions which desire to live should open themselves to the infusion of the popular principle. Shut them up in their old chrysalis state from this new atmosphere of life, and they inevitably perish. And these, my lord, are truths which I can more than see — I can also feel them. I am one of the people, full of the popular sympathies — it may be, of the popular prejudices. To no man do I yield in the love and respect which I bear to the Church of Scotland. I never signed the Confession of her Faith, but I do more — I believe it; and I deem her scheme of government at once the simplest and most practically beneficial that has been established since the time of the apostles. But it is the vital spirit, not the dead body, to which I am attached; it is to the free popular Church, established by our reformers, not to an unsubstantial form or an empty name, a mere creature of expediency and the state; and had she so far fallen below my estimate of her dignity and excellence as to have acquiesced in your lordship's decision, the leaf holds not more loosely by the tree when the October wind blows highest, than I would have held by a church so sunk and degraded. And these, my lord, are the feelings, not merely of a single individual, but of a class, which, though less learned, and, may be, less wise, than the classes above them, are beyond comparison more numerous, and promise, now that they are learning to think, to become immensely more powerful. Drive our better clergymen to extremities on this question, — let but three hundred of them throw up their livings, as the Puritans of England and the Presbyterians of our own country did in the times of Charles II., — and the Scottish Establishment inevitably falls. Your lordship is a sagacious and far-seeing man. How long, think you, would the English Establishment survive her humbler sister? and how long would the monarchy exist after the extinction of both?

You have entertained a too favorable opinion of the Scottish Church, and she has disappointed your expectations. Scotland is up in rebellion! The General Assembly refuse to settle Mr. Young. Take your seat, my lord, and try the members of this refractory court for their new and unheard-of offence. They believe "that the principle of non-intrusion is coeval with the existence of the Church, and forms an integral part of its constitution." Their consciences, too, are awakened on the subject; they see that forced settlements have done very little good, and a great deal of harm; and that intruded ministers have been the means of converting few souls to Christ, and have, it is feared, in a great many instances, been unconverted themselves. They have, besides, come to believe, with their fathers of old, that God himself is not indifferent in the matter, and are fearful lest "haply they should be found fighting against him." And in this assembly, my lord, there are wise and large-minded men — men admired for their genius, and revered for their piety, wherever the light of learning or religion has yet found its way. Now, a certain law of the country, which was passed rather more than a hundred and twenty years ago, through the influence of very bad men, and for a very bad purpose, has demanded that this assembly proceed forthwith to impose on a resisting people a singularly unpopular clergyman. And the assembly have refused; courteously and humbly, 't is true, but still most firmly. Give to this unpopular clergyman, they say, all the emoluments of the office. We lay no claim to these; we have no right to them whatever; nay, we hold even our own livings by sufferance, and you have the power to take them from us whenever you please. But we must not force this unpopular clergyman on the people: our consciences will not suffer us to do it; and as the laws which control our consciences cannot be altered, whereas those which govern the country are in a state of continual change, suffer us, we beseech you, to confer with the makers of those changing laws, that this bad law may be made so much better as to agree with the fixed law of our consciences. Now, such, my lord, is the heinous offence committed by these men. You could not believe they were so wicked; you could imagine the crime itself, but not in connection with them; you said it was indecorous, preposterous, monstrous, to believe that *they could* be so wicked. But you did ill to speak of Christ on the occasion. It is against Bolingbroke's law, not the law of Christ, that these men have offended.

Nay, my lord, you should have known the Church of Scotland better. Consult her history, and see whether she has not as determinedly opposed herself to wicked laws as to wicked men. The very act which first indicated her existence as a Church was her opposition to the law. And fearfully did she suffer for it. The law persecuted her children to death,—her Patrick Hamiltons, her George Wisharts, her Walter Mills,—and scattered their ashes to the winds. But there was a law to which she was not opposed—a fixed and immutable law; and God fought for her, and she waxed mighty in the midst of her great suffering; and at length, when her fierce and cruel persecutors had gone to their place, the unjust and intolerant law against which she had so long struggled in sorrow and great weakness was expunged from the statute-book. History tells me that, in all her after conflicts, it was not the Church that yielded to the law, but the law that yielded to the Church. Need I remind your lordship of her struggles in the days of Mary, of James, of Charles? Need I say that, subsequent to the Restoration, she opposed herself to the law for twenty-eight years together; and that the graves which lie solitary among our hills, and the tombs which occupy the malefactors' corner in our public burying-grounds, remain to testify of the heavy penalty which she paid? But the curse denounced against Cain of old fell on the unrighteous shedders of innocent blood: the descendants of our ancient monarchs became fugitive and vagabond on the face of the earth. The law to which our Church would not yield, yielded to her; and that better law which your lordship so pointedly condemns as unworthy of the Revolution, but which thousands among the wise and good of my countrymen, and many, many thousands of humble individuals like myself, have been accustomed to regard as so entirely in its purest spirit, was made to occupy their place. We do not think the worse of our Church, my lord, for her many contests with the law; not a whit the better of her opposers for their having had the law on their side. The public prosecutor in the time of Charles II. was perhaps as able a lawyer as even your lordship, but we have been accustomed to execrate his memory as "the bloody Mackenzie."

The Church has offended many of her noblest and wealthiest, it is said, and they are flying from her in crowds. Well, what matters it?—let the chaff fly! We care not though she shake off, in her wholesome exercise, some of the indolent humors which have hung about her so long. The vital principle will act with all the more vigor when they are gone. She may yet have to pour forth her life's blood through some incurable and deadly wound; for do we not know that though *the Church* be eternal, churches are born and die? But the blow will be dealt in a different quarrel, and on other and lower ground,—not when her ministers, for the sake of the spiritual, lessen their hold of the secular; not when, convinced of the justice of the old quarrel, they take up their position on the well-trodden battle-field of her saints and her martyrs; not when they stand side by side with her people, to contend for their common rights, in accordance with the dictates of their consciences, and agreeably to the law of their God. The reforming spirit is vigorous within her, and her hour is not yet come.

I am, my lord, with profound respect,
Your lordship's most humble,
Most obedient servant,

HUGH MILLER.

CROMARTY, JUNE, 1839.

WHIGGISM OF THE OLD SCHOOL, ETC.

"So filled was my mind with our ecclesiastical controversy, that, while yet unacquainted with the fate of my first *brochure*, I was busily engaged with a second." In these words Mr. Miller has sufficiently indicated the relation of the following Essay to that which precedes it. It is essentially a continuation of the same discussion; the question of patronage, in its historical, philosophical, and religious aspect, being probed in a manner equally searching, and perhaps more deliberate and comprehensive. The absence of a personal opponent may detract somewhat from the vivacity of the composition; but the place occupied by Lord Brougham on the previous occasion is here partially held by the President of the Court of Session. The opinion pronounced by his lordship against the claims of the Church in the Lethendy case had exposed him to the particular animadversion of Mr. Miller. — ED.

One of the most important views of the Christian religion, in its political effects, which I have anywhere met with, is to be found in Voltaire. It occurs in his "Age of Louis XIV.," in the chapter devoted to Calvinism, and serves admirably to show, that though infidelity owes much to a false philosophy, it has nothing to hope from the true. The historian tells us, after descanting, in his usual style, on "the furious zeal, unknown to paganism," which first gave rise to religious wars, that he had often endeavored to find out why the dogmatical spirit, so harmless in the schools of antiquity, should be productive of so many disorders among us. Fanaticism could not be the cause; men quite as fanatical as Christians did harm to none but themselves. The origin of this "new pest," he says, is rather to be found "in the *republican spirit* which animated the first churches. Those secret assemblies which, from their caves and recesses, braved the authority of the Roman emperors, formed by degrees a state within a state — a concealed republic within the empire." But after Constantine had drawn this stubborn religion from its retreat under ground, to place it on a level with the throne, there was a gradual softening of its character. Prosperity imparted a new nature to it. "The authority attached to the great sees ran counter to the popular spirit;" and in the end, so unlike itself did it become, that the powers which it had at first so determinedly opposed found in it eventually one of their surest and most efficient supports. But, in laying down its primitive character, it had also relinquished its *original opinions;* and no sooner, says the historian, were *these revived* by Luther, Zuinglius, and Calvin, than the ancient spirit also awoke. The identical principle which had opposed itself so determinedly to the tyranny of ancient Rome arose, from under the enormous mass which the guilt and superstition of ages had accumulated over it, to do battle with the despotisms of modern Europe. It opposed itself, though miserably oppressed and overborne, to the iron sway of Mary of England; took up arms in our own country against Mary of Guise; contended in France with the ghostly authority of kings and cardinals; and set limits in Germany to the encroachments of the emperors.

It may be remarked in the passing, however, that what Voltaire has termed the *republican spirit* of Christianity is by no means exclusively republican; for, though it has an inevitable tendency to limit the power of kings, it has none whatever to abrogate their office. On the contrary, the just restrictions which it imposes on their authority do not serve more as barriers to confine than as ramparts to protect them. And nothing, surely, can be more simple than the mode in which it acts, or more in accordance with the moral and intellectual dignity of man. Homer tells us that the day which makes man a slave robs him of half his worth: Christianity more than doubles it. He who becomes a Christian, becomes, of necessity, subject to an immutable and paramount code, to which every other code must be subordinate; his obedience to kings and magistrates becomes, in consequence, a conditional obedience — his prince a limited prince; he finds his subjection to every merely human law restricted by the simple but unanswerable argument of Peter and John; nor must his oath of allegiance interfere with the more sacred oath which, according to Pliny, binds him that he commit no evil. What are the persecutions, whether those of our own or of other countries, but just so many illustrations of this principle in its necessary attitude, — opposed alike to domination in the priest and to despotism in the ruler, — and of that deadly and exterminating hatred with which the antagonist principles, tyranny, bigotry, and the secular spirit, have ever regarded it? The entire history of the Church is corroborative of the view so unwittingly given us by Voltaire; and in none of its various sections is the evidence more complete than in the history of our own. There is a little tract by John Knox — his "Admonition to his Dearly Beloved Brethren, the Commonality of Scotland" — which is of itself sufficient to establish the point. It was first published in the year 1558 (only two months after Walter Miln had been cruelly put to death by the Archbishop of St. Andrews), and exhibits in a truly admirable light the large heart and masculine understanding of its extraordinary author. The truths which it embodies have since become common; not so, however, the power with which these are enforced; and with how deep and startling an effect must they have fallen for the first time on the ears of the serf and the vassal, sunk almost below the level of our nature by a hereditary course of servitude, that wears out the very mind, and with well-nigh all their natural rights as men absorbed in the exclusive and long-established privileges of their masters.[1]

1 "Neither would I," says the reformer, in his address to the common people, "that ye should esteem the Reformation and care of religion less to appertain to you than to the rulers and judges set over you in authority. Beloved brethren, ye are God's creatures, created and formed to his own image and similitude, for whose redemption was shed the most precious blood of the only beloved Son of God, to whom he hath commended his gospel and glad tidings to be preached, and for whom he hath prepared the heavenly inheritance, if so that you do not obstinately refuse and disdainfully contemn the means which he hath appointed to obtain the same, namely, his blessed gospel, which he now offereth unto you, to the end that ye may be saved. For the gospel and glad tidings of the kingdom, truly preached, is the power of God to the salvation of every true believer. Which to credit and recieve, you, the commonality, are no less addebted than are your rulers and princes; for, albeit God hath ordained distinction and difference in the administration of civil policies betwixt kings and subjects, rulers and common people, *yet in the hope of the life to come he hath made all equal*. For as in Christ Jesus the Jew hath no greater prerogative than hath the Gentile, the man than hath the woman, the learned than the unlearned, the lord than the servant, but all are one in him, so is there but one way and means to attain to the participation of his benefits and spiritual grace, which is a lively faith working by charity. . . . . Surely, then, it behooveth you to be careful and diligent in this so weighty a matter, lest that ye, contemning the occasion which God now offereth, find not the like again, even although that ye seek after it with sighings and tears. And that ye be not ignorant of what occasion I mean, in few words I shall express it.

"Not only I, but with me also divers godly and learned men, offer unto you our labor, faithfully to instruct you in the ways of the Eternal, our God, and in the sincerity of Christ's gospel, which this day, by the pestilent generation of Antichrist, are almost hid from the eyes of men. *We offer to jeopard our lives for the salvation of your souls*, and by manifest Scriptures to prove that religion that amongst you is maintained by fire and sword, to be false, vain, and diabolical. We require nothing of you but that patiently ye will hear our doctrine, which is not ours, but the doctrine of salvation revealed to the world by the only Son of God, and that *ye will examine our reasons* by which we offer to prove the Papistical religion to be abominable before God; and, lastly, we require that *by your power* the tyranny of these cruel priests and friars may be bridled, till we have uttered our minds in all matters this day debatable in religion. If these things, in the fear of God, ye grant unto us, I am assured that of God ye shall be blessed, whatsoever Satan shall devise against you. But if ye contemn or refuse God, who thus lovingly offereth unto you salvation and life, ye shall neither escape plagues temporal, which shortly shall apprehend you, neither yet the torment prepared for the devil and his angels."

The quotation is not too long. To use the scarcely more powerful language of Milton: "It was Knox himself, the reformer of a kingdom, that spake it; and

There is another important principle involved in what has been termed the republican spirit of the first churches. The spread of political power as necessarily accompanies the spread of intelligence as the heat of the sun accompanies its light; and it is quite as idle to affirm that the case should be otherwise as to challenge the law of gravitation, or any of the other great laws which regulate the government of the universe. If the progress of mind cannot be arrested, it is quite as impossible to arrest the growth of the power which necessarily accompanies it. Now, Christianity is essentially an intellectual religion, which, by increasing the popular intelligence, adds necessarily to the popular power. It is a system not of rites and ceremonies, but of morals and doctrines, — of morals that exercise those useful faculties which find fit employment in regu-

though his sentence seemeth of a venturous edge, uttered in the height of zeal, and perchance not suited to every low decrepit humor of the time, yet who knoweth whether it might not have proceeded from the dictat of a Divine Spirit?" The whole passage is pregnant with what may be termed the political influences of Christianity, as recognized by our Saviour himself, when he declared that he had come not to send peace on the earth, but a sword.

The concluding portion of this interesting little tract is conceived in the very vein in which Paul addressed himself to Felix, and rouses like the blast of a trumpet. The reformer speaks of perilous times — of blood spilt for the testimony of Christ by unjust princes and rulers who had set their faces against the truth — of proud and cruel Churchmen, embruted in their lusts. "Their lives," he says, "infect the air. The idolatry which openly they commit defileth the whole land. The innocent blood which they shed crieth for vengeance in the ears of our God; and none among you do unfeignedly seek after any redress for such foul enormities. Will God in this behalf hold you as innocent? Be not deceived, dear brethren. God hath punished not only proud tyrants and cruel murderers, but also such as with them did draw the yoke of iniquity, whether by flattering their offences, *obeying their unjust commandments*, or winking at their manifold and most grievous oppressions; — all such, I say, God once punished with the chief offenders. Be assured, brethren, that as he is immutable of nature, so will he not pardon you in that which he hath punished in others; and now the less because he hath plainly admonished you of the danger to come, and offered you his mercy before that he pour forth his wrath and displeasure on the gainsayer and the disobedient." The writer concludes with an emphatic prayer that his "dearly beloved countrymen" might "be partakers of the glorious inheritance prepared for such as refuse themselves, and fight under the banner of Christ Jesus *in the day of this his hot battle*; and that, in deep consideration of the same, they might learn to prefer the invisible and eternal joys to the vain pleasures that are present." For these quotations see Oliver & Boyd's edition of Knox, 1816, vol. ii. pp. 259, 275, and 278.

lating the human conduct, and of doctrines that, in their unexaggerated magnitude, fill, and more than fill, the widest grasp of the human understanding. There is scarce a question in the philosophy of mind of which at least the germ is not to be found in the Bible; and instead of leaving these to be discussed at pleasure by a few intellectual natures, it renders the study of them in some degree imperative on all. The same revealed truths which, as rudiments of thought, serve to awaken the faculties, constitute that identical "mind of God," which it is the essential duty of all men to know. And hence it is that conversion, in so many instances, is scarcely less marked in its intellectual than in its moral effects, and that wherever the Christian religion is established in the integrity of its first promulgation, men in even the humblest condition learn to reason and to observe. We find it stated by Locke, that among the Huguenots of France the common people were better instructed in their religion than even the higher classes in most of the other countries in Europe. We are told by Sir James Mackintosh, that "the uniform effect of Calvinism, in disposing its adherents to metaphysical speculation (which survives at times even the beliefs in which it originates), cannot be doubted to have influenced the mind of Butler." Christianity formed the sole learning of Bunyan. It constituted, in its reflex influences, the sole education of Burns. But by no class of writers, or no series of facts, is this sound principle better illustrated than by the history of the Reformed Church in Scotland.

The Reformation found the great bulk of our people parcelled out, through the influence of the feudal system, into detached masses,—possessed, like so many machines, of a merely physical power, and ready to be employed, whether for good or evil, as the caprice of a few ill-regulated minds chanced to direct. Pageants and ceremonies, with a multitude of vague, ill-defined beliefs, to which there attached no discipline of purity, and the tendency of which was to deaden, not to stimulate the intellect, constituted the entire religion of the country. But the "revival of the ancient opinions" led to a very different state of things; partly, doubtless, through the more covert workings of the principle described, and partly through the educational institutions established for the direct purpose. The religion of the reformers was a religion which sought the light, and which, in calling upon the masses to reason and to judge, laid it down as a first principle, that "for the soul to be without knowledge is not good." The scheme of education drawn up by Knox and his brethren was at once the most liberal and comprehensive which the world had yet seen, and bears reference in all its provisions to that spiritual nature, the common inheritance of the species, on whose high level all men meet and are equal. It provided that even the humblest of our craftsmen and peasants should be furnished with the data necessary to just thinking, and brought acquainted with the rules which regulate the reasoning faculties. Almost all the knowledge which books could supply was locked up in the learned languages. It was appointed, therefore, "that young men who purposed to travel in some handicraft, or other profitable exercise, for the good of the commonwealth, should (after devoting a certain time to reading and the catechism) devote a certain time to grammar and the Latin tongue; and then a certain time further to the study of the other tongues, and to the arts of philosophy."[1] It must have been surely a strange fanaticism that could have formed a system such as this. Despite the utmost efforts of the reformers, however, the system was only partially established, for its enemies were numerous and powerful. But the pure and intellectual religion in which it originated had freer course; and such were the effects of the latter, that in little more than half a century it had filled even the humblest cottages of our country with thinking men, who had learned to read and to pray over their

1 "First Book of Discipline," chap. VII. part I. clause 5.

Bibles. The fact is happily illustrated by the two great persecutions to which our Church has been subjected,—that which preceded the first establishment of the reformed religion, and that of the reign of Charles II. The martyrs of the one were mostly men of rank and learning. Hamilton was the scion of a noble family, Wishart a gentleman and deeply learned, Miln a priest, Straiton well born and a person of erudition. The victims of the other, on the contrary, were taken, in most instances, from among our common people — our farmers, mechanics, and shopkeepers. The testimony of Bishop Burnet to the intelligence of this class, as adduced by the Rev. Andrew Gray, in his masterly pamphlet, is very conclusive. Burnet was one of six Episcopal divines employed by Leighton in the year 1670 to go among the people and combat their Presbyterian prejudices; but the mission proved, it would seem, of little effect. "We were indeed amazed," he states, "to see a poor community so capable of arguing on points of government, and on the bounds to be set to the power of princes in matters of religion. Upon all these topics they had texts of Scripture at hand, and were ready with their answers to anything which was said to them. And this measure of knowledge was spread among the very meanest of them, even their cottagers and their servants." We find evidence equally direct, though of a somewhat different character, in the "death testimonies" preserved in such works as "Naphtali" and the "Cloud of Witnesses." Many of these were written by yeomen and mechanics,—by Glasgow shopkeepers, shoemakers from Edinburgh, and weavers from the Stewartry of Kirkcudbright; and yet, though sufficiently humble regarded merely as compositions, there are none of them so imperfect as not to embody the thoughts and give expression to the feelings of their respective authors. Be it remembered, too, that they are the productions of a period when it was no uncommon matter, in at least the northern parts of the kingdom, to find persons in the grade of gentlemen unable to sign their names.

The defects and errors of the Scottish Church in the earlier and better part of her history it is no difficult task to point out. We do not live among greater or better men than the Knoxes and Melvilles of the sixteenth century, or the Hendersons and Rutherfords of the seventeenth; but we live in an age considerably in advance of theirs. Let us remember, however, that the knowledge of truths which perchance we could never have discovered for ourselves does not entitle us to look down with any very marked contempt on the vigorous-minded worthies who flourished before their promulgation; and that we would do well to enjoy with moderation the chance eminence which raises our dapper little persons over the giants who stand on a lower level. The age of Knox and of Craig was essentially a despotic age. The Church in which they had spent that earlier portion of their lives in which habits of thought and feeling are most readily formed, was inevitably and constitutionally a despotic Church. The principles of toleration were altogether the discovery of a later time. It is undeniable, too, that some of the better members of the Church, in her seasons of suffering, were goaded into blamable excesses by that exasperating spirit of persecution which, according to Solomon, maketh even wise men mad. It is equally undeniable that she must have included within her pale, in her times of triumph, a considerable amount of the volatile rascality which ever delights to attach itself to a dominant party. Do we not know that the blood-thirsty Lauderdale and the crafty and cruel Sharpe were at one period of their lives zealous and influential Covenanters? Let us not confound, however, the excesses of either her true or her renegade members with her own proper acts, or the grosser spirit which sometimes influenced her from without with the infinitely purer principle which dwelt within. Nor yet let us forget that the great bulk of our countrymen in the sixteenth and seventeenth centuries had not attained to that full moral and intellectual stature which is incompatible with a state of tutelage and subserviency. We treat children after one fashion, and men after another, in even the freest states, and under the most equal laws. And in deciding regarding the spirit of the Scottish Church, there can be nothing more illiberal than to mix up into one heterogeneous idea two such opposite principles as the absolute rule of a schoolmaster, whose very vocation it is to forward the progress of the human mind, and the iron despotism of a tyrant, who, to accomplish his own base purposes, would plunge the millions into barbarism. Let our Church be tried, as we try the characters of our fellow-men, by the main scope of her conduct, and the intrinsic value and ascertained effects of her grand principles. Let us try her enemies and antagonists by the same rule, separating their general conduct from all such accidental circumstances as the beauty and fascinating elegance of Mary, the dignity under suffering of Charles I., or the military genius of Montrose and Dundee. It will be found that the Church has much to hope and nothing to dread from such a trial, —that ignorance, tyranny, cruelty, superstition, the ignoble selfishness that would sacrifice the welfare of the many to the little interests of the few, and criminally repress the moral and intellectual growth of the species, have ever formed the chief characteristics of her opponents,—that a regard for the souls of men, a zeal for the spread of knowledge, a love of liberty and of morals, an all-pervading reverence for the law of God—in short, the "antient opinions," joined to the original spirit of Christianity, have ever constituted her own.

The gist of the argument lies in least compass when we regard it simply as a question of history. The inevitable hostility of Christianity, in its purer forms, to irresponsible authority, however strengthened by ancient prejudice or unjust laws, arises, as has been shown, from two grand principles,—the recognition of a paramount code, to which every other code must yield, and an intellectual discipline, through which men are raised to a freedom and dignity of thought incompatible with a state of political servitude. And what wonder that principles so formidable should have found bitter enemies in absolute kings and tyrannical nobles, men whose widely extended privileges were encroachments on the unalienable rights of the species? Prerogative urged its claims on the one side, men asserted their rights on the other. But though such formed the actual merits of the controversy, they were otherwise stated and understood. The reformers contended that to Cæsar should be rendered the things which were Cæsar's, and nothing more; and that they should be permitted to render directly unto God himself the things which pertained to God. Cæsar contended, on the other hand, that he should be put in possession of the whole,—one part, of course, in his own proper right, the other in an assumed capacity of steward or middleman. The reformers maintained that their religion was a pure and scriptural religion, and that they could not in conscience receive any other. Cæsar insisted on taking this scriptural religion from them, and setting what he deemed a better in its place—a religion whose laws he had made to agree with his own. In all history there are not three characters better or more generally understood than those of James and the two Charleses. We are as intimately acquainted with not only the general scope of their conduct, but even their little individual peculiarities, as if our knowledge of them had been the result of personal observation. Who will venture to affirm that any one of the three, even the alleged author of the *Icon Basilike* himself, was actuated for a single day by that pure missionary spirit which can unhesitatingly sacrifice the lower regards of self to the glory of God or the general good of men; or that they preferred the Episcopacy they were so zealous to establish, to the Presbyterianism they would so fain have annihilated, merely because they deemed it more purely scriptural, or better suited to advance the true interests of their subjects? James, whose very considerable shrewdness was balanced by a singularly great amount of folly and weakness; and who was by much too vain to enjoy his wisdom in secret, divulged the principle on which both himself and his successors acted, in one of those "short speeches" which, according to Bacon, have the double quality of indicating men's real designs and of flying about like arrows. "No bishop, no king." The Episcopacy which these princes labored to introduce was virtually a modified Christianity, which, to use the language of Voltaire, "ran counter to the popular spirit," necessarily associated with the "antient opinions," now happily "revived." The institution of bishops was a piece of mere political machinery on which to rest the ghostly authority of the king. And the character of the men best suited for the office throws light, like that of the princes by whose authority they were appointed to it, on the secular nature of the purposes which they were intended to serve. We have been lately instructed by an eminent judge, on the strength of a Greek etymology, that this order of Churchmen and the Presbyterian superintendents of our "First Book of Discipline" were in reality identical. Perhaps, however, a slight acquaintance with history might have stood his lordship in better stead on the occasion than even the nicest knowledge of Greek. The Scotchman knows very little of his Church who does not know that the more fitted a minister was to be a superintendent, the less fitted was he to be a bishop. The superintendent was a faithful and able clergyman, "a man endowed with singular graces," chosen by the people and his brethren to be, like the apostle of the Gentiles, "more abundant in labors" than men of ordinary gifts; to be a journeyer from place to place, in districts where ministers were few; to "preach at least thrice every week;" to take note of crimes and defections; to "admonish where admonition was needed;" to give good counsel where it was required; to consider how the "poor were to be provided for," the "youth instructed;" to watch over the "manners of the people," the lives of ministers, the order of churches.[1] The men best fitted to be bishops, on the contrary, were the Montgomeries, Adamsons, Sharpes — Judas Iscariots of the Church. It was essential that the Scotch superintendent should have much religion; it was necessary that the Scotch bishop should have none. Leighton was a truly good man; and, after giving the office a fair trial, he found himself entirely unfitted for it.

It may be remarked, however, that though the Reformed Church of Scotland has always been opposed to bishops in the king's sense of the term, she has ever loved and cherished them in the true apostolical sense; and that the republican level on which she has placed her ministers has proved the most direct means of securing to her the services of real bishops, and of guarding her against the intrusion of counterfeits. It has secured to her that the John Newtons, Thomas Scotts, and Richard Cecils of the corporation should not remain in inferior, uninfluential offices, when right reverend infidels, high in spiritual authority, should be lending the full weight of their influence to degrade to the merely human level the adorable and sole Redeemer. The bishops of our Presbyterian Church have been men of larger minds and greater moral force than their brethren, and their widely-extended dioceses have been the hearts and understandings of the people of Scotland. Knox, Craig, Melville, Bruce, Rutherford, Henderson, Witherspoon, Erskine, Moncreiff, Thomson, — all these, and many others, were eminent Presbyterian bishops of the first rank; and, though their claims may seem more than a little doubtful when tried by the Puseyite argument, we have no unwillingness whatever to subject them to the test of reason and of Scripture.

Such is the true and rational Episcopacy of the Church of Scotland — an Episcopacy founded on principles which secure, agreeably to the spirit of the apostolical church, that the best and wisest men shall exercise the greatest

1 First Book of Discipline, chap. VI. part II.

authority, and which the counterfeit Episcopacy of James and the Charleses labored so zealously to subvert. But there is a principle whose hostility to the Church's true interest is even less defensible, because more unequivocally secular, than that of the nominal religion by which the Church, in the earlier portion of her history, was so long and so grievously oppressed. It is not difficult to conceive how, through a little perverted ingenuity, the identical arguments which support the better Episcopacy may be converted into sophisms to defend the worse. Nothing easier than to prove the immense value of such master-spirits as our Knoxes and Hendersons; and it is only necessary to confound the distinctions conferred on Churchmen by kings and laws, with the distinctions created among them by grace and nature, in order to arrogate an equal importance to the hierarchy appointed by men as to the hierarchy instituted by God. Or the argument may be differently grounded. It may be asserted that a nominal Episcopacy in the Church is a mere recognition of its real Episcopacy — a mere system of sanctions extended by human law to the natural and divinely-instituted authority of great and good men. And to give the assertion weight and plausibility in its bearing on the Scottish Church, we have merely to set aside our histories, and to forget that it was the Montgomeries, Adamsons, and Sharpes, to whose authority the law extended its sanction, while our untitled, though surely most venerable and divinely-instituted bishops were compelled to flee for their lives to the hill-side. But the other great expedient for secularizing the Church, — the *patronage principle*, — even sophistry itself has scarcely ingenuity enough to defend. It is one of those legalized enormities which disdain to assume even the color of good, and which base their claims to the respect and obedience of the masses whom they oppress, not on their being just and rational, but on their being law. Episcopacy, notwithstanding its grovelling and earthly spirit, was ostensibly a form of religion as truly as Presbyterianism itself;

5*

and the controversy assumed, in consequence, a theological aspect. The patronage principle, on the contrary, is avowedly secular. It interferes with spiritual concerns, with no spiritual character to assert, and intermeddles with matters of conscience, with no conscientious motives to urge.

True it is, however, that the difference is rather apparent than real. It will be found that it is virtually the same modifying power in its attempts to render the Church a merely secular institution, subservient to merely secular purposes, which assumed an Episcopal form in the earlier portion of her history, and embodied itself into a patronage principle in the latter. It will be found, too, that identically the same class of men who were so ready to lay down their lives in resisting the encroachments of the one, have been ever the staunchest and most uncompromising opponents of the other; that though the assaulting principle from without has altered its form and mode of attack, it has not altered its nature; and that the resisting principle within, still more thoroughly consistent, has retained both its form and its nature too. The two conflicts, at once dissimilar and alike, have agitated the Church during two nearly equal periods of her history, — the one from early in the reign of James VI. until the Revolution, the other from the latter years of Anne until the present day. Patronage existed during the earlier period; and broadly was it denounced, and the "free election" principle asserted, by even the first fathers of the Reformation; but the field was occupied by questions embodying the same antagonist principles in a different form, and the abuse on the one hand, and the popular right on the other, were assigned subordinate places in the controversy. It is perhaps not unworthy of remark, that the truly liberal educational scheme of the reformers shared (also in a subordinate form) in exactly the same prosperity and the same reverses with the non-intrusion principle; that the cause of ignorance and of patronage on the part of the court, of the popular right and of popular instruction on the part of the Church, triumphed and suffered together. During the earlier part of the seventeenth century, the educational scheme, with only its true excellence to recommend it, retained its first unauthorized and unsanctioned character. No sooner, however, did the Church become dominant, at the close of the reign of Charles I., than it passed into a law, — "a law," says Currie, the elegant biographer of Burns, "which may challenge comparison with any act of legislation to be found in the records of history, whether we consider the wisdom of the ends in view, the simplicity of the means employed, or the provisions made to render these means effectual to their purpose."[1] The Church sank on the Restoration, and the educational law sank with it, together with all the other laws unsanctioned by the royal assent. It slept during the reigns of Charles and James; but on the Revolution the Church again became dominant, and this wise and good law was again enacted in identically the original terms. I need hardly remind the reader that it had for its meet companion an anti-patronage law, which was established, abolished, and reënacted at precisely the same periods, and through exactly the same influences.

The origin of the singularly metaphysical right of patronage has been variously accounted for. It has been asserted that it may be traced simply to the circumstance that, in the earlier periods of our ecclesiastical history, churches were sometimes built and endowed by private individuals, who retained to themselves and their successors the right of nominating the ecclesiastics by whom the duties attached to these erections were to be performed, and the revenues enjoyed; and that this merely civil right escaped the general confiscation of church property which took place at the Reformation, and has come down, with a few interruptions, to our own times. It will be found, however, that this, though a sufficiently clear, is but a partial statement of the case. In whom, I ask, were the rights of

1 Dr. Currie's Prefatory Remarks, Life of Burns.

patronage vested in 1560, on the first documentary recognition of Protestantism by the Lords of the Congregation? — Not, certainly, in the Argyles, Glencairns, Lindsays, Boyds, Hays, Lochinvars, Marshals, Drumlanrigs, of Scottish story. I find the names of these noblemen, with those of many others, attached to the First Book of Discipline, in which the free election principle is so broadly and uncompromisingly laid down. I find, too, that in pledging themselves to support the various important principles which the book embodies, as altogether "good and conform to God's word," they could stipulate as a condition that the Churchmen of the exploded faith should be permitted to enjoy their benefices during the course of their lives. But there is no stipulation regarding the "free election" principle; no mention made of a right vested in either themselves or others, which it threatened to subvert; in short, nothing whatever to show that they deemed the claims of patronage more Protestant in principle, or less entirely abrogated by the triumph of the "antient opinions," than even the worship of saints and images, or the doctrine of transubstantiation itself. The Reformation interposed at this period a wide gulf between the abuses of the old system and the usages of the new, and not a single right of patronage had as yet strided across the chasm.

The revival of these rights was evidently an afterthought, — one of the many expedients of the time for secularizing the Church. We read its true character in that of the party in whom it originated, — in the appointment of the *tulchan* bishops, in the violence of Morton and his associates in 1571, in the Black Acts of 1584, — in short, in the entire history of James, and in that of his son. Nor can we well conceive a greater contrast than that which existed between the spirit in which these rights of patronage were asserted by the court party on the one side, and the modified and well-restricted sense in which they were recognized by the Church on the other. The highest civil authority was of course that of the king; nor was his power yet compressed within its true limits by the just rights of the people; for, though a few enlightened minds of the Knox and Buchanan calibre could mark out the separating boundary with a skill and precision not surpassed in any after period, there existed no tidal influences of opinion powerful enough to raise and propel the masses to the proper line. Liberty had almost all its battles yet to fight, and prerogative almost all its defeats yet to sustain. The king was the first magistrate of the country; but he was also a great deal more; and the national property held by him for the public good was too often confounded with a thing so entirely different as the personal property held by him for his own benefit. But though the Church shared, in some degree, in this confusion of ideas, her high principles assisted materially in clearing her views; and she could assert in her Book of Discipline that not even by the king himself should ministers be obtruded on congregations contrary to the will of the people. In his connection with her patrimony, however, — a connection which, now that such matters are better understood, resolves itself into merely the care of the magistracy extended to public property employed for the public advantage, — she recognized his rights of patronage. Nor is it at all difficult to conceive how, in her view of the matter, these rights, and even a free-election principle, should be perfectly compatible with each other. She had but one code of laws and one rule of duty for all men, with no peculiar license for kings; and, deeming the monarch as certainly an accountable creature as any of his subjects, and recognizing but one way in which his privileges could be employed, she held that his right of patronage was a sacred trust, which he could only properly exercise by extending to the people, as the occasion offered, a liberty of choice; and that the intrusion upon them of an unpopular minister was a gross and criminal abuse of power, which, as being contrary to justice, no law could sanction. There are, fortunately, Scottish patrons of the present day who view the privilege as vested in themselves in a light exactly similar to that in which the Church regarded it in its connection with the king, and who find no disagreement between its wise and conscientious exercise and a scrupulous regard to the welfare and wishes of the people; nor is the right a merely nominal one, when thus exercised by these men, if the gratitude and good-will of thousands, and the approval of their own conscience, be matters of any value. Even we of the present time have no other objection to patronage in such hands than the one which a Roman of the empire might have urged against the despotism of an Antonine or an Aurelian; — it is merely the irresponsible power, and the Neros and Domitians, that we dread.

But James VI., the true son of Mary and of Darnley, and, if we except his ancestor, James III., the most contemptible of all our Scottish kings, was a patron of a very different stamp from either Sir George Sinclair or the Marquis of Bute. At once timid and unscrupulous, grasping and profuse, facile and ungenerous, childishly attached to a few, though indifferent to the good of the many, ever eager to extend his power beyond the just limits, and yet ever subject to some petty tyranny of his own creating, with almost vanity and folly enough to neutralize his cunning, and nearly weakness enough to balance his wickedness, — there was scarce an opportunity of good or of advantage which he did not misimprove, scarce a privilege which he did not abuse, scarce a duty in which he did not fail. Nay, such was the nature of the man, that he was hardly more faithful to his own selfish aims than to the just rights of his subjects. Robertson shows us with how careless a hand he portioned out, among his flatterers and favorites, the church lands annexed by Parliament to the Crown, and which, if retained, would have so mightily strengthened the power he was so anxious to establish. And Calderwood relates that he dealt after exactly the same manner with the rights of patronage, which he had for the purpose created, contrary to law, when they had ceased to exist — scattering them as thoughtlessly and profusely among his courtiers and minions as he could have done the counters which he used in play, when the game was over.[1] The Church seriously remonstrated against an abuse of the kingly power so weak in itself, and so pregnant with evil, and urged, somewhat in the spirit of the last General Assembly, that gifts of such ill omen should be instantly recalled, and that commissioners and presbyteries should not be "processed and horned" for not giving admission to "persons presented by the new patrons." But supplications and remonstrances with only justice and reason to recommend them proved of little avail; and the king's gifts, in all their portentous absurdity, were confirmed, not recalled. Certainly the origin of patronage in the Reformed Church of Scotland had not been such as to entitle it to much reverence. It has been truly remarked, that the cause of justice and of truth stands in need of no pedigree to ennoble it; but the reverse is not equally true; and it is well to know of an antagonist cause, that the meanness of its descent corresponds with the flagitiousness of its principles. It does not in any degree tend to increase our respect for the rights of patronage — rights so continually associated with wrong — to find that they should have originated in the grasping rapacity of a selfish aristocracy, who, to accomplish their sordid purposes of personal or family aggrandizement, could have sacrificed the spiritual welfare of a whole country, in the mistaken notions of a comparatively uninformed age, only partially won from slavery and barbarism, and in the criminal usurpation and weak profusion of a silly and unprincipled king.

To the reënactment of patronage by the last Parliament of Anne it is unnecessary to allude. All the more honor-

1 Calderwood, p. 227. (Sir George M'Kenzie, Observ. Act 1692, c. 121, observes: "There can be nothing so unjust and illegal as these patronages were.")

able friends of the principle which the law embodies freely admit that the measure, whatever it was in itself, was disgracefully carried, and that the accomplishment of its main object would have proved the ruin of the country. There is no one reckless or unprincipled enough to justify it in its first character as a conspiracy. Brougham himself does no more than shut his eyes on the history of the time, and observe a profound silence regarding the facts. The apologists of the law ground their defence on an entirely different basis. They remark, with Paley, that there are measures which have presented, on their first establisment, an apparently doubtful or indifferent character, which are found eventually to involve principles little dreamed of by either their friends or their enemies, and to serve other and more important purposes than those for which they were originally designed, and that the law of patronage is one of these. They are ingenuous enough, in most instances, to confess, wlth the honorable Sir Walter, that the law was badly conceived and ill-intended; they only assert that it has wrought well. Now, most broadly and pointedly do we deny the fact. It has not wrought well. It has wrought ill — decidedly, unequivocally, emphatically ill. It has ever breathed in its influences the spirit of its first enactment; its character has ever corresponded with the baseness of its origin; it has done more to unchristianize the people of Scotland than all the learned and ingenious infidelity of the eighteenth century; it has inflicted a severer injury on the Church than all the long-protracted and bloody persecutions of the seventeenth.

The subject is one of great multiplicity; but nothing can well be simpler or more obvious than the principles which it involves; and the light of reason and of history exhibit it in exactly the same point of view. No one can assert, without either a strange abuse of words or a scarcely conceivable confusion of ideas, that a law works for the benefit of any institution, if it be the direct and palpable tendency of that law to overturn and destroy it.

And it is not less obvious, that if the institution be good, and positively useful, the law which tends to its overthrow must be bad, and positively mischievous. It is a poison introduced into the system, a "law which kills." Now, it is an undisputed fact, that little more than a century has passed since a Commission of the General Assembly "loosened the pastoral relation" of four of our worthiest clergymen "to their respective charges," and declared them to be "no longer ministers of the Church;" and this for no other crime than that of daring openly to avow the same detestation of the intrusive principle which, during the two preceding centuries, all the better Presbyterians of the country had been openly avowing before them. It is not less a fact, that in the Edinburgh Almanac for the present year there are no fewer than twelve closely-printed pages of names of Scottish clergymen located within the country, each of these holding by the same catechism and confession of faith with the Church itself; each and all of them deriving their distinctive designation from the four ejected ministers, and their separate existence, either directly or indirectly, from the abuse of patronage; each furnished with an attached congregation, who, but for the tyranny of the deprecated law, would have been at this moment within the pale of the Establishment, constituting its strength; and that, in the proportion of about seven-eighths to the entire amount, this numerous and influential body, both ministers and people, are zealously laboring to overturn this very Establishment, and want only a little more of that power which has been accumulating among them in so formidable a ratio during the last fifty years, fully to accomplish their purpose. Nay, that they do not already possess this power, and that the Church is not already overthrown, is owing solely to the fact that the patrons of Scotland have been, in many instances, a great deal less wicked than the law of patronage, and have waived the exclusive rights which it conferred upon them in favor of the people.

And not only can it be shown that the law of patronage has a direct tendency to destroy the Church, but that it has also a tendency equally direct to render it worthy of being destroyed. The entire people of Scotland are judges in this matter; there is no need of framing arguments to convince them; it is only necessary to refer to well-known facts. When, and through what influence, I ask, was it that the Church of Scotland, long the most popular and influential of all establishments, ceased to so great an extent to impress its own character on that of the country, and, from being a guide and leader of the people, sunk in so marked a degree into a follower and dependent on the government and the aristocracy? When and through what influence was it that the children learned to look with coldness and suspicion on an order of men to whom their fathers had turned in every time of trouble for assistance and counsel, — whose sayings they delighted to treasure up, — the stories of whose lives and sufferings constituted their choicest literature, — whose very names they employed as watchwords whenever there was a right to be asserted or a wrong to be redressed, — whom they unhesitatingly followed to the hillside and the battle-field, into exile and captivity, to tortures and to death? When and through what influence was it that the old evangelical party sunk into a feeble and persecuted minority, — that party who subscribed the confession of our faith, believing it in their hearts, — who, fearing the curse denounced by John, delivered the whole truth of God, taking nothing therefrom, and adding nothing thereto, — who first asserted for themselves and their countrymen the high rights of the species, and dared to think and to act with the freedom of men ennobled by "the liberty with which Christ maketh his people free," — who so zealously strove, amid the darkness of ignorance and superstition, to extend to even the meanest vassal the blessings of religion and the light of learning, and who were ever so ready in the good cause to give their temporalities to the winds, and to hold their lives as nothing? When and through what influence was it that more than one-half the clergy of our Church, powerless for every good purpose, were made to stand on exactly the same ground which had been occupied by the curates and bishops of half a century before, and through which the pike and the musket came to be employed, as in the worst days of Charles II., to secure the settlement of ministers misnamed Presbyterian? Through what influence was it that, the more secular-minded the clergyman, the more certain was he of retaining his office in the Church, and through which men such as Fisher and the Erskines came to be regarded as the very pests and traitors of the institution, and the godly and inoffensive Gillespie — whose sole crime it was that he would neither offend against his own sense of duty nor yet outrage the conscience of others — came to be contemptuously thrust out? Through what influence was it that the clerical farmers and corn-factors of forty years ago were brought into the Church, — the men who were so ready, in what has been termed the natural course of society, to quit the *pastoral* for the *agricultural* life, and who, in years of scarcity, when the price of grain rose beyond all precedent, were either thriving on the miseries of the people, and accumulating to themselves, in the least popular of all characters, the bitter contempt and unmingled detestation of a whole country,[1] or, as the unhonored martyrs of unlucky speculation, were studying in jails, or under hiding, the restrictions and technicalities of the bankrupt statutes? Who of all the men of our country has not marked the difference which obtains between the faithful minister of Jesus Christ, alike equal in rank to the highest and to the lowest who have souls to be lost or saved, — between the zealous preacher of the truth, appointed by God himself to wrestle with men for their souls, and the mere clerical, half-

1 It is a fact which stands in need of no comment, that the person in the north of Scotland who first raised the price of oatmeal to three pounds per boll was a minister of the Established Church.

fashionable gentleman of "limited means," so little respected by the people, and so coldly regarded by the aristocracy, — the mere reader of sermons for a piece of bread, whose sole "vocation" consists in the perhaps purchased favor of some unprincipled courtier or ungodly patron? Truly the people of Scotland must forget a great deal before they can learn to love patronage even a very little; and the man must be wofully ignorant of both the facts of the question and the national character, or strangely confident in his own powers of persuasion, who hopes to convince us, in the face of ten thousand hostile recollections, that the secularizing, soul-destroying law of the infidel Bolingbroke has wrought well.

I heard sermon only a few weeks ago in the church of a country parish in the north of Scotland, where almost the entire people are separated from the clergyman. I had previously seen much of the evils of patronage. In the prosecution of a humble but honest calling, of which I am not mean enough to be ashamed, I had travelled over a considerable part of Scotland. I had been located for months together, at one period of my life, among the parishes of its southern districts, at another in those of the north; I had seen both the Highlands and the Low country; and if the powers of observation were not wanting, the opportunities were certainly very great. But the almost entire desertion of a pastor by his people was a thing I had not yet witnessed, and I was desirous to see and judge for myself. There are associations of a high and peculiar character connected with this northern parish. For more than a thousand years it has formed part of the patrimony of a truly noble family, celebrated by Philip Doddridge for its great moral worth, and by Sir Walter Scott for its high military genius, and through whose influence the light of the Reformation had been introduced into this remote corner, at a period when all the neighboring districts were enveloped in the original darkness. In a later age it had been honored by the fines and proscriptions of Charles II.; and its minister — one of those men of God whose names still live in the memory of the country, and whose biography occupies no small space in the recorded history of her "worthies" — had rendered himself so obnoxious to the tyranny and irreligion of the time, that he was ejected from his charge more than a year before any of the other non-conforming clergymen of the Church. I approached the parish from the east. The day was warm and pleasant; the scenery through which I passed, some of the finest in Scotland. The mountains rose on the right in huge Titanic masses, that seemed to soften their purple and blue in the clear sunshine to the delicate tone of the deep sky beyond, and I could see the yet unwasted snows of summer glittering in little detached masses along their summits; the hills of the middle region were feathered with wood; a forest of mingled oaks and larches, which still blended the tender softness of spring with the full foliage of summer, swept down to the path; the wide undulating plain below was laid out into fields, mottled with cottages, and waving with the yet unshot corn; and a noble arm of the sea winded along the lower edge for nearly twenty miles, losing itself to the west among blue hills and jutting headlands, and opening in the east to the main ocean through a magnificent gateway of rock. But the little groups which I encountered at every turning of the path, as they journeyed, with all the sober, well-marked decency of a Scottish Sabbath morning, towards the church of a neighboring parish, interested me more than even the scenery. The clan which inhabited this part of the country had borne a well-marked character in Scottish story. Buchanan has described it as one of the most fearless and warlike in the north. It served under the Bruce at Bannockburn; it was the first to rise in arms to protect Queen Mary, on her visit to Inverness, from the intended violence of Huntly; it fought the battles of Protestantism in Germany under

Gustavus Adolphus;[1] it covered the retreat of the English at Fontenoy, and presented an unbroken front to the enemy after all the other allied troops had quitted the field. And it was the descendants of these very men who were now passing me on the road. The rugged, robust form, half bone, half muscle; the springy firmness of the tread; the grave, manly countenance,—all gave indication that the original characteristics survived in their full strength; and it was a strength that inspired confidence, not fear. There were gray-haired, patriarchal-looking men among the groups, whose very air seemed impressed by a sense of the duties of the day; nor was there aught that did not agree with the object of the journey in the appearance of even the youngest and least thoughtful.

As I proceeded, I came up with a few people who were travelling in a contrary direction. A Secession meeting-house has lately sprung up in the parish, and these formed part of the congregation. A path nearly obscured by grass and weeds leads from the main road to the parish church. It was with difficulty I could trace it, and there were none to direct me, for I was now walking alone. The parish burying-ground, thickly sprinkled with graves and tombstones, surrounds the church. It is a quiet, solitary spot of great beauty, lying beside the sea-shore; and as service had not yet commenced, I whiled away half an hour in sauntering among the stones, and deciphering the inscriptions. I could trace in the rude monuments of this retired little spot a brief but impressive history of the district. The older tablets, gray and shaggy with the mosses and lichens of three centuries, bear, in their uncouth semblances of the unwieldy battle-axe and double-handed sword of ancient warfare, the meet and appropriate symbols of the earlier time. But the more modern testify to the

[1] It is an interesting fact, and illustrates happily the high respect with which the clansmen must have regarded their general, that, even in the present day, the name Gustavus is scarcely more common in Sweden itself than in this part of the country.

introduction of a humanizing influence. They speak of a life after death in the "holy texts" described by the poet, or certify, in a quiet humility of style which almost vouches for their truth, that the sleepers below were "honest men, of blameless character, and who feared God." There is one tombstone, however, more remarkable than all the others. It lies beside the church door, and testifies, in an antique inscription, that it covers the remains of the "GREAT.MAN.OF.GOD.AND.FAITHFVL.MINISTER.OF.IESVS CHRIST," who had endured persecution for the truth in the dark days of Charles and his brother. He had outlived the tyranny of the Stuarts, and, though worn by years and sufferings, had returned to his parish on the Revolution, to end his course as it had begun. He saw, ere his death, the law of patronage abolished, and the popular right virtually secured; and fearing lest his people might be led to abuse the important privilege conferred on them, and calculating aright on the abiding influence of his own character among them, he gave charge on his death-bed to dig his grave in the threshold of the church, that they might regard him as a sentinel placed at the door, and that his tombstone might speak to them as they passed out and in. The inscription, which, after the lapse of nearly a century and a half, is still perfectly legible, concludes with the following remarkable works: — "THIS.STONE.SHALL.BEAR.WITNESS.AGAINST. THE.PARISHIONERS.OF. . . . . IF.THEY.BRING.ANE.UNGODLY. MINISTER.IN.HERE." Could the imagination of a poet have originated a more striking conception in connection with a church deserted by all its better people, and whose minister fattens on his hire, useless and contented?

I entered the church, for the clergyman had just gone in. There were from eight to ten persons scattered over the pews below, and seven in the galleries above; and these, as there were no more "*John Clerks*" and "*Michael Tods*"[1]

[1] "Peter Clark and Michael Tod were the only individuals who, in a population of three thousand souls, attached their signatures to the *call* of the obnoxious presentee, Mr. Young, in the famous Auchterarder case." — *Note appended to "My Schools and Schoolmasters."*

in the parish, composed the entire congregation. I wrapped myself up in my plaid and sat down, and the service went on in the usual course; but it sounded in my ears like a miserable mockery. The precentor sung almost alone; and, ere the clergyman had reached the middle of his discourse, which he read in an unimpassioned, monotonous tone, nearly one half his skeleton congregation had fallen asleep; and the drowsy, listless expression of the others showed that, for every good purpose, they might have been asleep too. And Sabbath after Sabbath has this unfortunate man gone the same tiresome round, and with exactly the same effects, for the last twenty-three years, at no time regarded by the better clergymen of the district as really their brother, on no occasion recognized by the parish as virtually its minister, with a dreary vacancy and a few indifferent hearts inside his church, and the stone of the Covenanter at the door! Against whom does the inscription testify? — for the people have escaped. Against the patron, the intruder, and the law of Bolingbroke, — the Dr. Robertsons of the last age, and the Dr. Cooks of the present. It is well to learn from this hapless parish the exact sense in which, in a different state of matters, the Rev. Mr. Young would have been constituted minister of Auchterarder. It is well, too, to learn, that there may be vacancies in the Church where no blank appears in the Almanac.

It is scarce necessary to remark, that the present position of the Church is a position which she has often occupied, or that the agitated question is one which she has agitated a thousand times before. There is comfort in the fact that we need only refer to her history, to show that all her better names have been invariably on the one side; and that the highest praise to which her opponents can pretend is that some of them have been fortunate enough to have attained to a negative character, and that some of them have had the merit of being equivocal. There is comfort, too, in the reflection that what is morally wrong cannot be logically right; and that not only the worthier men, but also the sounder arguments, are to be found on the better side. It is indeed no easy matter to prove that our clergymen should not receive the people's money for the people's good, unless they first recognize *an uncontrollable right of misapplication* in the patron; that Bolingbroke's Act and the Reform Bill should alike remain the law of the land, to blend more than the civil liberty of the freest states of antiquity with well-nigh the ghostly despotism of Turkey or of Rome; or that men, through a sense of the high duty which they owe to God, should obey an unjust law, through which God's own laws are to be nullified, his gospel repressed, and the consciences of his people wronged and offended. And yet such are the difficulties of at least our more extreme opposers. The Lord President of the Court of Session is unquestionably an able and respectable lawyer; but it is an over-task for even the Lord President himself to be correct and rational when in the wrong; and his address in the Lethendy case is perhaps not less valuable as an illustration of the kind of facts and arguments of which our opponents can alone avail themselves, than even his lordship's ablest and most impressive addresses in their direct and proper character.

We are shown by Locke, in his wonderful Essay, that "confusions making it a difficulty to separate two things that should be separated, concern always two ideas, and those most which most approach one another." His lordship, however, confounds ideas the most distinct — things which do not belong to even the same category. He mistakes a duty enjoined for a power conferred; and finds a mystery, which he confesses himself unable to comprehend, in the absurdity into which the mistake necessarily leads. The article in our Confession quoted by his lordship instructs the civil magistrate "to take order that unity and peace be preserved in the Church; that the truth of God be kept pure and entire; that blasphemies and heresies be suppressed; corruptions and abuses in worship and discipline prevented or reformed;" and it empowers him, the better to fulfil the enjoined duty, to call synods, regarding which he is instructed "to provide that whatever is transacted in them *be according to the mind of God.*" Now, what, I ask, can well be simpler than this, especially the concluding portion of the passage, which seems intended to guard against the very possibility of misconception, and throws so clear a light on what goes before? The *mind of God* is the pure and perfect code embodied in God's word,—the sublime doctrines which God reveals, the high duties which he enjoins, the pure morality which he inculcates; and the magistrate, as the responsible subject of this absolute and immutable code, is commanded to take order that he not only conform to it himself, but that the Church conform to it too. Strange, however, as it may seem, this explanatory and restricting clause—this clause which lowers the delegated trust into a strictly defined duty—his lordship confesses himself totally unable to understand.[1] He had explored the passage with so engrossing and definite a conception of the meaning he had expected to find in it, as to have no eyes for the meaning which it actually conveys. The determining and defining clause, which asserts the supremacy of the Divine law, appeared to him somehow as merely a splendid obscurity, which sanctioned the exercise of a great, though mysterious and undefinable, power. I doubt not that the ministers at the bar understood the passage a little better, and accepted

[1] "What is the precise meaning of that passage I am sure I don't know, or what is the jurisdiction it gives to the civil magistrate: but it must allude to something which is not temporal. The mind of God is a spiritual concern, and they [magistrates] are to take care that the things transacted in synods be according to the mind of God. Surely this does not exclude the civil magistrate from interfering in ecclesiastical concerns. If words be capable of conveying a meaning, it certainly gives to the civil authority more power than they have ever exercised, or than, I believe, it was ever meant they should exercise; but it must allude to more than mere temporal concerns. In short, I hope that, on sober reflection, the Church will see that they cannot remain in the position of an Established Church, and yet resist the law which has made them an Established Church."—*Lord President's Address, Report, Scot. Guard.*, 18*th June*, 1839.

it as a sign that they were not standing on unsafe or dishonorable ground. It proved perfectly impracticable on this occasion for every purpose of the court. It passed no censure on the minister of Lethendy; denounced no threat against the Presbytery of Dunkeld; and if it empowers Lords of Session and their presidents to enter our church courts, it gives them at least no encouragement to vote on the secular side. The passage was introduced into our Confession, in its present form, rather more than a hundred and ninety years ago; and there has it remained ever since, as unchanged to suit the profligacy of Charles II., or the prostitution and subserviency of his courts of law, as when the good President Forbes employed his whole Sabbaths in studying the "mind of God," and the rest of the week in advancing the weal of his country, and in the conscientious discharge of the high duties of his office. It extended to the magistracy exactly the same power which it does now, and breathed exactly the same spirit, when Middleton introduced the unhappy act which overturned Presbyterianism in Scotland, — when the apostate Lauderdale renounced the Covenant, to become the remorseless persecutor of his brethren, — when the criminals of our courts were the martyrs of our Church, — when the heroic Mackail stood before the Lords of Council with his leg fixed in the boot, and the executioner struck the wedge till the bone was splintered, and the blood and marrow spurted in their faces.

Some of his lordship's other mistakes and misconceptions are scarcely less striking than the one just exposed. Error and misstatement creep into his very facts, — error, too, of so important a nature as entirely to alter their illustrative scope and character. It is unnecessary to allude a second time to his lordship's Episcopal argument, so well backed by Greek, and so ill supported by history. In his allusion to the eminent Father of the Secession, he is still more palpably unfortunate. He tells our better clergymen that they have but one alternative in the matter; that an implicit submission to the law of patronage is one of the express conditions on which they receive the support of the state; and that they must either unresistingly subject themselves to this conditional law, or, like the good Ebenezer Erskine, throw up their livings, and quit the Establishment: for this excellent and eminent man, finding, as his lordship states the case, that he could neither remain in the Establishment without submitting to the law, nor yet submit to the law without offending against his conscience, judiciously and honestly settled the point by withdrawing from the Church and founding the Secession. What obscure and nameless historian could have so entirely misled his lordship? The statement is totally untrue. Erskine did not withdraw from the Establishment: he was thrust out, and thrust out for this, — that he broadly and pointedly condemned the Church for doing what the court now requires of it to do, and for not doing what, in direct opposition to the court, it has now done. He took his stand, with his three brethren, on the broad constitutional ground which had been occupied by all the better men of the Church from the Reformation downwards; and, outnumbered and overborne in an inferior ecclesiastical court, he appealed to the highest. And there, too, he was outnumbered and overborne; but, strong in the goodness of his cause and the approval of his conscience, he would neither recognize its censures as just, nor succumb to its authority. And the court, by a commission of its members, proceeded to cast him out as a disturber of its peace. It "loosened his pastoral relation to his charge," declared his "parish vacant," pronounced him "no longer a minister of the Church of Scotland," and prohibited all the acknowledged ministers of the Church from "employing him in any ministerial function." Against this unjust sentence Erskine protested and appealed; and the document is recorded, not in the journals of the assembly, but in the heart and mind of the country. He "protested that his pastoral relation to his people should still be held firm and valid;"

that he should "still hold communion with all and every one who adhered to the principles of the true Presbyterian Church of Scotland;" that it should "still be held lawful for him to exercise the keys of doctrine, discipline, and government, according to the word of God, the Confession of Faith, and the constitution" of this, the "Covenanted Church," by which he so tenaciously held; and finally, in the hope of a better spirit in the future, he "*appealed to the first free, faithful, and reforming General Assembly of the Church of Scotland;*"[1] nor are there many of our worthier ministers who do not recognize the full justice of the appeal. Such are the facts of the case, as sanctioned by authentic history, in opposition to those adduced by his lordship. But in passing from the illustration to the principle illustrated, it cannot be improper to ask, what sort of estimate has this shrewd and able magistrate formed of the strength and importance of the party which he so coolly recommends either to submit to the law of patronage, or to retire from the Church? Has he not mistaken the staff, on this occasion, for the main army, — the representatives of the million for the million itself? Or is it really the tens and hundreds of thousands — the preponderating majority and strength of the country, with all their hereditary hatred and acquired dislike of the iniquitous and deprecated law — to whom he submits the alternative? Retire from the Church! The Church cannot exist without us. We are the thews and sinews, the blood and nerves, of the Church. Our support is essentially necessary to secure their temporalities to even the clergymen who value us least; and the secession of our party would be the inevitable ruin of our opponents.

The misfortune of the Lord President's address consisted simply in this, — it was a great deal too clear. His lordship had to defend what was in itself radically wrong;

1 For an impartial and well-written account of the origin of the Secession, see "Chambers's Lives of Eminent Scotsmen," "Life of Erskine," vol. ii. p. 280, etc.

and, instead of entrenching himself behind acts of Parliament happy in their ambiguities, and precedents of the Court which may in some instances be but recorded mistakes, he came imprudently out into the open field of reason and of Scripture. Arguments drawn from the mere law of the case could have been combated by few; but in drawing them from the Bible — a book at once the most decided on questions of morals, and the most extensively known — and from reason, the common gift and distinguishing characteristic of the species, he addressed himself to the understandings of the entire community. And hence, obviously enough, the people have been enabled to change places with his lordship. It is alike contrary to the whole scope of reason and of Scripture that obedience be rendered to an unjust law; nor can there be anything more exquisitely absurd than to confound such an obedience with the mere recognition of the power and authority of the magistrate. "Our Saviour," says his lordship, "pleaded no exemption from the jurisdiction of the Sanhedrim." True; but our Saviour never obeyed an unjust law. "Paul pleaded before Felix," Festus, "and Agrippa, and," as the edicts against the Christians were not yet framed, "he appealed to Cæsar." Undisputably; but Paul did not obey an unjust law. Nor are we left to mere inference in the matter. Peter and John, when brought before a council of rulers and Sadducee elders, assigned good and sufficient reasons why they should not submit themselves to the will or authority of *men*, if opposed to that of God; and the argument still survives to urge on our consciences, that we yield not obedience to an unjust law. Nay, it is only necessary, in deciding the question, to inquire why the churches have been persecuted and the martyrs slain. His lordship's law does not lie so much within reach as his lordships facts and arguments. It is exceedingly natural, however, to judge of it from the company which it keeps, and to bear in mind that very eminent lawyers have arrived at very opposite conclusions on the point, and entertain very different opinions. The independence of the Church seems as decidedly recognized by statute as the rights of the patron; and, besides, are we not assured "*that the law and the opinion of the judge are not always convertible terms, or one and the same thing, since it sometimes may happen that the judge may mistake the law*"? Now, this must surely be good sense, for it is according to reason and experience; and it must necessarily be good law, for it occurs in Blackstone.

It is fully admitted, however, that the decision of our courts has practically determined the law, and that the Church is at this moment as entirely at the mercy of the patron as if her liberties had never been asserted nor her independence recognized. The Court of Session has means at command, far more convincing than argument, to compel the admission; and the readiness to employ these is fully equal to the ability. We have already seen one of the Presbyteries of our Church honored by a public rebuke, and fines and imprisonment hang over another. But the duty of our ministers is not the less clear. They owe it to themselves and to their people, to their country and to their God, that they neither obey this iniquitous law, nor yet quit the Establishment. Either alternative involves the ruin of the Church of Scotland; and who is there that has studied our country's history in the true spirit, or has acquainted himself with the temper of the present time, and the depth and force of the national character, who can believe that the Church of Scotland is destined to fall alone? There is more at stake in the agitated question than either rights of patronage or the temporalities of the Church; and our Earls of Kinnoull, who have wealth, and lands, and titles, as well as patronages, to lose, and our Lord Chancellors and Lord Presidents, who, like our clergy, derive their support from an establishment, would do well to beware that in this season of tempests and tornadoes they unsettle not the ballast of the state. There are elements of tremendous power slumbering, and but partially slumbering, among the masses; and woe to the people — a double woe to the aristocracy of the land — if these once awaken in the fierce and untamable fury of their nature, to bid defiance to every law, and to trample on every privilege. God, to avert the calamity, and in his great and wonted care for our country, is awakening the old spirit of the Church, — that free and noble spirit which, alike opposed to despotism in the ruler and to license in the people, can brook neither the grinding tyranny of the few, nor yet the fiercer and more savage intolerance of the many; and if his design of mercy be thwarted through a selfish and short-sighted policy, the judgment shall assuredly fall heaviest on the classes which offend most. In the event of a popular convulsion, all must necessarily suffer, and suffer to no good end. It is an immutable law of Deity that the blessings of freedom can be enjoyed by only wise and virtuous men, and that the uncultured and the vicious, in their vain attempts to secure to themselves an ideal liberty, for which they are unfitted, shall struggle fruitlessly in a miserable and delusive cycle of crime and sorrow, that ever returns into itself. All would necessarily suffer. But it could not be by the common people that the infliction would be felt most severely; nor, were the hour already come, would the writer of these pages exchange his humble lot, with its various adjuncts, necessary or peculiar, for perhaps even the highest. He has but little to lose or to provoke envy; he has been accustomed to hardship and fatigue; he is in the full vigor of manhood; he could fight as a common soldier in the ranks; and, if he survived the struggle, he might find himself occupying a not lower level at its close than at its commencement. But the aged judges, the wealthy patrons, the delicately-nurtured aristocracy of Scotland, the men who have so much to lose, which in a popular convulsion could not fail to be lost, nay, even the more eloquent orators and more vigorous thinkers of the age, who have yet to give their first proof of military talent, — what fate do they augur to themselves? Have they secured the position which they are to occupy in the struggle, or ascertained the exact rank which they are to bear among the new aristocracy, or under the second Cromwell? They think miserably amiss if they think the people could not find leaders without employing them; nor do they well if, instead of calculating upon the formidable depth and momentum of the yet unbroken waters, they merely look (with, I grant, the natural and proper contempt) on the froth and spume which idly bubbles on the surface,—on the shallow and futile talent of demagogues and declaimers, so noisy and obtrusive now, but which, with the first breach in the barrier, would be forever engulfed in the torrent.

It is an unchallenged truth, that it is not from reason we derive our highest degree of knowledge, and that we lower the certainty of the intuitive if we but equal it with the merely inferable. It is according to the nature of the human mind that an ascertained fact should weigh more than even the most ingenious argument; and it is on this principle that the experience of fourteen years, spent in the workshed and the barrack, in almost every district of the country, and among almost every class of the common people, has had infinitely more to do in influencing my opinion regarding the high importance of the present struggle, and the imminent danger of the community, than all that even the more rational waiters for a merely intellectual millennium have urged on the one hand, or all that ever the abler and better Voluntaries have argued on the other. I have not yet discovered the elements of the coming happiness among the immense masses broken loose from religion. And though I can believe, with even Voltaire, that great prosperity has proved prejudicial to the Church, I cannot see that it is from prosperity the Church of Scotland has most to dread at present; nor have I found much satisfaction in balancing matters between the ascetics of Upper Egypt, or the more than half-infidel gnostics of the East, and the corrupt and tyrannical churchmen established by Constantine. Arguments drawn from so remote and misty a period have but the effect of rendering the discussion long and the inference uncertain. I have been enabled to arrive at conclusions much more satisfactory, to at least my own judgment, than what I have found among the Voluntaries themselves. I am not ignorant that the party has its truly excellent lay adherents — its good and faithful ministers. I have associated for months together with pious Voluntaries from whom I differed wonderfully little; and Sabbath after Sabbath have I accompanied them to the meeting-house, to listen with, I trust, more than pleasure to some of their better divines; and this in districts — and there are still too many such — where the gospel is not preached in the Establishment. It has not escaped me, however, that the religious men of the party are comparatively few; that, save for purely political purposes, they act but feebly on the mass to which they are attached, and not at all for good on the formidable masses beyond; that, in short, they form merely the "silver lining of the cloud," and that there is enough of the smoke and stench of infidelity in its obscurer recesses to render a Voluntary triumph the bane of the country. The conscientious motives of Dr. Wardlaw and his better friends operate but feebly and inefficiently on the thousands who, holding ostensibly by the same opinions, make common cause with these good but mistaken men, for accomplishing the same object. I have met with other than pious Voluntaries — and this, too, in immensely greater numbers — with unsatisfied and restless spirits, who, had not the controversy been agitated in its present form, would have opposed themselves, not to the Establishment, but to Christianity itself; and, with no secular interest involved in the quarrel, save in its remoter consequences, I have deliberately taken my stand on the side of the Church of Scotland, not more influenced by a cherished recollection of her past services in the cause of God and humanity, or by a well-grounded confidence in those pregnant elements of good which she still so largely retains in her constitution, than from an assured conviction that the animating spirit of her opponents is less an inspiration than a possession. It is not this spirit of modern Voluntaryism, so unlike that of the missionary, which is to reëstablish the old character of our country, — to substitute a pure Christianity for the semi-barbarous and unreasoning infidelity of our larger towns, — to fill our hamlets with such men as the cotter described by the poet, — to sanction the testimony of some second Kirkton, or to justify the eulogium of some future Whitefield. It is easy to distinguish between a disorganizing influence and a reforming principle, — between the "revived opinions" of the sixteenth century and the new opinions of the nineteenth, — between a Scotch Parliament suppressing a corrupt Establishment because it was Popish, and a French convention annihilating a similar institution because it was Christian. It is reformation, not change, — Christianity, not Voluntaryism, — that can alone save our country.

There is a palpable confusion of idea in the main argument of the party. It confounds things essentially different — the provided temporalities with the secular spirit. It regards a mere accidental connection as a necessary and inevitable consequence; and could the absurdity occur in any other than a semi-theological controversy, we might hear the incompetency of Cope or Burgoyne attributed to the parliamentary grant for the pay of the army, and the brutality and gross injustice of Jeffries to the establishment of the court over which he presided. We are content to trace the well-marked distinction in both the past history and present position of the Church of Scotland; and are in no danger whatever of confounding the vantage-ground which her better ministers have occupied to such good purpose, from the days of Knox until now, with that secular spirit which has oppressed and persecuted her in both the earlier and later periods of her existence,—in the one as an Episcopal form, in the other as a Patronage principle.

LITERARY CHARACTER OF KNOX.

It is one of the main distinctions of works produced by the master minds, whether in literature or the fine arts, that they contain a large amount of thought. There are books of no great bulk which it seems scarce possible to exhaust, and pictures which, after one had looked at them for hours together, appear just as fresh and new as at first when one comes to look at them again. The works of Hogarth are scarcely less remarkable for vigor and condensation of thought than the works of Shakspeare; nor is Sir David Wilkie a less fascinating author than Sir Walter Scott, or a less masterly delineator of character. Both these great artists—the living and the dead one, Hogarth and Sir David—have shown how possible it is for men of genius to think vigorously upon canvas; and that a clear, readable, condensed style may be attained in painting as certainly as in writing. One never tires of their productions. They tell admirable stories in so admirable a manner, that the oftener we peruse them the better are we pleased; and almost every story has its moral. There is, however, one of the most readable of Sir David's pictures which contains what we have been inclined to think a gross historical error, and belies the character of a very great man. His "Knox preaching before the Lords of the Congregation" is unquestionably a splendid composition, full of thought and sentiment; but the main figure is defective. It represents not the powerful and persuasive orator, whose unmatched eloquence led captive the great minds of the country, but the mere fanatical leader of an unthinking rabble. It reminds us of the narrow-minded heresiarch described by Hume and Gilbert Stuart, not of the vigorous-thoughted worthy apostrophized by the noble Milton as "Knox, the reformer of a kingdom," — "a great man, animated by the Spirit of God."[1]

The labors of the late Dr. M'Crie have done much to disabuse the public mind regarding the true character of Knox, moral and intellectual. Never before did an honest and able man turn the stream of truth through such an

[1] Mr. Carlyle, in his letter to David Laing, Esq., of the Signet Library, Edinburgh, on the project of a National Exhibition of Scottish Portraits, refers to this work of Wilkie's in the following terms: "No picture that I ever saw by a man of genius can well be, in regard to all earnest purposes, a more perfect failure. Can anything, in fact, be more entirely *useless* for earnest purposes, more *un*like what ever could have been the reality, than that gross Energumen, more like a boxing-butcher, whom he has set into a pulpit surrounded with draperies, with fat-shouldered women and play-actor men in mail, and labelled Knox?" With all deference to authority so high and emphasis so great, it may be permitted us to doubt whether Mr. Miller and Mr. Carlyle have done full justice to Wilkie's picture. It was legitimate for the artist to paint Knox as a preacher, and in this character his representation is certainly not unlike what the reality would have been. Knox in the pulpit was one of the fieriest incarnations of the *perfervidum ingenium* of his countrymen — more fiery even, were that possible, than Chalmers. James Melville heard him preach in 1571, the year before his death. Such was his weakness, that he went leaning on a staff, his neck wrapped in furs, and supported by Richard Ballenden. It was necessary to lift him to the pulpit, and on first entering it he had to lean for a time to draw breath; "bot," says James, in his old dialect, "er he haid done with his sermone, he was sa active and vigorous, that he was lyk to ding the pulpit in blads, and flie out of it." Wilkie had probably this passage in view when he designed his picture, and the gestures of his Knox correspond as closely as possible to Melville's last words. The question whether Wilkie's choice of a moment for representing Knox was just and felicitous — whether it is thus we ought to realize to ourselves the Reformer of Scotland — resolves itself into this other, how far the character and work of Knox were revealed or typified in his pulpit appearances. Restrained by the conditions of his art, Wilkie was forced to choose between the Knox of the council chamber, or of the General Assembly, or of the study, and the Knox of the pulpit. Perhaps he ought to have painted him in some one of the former characters rather than in the latter. But the Reformation was much the work of preaching, and the painter's eye of Wilkie was correct in discerning how Knox preached. It may be suggested that before the Lords of the Congregation he would have subdued his fire. It is not likely. In the pulpit least of all would he fear or respect the face of man. The "fat-shouldered women, and play-actor men in mail," are of course conventional and absurd. — ED.

Augean stable of calumny and falsehood as this admirable writer in elucidating the history of the Reformation. He accomplished such a revolution in public opinion regarding the characters and events of the period, as the well-chosen hero of his first biography accomplished in its religion.

The reign of the dissolute and totally unprincipled Charles II. affected more than the mode and framework of English literature; it affected its spirit also. It substituted for that indigenous school to which Shakspeare and Milton belong, and which, in a later time, has been restored by Cowper and Wordsworth, the feeble elegances of French literature in the reign of Louis XIV. It substituted also for the native spirit of liberty and the zeal of truth, the servilities of French flattery and French falsehood. It was in this reign of degradation — the reign in which the glorious "Paradise Lost" was described by a servile versifier as a "poem remarkable for only its length" — that Knox came to be represented, like the blind poet who so honored and cherished his memory, as a rude and unmannerly fanatic. He had taught kings that the divine right is not on the side of irresponsible power, but on the side of a well-regulated popular liberty. He had shown, with irresistible effect, that whatever God has commanded, men have a "divine right" to obey; and that in such matters kings and law-makers have no right whatever to interfere. And the hereditary despots could neither overturn his logic nor forgive him the lesson. But they could revile and calumniate; and the creatures whom they half fed, half starved, fixed the calumny in the literature of the time. There was a decided improvement in the following age; but the tone of its theology, in at least the sister kingdom, was unfavorable to the character of Knox. It was a time of spiritual death in the English Church; and the cry of fanaticism raised against the reformer, chiefly on a civil plea, in the reign of Charles II., was prolonged, in the reign of Anne and the earlier Georges, on a purely religious one. Naturally enough, his beliefs were deemed absurd and irrational by the defamers and depreciators of Whitefield; and there was no M'Crie to tell the Rundles and Atterburys of the time that the zealot whom they contemned and undervalued had been a fellow-laborer in the English Church with its Latimers and Cranmers, and had lent his assistance in framing the code of belief which they themselves had professed to receive, but for which in reality they cared so little.

The tone of our Scottish literature in the last century was borrowed in part from our English neighbors, and in part from the French. Hume, with less liveliness but greater original powers than Voltaire, condescended, in a considerable degree, to imitate the historical style of that volatile and accomplished writer, and evinced a hostility equally bitter to whatever had the sacredness of religion to recommend it. Robertson, Smollett, Kaimes, Adam Smith, Gilbert Stuart, Tytler, and Moore, had all caught the English mode and the English spirit, and were, in at least as marked a degree as any of their English contemporaries, tinctured with infidelity. Hence, in part, the disrespect shown by almost all these writers to the memory of Knox. Many of them, too, had imagination enough to evince a sympathy for the misfortunes of Mary, which a sense of her crimes and infamies seems to have checked in the friends and followers who would not fight for her at Carberry Hill, and who struck only a half-blow in her quarrel at Langside; and the man who could attach more importance to the religion of a country than to the smiles of so fine a woman, was characterized as rude and brutal. Robertson's hostility to Knox is well known. Even Hume — who was by much too cool and too sagacious a man to share in the general admiration of Mary — could urge with him, as an argument of weight, that, if he only gave him up the princess, "he would have the compensatory satisfaction of seeing the reformer made sufficiently ridiculous." We are in possession of a volume of the "Edinburgh Magazine," of the time when that periodical was edited by Gilbert Stuart, and when the Moderate clergy of the south of Scotland were the chief contributors. The articles are temperate throughout, except on two subjects, — the Secession and John Knox; but when these are introduced, we find that the writers seem to have lost all command of temper, or to have regarded as legitimate the foulest epithets of opprobrium and reproach. There is, in particular, one article on Knox, written apparently by the editor, in which our venerable reformer is described as mean, illiterate, narrow-minded, cruel, and libidinous; and so completely does the engraver for the work appear to have entered into the writer's spirit, that the figure in an accompanying print wants only horns and a tail to render it complete.

But whatever Gilbert Stuart might have thought of the literature of John Knox, it is certain the contemporaries of the reformer, both friends and enemies, estimated it very high. Nor in the present time are we without data on which to decide. The art of writing history in the vernacular tongue was not an art of the age. Even the great Bacon failed utterly in this department, nearly an age after, and produced, in his History of Henry VII., a work which has been quoted liberally by both Lord Kaimes and Sir Richard Steele, to show how very badly history may be written. Knox's "History of the Reformation" is immensely superior to the history of Bacon. It displays more freedom and more power. There is a dramatic effect in some of the dialogues altogether fascinating, and there are touches of such simple pathos in the narrative that they affect even to tears. We would instance the closing scene in the life of the martyr Wishart, as described in the first volume. No one can glance over the passage without being convinced that the heart of the writer was a heart tender and compassionate in the first degree. We doubt not that it was written with wet eyes and a swelling heart. He relates, with almost New Testament simplicity, how the "said Mr. George Wishart, departing from the town of Haddington" under a presentiment of death, "took good night forever of all his acquaintances," and "how John Knox pressing hard to go with him," the devoted man said, "Nay, return to your children, God's people, and God bless you; one is sufficient for a sacrifice:" and how "the said John Knox unwillingly obeyed." He relates, further, after narrating the apprehension and trial of the martyr, "that the fire was made ready, and the stake, at the west port of the Castle of St. Andrews, near to the Priory; and that, directly over against the place, the castle windows were hung with rich hangings, and velvet cushions laid for the cardinal and the prelates, who came to feast their eyes with the torments of this innocent man;" how that, "dreading lest he should be rescued by his friends, the cardinal had commanded that all the ordnance of the castle should be bent right against the place of execution, and had ordered the gunners to be ready standing by their guns, until such time as his victim was burnt to ashes;" how, "all this being done, they bound Mr. George's hands behind his back, and with sound of trumpet led him forth with the soldiers from the castle to the place of their cruel and wicked execution;" how, "*as he came forth of the castle gate, there met him certain beggars, asking of him alms, for God's sake, to whom he answered, 'I want my hands wherewith I was wont to give you alms; but the merciful Lord, of his benignity and abundant grace, that feedeth all men, vouchsafe to give you necessaries, both unto your body and souls;*'" how, "after this, he was led to the fire with a rope about his neck and a chain of iron about his middle; and how, kneeling down beside the faggots, he rose again, and thrice said these words, 'O thou Sovereign of the world, have mercy upon me; Father of Heaven, I commend my spirit into thy holy hands;'" how, "when he had made this prayer, he turned unto the people and said, 'I beseech you, Christian brethren and sisters, that ye be not offended at the Word of God, for the affliction and torment which ye see ready prepared for me; but I exhort you that you love the Word of God, and suffer patiently, and with a comfortable heart, for the Word's sake, which is your undoubted salvation and everlasting comfort;'" how that "many more faithful words he spake unto them, taking no heed or care of the cruel tortures prepared for him;" and how, "by and by, the trumpet sounding, he was tied to the stake, and the fire kindled;" how "*the captain of the castle, for the love he bore to Mr. Wishart, drew so near to the fire that the flame thereof did him harm*, and urged him to be of good courage, and to beg from God the forgiveness of his sins;" and how the martyr answered him thus from the flames, "'The fire torments my body, but no ways abates my spirit;'" how "then Mr. Wishart, looking steadfastly towards the cardinal, said, 'He who in such state from that high place feedeth his eyes with my torments, within few days shall be hanged out at the same window, to be seen with as much ignominy as he now leaneth there in pride;'" how, finally, "in short space thereafter, the fire being very great, he was consumed to powder." We can believe that the man who wrote this affecting narrative — the "ruffian Knox," the "barbarian who made Mary weep" — told his queen the very truth when he assured her that "he delighted not in the weeping of any of God's creatures; yea, that he could scarce abide the tears of his own boys when his own hands corrected them." Love and pity were assuredly no unwonted emotions in the large heart of him who "never feared the face of man."

It is not as a historian, however, that the literary character of Knox can be rated highest. His history, unlike Bacon's, which is rather overlabored than the reverse, seems, so far as regards composition, to have been carelessly written, — in the midst, doubtless, of the ceaseless round of harassing employments in which the latter portion of his life was spent. It is in his shorter compositions that his great ability as a writer is best shown; and, with some of these before us, we speak advisedly when we assert that he was decidedly the first man of either kingdom who wrote what would be deemed a good English style, tested by the present standard. There is a mellifluous flow and thorough ease in his sentences altogether astonishing, when we take into account the stiff inflexibility of the English language at that period, as shown in the prose writings of even his abler contemporaries. Whole colonies of half-naturalized Greek and Latin words had been just brought into the language; and, as if unsuited to its genius, they performed their work clumsily and heavily in even the hands of superior men. We instance the earlier homilies of the English Church. Almost every member of every sentence in these compositions is broken into two parts, the last of which generally repeats in *Saxon* English the idea which in the first is expressed in *Latinized* English. And hence their stiff and peculiar verbosity of style. In the more carefully written compositions of Knox there is none of this. Johnson has remarked of Milton, that the "heat of his genius sublimed his learning," and threw off merely the finer and more subtle parts into his poetry. In the same way, the genius of the great reformer seems to have fused into one pliant and homogeneous mass the language which, when employed by men of a lower order, was so heterogeneous and untractable. He seemed as if born to anticipate the improvements and refinements of an age yet distant, and this not merely in his knowledge of things, but in his command of words. Sir Walter Raleigh has been described by some of our higher critics as the first good prose writer of England; we beg to submit to the reader the following prayer, written by Knox during the reign of Mary of Guise, nearly an age, be it remarked, before Sir Walter produced the great work on which his fame as a writer chiefly rests. We know not in the compass of our literature a more interesting composition. It was written at a time when the ashes of Walter Mill still blackened the public square of St. Andrews, and gives us no inadequate idea of the power of that eloquence chosen by Deity as his honored instrument for the reformation of a kingdom. We adopt the punctuation and spelling of the oldest edition we have yet seen, — that of the year 1600.

A Complaint of the Tyrannie used against the Saincts of God, containing a Confession of our Sinnes, and a Prayer for the Deliverance and Preservation of the Church, and Confusion of the Enemies.

Eternall and everlasting God, Father of our Lord Jesus Christ, who hast commanded us to pray, and promised to hear us, even when we doe call from the pit of desperation, the miseries of these our most wicked dayes compel us to poure forth before thee the complaintes of our wretched hearts, oppressed with sorrow. Our eyes doe behold, and our eares doe heare, the calamities and oppression which no tongue can expresse, neither yet, alas, doe our dull hearts rightlie consider the same; for the heathen are entred into thine inheritance, they have polluted thy sanctuarie, prophaned and abolished thy blessed institutions, moste cruellie murthered, and daylie doe murther thy deare children; thou hast exalted the arm and force of our enemies, thou hast exposed us a prey to ignominie and shame, before such as persecute thy trueth; their wayes doe prosper, they glorie in mischiefe, and speake proudlie against the honour of thy name; thou goest not forth as captaine before our hostes; the edge of our sworde, which sometimes was most sharpe, is now blunte, and doeth returne without victorie in battell.

It appeareth to our enemies, O Lord, that thou hast broken that league which of thy mercie and goodnesse thou hast made with thy Church: For the libertie which they have to kill thy children like sheep, and to shed their blood, no man resisting, doeth so blind and puffe them up with pride, that they ashame not to affirme, that thou regardest not our intreating. Thy long suffering and patience maketh them bold from crueltie to proceed to the blasphemie of thy name. And in the mean season, alas, we do not consider the heavenesse of our sinnes, which long have deserved at thy hands not onlie these temporall plagues, but also the torments prepared for the inobedient; for we knowing thy blessed will, have not applyed our diligence to obey the same, but have followed, for the most part, the vaine conversation of the blinde world: and therefore in verie justice hast thou visited our unthankfulnesse. But, O Lord, if thou shalt observe and keep in mind for ever the iniquities of thy children, then shall no flesh abide nor be saved in thy presence. And therefore we, convicted in our own conscience, that most justlie we suffer, as punished by thy hand, doe nevertheless call for mercie, according to promise: And first we desire to be corrected with the rodde of thy children, by the which we may be brought to a perfect hatred of sinne, and of ourselves; and therefore, that it would please thee, for Christ Jesus thy Sonne's sake, to shew us, and to thy whole Church universally persecuted, the same favour and grace that sometimes thou diddest, when the chief members of the same for anguish and fear were compelled to crie, Why have the nations raged? Why have the people made uproares? And why have princes and kings conjured against thine anointed Christ Jesus? Then diddest thou wonderfullie assist and preserve thy small and dispersed flock; then diddest thou burst the barres and gates of yron; then diddest thou shake the foundations of strong prisons; then diddest thou plague the cruell persecutors; and then gavest thou tranquilitie and rest, after those raging stormes and cruell afflictions.

O Lord, thou remainest one for ever; we have offended, and are unworthie of anie deliverance; but worthie art thou to be a true and constant God, and worthie is thy deare Sonne, Christ Jesus, that thou shouldest glorifie his name, and revenge the blaspemie spoken against the trueth of his gospel, which is by our adversaries damned as a doctrine deceaveable and false. Yea, the blood of thy Sonne is trodden under feet, in that the blood of his members is shed for witnessing of thy trueth; and therefore, O Lord, behold not the unworthinesse of us that call for the redresse of these enormities, neither let our imperfections stop thy mercies from us; but behold the face of thine anointed Christ Jesus, and let the equitie of our cause prevaile in thy presence; let the blood of thy saincts which is shed be openlie revenged in the eyes of thy Church, that mortall men may know the vanitie of their counsells, and that thy children may have a taste of thine eternal goodness. And seeing that from that man of sinne, that *Romane* Antichrist, the chiefe adversarie to thy deare Sonne, doth all iniquitie spring, and mischiefe proceede, let it please thy Fatherlie mercie, more and more to reveale his deceit and tyrannie to the world: open the eyes of princes and magistrates, that clearly they may see how shamefullie they have bene abused by his deceaveable wayes; how by him they are compelled most cruellie to shed the blood of thy saincts, and by violence refuse thy new and eternall Testament; that they in deep consideration of these grivous offences, may unfainedlie lament their horrible defection from Christ Jesus thy Sonne; from henceforth studying to promote his glorie in the dominions committed to their charges, that so yet once again the glorie of thy gospell may appeare to the world. And seeing also that the chief strength of that odious beast consisteth in the dissension of princes, let it please thee, O Father, which hast claimed to thyself to be called the God of Peace, to unite and knitte in perfect love the hearts of all those that look for the life everlasting. Let no craft of Sathan move them to warre one against another, neither yet to maintaine by their force and strength that kingdome of darknesse; but rather that godlie they may conspire (illuminated by thy Word), to root out from among them all superstition with the maintainers of the same.

These, thy graces, O Lord, we unfainedlie desire to be poured forth upon all realms and nations; but principallie, according to that duetie which thou requirest of us, we most earnestlie desire that the heartes of the inhabitants of *England* and *Scotland*, whom the malice and craft of Sathan, and of his supportes, of manie yeers have dissevered, may continue in that godlie unitie which now, of late, it hath pleased thee to give them, being knitted together in the unitie of thy Word: Open their eyes that clearlie they may behold the bondage and miserie which is purposed against them both; and give unto them wisdome to avoide the same, in such sort that, in their godlie concorde, thy name may be glorified, and thy dispersed flock comforted and relieved.

The commonwealthes, O Lord, where thy gospell is trulie preached, and harbour granted to the afflicted members of Christ's bodie, we commend to thy protection and mercie; be thou unto them a defence and buckler. Be thou a watchman to their walles, and a perpetuall safeguard to their cities, that the crafty assaults of their enemies, repulsed by thy power, thy gospell may have free passage from one nation to another; and let all preachers and ministers of the same have the gifts of thy Holie Spirit in such aboundance as thy godlie wisdome shall know to be expedient for the perfect instruction of that flock which thou hast redeemed with the precious blood of thine onlie and well-beloved Sonne Jesus Christ. Purge their hearts from all kind of superstition, from ambition, and vaine glorie, by which Sathan continuallie laboureth to stirre up ungodlie contention, and let them so consent in the unitie of thy trueth, that neither the estimation which they have of men, neither the vaine opinions which they have conceived by their writinges, prevaile in them against the cleare understanding of thy blessed Word.

And now, last, O Lord, we moste humblie beseech thee, according to that prayer of thy dear Sonne our Lord Jesus, so to sanctifie and confirme us in thine eternal veritie, that neither the love of life temporal, nor yet the feare of torments and corporall death, cause us to denie the same when the confession of our faith shall be required of us; but so assist us, with the power of thy Spirit, that not onlie boldlie we may confess thee, O Father of mercies, to be the true God alone, and whom thou hast sent, our Lord Jesus, to be the only Saviour of the world, but also, that constantlie we may withstand all doctrine repugning to thy eternall trueth, revealed to us in thy most blessed Word. Remove from our hearts the blind love of ourselves; and so rule thou all the actions of our life, that in us thy godlie name may be glorified, thy Church edified, and Sathan finally confounded by the power and means of our Lord Jesus Christ, to whom, with thee and the Holy Spirit, be all praise and glory, before thy congregation now and ever.

Arise, O Lord, and let thine enemies be ashamed, let them flee from thy presence that hate thy godly name; let the grones of thy prisoners enter in before thee, and preserve by thy power such as be appointed to death; let not thine enemies thus triumph to the end, but let them understand, that against thee they fight: preserve and defend the vine which thy right hand hath planted, and let all nations see the glory of thine Anointed.

Hasten, Lord, and tarrie not.

DR. THOMAS M'CRIE.

These articles upon Dr. Thomas M'Crie have no direct bearing upon the Disruption controversy. They illustrate, however, in a way eminently clear and pertinent, the precise manner in which the principles then at stake were apprehended by Mr. Miller, and constitute a masterly sketch of the beginnings of the contest in connection with the ecclesiastical history of Scotland in the present century. For these reasons, and on account of their intrinsic value as embracing a powerful and vivid delineation of one of the greatest Presbyterian divines, it has been deemed proper to give them a place in the volume. — Ed.

ARTICLE FIRST.

It is now sixteen years since we first saw the late Dr. M'Crie. We had learned to love and respect him at even an earlier period, not merely as an honest and truly able man, but also as a genuine type and representative of the Christian patriots of Scotland, — those worthies of other days, whose names we had been taught to pronounce in our childhood as at once the wisest and warmest friends of the people. All our sympathies, national, Presbyterian, and literary, had taken part together in our admiration of the historian of Knox. There was an air of positive romance about his history as a man of letters, which, by exciting our imagination, endeared him to us the more. Waller has remarked of the poet Denham, "that he broke out like the Irish rebellion, threescore thousand strong, when nobody was aware or in the least suspected it." But with how much more force does the remark apply to Dr. M'Crie? Half the literary power of the country had been employed for more than a hundred years in blackening the memory of our noble-hearted reformers. Hume, at once the shrewdest infidel that ever opposed the truth and the ablest historian that ever perverted it, had done his worst. Gilbert Stuart, no mean writer, had done his worst too, and in even a bitterer spirit. Tytler, Whitaker, and a whole host of others, including some of our most popular poets, had followed in their track; and the pictures of the more wary but not less insidious Robertson — pictures illustrative of the remark of Pope, that what men are taught to pity they soon learn to love — had prejudiced the public mind even more powerfully against the opponents of Mary than the attacks of more open assailants. The memory of Knox and his coadjutors was pilloried in the literature of the country; every witling, as he passed by, flung his handful of filth; and that portion of our Presbyterian people who, looking into the past through the religious medium, and believing that our reformers, as men awakened to a sense of the truth, were far different from what our literati represented them, could only retain for themselves the juster estimate of their fathers regarding them, without influencing in the least the opinions of their contemporaries. Such was the state of things when a nameless champion entered the lists, and threw down his gauntlet in the cause of Knox and the reformers. Who or what was he? A person who had been engaged a few years before in some obscure squabble, which he had seemed to think of vast importance, forsooth, but which had interested no one but himself and the opponents, who, with the aid of the Court of Session, had *put* him *down*, and which really no one had thought worth while trying to understand. Well, but what was the result on this occasion? The literature of a whole century went down before him, — Hume, Stuart, Tytler, Whitaker, Robertson, and the poets, — all the great names among the dead; and the living — men of a lower stature — he foiled with scarce half an effort. All went down who opposed him, and the rest stood warily aloof. The far known "Chaldee Manuscript," so much more witty than reverent, is happy in its description of this redoubtable champion; for, with all its mixture of the grotesque, it has at once the merit of being poetical and true. "And the Griffin," says the Manuscript, "came with a roll of the names of those whose blood had been shed, between his teeth; and I saw him standing over the body of one that had been buried long in the grave, defending it from all men; and, behold, there were none which durst come near him."

We had just passed our first week in this part of the country, a little out of town, early in 1824, and had walked into Edinburgh on the Sabbath morning to see the Doctor and hear him preach. Only two evenings before, we had been sauntering, after the labors of the day, along one of the green lanes of Liberton, and had met with a gentleman whose appearance had struck us as being as much the reverse of commonplace as any we had ever seen. He was an erect, spare, tall man — rather above, we should have supposed, than under six feet, though perhaps his carriage, which had much quiet dignity in it, and a good deal of the military air, might have led to an over-estimate. The countenance was pale, we would have said almost sallow, and the cast of expression somewhat melancholy; but there was a wakeful penetration in the dark eyes, and an air of sedate power and reflection so legibly stamped on every feature, that we were irresistibly impressed with the idea he could be no ordinary man. We stood looking after him. He wore a brown great-coat over a suit of black, the neck a good deal whitened by powder; and the rim of the hat behind, which was slightly turned up, bore a similar stain. Who can that possibly be? we thought. Shall we impart to the reader the recollection which flashed into our mind, — from an association awakened, doubtless, by what we deemed the half-military, half-clerical air of the stranger? — it was that of Sir Richard Steele's story of the devout old military chaplain, who, on being insulted by a foul-mouthed, blasphemous young officer, challenged him, fought and disarmed him, and then, ere he took him to mercy, made him kneel down and ask pardon, not of him, but of the Being whom he had blasphemed. On the Sunday morning we contrived to find our way to the Doctor's chapel about half an hour ere divine service began, and planted ourselves in one of the empty pews (for the congregation had not yet assembled) in front of the pulpit. The people began to gather; — we thought, but it might not be so, that more than the usual proportion were elderly; a respectable looking, well-dressed man, accompanied by his wife and family, entered the pew which we had so unceremoniously appropriated, and we rose to leave it for the passage, a good deal abashed at feeling, for the first time, that we were an intruder, for we had thought previously of only the Doctor. The man, however, politely insisted that we should keep our seat. On sitting down again, we found that the Doctor had meanwhile entered the pulpit, and we at once recognized in the historian of Knox and Melville the military chaplain whom we had met in the green lane.

We were first struck by the great simplicity of his manner. It reminded us of a remark of Robertson's, on his return from his visit to London, immediately after the publication of his History of Scotland. The extraordinary merit of the work had introduced him to all the more eminent literati of the time; and he was asked, on coming back, by a friend in Edinburgh, whether he thought the celebrated men, his new acquaintances, varied as they were in genius and acquirement, had any one trait in common. "Yes," replied the historian, "one trait at least, and a very striking one; all the truly great among them are marked by a child-like simplicity of manner." The service went on. There was a solemn impressiveness about the Doctor's prayers, which were, in the best sense of the term, extempore, that was well suited to lead our thoughts from himself to the Being whom he addressed. There was little exertion of voice, and no striking combinations of set phrases, fine, doubtless, when they are new, but on which it is possible to ring the changes until they become commonplace and lose their meaning; but there was what was much better, — a continuous stream of thought, sobered by a feeling of devout reverence, which found ready entrance into the mind, and subdued it into seriousness. He entered upon his discourse. We were again struck by the great simplicity of his manner and style, and listened, rather soothed and pleased by his lucid statements of important truths, grounded, if we may so express ourselves, on a deep substratum of serious feeling, than surprised by any marked originality of view. By and by, however, when the first obvious principles were laid down, the Doctor began to draw inferences. Ah! thought we, as we sat up erect in the pew, there now is something we never heard before. The discourse, simple and quiet at its commencement, had assumed a new character. The unquestioned but common truths were but the foundations of the edifice; the edifice itself was such a one as the historian of Knox and Melville could alone have erected. There were remarks on human nature, that, from their graphic shrewdness, reminded us of Crabbe, and yet the mode was entirely different; there were gleams of fancy, that, falling for a moment on some of the remoter recesses of the subject, lighted them up into sudden brightness, and, when fully shown, the gleam disappeared; there were strokes of eloquence, condensed at times into a single sentence, that found their way direct to the heart; and far conclusions attained by a few steps through vistas of thought unopened before. We would perhaps not have termed the discourse a philosophic one at the time we were listening to it: men are misled by the mere conventionalities of thought — the set terms and phrases in which thought is usually embodied; and according to the pattern of these are they apt to judge and classify the thoughts themselves. But the reverse process is surely the true one: it is the man, not the dress, to which we are to look, — the soul, not the body; and, tried by this process, the Doctor's discourse was philosophic in the best and highest sense of the term; for what is philosophy but good sense, on an extended scale, employed in discovering the remote causes of things, or in anticipating their distant effects? His plain, simple style reminded us of Swift's definition — "Proper words in their proper places." There was nothing very striking in the general groundwork, only it would be found no easy matter to alter any one of his words for a better. Even his occasional Scotticisms had invariably more point and a larger meaning than the nearly synonymous English phrases which a fastidious critic might have substituted for them. But style, and even thought, were but subordinate matters in the pulpit ministrations of Dr. M'Crie. Never have we listened to a preacher — and from that day until we quitted the district he was almost our only minister — on whose judgment and integrity we could more thoroughly depend. Scotchmen, especially the Presbyterian Scotch, are naturally sticklers for the right of private judgment, and less disposed than almost any other people to yield themselves up implicitly to their religious teachers; and hence it is that, though Moderatism has been encamped in the Church for more than a century, it has acquired no popular basis. To the Doctor, however, we soon learned to give ourselves up entirely. Not that he saved us the trouble of thought; — his discourses were by much too intellectual for that, and his remarks had a germinative quality, suited to fill the mind which received them in their unbroken vitality: but if he did not save us the trouble of thought, he at least saved us the trouble of suspicion. We could lean ourselves unsuspectingly on his judgment; nature had formed him for a leader; and his capacious understanding and almost instinctive sagacity were heightened and strengthened by other and even more valuable qualities—the depth of his devotional feelings, and the high-toned rectitude of the moral sense.

The Sunday on which we first heard Dr. M'Crie was, as we have said, early in the season. There had been a sudden change of weather a few days before, and there was a great deal of coughing in the chapel. We were annoyed by finding some of the pithiest remarks in the discourse broken in upon by some remorseless cougher, and mutilated, so far at least as the listeners were concerned; and the Doctor seemed somewhat annoyed too. He knew better, however, than we did, in what degree even coughing lies under the restraint of the will; he knew, too, what we did not, that when people are very much surprised they cease to cough. Suddenly the Doctor stopped short in the middle of his argument; every face in the chapel was turned to the pulpit, and for a full minute so dead was the stillness that a pin might be heard to drop. "I see, my friends," he said, with a suppressed smile, "you can all be quiet enough when I am quiet." It would be difficult to imagine a better humored rebuke, but certainly never was there a more effectual one. A suppressed cough might occasionally be heard during the rest of the service, but not even the tithe of what had disturbed it before. Simple as the incident may seem, we remember being much struck by it, as illustrative of the peculiar shrewdness of the character.

We have but just risen from the perusal of the Life of Dr. M'Crie by his son, the bulkiest volume we ever ran over at a sitting, and certainly one of the most interesting we have ever read. We had thought that the subject of the memoir could not have risen in our esteem, and, now that we have communicated our sentiments and recollections of him to the reader, others might perhaps have thought so too; but we have been mistaken; our respect for his memory is higher now than it ever was before. The whole character lies open before us,—magnanimous, wise, sincere, humble, affectionate, invincibly honest, consistently devout; and the more thoroughly we study it, the more do we find to love and admire. It forms a mirror by which to dress the heart; it furnishes a rule by which to regulate the understanding. We contemplate with a feeling of awe the far-sighted character of his intellect,—to use the language of Cowper, "the terrible sagacity that informed his heart," in anticipating coming events. We have alluded to his first controversy. It commenced just thirty-seven years ago, and involved him in great difficulty and distress; many of his friends and his people forsook him; he was dispossessed of his chapel by the strong arm of the law; he was *deposed* and *excommunicated* by his brethren. Yes, the greatest and ablest, and certainly one of the best and most devout Dissenters Scotland ever produced, was deposed and excommunicated: for what?—simply for contumacy and disobedience to the synod of which he was a member. But disobedience in what? That could not be understood: it involved some metaphysical point about the civil magistrate, and the duty of nations as such in their religious character. Lawyers and judges could see nothing in it; and they decided the case merely as one of contumacy. The press and the pulpit were alike silent. The matter was one of no interest or importance whatever, except to the sufferer for conscience' sake; and he published a "Statement" on the subject, which no one read, and asserted that the principles which he opposed were soon to shake the whole country, and subvert all its religious institutions. "But we will not live to see that day," said one of his humbler friends. "I don't know that," was the reply; "I feel persuaded you will see the fruits of these principles *in a quarter of a century*." Men know something better about them now. It was the great Voluntary contest which this remarkable man saw so clearly at this early period; and his "Statement" has since been eagerly sought after and reprinted, as the ablest defence of religious establishments which has yet appeared. To employ his own striking figure, he had seen "in the cloud like the man's hand, the tempest which was soon to darken the heavens, the earth, and the sea." Contrast with this wonderful power the benevolence and humility of the character. "People of less reach of mind," says one of his friends, "never can appreciate aright the disinterested patience with which he would hear out a long story from some prosy person, or walk far to see some poor body, or even, as I have known him do, go six miles out of town, that he might communicate by word of mouth, and with the greatest delicacy, some painful news to a servant maid."

ARTICLE SECOND.

Thomas M'Crie was born in the year 1772, at Dunse, in Berwickshire, a town which has been the birthplace of at least two other distinguished men,—Duns Scotus, the famous scholastic doctor of the fourteenth century, and Thomas Boston, the well-known author of the "Fourfold State." His parents, persons of great worth, belonged to that middle class among the people which may be regarded as forming the staple of our population, and on whose general character that of the country always depends. His father, whose name was also Thomas, a strictly religious man, of strong good sense and much general intelligence, was a manufacturer and merchant. His mother, Mary Hood, a tender-hearted and affectionate woman, of singular piety and devotedness, was the daughter of a respectable farmer. Thomas, their first-born, seemed to share in the character of both. He was a manly little fellow, rational beyond his years, fond of robust exercises, skilled in athletic games, and a fearless rider; but there were other and gentler elements in his nature, — a tenderness and sensibility of heart almost feminine, and a warmth and strength of affection not often equalled. Never, in any instance, were mother and son more thoroughly attached. She was long in delicate health; and the hours wasted by his companions in play were spent by Thomas in watching beside his mother's sick-bed, and in performing for her all the little acts of kindness which her situation required. And well was his tenderness repaid; in after-life he has frequently been heard to trace to her example, her instructions, and her prayers, his first serious impressions of religion.

"Common birds fly in crowds," says the romantic Sir Philip Sydney, "but the eagle goes forth alone." It was soon found that the little boy, the manufacturer's son, differed from all his fellows. He had an insatiable appetite for knowledge, that, the more it was fed, strengthened the more. He was sedate, too, and studious; and often, when he wandered out alone into the fields to pore over his books, food and play and his companions were all alike forgotten, and the live-long day passed happily in the solitude. His father rather discouraged the prosecution of his studies; "he would not," he said, "make one of his sons a gentleman at the expense of the rest;" but the hopes of the affectionate mother had been awakened in the behalf of her favorite son; and, through the kind interference of the boy's maternal grandfather, he was permitted to pursue what he so ardently inclined. Had the decision been otherwise, the world would probably have heard of him, not as the deeply-learned historian of Knox and Melville, but as a self-taught writer of powerful genius; for unquestionably the development of the larger minds is but little dependent on circumstances, and the mind of M'Crie belonged to the larger order. And yet we have little doubt, when we consider how much the world has owed to his unequalled powers of research, that his usefulness, if not his celebrity, depended materially on the decision.

In his sixteenth year he set out for the first time to attend the classes at the University of Edinburgh, and his pious and attached mother, whom he lost in about a twelvemonth after, but whom he never forgot, accompanied him part of the way, and parted from him on Coldingham Moor. Before bidding him farewell, she led him behind a rock, a little way off the road, and there, kneeling down with him, she affectionately and solemnly devoted him to the service of God, and earnestly commended him to his fatherly care. The grave closed over her; nearly half a century passed by; the time had well-nigh arrived when the son whom she had blessed, and for whom she had prayed, was to rest from his labors; and then she appeared to him in a dream, as he had seen her behind the rock upon the moor, and beckoned upon him to follow her, which he promised to do. Dr. M'Crie was no weak or superstitious man, but he did not on this occasion slight the solemn warning, and the result showed that he only regarded it in the proper light.

He passed through college with little show, but with great profit: knowledge was his daily food, and he could not exist without it. The languages, moral and political science, history, philology, eloquence, and in some degree poetry, were his favorite studies. His every-day companions among the classics were Tacitus, Livy, and Cicero; and he sedulously kept up his Latin reading to the close of his life. He excelled, too, in his knowledge of Greek. The English authors he most valued were the masculine thinkers of our literature; the Lockes, Smiths, Butlers, Reids, and Humes. He was a thorough admirer of the character and the writings of one who, at an after period, expressed an equally high admiration of him and of his productions, —his professor, Dugald Stewart. We need hardly add, that he was not content with being merely a reader of books; he cultivated a close acquaintance with his humbler countrymen; and the future historian might often be found in some back shop, ensconced among the members of a reading club, listening to the news of the day, and the accompanying remarks. He had thrown himself at an early period on his own resources: he had taught successively two country schools in the neighborhood of Dunse before completing his fifteenth year, and had contrived — a task of some difficulty, one should think — both to control his pupils when under his charge in school, and to play with them when they got out. In his eighteenth year he removed to Brechin, where he continued to teach a school for three years longer, and of which he may be regarded as the founder; for he began with only three pupils, and ere he quitted it he had well-nigh filled the house. It still continues to exist. His character at this early period of his life, including the space between his eighteenth and his twenty-first year, is well described by one of his old pupils, the Rev. Mr. Gray of Brechin, as a happy mixture of playfulness and sobriety. Exemplary in conduct, a frequenter of fellowship meetings, attached to the company and converse of unlettered Christians, strict in his observance of the Sabbath, and much in religious duty, a great consumer, withal, of the midnight oil, — he was yet one of the most playful, ready-witted, buoyant-spirited, happy young men in the country side. No one could be readier for an adventure, or fonder of innocent amusement; and in exercises of skill or peril he distanced competition. It could not be anticipated at this stage of his life that he was to write the Lives of Knox and Melville; "but those who best knew him," says Mr. Gray, "had already set him down as a very likely person, did the occasion offer, for accomplishing some of their boldest deeds." We were not mistaken, it seems, in our first impression of the Doctor, or in recognizing in his quiet and yet dignified air a mixture of the clerical and the military. He was as fitted by nature to lead a battalion to the charge, as qualified by grace to direct the devotions of a congregation.

The native weight of his character began to be felt. He was licensed to be a preacher of the gospel by the Associate Synod of Kelso, in 1795, and received, only a month after, a unanimous call to become minister of an Associate congregation in Edinburgh, which anticipated and frustrated the call of another respectable congregation of the same body who were likewise solicitous to secure him as their pastor. The people do sometimes discern merit, and make amends for their rejection of Youngs and Edwardses[1] by their anxiety to secure the services of M'Cries. It is an interesting fact, that he had a strong presentiment, long ere his appointment, of being settled as a minister in Edinburgh, — the only field, be it remembered, in which his truly important historical labors could be profitably pursued. Shortly after his settlement he was united in marriage to a lady to whom he had been long and ardently attached — a person of great sweetness of disposition, exemplary prudence and affection, and with whom he enjoyed much happiness. He was assiduous in his ministerial labors; our readers already know the character of his pulpit ministrations. His week-day services were not less valuable; and there was a frankness and kindness of disposition about him that recommended him powerfully to the affections of his people. The Doctor was one of those rare individuals who always think of the interests of others in the first place, and of their own last. His congregation rapidly increased; but it was composed mostly of the humbler classes of society; and his income, which had not been growing in proportion, was inadequate to support his station in a large city, and provide for the wants of an increasing family. Years of scarcity, and the revolutionary war, bore heavily upon all classes; and the price of provisions about the year 1799 rose to a height unequalled at any previous period. His people felt that duty demanded an effort, and they met among themselves to propose an addition to his stipend. No sooner, however, had

[1] Mr. Young and Mr. Edwards were the rejected presentees to Auchterarder and Strathbogie.

the intention reached their minister's ears than he clapped his veto upon it at once. The times, to be sure, might bear somewhat hardly upon him, but then they could not bear less hardly upon his people. The expense of living, he remarked, in a letter which he addressed to them on the subject, and which they gratefully inscribed among the congregational minutes, had, indeed, been increasing for some time past, but the income of tradespeople had not increased in proportion; and as the greater part of the body were of that description, he could not permit the sacrifice which their feelings had so kindly suggested. Worse times soon followed; and in the long-remembered year 1800, when our fields, according to Wordsworth, "were left with half a harvest," and a general scarcity of employment immensely heightened the evil, he came unhesitatingly forward, and proposed in form to give up a portion of his already too scanty income. His people, however, were not to be thus overcome by their disinterested and generous pastor, and the proposal, therefore, was gratefully but firmly declined. It would be no difficult matter to find striking foils to these instances of high-toned and unselfish feeling among some of the most noisy advocates of Voluntaryism.

He was now on the eve of entering his first great controversy. At the period of his license the synod were contemplating certain changes in the profession of their body, affecting, among other things, the old received opinion regarding the power of the civil magistrate in religious matters. Young, fearless, and ardent, the frank and open-hearted probationer had adopted all the more liberal opinions of the age. He had been smit with the opening glories of the French Revolution, so soon to be quenched in blood; his views of ecclesiastical polity had been taken through a somewhat similar medium, and the contemplated changes accorded well with his hastily-formed conclusions. He objected, therefore, against taking the formula as it then stood, without some qualification corresponding with the anticipated change; and the objection was more than sustained — it was highly approved of, and made the groundwork of a general declaration. Bitterly did he afterwards regret this rash step, and the result to which it had led. His mind was not one of the superficial and ordinary class, that are content to flutter over the surfaces of things. He deeply revolved the subject; applied the principle which it embodied to the events of the past; followed it, with that far-seeing sagacity in which he excelled all his contemporaries, into its remote consequences; and, convinced that he had erred egregiously, he joined with five of his brethren, all men of the highest character, in remonstrating with the synod against the proposed change of the formula. He felt the mortifying awkwardness of his position; but principle demanded, not that he should appear consistent, but that he should do what he had ascertained to be right; and feeling, therefore, was sacrificed to duty. The great bulk of his brethren deemed the matter one of little consequence. He had come to know better: that principle could not be one of slight importance which, if it had been generally operative in the past, would have effectually prevented the Protestant Reformation, and which, if carried out to its legitimate effects, would shake the whole country, and overturn all its religious institutions. And such was the gloomy result which he at this period ominously anticipated. He petitioned the synod, and, referring to his former ill-weighed scruples, expressed his deep regret for the rash step to which they had led, and the great distress in which he had been plunged by the reflection that he might have been thus instrumental in unhinging the principles of others. There is no portion of his biography in which we find the moral sense more nobly predominant than during this period of distress. The intensity of his feelings visibly affected his health. "What would I give," he says, in a letter to one of his friends at this period, "to have some of my years blotted out! I think my situation worse than that of the other brethren, and need to be taught the lesson of the apostle, 'There hath no temptation taken you but such as is common to men.'" His history at this period, with that of the few friends who made common cause with him, closely resembles the history of the first founders of the Secession. They alike stood upon the old ground, a small and despised minority, accused of sectarian narrowness and a want of charity, protesting and remonstrating against what they deemed dangerous and unconstitutional innovations, but protesting and remonstrating in vain. Matters soon reached their crisis. The synod enacted their new Narrative and Testimony into a term of communion. The protesters stood firm; and though the innovators were liberal enough to propose receiving them into their body, it was only on condition that, whatever they might think of the new principles themselves, they should neither impugn nor oppose them from the pulpit or the press. Moderatism would have received Fisher and the Erskines on exactly the same terms; and neither the Doctor nor his coadjutors were unworthy of the first fathers of the Secession, nor disposed to act a part which involved a dereliction of principle so gross. The protesters, therefore, as they were termed, now reduced to four, — for death had recently been thinning their numbers, — formed themselves into a Presbytery, and drew up a deed of constitution, in which they declared that, finding themselves virtually secluded from ministerial and Christian communion, and unable, with a good conscience, and consistently with their vows, to comply with the new terms, they were reluctantly driven in this state of seclusion to constitute themselves an independent body, adhering to the true constitution of the Reformed Church of Scotland and the original Testimony. The synod, meanwhile, unconscious of what was passing, was employed in deposing one of the refractory four, — a person who had rendered himself particularly obnoxious to some of the leading members, as "disorderly and a schismatic;" they were still sitting when the intelligence reached them of the act of independence; and, with a haste which was at least indecent, they proceeded, without the formalities of a legal process, to pass sentence of deposition and excommunication on a still more obnoxious and formidable member of the body — Thomas M'Crie. He was deposed and excommunicated, therefore, — thrust out of the synagogue for conscience' sake, — on the 2d September, 1806.

A time of great suffering ensued. Very brave men may bear very tender hearts, and the subject of our brief memoir, though there never lived a more determined asserter of a good cause, was no hard, unfeeling stoic. The sentence of his deposition was intimated by one of the estranged brethren of the majority, from his own pulpit; many of his old friends forsook him, and more than half his people. There was an action raised against him in the Court of Session, which terminated in wresting from him his chapel. He saw his brethren involved in the same general calamity; interdicts, sheriff officers, legal prosecutions, and even military force, called into action against them, and employed, strange to say, in carrying into effect sentences grounded expressly on ecclesiastical censures, and at the instance of enemies to all magisterial interference in things sacred. But error is ever inconsistent. Nor is the sum of his sufferings on this occasion yet complete. He heard the gibes of his brethren in the Church reëchoed by the wits of the bar and the judges on the bench; he found himself isolated in the midst of society, — shunned even by all the evangelical ministers of Edinburgh as a narrow-minded and obstinate bigot, — a man who could bring his wife and family to poverty and contempt rather than abate one jot of his antiquated and metaphysical scruples. What supported him meanwhile? A firm reliance on Divine guidance and support, and a thorough conviction of the goodness of his cause. "What am I," he has exclaimed, "that I should be counted worthy to suffer shame for his name?" He knew well upon what ground he had planted his foot. If he was in the wrong, then were our ancestors in the wrong in legalizing the profession of the true religion; they were in the wrong in passing laws in its favor; they were in the wrong in protecting the Sabbath; they were in the wrong in repressing gross violations of the first table of the law; they were in the wrong in all their solemn contracts,—in the covenants by which the Reformation, at both its periods, was confirmed; they were in the wrong in recognizing religion in the education of youth, in the administration of oaths, and in the admission to all places of power and trust. A question involving points of such mighty importance might seem merely metaphysical to others, but not so to him. He contended for what he deemed a great practical principle, which was in all time to affect the destinies of the British empire. He held, too, that the principle to which it was opposed—that of the Voluntary—was incapable of defence, except on grounds inconsistent with a belief in divine revelation; that indirectly but infallibly it led to infidelity; and, looking far into the future, he could discern through the gloom, impenetrable to other eyes, the field of the coming warfare thronged with dim shapes of terror—with the threatening faces and fiery arms of the yet unawakened, perhaps unborn, combatants. Nor were there more melancholy moments wanting, when he saw amid the darkness the fall of age-hallowed institutions, and the short-lived, but for the time complete, eclipse of religion itself. In referring in after years to this period of suffering and trial, he ever spoke of his opponents in a subdued and placid spirit. "Well," said he one morning to a friend, "there's a man dead who took the trouble of coming eighty miles to depose me from the ministry. I am sure I have had no resentment toward him. No doubt he did what he considered it his duty to do. Yet it was hard, with a wife and family, to be thrown upon the world."

ARTICLE THIRD.

The Court of Session decided that Thomas M'Crie, and the portion of his congregation which continued to hold by him, had forfeited all right to their chapel. There could not be a clearer case. They were found guilty of adherence to the old standards; they had obstinately refused to alter the Confession of Faith; they had continued to cling to the original Testimony; they had even gone so far as to assert that magistrates, as such, have religious duties to perform; and it was but strict justice, therefore, that they should lose their chapel. The case was decided against them in March, 1809, and the decision has no doubt been carefully registered among the archives of the court as a valuable precedent. The poor people who suffered by it were not numerous, and we use the right phrase when we say that they were poor; and so, in providing their deposed and excommunicated minister with another chapel, they had just to content themselves with an obscure building, that lay hid among old and blackened tenements at the foot of Carrubber's Close. Rarely has there been a preacher or congregation less generally known. "There now," said the late Dr. Andrew Thomson to a friend, after listening, at a subsequent period, to one of Dr. M'Crie's discourses,—"There now is something far beyond the compass of any minister in our Establishment." What would have been thought of the man who would have said as much in the year 1810 of the deposed minister who preached in Carrubber's Close?

During this period of obscurity he was silently employed on his first great work—the "Life of Knox." He had been engaged in storing up materials of thought from even his earliest boyhood; and for at least the last seven years he had been contributing largely to the "Christian Magazine," a religious periodical edited by one of his friends. But "can any good come out of Galilee?" No one looked for powerful writing and profound research in the humble pages of a Secession Magazine; nor was it discovered by more than a few friends, as obscure as himself, that his "Sketches of the Reformation in Spain," or his biographies of French and Scotch ministers of the sixteenth and seventeenth centuries, were fraught with interesting information, pleasingly conveyed, and which no other writer of the age could communicate. "It is pleasing," says Johnson, "to see great works in their seminal state, pregnant with latent possibilities of excellence." In some of these earlier pieces may be found the unexpanded germ of the "Life of Knox;" and as early as the year 1803 he had struck out his plan—never, alas! fully completed—of writing the history of the Church of Scotland in a series of biographies. But the more immediate cause of his undertaking was unquestionably his recent controversy. The pillar of history is sagaciously placed by Bunyan in the immediate neighborhood of the den of Giant Pope; and fain, he tells us, would the giant deface its inscriptions, were it not carefully guarded. The historian felt how necessary it was to erect a similar pillar among the people of Scotland—a pillar which none of the enemies of the Church, whether they sheltered under a pretended liberalism, like the men who had cast him out of their communion, or accomplished similar ends by opposite means, and under a different profession, would be able to obliterate or pull down. He had thoroughly satisfied himself that the system of doctrine and discipline introduced by our first "Reformers and Confessors" was not more consonant to the oracles of truth than conducive to the best interests, temporal and spiritual, of the nation. He had set himself, therefore, minutely to study their history;—to use his own striking language, "then the fire began to burn:" nor could he forbear imparting to others what he himself had felt so strongly. But his feeling of admiration was not for the men,—they were all deceased, and had rendered in their accounts,—but for the grace and gifts with which God had endowed them, and for the fabric which they had been honored to rear. Late in the year 1811 his "Life of Knox" was submitted to the public.

There is much interest in marking the first reception of works of great genius, destined powerfully to influence public opinion, and to become the heir-looms of civilized man in all after ages;—to see them at times painfully struggling with neglect, at times well-nigh borne down by the malignancy of envious opposition,—now contending with some blind prejudice, now with some selfish interest,—awhile repressed by the severity of vulgar and undiscerning criticism, awhile by the conventionalities of some artificial, but, for the time, established mode; and then to mark them rising variously, but invariably, to their proper place,—in some instances by a slow and gradual process, in others suddenly and at once, through the influence of happy accidents. Cowper was told by one of his first reviewers that he might be a very honest man, but most assuredly he was no poet; and poor Kirke White was represented as a beggar, who had made a worthless book a pretence for gathering money. The "Life of Knox" was destined to no long probation, for it soon fell under the notice of very superior men. Shortly after its publication, the author's old favorite professor, Dugald Stewart,—certainly the most eloquent, if not the most profound, of all our Scottish metaphysicians,—was confined one Sunday to the house by a slight indisposition. All the family were at church except his man-servant, an old and faithful attendant; and the Professor, on some occasion which required his services, summoned him by the bell. To his surprise, however, the careful domestic did not appear, and the bell was rung again and again, but with no better effect. The Professor then stepped down stairs to see what could have possibly befallen John, and threw open the door of the old man's apartment. And there, sure enough, was John, leaning over a little table, and engrossed heart and soul in the perusal of a book, as unconscious of the presence of his master as he had been an instant before of the ringing of the bell. The Professor's curiosity was aroused; — literature was rather a new pursuit to John; — and, shaking him by the shoulder, he inquired what book it was that had so wonderfully captivated his fancy. "Why, sir," said John, "it's a book that *my minister* has written, and really it's a grand ane." The Professor brought it with him to his room, to try what he could make of John's minister's book; and, when once fairly engaged, found it as impossible to withdraw himself from it as John himself had. He finished it at a sitting, and waited next day on the author to express the admiration he entertained for his performance. The Doctor bowed to the praises of his old Professor with the modesty of real genius, and replied in one of those happy compliments which show the elegant and delicate mind, "*Pulchrum est laudari a laudato,*" — "It is delightful to be praised by one who has himself gained the applauses of mankind."

The "Edinburgh Review" — at this period beyond comparison the most powerful periodical in Europe — took up the biography of Knox in the same spirit with Dugald Stewart. An air of surprise and admiration so thoroughly pervades the able article in which the work is reviewed, that it seems to constitute a part of its very style, and certainly a very refreshing part of it. M'Kenzie has been praised for the shrewdness he evinced in at once placing Burns among the great masters of undying song, at a period when at least nine-tenths of his contemporaries thought of him as merely a clever ploughman, who made very passable verses, considering that he was but an untaught man. Lord Jeffrey was equally happy in marking out the proper place of M'Crie. He at once characterized his work as one which united opposite qualities of excellence, and as by far the best piece of history which had appeared since the commencement of the reviewer's critical career, — as accurate, learned, and concise, and yet not the less full of spirit and animation; as a rare union of patient research and sober judgment, with boldness of thinking and force of imagination. Nothing had he ever read on the subject, he said, which had afforded him so much amusement and so much instruction; and yet this noble production was the work of an author of whose very existence, though residing in the same city with himself, he had never heard before. The Quarterly Reviewers, in spite of their Episcopacy, said well-nigh as much. With them, as with their contemporary, "Dr. M'Crie was really a great biographer." Compact, precise, discriminating, simple, vigorous, profound in his researches, and candid in his statements, he told the story of a hero as a hero would wish to have it told. Neither Luther nor Calvin, they said, had found a biographer like the present: and yet, true it was that his principles were bad. He held by the reformers in all their extremes; and had he been born in the sixteenth century, "less," they were persuaded, "would have been heard of Rowe or Willox as auxiliaries of Knox than of M'Crie." We believe they were perfectly in the right, and yet think none the worse of the Doctor.

He rose at once into eminence. The University of Edinburgh honored itself by conferring upon him his degree, the first ever extended in Scotland to a dissenting clergyman. His work was translated into the French, Dutch, and German languages, and spread extensively over the continent. History assumed a new tone when it spoke of the deeds and the character of Knox; monuments were erected and clubs instituted to his memory; candid and honorable men, of all persuasions, filled the periodicals of the time with their recantations of the error into which they had fallen regarding his character; and the powerful and manly reasonings and well-attested facts of his biographer were only met by the contemptible puerilities and garbled misstatements of a few embryo Puseyites, and at an after period by the denunciations of the Court of Rome. In the list of those peculiarly dangerous writings, among which the Bible stands preëminent, the infallible church has placed at least one of the productions of Dr. M'Crie, — by far the highest compliment which he has yet received. But the effect of a personal nature resulting from his sudden celebrity, which the Doctor himself probably valued most, was the degree of friendship and esteem which it secured to him from kindred spirits. Dr. Andrew Thomson — whose star, of, alas! brief but matchless brilliancy, had at that time just risen above the horizon — found him out; and a friendship, based on mutual admiration and respect, was formed between these two great and good men, whose duration, it is probable, is not to be measured by periods of time. Except on one unhappy occasion, they stood side by side in all their after controversies, employing somewhat dissimilar weapons, but fighting under the same shield. Was the historian assailed by the Episcopalian critics of our own country or of the south? — a discharge of merciless ridicule and resistless argument from his friend the Churchman prostrated the assailants. Did his friend the Churchman refuse opening St. George's at the bidding of the state, just because he held that the Church of Scotland was not an Erastian church? — out stepped the historian in his defence, and opposition sunk overawed. They were often together, and the happy temper of both, added to the rich humor of Dr. Thomson, threw an air of peculiar cheerfulness over their intercourse. There is a sunshiny freshness in the few notes which have been preserved of the many that passed between them; and when at any time the frequent and hearty laugh was heard proceeding from the historian's study, all the household at once concluded that Dr. Andrew Thomson was there. The Doctor was more than half a phrenologist, and used at times to try whether he could not accommodate the cranial development of his friend the historian to the well-known powers of his mind. In some respects he was singularly unlucky, and his blunders seem to have furnished large occasion of mirth. The Doctor flattered himself on one occasion that he had discovered a large development of the organ of music on the corners of his friend's forehead, and when he had fully assured himself of the fact, his friend quietly informed him that the accompanying musical ear was, notwithstanding, particularly dull, and that one of the most arduous tasks which he had ever seen accomplished was the task undertaken by one of his acquaintances, an old weaver, who had set himself to beat into his head the familiar tune of *St. Paul's.* We find humorous allusions to the new *science* in some of Dr. M'Crie's notes referring to contributions for the "Christian Instructor." "You are prodigiously moderate," he says, "in your expectations, when you look for two reviews from me in one month. You imagine, I suppose, that my brain is as large and as fertile as your own, — a mistake which you might have avoided without the assistance of Dr. Spurzheim." The two champions stood, as we have said, side by side, the unflinching opponents of slavery in the colonies and of patronage in the Church, — of the superstition that would debase religion, and of the infidelity that would overturn it, — of the hirelings of Moderatism, the wild visionaries of Roweism, and the incendiaries of Voluntaryism, — till the younger champion dropped, and died, we may well say, in his harness, cut down in his mid career of usefulness, "when best employed and wanted most." Deeply was the survivor affected; and many of those who on the succeeding Sabbath heard him give vent to his feelings in a sudden and impassioned burst, have not yet forgotten what the passage conveyed, and never will. "Brethren, pray for us, and let your first and last petition be *humility.* Once, yea twice, has a voice cried to the ministers of this city, and again, since we last met, it hath cried with the sound of a trumpet, 'All flesh is grass, and all the goodliness thereof is as the flower of the field!' The time has not come at which ceremony permits the dead to be spoken of in public. But I hasten to say the little which I have to say, especially as it is not in the way of eulogy. Others will praise him: as for me, I can only deplore him. And my deploration shall not turn on the splendid talents with which his Master adorned him,—the vigor of his understanding, the grasp of his intellect, or the unrivalled force of his masculine eloquence; but on his honest, firm, unflinching, fearless independence of mind,—a quality eminently required in the present time,—in which, I may say, he was single among his fellows, and which claimed for him respect as well as forbearance, even when it betrayed its possessor into excess." We are reminded strongly by this truly eloquent passage of a passage which has been long regarded as one of the most powerful in English literature,—the concluding part of the last chapter of Sir Walter Raleigh's "History of the World:" "O earth, earth, earth! thou art the true proprietor and lord paramount of all that is here below. Thou givest forth nothing but what thou receivest again, and thou receivest thine own with usury. Grass, herbs, trees, plants, houses, metals base and precious, and man himself, who hath rifled thee of all these, and who tears thy bosom and digs into thy bowels, and, measuring thy length and thy breadth, proudly walks over thee as if he were more than dust,—all shall return to thee, and find a grave in the womb from which they sprang."

ARTICLE FOURTH.

Dr. Johnson has occupied a whole paper of the "Idler" in showing that the biographies of authors may be as rich in interest as the biographies of any class of persons whatever. No lives, he remarks, more abound in sudden vicissitudes of fortune, and over no class of men do hope and fear, expectation and disappointment, grief and joy, exercise a larger influence. Goldsmith, in his Life of Parnell, has recorded an opposite opinion; but Goldsmith did not sufficiently attend to his own history—a history quite as striking in its details as any piece of fiction, not excepting even his own exquisite "Vicar of Wakefield." The obscure surgeon-assistant, whom the faculty were afraid to employ because his brogue was so strong and his appearance so uncouth; the imprudent and ruined surety, who, forsaking his obscure little shop in a provincial town, fled from his creditors to avoid a jail; the poor scholar and itinerant musician, who wandered on foot over France, Belgium, and Italy, purchasing a supper and a bed with his tunes from the peasantry, and disputing on some philosophical question for the same meed and a piece of money additional with the learned of Ferrara and Padua, — was the elegant and accomplished author whose poetry, a few years after, was to be rated higher than that of Pope, and his prose superior to that of Addison. Dr. Johnson was so much in the right, that, to establish the point, one has but to appeal from the opinion of his opponent to his opponent's biography. We have already passed, in our rapid sketch, over that part of the life of Dr. M'Crie most marked by vicissitude. The novelist or the poet takes but a portion of individual or national history for his subject; — the curtain falls, or the tale closes, when the hero of the piece has passed from one extreme of fortune to another; even the boy hears no more of Whittington after he has become Lord Mayor of London, or of Pepin after he has become King of France. On the same principle, what may be termed the romance of the Doctor's life closes when the obscure and persecuted preacher of Carrubber's Close, known only, beyond the narrow circle of his friends, when known at all, as a narrow-minded and illiberal sectarian, takes his undisputed place among the literati of his country as beyond comparison the first historian of his age, — as a great master of public opinion, — as successful above all his contemporaries in removing long-cherished prejudice and misconception, and as singularly sagacious in seizing the events of the remote future in the imperfect and embryo rudiments of present occurrences, or in partially developed modes of feeling and thought. But in the portion of his history which remains, though little checkered by incident, there is interest of a different kind. It is something to know the part taken by such a man in the controversies of the time — controversies many of which still survive; for there were few judgments less liable to mistake, and no honest man ever questioned his integrity.

Dr. M'Crie was very much of the opinion of Cowley. Good men, says the prince of metaphysical poets, should pray not less frequently for the conversion of literature than for the Jews. No one better knew the importance of literature, or was more earnestly solicitous for its conversion, than the Doctor. He saw every species of power among men, whether for good or evil, founded in opinion; and recognized in the press an all-potent lever, through which the public mind may be either heightened or depressed. He was aware, too, that it is not always the grave or more elaborate works which produce the deepest impressions. Songs have hastened national revolutions, and a single romance has powerfully affected the character of a country; and in the first series of the "Tales of my Landlord," with its marvellously unfair representation of the Covenanters, he recognized a work of the most influential character, and influential chiefly for evil. Rarely, says the poet, has Spain had heroes since Cervantes laughed away the chivalry of his country; and it was a class beyond comparison nobler and better than the chivalry of Spain that the novelist had set himself to laugh down. Dr. M'Crie's review of the "Tales" appeared in the "Christian Instructor" for 1817, and produced a powerful impression. Sir Walter, secure in his strength, had felt for years before that he could well afford being indifferent to criticism. He had a firmer hold of the public mind than any of his reviewers; the occasional critique either reëchoed his praises in tones caught from the general voice, and then sank unheeded, or dared to dispute the justice of the almost universal decision in his favor and sank all the sooner in consequence. So far was he from deeming the strictures of a hostile reviewer worthy of reply, that he had ceased to deem them worthy of perusal. On this occasion, however, he found he had to deal with no ordinary critic; the stream of public opinion had been turned fairly against him; and, after recording his determination not even to read the Doctor's article, he eventually found it necessary not only to read, but also to attempt answering it, which he did in the "Quarterly," in the form of a critique on his own work. Hogg has informed us how invariably favorable Sir Walter as a critic was to Sir Walter as an author. He, of course, decided that his "Tales" were very excellent tales, and that the Covenanters were in no degree better than he had described them; referring for proof to a few insulated facts as valuable in proving general propositions, as if it were to be inferred from the history of the Rev. Titus Oates that all the clergy of England were perjured miscreants, or from that of the Rev. Dr. Dodd that they were all malefactors, and deserved to be hung. His article had its weight with a few High Churchmen, zealously prepared to believe on the side of Claverhouse without the trouble of thought or scrutiny; but in the estimate of the less prejudiced classes, both in England and our own country, victory remained as unequivocally on the side of Dr. M'Crie and the Covenanters as if the reply had never been written.

The "Life of Andrew Melville" appeared about two years after, in 1819. It may be regarded as a continuation of the history of the Scottish Church, so auspiciously begun in the "Life of Knox," and displays the same power and discrimination exhibited in that work, with even more than the same amazing profundity of research. It was remarked, it is said, by the present Lord Jeffrey, that one would require several years' additional reading to qualify one's self for the task of reviewing it. The Doctor had got into a walk of information, the intricacies of which were known to only himself; and critics of the highest class were content to set their craft aside, and, taking the place of ordinary readers under him, were fain, instead of leading others, to be followers themselves. Regarded simply as a piece of narrative, it has been found to possess less interest than the "Life of Knox." The writer has not performed his part less ably; but the subject of his memoir, if not less a hero than his great predecessor, the reformer, had lived a life of less stormy interest, and had found feebler, if not less insidious spirits, with which to contend. But the history of Melville will ever continue, notwithstanding, to be regarded as emphatically *the* history of the Scottish Church for the stirring and eventful period which it embraces. The High Churchmen of the "British Critic" were less candid and less knowing than the editor of the "Edinburgh Review;" and, making their own ignorance the measure of their censure, they were of course very severe. Authorities of which they knew nothing might be garbled and misquoted, they said, without their being aware of the fact; and it could not be held, therefore, that the "bold, rebellious fanatics who figured prominently in the early days of the Scottish Reformation" could be in reality the good, honest men which the Presbyterian historian had proved them to be. The argument seems unanswerable; and as ignorance in one set of men is quite as good as ignorance in any other set, there can be no faith in history so long as the Churchmen of the "British Critic," or any other sort of people, remain unacquainted with the data on which the historians have founded.

The Doctor rarely took any part in public meetings. Though an eloquent and impressive speaker, and at once qualified to delight by the manner and instruct by the matter of his addresses, his native modesty led him to rate his capabilities for the platform lower than every one else rated them. He felt, too, that he was not neglecting his duty so long as he was engaged in his own peculiar walk, — the walk in which he excelled all his contemporaries, — and so long as he saw every public measure in which he felt an interest furnished with its zealous and appropriate champions. His friend Andrew Thomson was the powerful assailant of the Apocrypha and the slave-trade; and the cause of the Scottish poor might well be entrusted to Dr. Chalmers. There were questions and causes, however, for which he could deem it a duty to mount the platform. Many of our readers will remember the apathy with which a large proportion of the British public regarded the long, protracted, and bloody struggle of the Greeks with their cruel and tyrannical taskmasters. The country had grown too mercantile to be generous; the interests of some of our trading bodies were compromised; it had become imprudent to be sympathetic. The Greeks had grown too base and degraded, it was affirmed, to be either deserving of freedom or capable of enjoying it; and so they were left to fight more than half the battle of liberty, not only without assistance, but without sympathy. But the Doctor indulged in other feelings, and reasoned on other principles. He could sympathize with the oppressed Greeks, not only as a scholar, richly imbued with the spirit of the ancient literature of their country, but also as a Christian, deeply interested in their welfare as men; nor had he learned, in the prosecution of his studies, to deem the struggles of even a semi-barbarous people as of little importance. The accident which befalls an individual in his immature childhood frequently influences his destiny for life; and it is so also with countries. The Irish were not a civilized people when conquered by the English under Strongbow, nor yet the Scotch when they baffled and defeated the same enemy under Cressingham and Edward II.; but who can doubt that the present state of Scotland and Ireland depends materially upon the very opposite results of their respective struggles? At the first meeting held in behalf of the Greeks in Scotland, — we believe in Britain, — Dr. M'Crie took the lead, and delivered an address of great eloquence and power, which had much the effect of exciting the public interest, and which united what is not often conjoined — a manner singularly popular and pleasing, with much profundity of thought, and information drawn from the less accessible sources. At an after period, when the struggle had terminated in the freedom of Greece, the ladies of Edinburgh exerted themselves in raising funds, through which it was proposed to extend the advantages of education to the long-neglected females of that country. The Doctor gave the scheme his warmest support; he preached in its behalf the sermon so highly eulogized by Andrew Thomson as something beyond the reach of his contemporary ministers of the Establishment, conducted the correspondence of the Association originated to carry it on, and at a public meeting appealed to the country in its favor. Some of the ladies, his coadjutors in the scheme, had conceived of the Doctor merely as a person of one talent — one of the most common conceptions imaginable; they had no idea that the man who excelled all his contemporaries in research could excel most of them in eloquence also. They knew that no one could surpass him in argument or narrative, and therefore for argument and narrative they looked to him; but to delight the meeting with the poetry of the subject, to recall the old classic associations, to appeal powerfully to the feelings, — to do all they supposed the Doctor was not capable of doing, — they secured the services of the late Sir James Mackintosh. One of them even went so far as to tell the Doctor of their arrangement, in which he readily acquiesced. When the meeting came, however, they were all convincingly shown that he could do more than argue and narrate. "His address," says a writer in an English periodical, "distinguished throughout by the most thorough acquaintance with the politics, philosophy, mythology, and poetry of ancient Greece, commingled with the happiest allusions to these so fervid a contrast of her ancient glory with her modern degradation, that, new and foreign as such topics were thought to be to the habits of the good Doctor, his speech reminded many of his hearers of the finest speeches of Burke."

The year 1827 was what we would have termed a year of triumph to Dr. M'Crie, had the conscientious stand for what he deemed a great principle, which had subjected him to so much persecution rather more than twenty years before, borne any reference to the opinion or the approval of men. He had stood with his few brethren on the ground occupied by the fathers of the Secession and the first reformers of the Church, and had seen well-nigh the entire body to whom he had been united, but who had cast him off, carried away on a new and untried course of peril and defection, which would terminate, he augured, in the wreck of all those principles for which their fathers had so zealously contended. The body, however, had contained many excellent men, who, less sagacious than the Doctor, were yet not less attached to the original principles of the Secession, and who had been led from off the ground occupied by the first reformers, merely in the hope of reforming a little further. But the experience of twenty years had sufficed to teach them that their liberalism had led them astray. About seven years before, on the union of the Burgher and Antiburgher synods, a considerable body of this class, thoroughly convinced that the Secession was drifting from its original moorings, had formed themselves into a separate synod; and now in this year, finding that they were contending for the same grand truths with the Doctor and his brethren, they again entered, through mutual agreement, into communion with them, and were reunited, as of old, into one body. They virtually confessed that the excommunicated and deposed minority had occupied all along the true position — a position to which they themselves now deemed it necessary to return. Such are some of the honors reserved for the men who, through good and evil report, steadily adhere to the truth. With a magnanimity, however, natural to his character, Dr. M'Crie "steadily refused," says his biographer, "either to exact or receive from his former associates any acknowledgment of the illegality or severity of the sentences passed by the General Synod against himself or his brethren. The honor of the truth was all that he cared to vindicate; his own he left in the hands of his Divine Master."

ARTICLE FIFTH.

Two of the later literary works of Dr. M'Crie bear in history such a relation to his two earlier productions, the Lives of Melville and Knox, as, in the drama, tragedy bears to comedy. A cloud of disaster darkened the closing scene of the life of Melville, but the existence of the Scottish Church in the present day shows that he did not dare and suffer in vain. The cloud was a temporary one. The seed which he had sown lay dormant for a while, but it ultimately sprang up and bore fruit abundantly. The biographies of Melville and Knox constitute, therefore, the history of a successful reformation; his later works — the Sketches of the Reformation in Spain and Italy — form the histories of unsuccessful ones. The beacon-light was kindled but to be extinguished; the seed was sown but to die. Both works read an important lesson, and both are probably destined to produce important effects, in the future, in the countries to which they relate. The "History of the Reformation in Italy" has been translated into the Dutch, French, and German languages; and in the fear, doubtless, of its being translated into the Italian also, the Court of Rome has done it the honor of inserting it in the "Index Expurgatorius," as a work peculiarly obnoxious. The "History of the Reformation in Spain" has lately been translated into German. Both works are acquiring a continental celebrity; and when the time shall come — and it may not now be very distant — when, according to Milton, the "blood and ashes" sown over the fields "where still doth sway the triple tyrant," shall begin to bear fruit, the faithful record of the fierce and relentless hatred of the persecutor, and of the sufferings unflinchingly endured and the deaths joyfully welcomed for the truth's sake by his oppressed victims, may exert no little influence in hastening the fall of the one and leading to an imitation of the other.

The Doctor was employed in pursuing his researches, adding instance to instance of the cruelty and perfidy of Popery, and accumulating proof upon proof that its atrocities have not been restricted to one country or confined to one age, when the bill for admitting Roman Catholics into places of power and trust was introduced by the government. In the preceding year he had taken an active interest in petitioning for the abolition of the Test and Corporation acts. He was too shrewd not to recognize the measure as merely a preparatory one, and which could not fail to terminate in Catholic emancipation. But he was not one of the class who can withhold from doing what is right in itself because something not so right may follow. He believed, with Cowper, that these acts involved a gross profanation of things sacred; that they converted the symbols of "redeeming grace" into mere "picklocks," through which the unscrupulous entered into office, but by which the conscientious were excluded; and hence the zeal with which he urged their abolition. He now took as active a part, and on quite the same principle, in opposing the emancipation of the Catholics. He advocated the preliminary measure because he deemed it essentially right, and denounced and opposed the measure to which it had led as radically wrong, — as a measure, too, to be dreaded and deprecated in its effects as one of the most ruinous of modern legislation. He was convinced, he said, that the ministry of the day would succeed in carrying their object; such seemed to be the intention of Providence in permitting the union of parties hitherto opposed, and in suffering even "our prophets" to be carried away by a spirit of delusion; but he felt it necessary to do all he could in the matter, by way of personal exoneration; he felt opposition, however fruitless, to be his duty. "We have been told," he said, "from a high quarter, to avoid such subjects, unless we wish to rekindle the flames of Smithfield, now long forgotten. Long forgotten! where forgotten? In heaven? No. In Britain? God forbid. They may be forgotten at St. Stephen's or Westminster Abbey, but they are not forgotten in Britain. And if ever such a day arrives, the hours of Britain's prosperity have been numbered." A petition to the Legislature against the Catholic claims, which, whatever might be thought of its object, could not be regarded as other than a document of extraordinary ability, was drawn up by Dr. M'Crie, and received the signatures of rather more than thirteen thousand persons. We are ill qualified to decide on the part taken on this occasion by the Doctor. There were very excellent and very sagacious men — men little moved by the arguments of mere expediency — who exerted themselves on the opposite side; nor was it easy to see what other course remained for our legislators, in the peculiar circumstances of the country, than the course which they adopted. The Catholics seemed prepared for a civil war, and at least nine-tenths of our Protestants were determined not to fight in such a quarrel. We would not have signed Dr. M'Crie's petition at the time; had an opportunity occurred, we would have readily appended our signature to the list which contained the names of Thomson and of Chalmers. Eleven years, however, have since passed: the government of Ireland is well-nigh as great a problem now as it was then; the struggle between Protestantism and Popery still continues, with this difference, that the advantage is now more on the side of the enemy, without his being in any degree less bitter in his enmity; the power of the priest is nothing lessened; the success of the missionary or the triumph of the Bible is nothing increased. We are afraid, in short, that the part taken by the Doctor did not run so counter to his profound sagacity in such matters as at one time we might possibly have thought; nay, more, we are somewhat afraid that events are in the course of showing it did not run counter to it at all. As little, however, can we avoid feeling that, should the worst come to the worst, Protestantism on its present ground would have at least a clearer, if not a better quarrel than on its former post of advantage; and that if Popery, unlike an ancient wrestler, could not have contended with most success when beneath its opponent, it would at least have to contend with an opposition less hearty, and encouraged by a sympathy deeper and more general.

Three years after, Dr. M'Crie again deemed it his duty to come publicly forward and record his conscientious disapproval of another political measure, — the Irish Educational scheme, with its carefully culled scriptural lesson-book. His estimate of the statesmanship of the present day was far from high; but it was not an estimate that any one party would choose to quote with the view of bettering their own character at the expense of that of the party opposed to them. Nor was it much more favorable to the people than to the people's rulers; for, though the Doctor loved, he could not flatter them. "It has been my opinion fixedly for some time," he remarks, in a letter to a friend, "that any administration to be formed at present, whig or tory, would sacrifice religion on the shrine of political expediency; and 'my people,' provided their temporary and worldly views were gratified, would 'love to have it so.' This is my political creed." He held that the scheme which he opposed involved a principle on which the very foundations of Protestantism rested; and that it was taking a view of the subject radically false to regard the book of selected extracts in the same light with collections of passages drawn up for purposes of mere economy; seeing that these extracts were confessedly made to conciliate the prejudices of a class who deny the right of the laity to the use of the whole Bible. We are not unacquainted with the arguments which have been urged on the opposite side, and they are at least plausible. We have little doubt, however, that ultimately it will be found that the Doctor was in the right; and we are inclined to think that by placing the question, through a slight alteration of the terms, more in a secular light, the soundness of his views would be more generally recognized. Suppose the entire Scriptures consisted of the decalogue alone; that a sound criticism had proved, as it has proved, the integrity of every one of the ten commandments which compose it, and that all Protestants were thoroughly convinced of their Divine origin; suppose that Popery treated four of the ten in exactly the way in which it sometimes treats one of the ten,—that it had not only struck out the Divine prohibition of idolatry, but the prohibition also against theft, murder, and adultery,—would any government, five-sixths of which were Protestants, so much as dream of forming an educational scheme for both Protestants and Papists, through which, out of respect to the prejudices of the latter, only six of the commandments—the permitted six—would be taught? And yet, either the Bible, as a whole, is no revelation, addressed as it is to the people as a body, not to any particular class of functionaries, or the same rule must apply to it too. Or, again, suppose that Popery, instead of forbidding the perusal of the whole Scriptures, forbade the acquirement of the art of reading altogether, leaving the other branches of education open, such as arithmetic, drawing, and the mathematics,—would a liberal government once think of closing with it on such terms, or exclude reading from its schools, in deference to a prejudice so illiberal? And if a prejudice against secular knowledge is to be overborne and denounced, why respect a prejudice against religious knowledge? But our limits, and the character of our sketch, forbid an examination of the question; and we refer the reader to the powerful and eloquent speech of the Doctor on the subject, appended to his biography. He was no way appalled at finding himself standing in a slender minority; he had been in the minority, he said, all his life long; and the truth has often shared the same fate with Dr. M'Crie. On an attempt being made to disturb the meeting, of that low and disreputable character so often resorted to on similar occasions, and in which brute noise is brought to bear against argument, — the mere animal against the moral and rational agent, — the Doctor stepped forward, and told the disturbers, with much emphasis, to "recollect that they had to do with men, and with men who were not accustomed to be browbeat." His spirit rose with opposition, and kindled at every show of oppression and injustice; and though the shouts and bellowings of a score or two of *Liberals*, determined to tolerate only the principles of their own party, might drown his voice, just as the kettle-drums of Dalyell and Claverhouse drowned the voices of the Covenanters in their scaffold addresses, no one could better exert the influence of that moral force before which all such brute violence must ultimately quail.

The Voluntary controversy, in which he had entered so early, had become what he had predicted — an all-important conflict, recognized by every one as of the first importance. Men of some religion and men of none had made common cause, though with a different object, — the one against church establishments, the other against Christianity itself; and the Doctor could now look forward to a time when the better materials of the combination would be reduced to well-nigh the level of the worst, and the religious degradation of the men from whom he had parted company more than twenty years before would be rendered apparent to all. It was one of his first principles, "that society is a corporate body, and has rights and duties of the same kind as those of the individual;" nor could he believe, therefore, in his thorough conviction of the importance of religion, that religion would hold other than the first place among national concerns. Still, his anticipations were gloomy when he thought of the Establishment. Though persuaded, as we have already said, that "the Voluntary principle was not only untenable, but incapable of defence, except on grounds inconsistent with a belief in Divine revelation, and directly but infallibly leading to infidelity," no man could see better how much of abuse and corruption had crept into our national Church, and how strenuously every measure of reform would be resisted through the blind and suicidal selfishness of her professed but hollow friends, and the hostility of her clearer-sighted enemies. He often anticipated, therefore, a disastrous result of the controversy, and a season of general suffering and perturbation, in which all classes would be fearfully taught the value of religion through the want of it. At times, however, his views would brighten; and we find him, in one of his happier moods, thus addressing a correspondent: "Is it yet time for me to commence a canvass for John Knox's Church? I have heard that Adam Gib, to a considerably late period in his life, expressed the hope that he would preach in St. Giles's. You know the practical inference. Yet we do injury to more than our own happiness by dealing harshly with kind hope, repressing her ardor, and chiding her for those lamb-like friskings in which she indulges to please us."

And he *did* bestir himself in the behalf "of John Knox's church;" but it was not by striking at her enemies, but by striking at one of the main abuses which had entered into her system — the abuse of patronage. And the blow was dealt by no feeble or unpractised hand. The cause was of importance enough to bring him to the platform. He attended, in the beginning of 1833, a meeting of the Anti-Patronage Society, and delivered a powerful and impressive speech, in which he advocated the total abolition of patronage, as the sole means of saving the Establishment. And perhaps on no occasion was the magnanimity of the man more strikingly shown than in the concluding portion of this address, or brought out in broader contrast with the no doubt widely opposite but equally selfish feelings of the class who, rather than relinquish their miserable powers of patronage, would stand and see the Church overwhelmed amid the surges of popular anarchy, or the class — anxious to fill their meeting-houses — who, like the wreckers of Cornwall, exert themselves with a view to her destruction, in the hope of profiting by the wreck. "If you succeed in your object," said the Doctor, "you will do much harm, — you will thin, much thin, my congregation. For I must say that, though patronage were abolished to-morrow, I could not forthwith enter into the Establishment. But I am not so blind or so ignorant of the dispositions of the people as to suppose they would act in that manner. Your cause will soon come into honor; the restoration of long-lost rights will convert popular apathy into popular favor, and in their enthusiasm the people will forget that there are such things as erroneous teachers and neglect of discipline. Do I therefore dread your success, or stand aloof from you, on the ground mentioned? Assuredly not. The truth is, that I think I may be of more service to you by declining to be in your council. I have only to say, therefore, Go on and prosper; though your beginnings have been but small, may your latter end greatly increase. You have my best wishes and prayers." These surely are the sentiments of a man who, to employ the striking figure of Burns, held a patent of nobility direct from Deity himself, and who had trained and cultivated his heart as sedulously and successfully as his head.

He published, in the May of the same year, his now well-known but at the time neglected pamphlet, "What ought the General Assembly to do at the present Crisis?" It had one great defect — it wanted the author's name; and told, in consequence, with less power on the body for whose benefit it was chiefly intended. But in none of all the Doctor's writings is his wonderful sagacity more clearly and unequivocally shown, and there are none of them on which subsequent events have read a more striking comment. His advice to the Assembly forms an emphatic reply to the query in the title: "WITHOUT DELAY PETITION THE LEGISLATURE FOR THE ABOLITION OF PATRONAGE." But he neither did anticipate, nor could have anticipated, the present position of the Church; for to have done so would have required not simply human sagacity, but a superhuman prescience. "No meaning," says Pope, "puzzles more than wit." "It is almost impossible," says Robertson, "to form any satisfactory conjecture concerning the motives which influence capricious and irregular minds." No one could have presaged more justly than Dr. M'Crie the manner in which the Court of Session would have decided any ecclesiastical case according to law; but it was not in the nature of things that he could have presaged the manner in which the court was to decide ecclesiastical cases contrary to law. There was no clew to surmise, no guide to conjecture. One of the first principles laid down in his profound and masterly pamphlet—a principle from which he deduces the necessity of a popular check in the appointment of ministers—must have as effectually prevented him from premising the possibility of such interdicts as have been granted to the suspended functionaries of Strathbogie or the rejected licentiate of Lethendy, as it ought to have stood in the way of the court itself in rendering them possible. "According to law," says the Doctor, "there lies no appeal from the decisions of a church court to any civil tribunal, not to the Parliament itself, in any case properly ecclesiastical. Everything of this kind is finally settled by the decision of the General Assembly, which, in addition to its judicial and executive power, claims a legislative authority, or at least a power of making authoritative acts, and, with the concurrence of a majority of Presbyteries, of enacting standing laws which are binding on all the members of the Church, laity as well as clergy." The decision of the historian of Knox and Melville in a question of this kind bears a very different sort of value from that of the Dean of Faculty or the Earl of Aberdeen. Mark, too, the shrewdness of his conclusion regarding the more thorough-going Voluntaries: "You will not find one of them taking part in a society for promoting church reform;

you will not see one of their names at a petition for abolishing patronage. They affect to laugh at such attempts to reform minor abuses, although, in fact, they dread them more than the most able and elaborate vindication of ecclesiastical establishments."

CONCLUDING ARTICLE.

We passed a Sabbath in Edinburgh early in 1835,—the first after a lapse of nearly ten years,—and sought out the well-known chapel of our favorite preacher. There was no change there; the same people seemed to occupy the same pews; but so marked was the change in the appearance of the Doctor, that at first we scarce recognized him. "Can it be thought," says a living writer, "that the human soul, so nobly impressed by the hand of Deity, is but the creature of a passing day, when a brick of Thebes or of Luxor retains, undefaced, its original stamp for thousands and thousands of years?" The intervening decade had borne heavily on the Doctor. He had lost his elasticity of tread, and his erect and semi-military bearing; and the complexion, darker and less pale than formerly, bore, after slight exertion, an apoplectic flush, that indicated some perilous derangement in the springs of life. But the too apparent decay affected only the earthy and material frame: the mind retained all its original vigor. We have never listened to the Doctor with deeper interest, or a more thorough admiration of his sound and powerful judgment, than on that Sabbath; and we fancied, but it might not be so, that his manner was more impressively earnest, even, than usual,—impressive and earnest as it always was,—and that he was "laboring with all his might," in the belief that the long night was fast closing over him, in which "he could no longer work." We stood beside the chapel-door as the congregation slowly dismissed, and took our last look of the Doctor, believing it to be such, as he entered a hackney coach, assisted by a friend. The assistance did not seem necessary, but it was sedulously rendered.

His death took place in the following autumn. Melancthon, in his latter days, evinced a weariness of the world. The folly and villany of mankind, the littleness of their aims, and the base and ungenerous spirit in which they so often pursued them, sickened and disgusted him, and he longed earnestly to be "away from them, and at rest." Cowper's wish was of a similar character. The ever-swelling rumor of outrage and wrong, of oppression, cruelty, and deceit, disturbed and pained his gentle spirit, and he longed for a "lodge in some vast wilderness," where he might never hear it more. There were seasons, towards the close of his life, in which Dr. M'Crie experienced a weariness such as that of Melancthon, a feeling such as that of Cowper. "His heart," says his biographer, "was greatly alienated from the world, and tired of the troubled scenes of its politics, civil and ecclesiastical." There was an impression, too, borne in upon his mind that he was soon to be called away, and that his death, like that of his friend Andrew Thomson, was to be sudden. He felt his little remaining strength fast sinking, and the remarkable dream to which we adverted in an early article mingled its warning with his waking presentiments, like the morning dreams described by Michael Bruce in his Elegy. He had seen the hand beckoning him away, which, nearly half a century before, had so solemnly devoted him to the service of God. Not the less, however, did he continue to urge his labors, to walk his round of professional duty, to ply his literary occupations, — for he had now engaged in a life of Calvin, — and to meet the unceasing demands made upon him for counsel and assistance. He was too little sedulous, perhaps, to "keep life's flame from wasting by repose;" an accumulation of toil was suffered to press on his health and spirits; but in the benignity of his disposition he could not find heart to refuse an application, and so he toiled on. "Some people," he said, with reference to a task to which he had just submitted, and which was to engage him for a whole week, — "some people seem born to be beasts of burden." Nor did the presentiment of his approaching dissolution lessen his interest in the fortunes of the Church of Scotland. Nothing so delighted him as any indication among her ministers of a "disposition to return to the good old way of their fathers." The Assembly of May, 1835, appointed a day of general fasting — "an assertion," says the Doctor's biographer, "of the intrinsic power of the Church which he did not anticipate, and which, reminding him of her better days, appeared a token for good." "Will they venture," he said, unacquainted with what the Assembly had intended, "to appoint a fast on their own authority?" and he received the intelligence with hardly less surprise than pleasure, that what he had been scarce sanguine enough to anticipate from them they had actually done. The Doctor had never held public worship on a king's fast, but readily and willingly on this occasion did he join with the Church. His resentments, however, were all over; and he anticipated, more in sorrow than in anger, and anticipated justly, that the Dissenters, as a body, "would keep their shops open and their churches shut." "They did not use to do that," he said, "on days of royal appointment."

But if no man could evince a deeper interest in the welfare of the Church of Scotland, there was no man, on the other hand, who could feel more painfully for what he deemed the imprudence of her ministers, or for any general act on the part of her friends, which compromised, as he believed, either her safety or her usefulness. The following remark in a letter to a friend — a remark full of shrewd meaning, and on which recent events have been reading a comment of tremendous emphasis — belongs to the closing year of his life, and craves careful study: "What fools our church folks are, to identify their cause with Toryism at the present day, — to alienate the whigs, and oblige them to league with radicals, — to give them an excuse for deserting the defence of the Church whenever they shall find it safe or politically wise to do so! Don't you think that our times bear a great resemblance to those of 1640 in England, with the difference (great indeed), that there is not the same religious spirit in Parliament and in the public which existed at that period? How a collision between the aristocracy and the commons (not to speak of the monarchy) is to be avoided, I do not see. The public mind is much more extensively enlightened as to politics than it was in 1793; and it has got a power — a lever — which it did not then possess. I have no doubt I have got a great portion of the incredulity of my namesake, and would wish to say with respect to public prospects, 'Lord, I believe; help thou my unbelief.'"

He had held, as we have said, the Assembly's fast; and never, it was remarked, had he addressed his people with more solemn effect than on that occasion. On the Sabbath after, he preached twice from the striking text in Matthew, "Whose fan is in his hand, and he will thoroughly purge his floor, and gather his wheat into the garner; but he will burn up the chaff with unquenchable fire." At the close of the service he seated himself at the door of the vestry, contrary to his usual practice, "and watched the people while they were retiring, until they had all gone out." On the afternoon of the Tuesday following, after spending the early part of the day in visiting some of his congregation, he was seized, immediately on his return home, with a severe pain in the bowels; and, after experiencing an interval of partial relief, fell into a slumber, out of which he never awoke. He continued to breathe until the middle of the next day; and then, surrounded by his friends, and by many of his beloved flock, who had collected to witness his last moments, he passed to his reward, without a groan or a struggle. He had entered the sixty-third year of his age, and the fortieth of his ministry.

His funeral was attended by nearly fifteen hundred persons, including the magistracy of Edinburgh, its ministers of all persuasions, the preachers and students attending the halls of the Establishment and the United Secession, and by a deputation from the Assembly's Commission, headed by the clerk and the moderator. Nor could his remains have found a more appropriate resting-place than the ancient cemetery to which they were conveyed,—the burial ground of the Greyfriars. It contains the dust of Alexander Henderson, the great leader of the Church during the troubles of the first Charles; it contains also, in its malefactor's corner, the remains and the monument of the martyrs who, in the cause of Christ and of Presbytery, laid down their lives in Edinburgh during the dissolute and bloody reign of Charles the Second; and for an entire twelvemonth its open area was the prison in which the captive Covenanters of Bothwell Bridge were exposed to every inclemency of the seasons, and to the mockeries and revilings of their fierce and cruel jailers. Nor is there any lack of the kindred dust once animated by genius. There occur on the surrounding tombs the names of Colin M'Laren, of Allan Ramsay, of Hugh Blair, and of William Robertson. But the talents which the Task-Master entrusts to his servants, whether the sum total consists of one or of ten, are of but little value, compared with the use to which they have been devoted, and the effects which the possessors have accomplished through their means. We have stood beside the Doctor's grave, and felt, amid the deep silence of the place where knowledge and device faileth, and where there is no work and no wisdom, how well and honestly he had "occupied" his. His important labors are over; the work set him to do has been faithfully performed. Though during his life he stood apart from the Church which he loved, it was only as a watchman on some outer tower, or like a sentinel of the times of the persecution, stationed on some eminence of the waste, to warn the assembled congregation of coming danger; and the imperishable monuments which he has reared stand forth to shed on the present the light of the past, and as beacons which, however times may darken, will continue to mark out the course which churches and nations will ultimately find it their interest as well as their duty to pursue. A massy and tasteful monument of white stone, erected by his sorrowing flock, as a memorial of "his worth and of their gratitude," marks out his final resting-place, and bears an inscription whose rare merit it is to be at once highly eulogistic and strictly true.

Our sketch has been miserably imperfect indeed if the reader has not been enabled to form from it some estimate, correct though not adequate, of the character of Dr. M'Crie. His whole life was a powerful illustration of how much a superior mind can be improved and ennobled by Christian principle. It shows also how necessary integrity is to the development of a high order of intellect. Had the Doctor been less honest, he would have been less sagacious also. His mind, like a fine instrument, took the measure and tendencies of passing events; and there were no disturbing influences of selfishness to throw their mixture of uncertainty and error into the process. His wisdom, in part at least, was a consequence of his magnanimity. It may seem a mere fancy to couple such men as Dr. M'Crie and the Duke of Wellington — the statesman and general with the historian and divine; but resembling minds may be placed in very opposite circumstances; and for sobriety of feeling, far-seeing sagacity, great firmness of purpose, an impregnable native honesty, uninfluenced by the small motives of party, — in short, for all that constitutes the safe and great leader, — the standing of both men, each in his own sphere, refers to a level to which very few attain. Plutarch has parallelisms that lie less parallel. We shall just refer, ere we close, to one or two detached points in the intellectual and literary character of Dr. M'Crie.

It was well remarked by Lord Jeffrey, in his admirable

review, that the Life of Knox "exhibited a rare union of the patient research and sober judgment which characterize the more laborious class of historians, with the boldness of thinking and force of imagination which are sometimes substituted in their place." The remark strikingly illustrates a peculiar excellence of the Doctor's intellect. He could not rest on the surface of a subject, even if he had wished it. It was his nature to search to the very bottom, at whatever cost of labor, — to pursue some obscure fact through a hundred different authorities, until he had at length fixed it down before him as one of the unimpeachable certainties of history. The privileged friends whom he at times received in his study used to be utterly appalled by the huge masses of books and manuscripts which always lay piled up before him for constant reference; and so severely and conscientiously was his judgment exercised in every instance, that on not so much as one of his statements have even his abler antagonists succeeded in casting a shadow of doubt. Robertson was much his inferior in research. Hume, whose defects in patient investigation are now pretty generally known, was immeasurably so. In tracing the history of opinion and doctrine, where of necessity the evidence must be more shadowy and intangible than in whatever relates to conduct or action, the degree of certainty at which he invariably succeeded in arriving was truly wonderful. The whole bearing of bygone controversies, their after-effects on doctrine and belief, the degree in which they had led the parties they had divided to modify, retract, restate, — the influence on society of particular minds and peculiar modes of thought, — all seemed to open before him as he advanced, alone and unassisted, on his solitary and laborious course.

His style and manner fitted him no less for his task than his unwearied perseverance. To employ one of Johnson's figures, the heat of his genius sublimed his learning. It is related by Gibbon, that after he had formed his determination of devoting himself to literature, he perused the then recently published histories of Robertson and Hume. The measured and stately periods of Robertson delighted him; and yet he could hope, that with much pains and great study he might at length succeed in writing such a style. But he read Hume and despaired. Art might enable him to rival the exquisite art of the one, but art could not enable him to equal the still more exquisite nature of the other. Hume is one of the most readable of historians: he is invariably unaffected, invariably clear. Robertson palls: we admire his pages, but his volumes tire. Now, Dr. M'Crie in this respect resembles Hume. His pages are not so elegant as those of Robertson, but they are more attractive, and the reader turns over more of them at a sitting. We merely peruse the history of Scotland; we devour the biography of Knox. The number of editions which have appeared within the last few months, since the copyright has expired, evinces the degree of popularity which the latter work is destined to enjoy in the future. The last we saw formed a two-shilling volume; its price and appearance showed that it was intended for the common people; and we paid our respects to it, at once recognizing in it a formidable opponent of the Earl of Dalhousie's arguments, the Court of Session's encroachments, and the Earl of Aberdeen's bill.

We refer, ere we close our remarks, to but one other trait in the literary career of Dr. M'Crie. There is an occasional quaintness in some of his finer passages, that, to men deeply read in the theology of the Church's better days, constitues an additional charm. His eloquence is that of the divines of the Commonwealth, rendered classical through native taste and the study of the better models. We submit, as an example, the following exquisite passage: "Who would be a slave! is the exclamation of those who are themselves free, and sometimes of those who, provided they enjoy freedom themselves, care not though the whole world were in bondage. But there is a sentiment still more noble than that. Who would be a slave-dealer, a patron, an advocate for slavery! To be a slave has been the hard, but not dishonorable, lot of many a good man and noble spirit. But to be a tyrant, — that is disgrace! To trample on the rights of his fellow-creature; to treat him, whether it be with cruelty or kindness, as a dog; to hold him in chains, when he has perpetrated or threatens no violence; to carry him with a rope about his neck, not to the scaffold, but to the market; to sell him whom God made after his own image, and whom Christ redeemed, not with corruptible things, as silver and gold, and, by the act of transferrence, to tear him from his own bowels, — *that* is disgraceful! I protest before you that I would a thousand times rather have my brow branded with the name of *Slave*, than have written on the palm of my hand or the sole of my foot the initial letter of the word *Tyrant!*"

THE DEBATE ON MISSIONS.

PART FIRST.

It was forty-five years last May (1840) since the famous debate on missions took place in the General Assembly of the Church of Scotland. A race unborn at the time have now reached the term of middle life; and of those who either joined in the discussion, or recorded their votes at its close, very few survive. There are many important facts connected with the history of this memorable debate, which still read their lesson to the country; and during the present pause in the political world, our readers may deem themselves not ill employed in glancing over some of its more striking details. It furnishes a better illustration of the true character of Moderatism than they will be able to find for themselves almost anywhere else; and it were surely well they should all thoroughly know what sort of a *religion* it is which has so lately challenged for itself an exclusive right to be recognized as the state religion of Scotland.

Our materials are fortunately very ample. The art of the reporter was but in its infancy at the time, especially in Scotland; the contemporary debates of even the English Parliament appear but as mere skeleton sketches, that rather resemble lists of contents than series of speeches; and yet by a rare chance there exists a report of this singular debate, as ample and complete as any of the present day. Moderatism had its likeness taken at the time at full length, and in one of its worst attitudes, and, as if to prevent all suspicion regarding the truth of the picture, taken apparently not by an enemy. The unfortunate Robert Heron, the familiar friend of Burns, and whose melancholy history has been so touchingly recorded by D'Israeli in his "Calamities of Authors," lived at this period exclusively by his exertions as an "author of all work." He sat in the Assembly during the debate as an elder for his native burgh of New Galloway; he even took a prominent part in it; and to his singularly ready and masterly pen can we alone attribute a report so unlike, in its fulness and general literary tone, almost all the other reports of the age. It may be well, too, to mention that, though extensively circulated at the time in the form of a pamphlet, its faithfulness has never once been questioned.

It has been remarked by Carlyle, that "the history of whatever man has accomplished is at bottom only the history of great men, leaders of their brethren, who have been the modellers, and, in a wide sense, the creators, of whatsoever the general mass of men have contrived to do." Certainly, in the religious, as in the political world, we find all the more remarkable events, and all the more influential codes of belief, clustered, if we may so express ourselves, round a few great names. The history of Knox is the history of the Reformation in Scotland; the very name of Calvin expresses the religious code of half the churches of Protestantism. Apparently on a similar principle, we find the cause of general missionary exertion in this country connected in an especial manner with one great name. The reader of one of the most amusing novels of Scott — Guy Mannering — must remember that, on Colonel Mannering's visit to Edinburgh, the lawyer Pleydell brings him to the Greyfriars to hear Principal Robertson preach, and that, instead of the historian, he hears but the historian's colleague. Sir Walter had too often sat in the Greyfriars not to know that the pulpit ministrations of Robertson could have formed no proper subject of favorable or striking description. They were marked but by the dead inanity inseparable from an utter lack of earnestness and an ignorance of the gospel. And so he described, and in his happiest vein, a preacher of a very opposite stamp. A man of a remarkable though somewhat ungainly appearance entered the pulpit. His pale, fair complexion contrasted strangely with a black wig without a grain of powder. "A narrow chest and a stooping posture, no gown, not even that of Geneva, a tumbled band, and a gesture that seemed scarce voluntary, were the first circumstances that struck a stranger." They were all forgotten, however, as the preacher proceeded in his discourse — a discourse "in which the Calvinism of the Kirk of Scotland was ably supported, yet made the basis of a sound system of practical morals, which should neither shelter the sinner under the cloak of speculative faith or of peculiarity of opinion, nor yet leave him loose to the waves of unbelief and schism." "Something there was of an antiquated turn of argument and metaphor," continues Scott, "but it only served to give zest and peculiarity to the style of elocution. The sermon was not read. The enunciation, which at first seemed imperfect and embarrassed, became, as the preacher warmed in his progress, animated and distinct; and although the discourse could not be quoted as a correct specimen of pulpit eloquence, yet Mannering had seldom heard so much learning, metaphysical acuteness, and energy of argument, brought into the service of Christianity. 'Such,' he said, going out of the church, 'must have been the preachers to whose unfearing minds, and acute though sometimes rudely exercised talents, we owe the Reformation.'" He must have been assuredly no common man that could have thus mollified the anti-evangelical prejudices of Scott. The preacher described was Dr. John Erskine, of Edinburgh, for many years the revered leader of the Evangelical party in the Church of Scotland.

It was the fate of Dr. Erskine, as of many a good man besides, to contend on the losing side all his life long; but he fought on in hope, ever animated by the belief, in the midst of present defeat and disaster, that God himself was pledged to the principles which he maintained, and that their ultimate triumph was secure. He was the first man in Scotland to raise his voice against the war with the American colonies, as alike impolitic and unjust, — as opposed in principle to the sacred oracles, and as pregnant with disaster to the country. His little tract, "Shall I go to War with my American Brethren?" takes its place among the most powerful of his productions. But the warning voice was unheeded; and so, after much blood had been shed, and much treasure wasted, the colonies were lost to Britain. He was among the first Scotchmen, too, that took an active interest in the abolition of slavery; and when twitted with the fact, in his old age, by the Edinburgh lawyer who now sits on the bench, he rose, with all the spirit of his most vigorous days, "to acknowledge, and glory in the acknowledgment," — we employ his own words, — "that" he was "a member of the Slave Abolition Society. For why?" he added: "I wished to see justice done to cruelly oppressed fellow-creatures, dragged reluctantly from one quarter of the globe to another to satisfy the rapacity of our countrymen, — men who can boast proudly enough of their own freedom. I wished, too, to see a stain, the blackest that can be conceived, wiped away from the national character of Britain. This I wished, — this is still my wish; nor will all that the gentlemen opposite can say prevent me from effecting it, so far as God has given me the power." Dr. Erskine was long remarkable for the extent and expansiveness of his views in connection with the general interests of Christianity. They were not confined to one kingdom, nor even one quarter of the globe. When yet a young man, his attention had been strongly excited by the remarkable revival of religion which had taken place in North America, chiefly in connection with the labors of that truly eminent Christian and profound thinker, the metaphysician of the New World, President Edwards; and in order to obtain the earliest and most extensive religious intelligence from this quarter, in the hope of awakening a similar spirit at home, he had entered into an extensive correspondence with the distinguished President himself, and several of his fellow-laborers. With a similar purpose he also opened up a correspondence with many of the more eminent divines of the continent, which he maintained during the course of his long life. And, thus standing, like a prophet of old, on a hill-top, scarce a cloud could arise on the horizon of the religious world, or a gleam of sunshine break out in even its more solitary recesses, that escaped his notice. As he advanced in years, his interest in the survey increased. He saw some great convulsion at hand, which was perhaps to agitate all Europe; and so intense was his anxiety, that, at a period of life when the few who survive so long deem their time of exertion over, he set himself sedulously to the study of the German language, as a new medium of knowledge, and actually mastered its difficulties in a very few weeks. We may mention, as a proof of the unwearied zeal of the man, that even at his death, which took place in his eighty-second year, he was found to have collected materials for the current number of his periodical pamphlet, "Religious Intelligence from Abroad."

The storm which he had foreseen in "a cloud like a man's hand," at length burst out in all the horrors of the first French Revolution. A whole nation recognized the tenets of atheism as the moral and religious code of its people, and pronounced death to be an eternal sleep. No inconsiderable portion of the people of the other countries of Europe seemed fast treading in their footsteps. In the centre of the great moral earthquake which ensued, the gilded pinnacles of society were thrown down and broken in pieces; blood flowed in torrents; the whole face of things was fearfully changed. Men who had had no previous quarrel with skepticism — who, like Gibbon, rather had spent years of toilsome nights and laborious days in securing its spread — were struck aghast to see it resolve itself into its occult elements, convulsion and murder. Men who had held by a mere semblance of the truth — the *Moderates* of all churches — feared that the last days of the Christian religion had at length come, and that the general gloom betokened its setting. The popish hierarchy had fled in terror of their lives from France, routed by the Encyclopædists and the populace. Paine and his associates in our own country, backed by the previous labors of the bosom-friends and honored correspondents of Robertson and Blair, had commenced their ferocious attack on the religion of the Bible. Even to some not unacquainted with the vital energies of that Christianity which God himself has sworn to maintain, the time seemed a time of defeat and disaster, in which it behooved the cause of religion to yield, at least for a season, and take shelter till the fury of the assault might have spent itself in its own mad exertions. Very different indeed was the estimate of the aged and venerable leader of Evangelism in Scotland. The time might seem to others a time of inevitable retreat; he, on the contrary, deemed it a proper time for advance. For nearly sixty years had he now looked forth upon the long-protracted battle, in which the principles of good and evil contended for the mastery; and it was this dark hour, of all others, that he deemed fittest for the charge. He corresponded with his friends; he encouraged them to action in the missionary field. It was no time for them, he urged, to rest idly on their arms.

Nearly a century previous, a Society had been instituted in Scotland for the Propagation of Christian Knowledge; but its funds had been at no time sufficient to enable it to carry its exertions beyond the limits of the kingdom, or even adequately to supply the destitution of our Highlands and Islands, its more especial field. At a middle period in the century, the Moravians of Denmark had originated those arduous but *singularly* successful schemes for the spread of the gospel, through which the glad tidings of salvation had been carried to Greenland, the West Indies, and many parts of Africa and America. A very few years previous, some worthy Baptist ministers in Northampton and Leicestershire had set the missionary example to England, by originating a Society for the Diffusion of the Gospel; the London Society had been established the year previous; and now, in the spring of 1796, the first meeting of the Edinburgh Missionary Society was held in this city,—the truly venerable Dr. John Erskine, the father of the institution, then in his seventy-fifth year, in the chair. One of the first acts of the society was to address a circular to all the ministers of religion in the country, and to as many private individuals besides as were deemed able and willing to assist in forwarding its objects. All the ministers of the Church of Scotland were included in the list, as a matter of course; the society urged their coöperation, and entreated their prayers; considerable interest was excited over the country; the matter was discussed in synods and presbyteries; and the immediate result at this stage, in connection with the Church, was the transmission of two overtures to the General Assembly of the current year, recommendatory of a favorable consideration of the missionary scheme,—one from the Synod of Moray, the other from the Synod of Fife. The General Assembly met, and in arranging the order of business, the 27th day of May was fixed for its deliberations on the overtures on missions.

The generally recognized leaders of the two parties had been returned members of the Assembly—Dr. John Erskine, now, as we have said, in his seventy-sixth year, and Dr. George Hill, of St. Andrews, a man then in the prime of life. To the character of the first we have already introduced our readers,—an introduction unnecessary, we have little doubt, in the case of by far the greater number of them; that of the latter is also pretty generally known, *but certainly* much more variously estimated. "The boy," says Wordsworth, "is father to the man." We find the embryo Moderate leader, when yet a lad of eighteen, and at a time when Chesterfield was deemed a profound moralist, writing thus to his mother from London: "I am sure I am pliable enough, —*more than I think sometimes quite right.* I can laugh or be grave, talk nonsense on politics or philosophy, *just as it suits my company*, and can submit to any mortification to please those with whom I converse. I cannot flatter; but I can listen with attention, *and seem pleased with everything that anybody says.* By arts like these, *which have perhaps a little meanness in them*, but are *so convenient that one does not choose to lay them aside*, I have had the good luck to be a favorite in most places." "In the general scramble for the good things of this world," says one of the Doctor's biographers, "had such a man failed, who could ever hope to succeed?" George Hill did not fail. He was unlucky in one instance, in one of his patrons, through whose influence he might have risen high in the English Church; but, ere he had made up his mind to enter into orders in the more aristocratic Establishment, with a prospect of preferment superior to anything which Presbyterianism can offer, — a course much urged on him by his friends, — his patron unluckily died. Still, however, Presbytery has its good things also; at least, half a dozen of its tolerably good things make a very good thing when united; and both in practice and theory Hill was a pluralist. He made speeches in the Speculative Club in praise of the aristocracy, by which he acquired very considerable eclat. To favor a political friend, he became the holder of a paper vote in Nairnshire, which, under the dread of being possibly subjected to a prosecution for perjury, he again relinquished, after having once exercised the privilege which it conferred. In his twenty-second year he became Professor of Greek in the University of St. Andrews; he had been offered by the Earl of Haddington of those days the parish of Coldstream; but with prospects such as his, a country parish seemed a somewhat inconsiderable matter; and the result justified his prudence; for ere his thirtieth year he had united to his Greek professorship the second parochial charge of St. Andrews. A few years after, he became Professor of Divinity, and, in addition, Principal of the University. He was next nominated one of his Majesty's chaplains for Scotland; next, one of the deans of the Chapel Royal; and to all these profitable offices was superadded the merely honorary office of dean to the Order of the Thistle. If an aggregation of offices lead to an aggregated amount of character, never, surely, had church party a more honorable leader than the opponent of Dr. Erskine. One of the ministers of St. Andrews, its Professor of Theology, the Principal of its University, one of his Majesty's chaplains for Scotland, one of the deans of the Chapel Royal, and, finally, the dean of the Order of the Thistle, all walked into the General Assembly in the person of Dr. Hill.

Of the character of his measures as a public man it is not difficult at this time of day to form a correct estimate. They are now matters of history; and the experience of half a century has read its comment on the miserable narrowness of the policy by which they were dictated. "Frederick of Prussia," says Byron, "ran away from both the first and the last of his fields." Nearly the same thing may be said of Dr. Hill. He broke down as a leader in both his earlier and his concluding attempts. Though much superior as a theologian to Dr. Robertson, and apparently much more sincere in his beliefs, he was by many degrees a less prudent man. If the historian succeeded in prostrating the spirit of Presbytery, he deemed the achievement sufficient: its skeleton forms he suffered to remain. It was enough for him that he enveloped these in an atmosphere of death: there were risks connected with their removal which he was too wary and too far-seeing to run. He strenuously resisted, for instance, every attempt to set aside the Confession of Faith; he permitted the *Call* to survive in all its original integrity of form, deeming it sufficient that in practice he had reduced it to a dead letter; and during the whole of his reign — the most absolute, perhaps, of any ecclesiastical leader — he allowed the Assembly, without challenge, to raise every year its appeal to the Legislature against patronage. Dr. Hill, as we have said, was less prudent. Almost his first legislative attempt was an attempt to abolish the Call. The measure, however, though strenuously defended by Dr. Cook, in his biography, was regarded as too extreme by some of the more wary, and with these also by not a few, we may trust, of the better disposed Moderates. By the union of these with the Evangelical minority the design was defeated, and the Church was thus spared the signal disgrace of destroying by her own act one of the most important, and, surely, not the least sacred, of her liberties. He was again defeated still more signally, at a much later period, in his defence of the imposition of the miserably profane Test Act on members of the Established Church of Scotland. He deemed it no hardship, he said, for Presbyterians of liberal and enlightened minds to partake of the Lord's Supper according to the mode sanctioned by the sister church. He did not add that, regarded as a prelude to office, it could scarce be deemed other than a very agreeable ceremony indeed. But the majority of the Church thought differently, and so Dr. Hill was defeated. Unfortunately, however, for the character of his party, there were measures in which he was entirely successful. It was on a motion made by Dr. Hill, in the General Assembly of 1784, that the appeal against patronage to the Government of the country, which, year after year, from the times of Lord President Dundas, had been raised by the Church, was suffered to drop. He had the satisfaction, too, — though we doubt whether even his biographer, Dr. Cook, will now envy him the triumph, — of defeating, on the question of missions, the venerable Dr. Erskine and his party, and of thus branding *Moderatism*, though, surely, all unwittingly, full in the view of the religious world, as a principle essentially anti-Christian. It is but justice, however, to the character of Dr. Hill, to add one trait more. Very rarely is the thorough Moderate, though able and accomplished, a profound theologian. His lack of belief in the fundamental doctrines of theology — a lack of belief similar to that which obtains in the present age regarding the peculiar dogmas of the Schoolmen, and which prevents any very thorough study of their writings — has the effect of inducing superficiality. Why spend much time in acquainting one's self with doubtful complexities, that lead to no practical result? Such, however, was not the conclusion of Dr. Hill. His system of theology is not without its defects. His exposures of dangerous heresy and his exhibitions of Divine truth are alike characterized by a freezing chill of sentiment. But superficiality is not his fault: his work is that of a masterly theologian, who at least saw clearly, though he could not feel strongly. We know not whether we are to seek an explanation of the fact in a peculiarity of character adverted to by himself in one of his earlier letters: "I am, and perhaps all my life shall continue," he says, "a close student; but I hate learning."

PART SECOND.

The debate on missions opened with one of those disingenuous stratagems on the part of the Moderate leader, which, consorting thoroughly with the character and principles of the party, have ever constituted the staple of its policy, and in the management of which few men ever excelled Dr. Hill. Trick and finesse are the proper weapons of a false or unfaithful Church in a civilized age, whether she have to defend herself against the assaults of infidels and skeptics, whose doctrines, however congenial to her actual beliefs, would lead to the alienation of her temporalities, *or to oppose* herself a thousand times more thoroughly in earnest to the exertions of a very different class, animated by a desire of heightening her character and correcting her errors.

There were, as we have said, two overtures recommendatory of the missionary scheme before the Assembly,—one from the Synod of Moray, the other from the Synod of Fife. The Fife overture was of a general, though at the same time sufficiently definite character: it merely urged on the Assembly the consideration of the most effectual methods by which the Church of Scotland might be made to contribute to the diffusion of the gospel over the world. The Moray overture was more particular in what it recommended. Taking it somewhat too readily for granted that the course advised by the other overture the Assembly was already prepared to pursue, it went a step further, and earnestly urged the passing of an act recommendatory of a general collection in aid of the missionary scheme throughout the various parishes of Scotland. Both the leaders of the Assembly were shrewd and far-seeing men, and both intimately acquainted with the nature of the materials on which they had to operate. They alike saw that the Fife overture, if considered alone, and on its own merits, might very possibly pass into a law, which, however inoperative, would at least recognize the excellence of missionary exertion; they alike saw that the prevailing Moderatism of the Assembly would be at once roused to oppose the Moray overture, and that there was no chance whatever of *its* passing. The great object of Dr. Hill was to defeat both, and so get rid of the troublesome subject of missions altogether. The great object of Dr. Erskine was to get all passed in their favor that could possibly pass. Dr. Hill urged, therefore, that the overtures should be considered *conjunctly*. If he but succeeded in getting what he already deemed *the dead* tied about the neck of the living, he was secure, as he too justly augured, of soon seeing them both equally dead. Dr. Erskine contended, on the *contrary*, that they should be considered separately. The one, he argued, was "of a *general*, the other of a *specific* nature; and general propositions often command united assent, though men may differ widely regarding the time and manner of applying them to practice." But in deliberative assemblies, arguments fail when they have to contend with votes; and it was carried, on the motion of Dr. Hill, that the overtures should be considered, not separately, as became their character, but conjunctly, as consorted best with his own invidious policy. The preliminary motion virtually decided the fate of the whole discussion; but Evangelism fought on.

One of the first speakers in the debate was the Rev. Mr. M'Bean, of Alves—a worthy north country clergyman, uncle, we believe, of the present excellent minister of Forres. The good man had come from a remote rural district, in which he had been studying his Bible, and sedulously walking, in conformity with its injunctions, his useful round of duty; and in rising to support the Moray overture, it does not seem to have once entered his mind that there were two courses of conduct open regarding it. "The propagation of the glorious gospel of Jesus Christ!"—Had they not all been praying for it all their lives long? and was it not their duty to work as well as to pray—their duty, and not the less surely their high privilege and honor, that in this matter they could be fellow-workers with God? "Thy kingdom come." What Christian man could look forth without compassion on that vast portion of the earth which was still a region of thick darkness and horrid cruelty, and in which poor perishing fellow-creatures, born to immortality, enjoyed no opportunity of embracing the blessed gospel? And then, how great was their encouragement! Did not prophecy point their faith to a period when the knowledge of the Lord would be everywhere—all around and over this wide world, like the waters of a shoreless ocean? and should not they, strengthened by a hope so certain, be now up and doing,—using their every endeavor to hasten the happy time,—working, as well as praying, that the kingdom of grace might be advanced, and the kingdom of glory hastened? The good man sat down, and was succeeded by another speaker on the same side — the truly venerable Dr. Johnston, of North Leith.

It is scarce necessary that we advert to the character of this man. We stood not long ago in a humble domicile in Leith, before a rudely framed print of Dr. Johnston: it had been taken in his extreme age. The strongly marked and somewhat harsh features bore evidence to the ravages of time; but the course of years had worn into them the expression of his habitual mood, in characters which it was impossible to misinterpret, and the effect was something more powerful than beauty. Never have we seen thoughtful seriousness united to habitual benevolence more legibly impressed. "O, sir," said the inmate of the humble domicile, an aged woman, as she pointed to the print, — "O, sir, there were few like him. For many, many a year have I heard the precious gospel from those earnest, blessed lips." Dr. Johnston was one of the truly excellent of the earth. He rose on this occasion to signify his hearty approval of the two overtures on the table, but with evidently less confidence of success than was entertained by the north country minister; for he knew better than he the character of the party ranged on the opposite benches. In running over nearly the same line of argument, his fears were ever and anon breaking out. "Surely," he said, "however much they might differ from one another in matters of civil or ecclesiastical polity, they could not be other than united in whatever tended to promote the kingdom of their blessed Lord and Master!" What if he, in whose presence and in whose name they sat, and to whom one day they would have all to render their final account, was now waiting among them for some marked expression of their sincerity in his cause! Was the General Assembly of the Church of Scotland to declare against both him and it, by thwarting the means of promoting it? Means must be used; they are the instruments by which God works.

The advance of his kingdom among the heathen was the subject of their daily prayers, but it would not do to say, "Be ye warmed and clothed — be ye enlightened, reformed, and saved," without doing something more. They were called on to act as well as pray. Thousands, bound by only their common Christianity, were stepping forward to promote the missionary cause; their heathen brethren lay in their blood: would they, the Church of Scotland, pass by, like the Levite, on the other side? Paul reckoned himself "a debtor to the Greek and the barbarian." Did Scotland lie under no such debt? The fact that they themselves had been called from heathen darkness by missionary exertion in the remote past, had given a direct claim upon them to the perishing heathen of all time. Dr. Johnston ceased, and there rose a speaker on the Moderate side.

He was a tall, handsome man, in the prime of early manhood, fashionably dressed, and evidently a layman. Strange to relate, he rose, not to oppose, but strenuously to advocate the missionary cause. It is recorded in the biography of the Rev. Thomas Scott, that, when a thoughtless young man, he was severely reprimanded for some piece of wickedness by his master, — a person of no religion, and who pretended to none, — and that from this very circumstance the reprimand struck him more deeply than any that had ever been dealt him. Moderatism on the present occasion received a similar rebuke.

Robert Heron, a name introduced into one of the minor poems of Burns,[1] in a manner that too effectually precludes all idea of his having been a man of serious religion, was one of the many who seem born to illustrate the important truth, that without prudence and conduct there is no real value in talent or learning, and no virtue in genius. He was the son of a poor weaver; and in studying for the Church — for he had unluckily seen no other mode of rising from his miserably depressed level — he had struggled hard

1 Epistle to Dr. Blacklock.

with all the difficulties and hardships incidental to extreme poverty and an utter lack of friends. At the early age of eleven, he had both to support and educate himself, by mingling with his studies the labors of teaching. He fought his onward way bravely. In addition to his other acquirements, he completely mastered in his leisure hours the French language, attained to a thorough command of English, acquainted himself with general literature, wrote verses and essays; and, on removing to Edinburgh to attend the classes at college, he found means of introducing himself to the booksellers of the place, and of so impressing them with ideas of the force and versatility of his talents, that they furnished him with instant employment. He wrote translations by the score; produced original works, critical, historical, topographical, which, though now forgotten, were favorably received in their day. He delivered lectures on the law of nature and of nations, on subjects of taste and questions of science; and in the keen thirst of literary fame, and possessed of an iron constitution, which his sixteen hours a day employment failed for years sensibly to affect, he gave up his first-cherished hopes of a competency in connection with the Church, and devoted himself to literature exclusively. Rarely is the life of the literary aspirant a happy one; very rarely, except in the few cases in which religion exerts its influence over the whole conduct, is it even a comparatively innocent one. The literary man of the last century, too, was almost always an eccentric, unsettled being, ill-hafted in society, and licensed beyond his contemporaries by well-nigh general consent. Heron too soon acquired the character of his class. Periods of intense study were succeeded by occasional fits of dissipation. He was ambitious, too, of being deemed rather a gentleman than a man of literature, — no uncommon weakness among literary men, — and affected a fashionable style of living, which, joined to his unsettled habits, had soon the effect of placing him in great difficulties and distress. *It is* a melancholy fact, that no inconsiderable portion of his History of Scotland was written in jail. And yet, in the midst of his sore straits and signal imprudence, this unfortunate man of genius continued to cherish warm affections, and a conscience tenderly alive, even with reference to the religious standard, to the true nature of his own aberrations. We find him on one occasion thus writing to his poor parents: — "I hope, by living more piously and carefully, by managing my income frugally, and appropriating a part of it to the service of you and my sisters, to reconcile your affections more entirely to me, and give you more comfort than I have yet done. O, forget and forgive my follies; look on me as a son who will anxiously strive to comfort and please you, and, after all your misfortunes, to render the evening of your days as happy as possible." In another letter we find him thus speaking of his sisters: — "We must endeavor to settle our dear Grace comfortably in life, and to educate our dear little Betty and Mary aright." He brought a younger brother, a lad of promising talents, with him to Edinburgh, and supported him at college; but he saw him sink into an early grave, a victim to consumption. He then brought a favorite sister to live with him. The seeds of the same insidious disease were fixed in her constitution also, and she too sank into the grave. For a considerable period his mind seemed almost unhinged by this latter shock: he quitted Edinburgh, and forgot his griefs for a time in a round of unceasing literary occupation in London. For several years he employed his pen in the service of the English publishers, and this much more profitably than he had ever been able to do in Scotland; but his unsettled habits still clung by him, and kept him poor. His originally excellent constitution at length broke suddenly down, undermined by his arduous and long-protracted labors, ill relieved by life-wearing fits of dissipation; and he again became the inmate of a jail. And here, in the midst of squalor and distress, enfeebled in body, and with a mind bowed down by want and despair, he could yet derive a glimmering of comfort from the fact that he had never employed his pen against religion. He was now on the confines of the eternal world, for he quitted his place of confinement only to die in a hospital. Who that is "himself a sinner" shall venture to say that the mercy which found the penitent publican and the penitent thief did not visit his neglected death-bed, on which, alas! there was not a human friend to look? Be that as it may, it is at least justice to record, that in the memorable debate on missions Robert Heron originated the motion which Dr. John Erskine was well content to second.

His speech was characterized by clear good sense, with no assumption—for in his case the assumption could not have been other than offensive—of the devotional tone. It was a demonstrable truth, he said, that Christianity had a happy influence on society; that it contributed to the temporal prosperity of states no less than to the spiritual welfare of individuals. They had seen it gradually ameliorating the condition of the lower orders of society; it had extirpated, for instance, the domestic slavery of Europe, and taken its place in the very van of civilization, as the pioneer of improvement, whether intellectual or moral. If a spirit for its diffusion had now gone abroad, regulated by moderation and prudence, and if there existed at the same time circumstances more favorable for giving that spirit effect than at any former period,—and he was prepared to show that that spirit had gone abroad, and that these circumstances did exist,—he really did not see that in the General Assembly of the Church of Scotland there could be any ground for difference of opinion on the subject. As for favorable circumstances, the extensive commerce of the country, and the consequent vastness of its naval resources, might be rationally regarded as just the proper wings of missionary exertion. The country stood, too, on a high table-land of science and general knowledge, which could surely be made available in favorably *impressing*, for the best of purposes, the ignorant natives of barbarous or semi-barbarous lands. As for the missionary spirit which had been awakened, could there possibly be a more gratifying or joyful circumstance to men who had been long complaining of the progress of infidelity, and the consequent alarming decay of religion and good morals? It was a direct test of the vigor of religious feeling among them, and an evidence that infidelity was not destined to prevail. It was surely a good spirit. If Christianity be an excellent thing in itself, it is an excellent thing also to spread it widely. Prophecy points to a time in which, from the rising to the setting sun, the Gentile nations shall become willing subjects of the Redeemer's kingdom. He doubted not that the diffusion of a very general missionary spirit would be one of the means through which so desirable a result was to be produced; and who knew whether they might not, at that very time, be witnessing its first awakenings? At all events, he said, he could not avoid thinking that such a spirit should be encouraged, awake when it might, and that the only way for directing it well was just for men of character and abilities to take an active part in the exertions to which it led. The Church of Scotland had been complimented by a late distinguished philosopher, David Hume, as more favorable to the cause of deism than any other religious establishment. Now was the time for them to prove to the world that the compliment was undeserved, by zealously countenancing and assisting the honest endeavors of their fellow Christians throughout the country. Otherwise he did not see how the clergy could expatiate with a good grace on the general indifference about religion, if they themselves set so palpable an example of that very indifferency. He concluded, however, by moving, not that they should immediately adopt either of the overtures, but that they should appoint a committee for taking the subject of them into serious consideration, and on whose report the Assembly might afterwards act. A matter that promised so fair was at least worthy of examination: justice demanded that they should deal with it according to its merits; and it was imperatively their duty to ascertain what these merits were.

As he sat down, Dr. Erskine and the Rev. Mr. Hamilton, of Gladsmuir, rose together. The venerable Doctor yielded to his opponent, at that time a young man, merely remarking, that for the present, at least, he had risen but to second the motion of the "gentleman opposite," Mr. Heron. The Rev. Mr. Hamilton then proceeded with his speech, — one of the most carefully written, apparently, of any delivered during the course of the debate, — one of the most extraordinary ever delivered anywhere.

PART THIRD.

"The *bruit* goeth," said De Bracy shrewdly to his companion in arms, the Templar, "that the most holy order of the Temple of Zion nurseth not a few infidels within its bosom." David Hume, intending on one occasion to be very complimentary, said nearly the same thing of the Church of Scotland. Was the compliment deserved, and, if so, what peculiar aspect did the infidelity of our Scottish clergy assume? Was it gentlemanly and philosophic, like that of Hume himself? or highly seasoned with wit, like that of Voltaire? or dignified and pompous, like that of Gibbon? or romantic and chivalrous, like that of Lord Herbert of Cherbury? or steeped in ruffianism and vulgarity, like that of Paine? or redolent of nonsense, like that of Robert Owen? Or was it not rather of mark enough to have a character of its own? — an infidelity that purported to be anti-Christian on Bible authority, — that, at least, while it robed itself in the proper habiliments of unbelief, took the liberty of lacing them with Scripture edgings? May we crave the attention of the reader, instead of directly answering any of these queries, to the facts and reasonings employed by the Rev. Mr. Hamilton, of Gladsmuir, in opposing the motion of poor Robert Heron. Mr. Hamilton was one of the most respectable Moderates of his time. His party shortly afterwards honored him with the title of Doctor of Divinity; and when searching out among their soundest men for a Moderator of the General Assembly, they made choice of him. For the sake of brevity, we have taken very considerable liberties with the speakers whose more striking or more characteristic ideas we have already submitted to the reader; we have given the meaning, but not the words, of the first two, and only a few sentences of the last, in the language which he himself employed. But we shall take no such liberties with the speech of Mr. Hamilton. We cannot give the whole of it, for it occupies ten rather closely-printed pages; but our extracts will be all true to the original text. We could scarce translate the sentiments expressed in it into our own language, however fairly, without subjecting ourselves to a charge of exaggeration and injustice.

"I should blush, Moderator," said the reverend gentleman, "to rise in this venerable Assembly for the purpose of opposing a plan so beneficent in its first aspect as the present, did not mature reflection fully convince me *that its principles are not really good, but merely specious;* that no such honor could accrue to us from supporting and promoting it, as its friends among us have fondly anticipated; and because no such benefits could in all probability result from the execution of it to mankind as they have no less fondly imagined and described. Such being my decided sentiments on the subject, I feel no reluctance to rise and state them fully. I feel this declaration, indeed, incumbent on me; nor do I hesitate to say that, entertaining these sentiments, *it is as much my duty to wish that the house may be firm and unanimous in their opposition to these overtures*, as it appeared the duty of those who were of a very different opinion to be actuated by a very different desire. To diffuse among mankind the knowledge of a religion which we profess to believe and revere, is doubtless a good and important work; as to pray for its diffusion and to expect it is taught us in the sacred volume of Scripture. But as even the best things are liable to abuse, and as things the most excellent are most liable to abuse, so in the present case it happens, that *I cannot otherwise consider the enthusiasm on this subject than as the effect of sanguine and illusive views, the more dangerous because the object is plausible.*"

The reader will observe that the Rev. Mr. Hamilton, of Gladsmuir, was animated in his course by a strong sense of duty, and that he was not at all ashamed to boast, we make no doubt very honestly, and with all due modesty, of the sensitive tenderness of his conscience. He next proceeded to unfold the very occult principles on which his views of duty were based.

"To spread abroad the knowledge of the gospel among barbarous and heathen nations," he remarked, "seems to me highly preposterous, in as far as it anticipates, nay, as it even reverses, the order of nature. Men must be polished and refined in their manners before they can be properly enlightened in religious truths. Philosophy and learning must in the nature of things take the precedence. Indeed, it should seem hardly less absurd to make revelation precede civilization in the order of time, than to pretend to unfold to a child the *Principia* of Newton ere he is made at all acquainted with the letters in the alphabet. *These ideas seem to me alike founded in error, and therefore I must consider them both as equally romantic and visionary.*"

Mr. Hamilton next deduced very fairly from these first principles, that not only are there many millions of men who *have no* opportunities of embracing the gospel, but who as certainly, as he himself very pointedly said, "*ought to have none.*" The question of their responsibility naturally suggested itself to him; and his benevolent mind found in solution the following singularly comfortable but not the less somewhat extraordinary doctrine:

"To this question Scripture furnishes us with an answer, plain, natural, and just. We are in it told that 'a man is to be judged according to what he hath, not according to what he hath not.' We are, moreover, told by Paul to the same purpose 'that the Gentiles which have not the law are a law unto themselves;' and that 'they who are without law shall be judged without law.' *So that the gracious declaration of Scripture ought to liberate from groundless anxiety the minds of those who stated in such moving language the condition of the heathen.*"

He next proceeded to show how very excellent a condition that of the heathen may be, and caught, as he warmed in his description, the very spirit of Rousseau.

"Every state of society," he said, "has vices and virtues peculiar to itself, which balance each other, and are not incompatible with a large share of happiness. The untutored Indian or Otaheitan, whose daily toils produce his daily food, and who, when that is procured, basks with his family in the sun with little reflection or care, is not without his simple virtues. His breast can beat high with the feelings of friendship, his heart can burn with the ardor of patriotism; and although his mind have not comprehension enough to grasp the idea of general philanthropy, yet the houseless stranger finds a sure shelter under his hospitable though humble roof, and experiences that, though ignorant of the general principle, his soul is attuned to the feelings on which its practice must generally depend. But go—engraft on his simple manners the customs, refinements, and, may I not add, some of the vices of civilized society, *and the influence of that religion which you give as a compensation for the disadvantages attending such communications will not refine his morals nor insure his happiness.* Of the change of manners, the effect produced shall prove a heterogeneous and disagreeable combination; and of the change of opinion, the effects shall be a tormenting uncertainty respecting some things, a great misapprehension of others, and a misapplication perhaps of all."

It was surely no wonder that the Rev. Mr. Hamilton should have exerted himself, out of a high sense of duty, to shield from the contamination of the gospel the virtues of so happy a state. He then proceeded, with all the mingled zeal and knowledge of the philosopher and "qualified minister," to show how very mischievous and dangerous a thing this same gospel is, and how very terribly it would tend to brutalize savages.

"When they shall be told," he said, "that a man is saved not by good works, but by faith, what will be the consequence? We have too much experience of the difficulty of guarding our own people against the most deplorable misapplication of this principle; though here the people are instructed by stated and regular pastors, though their minds have been early imbued with a pious and virtuous education, and though they are daily warned of the folly and danger of immorality under this pretext, we have too much experience of this fatal tendency at home, I say, with all our refinement, to entertain a rational doubt that the wild inhabitants of uncivilized regions *would use it as a handle for the most flagrant violation of justice and morality.*"

Mr. Hamilton, early in his speech, had admitted that, could Christian missionaries be possibly found of the right stamp, — men of mildly tempered zeal, — and that could a heathen country blessed with civilization, and thus fitted for receiving them, be also found, — though evidently, according to his estimate, it required no small amount of civilization to neutralize the evils of but a very small amount of Christianity, — still he would have no very serious objection against sending the mildly tempered missionaries to the highly civilized land. On thinking over the matter, however, he deemed the admission rather too great, and he thus proceeded to qualify it:

"I formerly observed, that if missionaries were to be sent anywhere, it ought to be to that country whose state of civil society should appear to be fitted to receive it and improve by revelation. But even supposing such a nation could be found, I should still have weighty objections against sending missionaries thither. Why should we scatter our forces and spend our strength in foreign service, when our utmost vigilance is required at home?"

The concluding stroke in the following passage will scarce fail in provoking the smile of the reader. Most involuntarily, evidently, did the admission which it conveys fall from the speaker. It was a grace beyond the reach of art, — one at least which only our master dramatists could have equalled:

"What general," said Mr. Hamilton, "would desire to achieve distant conquests, and scatter for this purpose his troops over a distant and strange land, when the enemy's forces were already pouring into his own country, estranging the citizens from his interests, and directing the whole force of his artillery against the walls of his capital. *I cannot but reflect with surprise that the very men who in their sermons, by their speeches, by their publications, in short, by everything but their own lives, are anxious to show to the world the growing profligacy of the times at home,—I cannot but reflect with surprise that these are the very men most zealous in promoting this expedition abroad."*

We can give, as we have said, only a part of this speech; but the whole is infinitely curious. We add just two sentences more—the concluding ones.

"Upon the whole, *while we pray for the propagation of the gospel, and patiently await its period, let us unite in resolutely rejecting these overtures.* For my own part at least, I am obliged heartily to oppose the motion for a committee, and to substitute as a motion in its place, *That the overtures from the Synods of Fife and Moray be immediately dismissed."*

Mr. Hamilton ceased speaking, and sat down. On the table of the General Assembly there always lies a Bible. It lay there in even the darkest days of Moderate ascendency, and neither Hill nor Robertson had dared to recommend its removal. The venerable leader of Evangelism rose, and pointed to the table. "Moderator," he said,—and the brief and emphatic sentence that followed was one of those which men never forget,—"Moderator, RAX ME THAT BIBLE." The Church of Scotland has her appropriate Scripture motto, borne in reference to the burning bush seen by the prophet in the wilderness. Were she not so well provided,—were the label still to inscribe,—we could imagine many worse suggestions than that it should be occupied by the laconic though quaintly-expressed request of Erskine—RAX ME THAT BIBLE.

The Rev. Mr. Hamilton, of Gladsmuir, in the very spirit *of some of* our contemporaries of the press, who lie, in the present controversy, out of sheer policy, and supply "a plentiful lack" of argument by a no less marked fertility of fabrication, had accused his opponents of *dishonesty*. Like a reverend gentleman of the present day, he had, no doubt, felt it *to be his duty* to make the charge. The harvest of the preceding year had been scanty and inadequate. There obtained, in consequence, among the poorer people, a very considerable amount of distress, which a collection — and, to the honor of British liberality, it had been a very ample one — had recently been made to relieve; and, though the money was not yet expended, many and urgent, he stated, were the demands upon it. "Sorry, therefore, was he to say, that in such circumstances of calamity some of his brethren, without consulting any ecclesiastical court, had not only joined missionary societies, but had also set apart to their use the money collected for the poor. For such improper conduct," he added, "censure was by much too small a mark of disapprobation: it would, he doubted not, be a legal subject of penal prosecution." Dr. Erskine, old as he was, was not quite the man to suffer such a charge to pass unquestioned, and he now peremptorily demanded an explanation. The offence, he said, if really perpetrated, was a criminal offence, and ought to be dealt with as such; but it would not do thus to wound the character of innocent men by vague insinuations regarding it. He was entitled, he said, to urge that the cases of misappropriation should be specified, and the guilty individuals named; and to urge further that, should the accusation prove an unfounded calumny, it should meet with the merited contempt. He paused for a reply; and the pause was a long, and, to Mr. Hamilton, a singularly embarrassing one. But he at length stammered out an explanation. When he had said that money collected for the poor had been set apart for the use of missionary societies, he had not at all meant that money professedly collected for the poor had been set apart to their use. *He had* only meant that money collected at church-doors for missionary societies had been thus appropriated to missionary purposes; and that all money collected at church-doors seemed to him to belong to the poor. An offence for which censure was too small a mark of disapprobation — which ought rather to be made a subject of penal prosecution — resolved itself simply into the fact, that Dr. Erskine, and several other ministers besides, had made church-door collections for missionary objects, with the full consent of their several sessions, with full and public intimation to their several congregations beforehand of the purposes to which the money was to be applied, and, withal, with fair deduction from the amount received of the average Sunday collections for the poor. Moderatism in those days must surely have had a very nice perception of crime.

The minister of Gladsmuir was, it is said, a man of mild and insinuating manners, — very much a gentleman of the old school, — fluent and bland, and who ever deemed it a solecism in politeness to lose temper in company. We have been told, however, that there were four little words which he could never contrive to hear unmoved: they brought a singularly unpleasant scene to his recollection, and operated on him like the sight of the bodkin on Sir Percy Shafton. If an acquaintance wished to see him redden and get silent in even his gayest and most conversible moods, he had but to whisper in his ear, RAX ME THAT BIBLE. He had studied, when a very young man, what Dr. Johnson had termed the art of "labored gesticulation," in the belief, doubtless, that his facts and his arguments would be materially strengthened by the motions of his hands and his legs. He had had on this occasion much to prove; and therefore, to employ the language of the writer just named, he had "rolled his eyes, and puffed his cheeks, and spread abroad his arms, and stamped on the ground, and turned his eyes sometimes to the ceiling and sometimes to the floor." Dr. Erskine *regretted* that he could treat the Assembly to no such display of oratory. In *his* young days, he said, the art had been very little studied in Scotland. He had passed through his *curriculum* at a time when there had been even no professor of rhetoric in any Scotch college; his oratorical education had thus been sadly neglected; but he fain hoped the house would bear with him notwithstanding. He knew, he trusted, a little of church history, and a little of common sense; and his arguments, if solid, might just be permitted to stand "for what they were worth, though unembellished by the flowers of imagery or the graces of style."

He referred in terms of thorough approval to the sentiments expressed by Mr. Heron: they had left him nothing to add, he said, regarding the civilizing influence of Christianity, or in reference to the means possessed at that time by our country of spreading them abroad. He went on, therefore, to take a historical view of what had been already accomplished in the missionary field. He alluded to the missions of the Romish Church, and decided shrewdly on their character. They had left no traces behind them, he said, but traces of desolation and misery. It was a significant fact, too, that the countries chosen as the scene of them were either rich in mines, or amply furnished, through a fertile soil and genial climate, with the conveniences and delicacies of life. The fields selected for their operations were fields in which power or wealth, or at least a state of luxurious indulgence, might be attained to by the missionary; and their entire history, constituting, as it did, a record of rapine, cruelty, and secular aggrandizement, gave evidence of a false, not of a true church. Still, however, when Papists, priding themselves on their own exertions, turned to Protestant churches, and asked, in derision, what *they* had done to spread abroad the faith which they professed to value, or whether their indifferency regarding its promulgation did not argue the weakness of their convictions of its truth, the question was by much too rational to be *despised*. And it was a question which could be answered only by deeds. Something had already been done by Protestants;—more, as if to show that it was *will*, not *ability*, which was wanting, by one of the poorest and least considerable powers of Europe (Denmark) than by all the other Protestant states put together. He referred to the signal labors of the Moravians, as recorded by Crantz and Latrobe. He ran over the history of missions in connection with Great Britain; that of the London Missionary Society, instituted by royal authority in the days of William, which, for many years after its institution, had communicated precious light to multitudes who would otherwise have remained in darkness. He referred to the society established early in the century in Scotland. He alluded briefly to the more recently established societies of our several large towns—societies differently constituted, he said, from each other, and composed of various materials, but of all of which he approved more or less, for of all the great object was the same; and, however diverse might be the sects engaged in them, he deemed all points of inferior moment lost in the importance of the general cause. He paused briefly to consider the *arguments* of Mr. Hamilton. Was it really so absolutely necessary that learning and philosophy should precede the introduction of the gospel? He had been ever accustomed to consider it the peculiar glory of Christianity that it was adapted alike to the citizen and the savage; that it not only enlightened spiritual darkness, but promoted also temporal civilization. The "testimony of the Lord maketh *wise* the *simple*." Christ, in the days of the apostles, had been made "all in all" to barbarians and Scythians. Would it have been so if to barbarians and Scythians Christ had not been preached? Was it not the theme of prophecy, that the benign influences of the gospel should smooth down the shag of human nature in realms the most barbarous and uncivilized? How else did they interpret the bold metaphors of Isaiah? "*The desert* shall rejoice and blossom like the rose; and instead of the brier shall spring up the fir tree; and instead of the thorn, the myrtle tree." What was the testimony of history on the point? Did not the Fathers of the second century boast that the Mauritanians, the Getulians, and other savage nations, had submitted to the government of Zion's King? What was the experience of their own times? Had they heard nothing of the labors of Elliot, Brainerd, and the two Mayhews, among the fierce Indians of North America? Or had civilization visited the bleak coasts of Greenland and Labrador ere the *Unitas Fratrum* had preached the gospel there with such signal success? Some of his younger brethren opposite, no doubt, deemed him a fanatic, and might care little, therefore, for his *opinions;* but the question was not one of opinion; — he could assure them he was dealing in this matter with only solid and well authenticated facts. He alluded to the recent scarcity, and to Mr. Hamilton's terror of injuring the poor and exhausting the rich by their missionary claims. What signs of scarcity, he asked, did the tables, equipage, or general economy of the opulent among them exhibit? Had public calamity lessened either the power or inclination to extravagance? Was not rather the profusion in meats and drinks as marked, — were not the carriages in our streets as sumptuous, the attendants as numerous, — and were not theatres, assemblies, and card-tables, as much frequented as ever? "Besides," he added, "I early learned, and, though old, have not forgot the lesson, that the exercise of every habit naturally tends to strengthen and improve it; and therefore am I inclined to think that a wish to benefit our fellow-creatures in distant regions, and an occasional donation in their behalf, instead of lessening, will serve to increase the compassion of the givers for the needy at home, and thus widen, instead of contracting, the channels of general benevolence." He concluded by giving expression to his cordial approbation of the motion of Mr. Heron, which he had already seconded.

The Rev. Dr. Erskine was succeeded by the Rev. Dr. Alexander Carlyle, minister of Inveresk; and as the speech of this gentleman was a short and very extraordinary one, we shall give it entire. Dr. Carlyle was, of all his party, the boldest and most uncompromising advocate of the theatre, — one of the truly liberal in the case of Home and his tragedy, — in short, a man enlightened enough in his views of dramatic representation to have almost wiped away the stain of bigotry and narrowness from an entire Church. But there is, alas! no perfection in whatever is human; and there were matters in which even he, with all his general liberality, could be narrow and bigoted. He exhausted the charities of his nature in tolerating balls and the theatre; and for the gospel of Christ and the cause of its extension he had no tolerance and no charity.

"Moderator," he said, "my reverend brother, whose universal charity is so well known to me, has just been giving a new and extraordinary instance of it; — no less than *proposing as a model for our imitation the zeal for propagating the Christian religion displayed by Roman Catholics*. When we see the tide of infidelity and licentiousness so great, and so constantly increasing, in our own land, it would indeed be highly preposterous to carry our zeal to another and a far distant one. When our religion requires the most unremitted and strenuous defence against internal invasion, it would be highly absurd to think of making distant converts by external missionaries. This is indeed beginning where we should end. I have, on various occasions, during a *period of almost half a century, had the honor of being a member of the General Assembly. Yet this is the first time I remember to have ever heard such a proposal made*, and I cannot help also thinking it the worst time. As clergymen, let us pray that Christ's kingdom may come, *as we are assured it shall come in the course of Providence*. Let us, as clergymen, also instruct our people in their duty; and, both as clergymen and as Christians, let our light so shine before men, that, seeing our good works, they may be led to glorify our heavenly Father. This is the true mode of propagating the gospel; this is far preferable to giving countenance to a *plan which has well been styled visionary*. I, therefore, do heartily second the motion made some time ago by my young friend Mr. Hamilton, that the overtures be immediately dismissed."

PART FOURTH.

The characters in the debate on missions stand out in bold relief. There is a dramatic force and picturesqueness about them. Evangelism had to contend against the current of the age: it was alike denounced by the worlds of literature and fashion. The politically powerful exerted themselves to crush it as mischievous; the gay and dissipated denounced it as morose and intolerant; the widely-spread skepticism of the period characterized it as irrational and absurd; historians had written whole volumes to traduce and vilify it; and genius had striven to render it ridiculous in song. It behooved its more strenuous assertors, therefore, to be men of at least some force of character; and force of character never exists without those accompanying peculiarities which in the drama of life constitute well-marked individuality. Moderatism, on the other hand, enjoyed singular advantages, though of an opposite nature, of developing itself in its true proportions. It had not, as now, tamely and timidly to conform to the influence of the pressure from without; there was scarce any pressure from without at the time: it could venture on being well-nigh whatever it wished to be. And hence strongly marked character on the part of Moderatism also. From diametrically opposite but equally efficient causes, specimens of both parties, singularly characteristic, were exhibited in this debate. Erskine, Hill, Heron, Hamilton, the simple-hearted clergyman of Alves, and the venerable minister of Leith, appear all before us like the well-drawn *dramatis personæ* of a masterly play. But of all the characters exhibited, perhaps none were better marked than that of the last speaker, Dr. Carlyle. He was a Moderate on a larger scale than could be produced in the altered atmosphere of the present day. In digging him out, we feel as if we had fallen somehow on a *fossil* Moderate; and are struck, in contemplating the mighty fragments, with the degeneracy of his comparatively dwarfish successors. Dr. Bryce planted astride the shoulders of Dr. Cook would fail to overtop a single Dr. Alexander Carlyle.

"Both as clergymen and Christians let our light so shine before men," said the reverend Doctor, "that, seeing our good works, they may be led to glorify our heavenly Father. This is the true mode of propagating the gospel; this is far preferable to giving countenance to *a plan which has well been styled visionary*." Now, it is surely natural to ask, after what particular fashion was the light of the Rev. Dr. Carlyle made to shine before men? Or, what was its character as light? Or, was it light at all? We have already alluded to his liberality of opinion respecting theatrical representation. Milton had his prejudices against play-acting parsons, — "men who shamefully prostituted their ministry," he said, "by writhing and unboning their clergy limbs to all the antic and dishonest gestures of Trinculos, buffoons, and bawds." Not such, however, was the feeling of Dr. Carlyle: he was more than tolerant of play-acting parsons. He was a play-acting parson himself. On one occasion at least, when a select batch of Moderate divines rehearsed the tragedy of Douglas in the house of an Edinburgh actress, the Doctor, a large, dignified-looking man, well-known among the wags of the bar as Jupiter Tonans, performed to admiration the part of *Old Norval*. Dr. Hugh Blair personified the Lady Anna. Carlyle, from being an actor himself, proceeded next to be an instructor of actors. The Edinburgh playhouse of those days, as the reader of Ferguson's "Burlesque Elegy" must needs remember, was in the Canongate. The manager was a Mr. Digges, and one of the prettiest of his staff was a Mrs. Ward, an actress of considerable ability, but, as was common at the time to the profession, of equivocal character; and poor Jupiter Tonans, in urging his instructions, "had made his light so shine" that the tongue of scandal became busy. The case, among other matters, was brought before the Presbytery of Edinburgh; and the reverend Doctor, who seems to have been a man of infinite frankness, to save the Presbytery the trouble of leading proof, at once acknowledged that he had been not only in taverns with the actors, but also occasionally in Mr. Digges' house, hearing parts of the tragedy rehearsed by Mrs. Ward and the others; but that on no occasion had he ever ate or drank with the lady, or conversed with her farther than in agreeing or disagreeing to what was said about the play." This was of course satisfactory; for who could know so well as the Doctor himself? When the tragedy came at length to be acted, some of the clerical friends of the author were led, by the interest they felt in its success, to linger about the house, without actually appearing in the boxes. Hence the point of a stanza, the production of some Edinburgh wit of the period:

> "Hid close in the green-room some clergymen lay,
> Good actors themselves, — *their whole lives a play.*"

Dr. Carlyle, however, with a few others, had more courage. He appeared openly among the audience, armed with a bludgeon. In the course of the evening, two wild young fellows, reckless with intoxication, forced themselves into his box; and the Doctor, though known, says one of his biographers, from "his repeated exertions in favor of the law of patronage, and his strong dislike of *fanatics*, by the title of *the preserver of the Church from fanaticism*," stood up at once in the character of a Non-Intrusionist. He was perfectly sober at the time, and of great muscular strength; and succeeded, to the great delight of the lesser gods in the gallery, after a slight struggle, in ejecting both the intruders. Though a leading and influential man among his party, most of them seem to have regarded his character as somewhat too extreme. When appointed to preach before the Lord High Commissioner, in 1760, there was a solemn dissent entered on the part of some of his brethren, which still exists in the records of the Church; "and the case," says Morren, "is the only one on record in which the preacher proposed by the committee was objected to in the Assembly." Nearly thirty years afterwards, however, and but a short time before the debate on missions took place, he very nearly carried the principal clerkship in a struggle of unprecedented keenness. He shone as a wit; and succeeded at times in raising the laugh against Evangelism, by his narratives of the opinions entertained on doctrine or church policy by the fisher population of his parish. Some Janet Skatecreel, or Donald Mucklebacket, had come, he had found, to the same conclusion on a debated point with the Witherspoons and Erskines, his opponents; and he rarely failed in exciting the merriment of the brethren with whom he voted, by his ludicrous representations of the evangelic prejudices of Janet or Donald. There were cases, however, in which the laugh was turned very conclusively against himself. He had been all his life long a keen supporter of Toryism. In his exertions to support the policy of Pitt and Dundas, he had, to employ the language of one of his brethren, who spoke both for the Doctor and himself, "risked even the friendship of his flock, and his own usefulness as a pastor among them." He had taken a deep interest in the bill proposed in 1793 for the augmentation of ministers' stipends. It had been set aside, to his signal mortification, by his friends the Tories; and the reverend Doctor, in the ensuing Assembly, proved unable to conceal his disappointment and chagrin. He went the length even of charging the ministry with "ingratitude to their best friends," and in a style fully more lachrymose than pathetic; and the complaint was ludicrously paraphrased, in reply, by the singularly able and accomplished Dr. Bryce Johnstone, in the words of Balaam's ass, "Am I not thine ass, on whom thou hast ridden ever since I was thine until this day?" Dr. Johnstone followed up the allusion in a vein of the happiest ridicule, amid the irrepressible laughter of the house; the hint was caught by the eccentric Kay; and in his caricature, "*faithful service rewarded*," vol. II. p. 118, the reader may see a neatly etched head of Jupiter Tonans attached to a long-bodied, crocodile-looking jackass, bestridden by the late Lord Melville. In his latter days Dr. Carlyle tired, it is said, not only of preaching sermons, but also of hearing them preached. He furnished himself with an assistant; and leaving him to his prayers, as Hume did La Roche, he might himself be seen almost every fine Sunday, during the time of divine service, sauntering along the Musselburgh racecourse. The light of the reverend Doctor seems to have been a beacon light; it shone before men to show them, not the course which they ought to pursue, but the course which they were by all means to avoid.

He spoke just two sentences more during the course of the debate on missions. Principal Hill had made a long speech, which occupies nearly twelve pages of the printed report, in which he at once strenuously labored to defeat the missionary cause, and to deprecate, by a vein of general though singularly inconclusive concession in its favor, the odium which might, he feared, attach to such a course. Dr. Carlyle had no such fears, and no respect, apparently, for the tone of timid conciliation which they inspired. Though complimented by the Principal, who quoted his observations as excellent, and referred to him as his revered father, the old man rose in evident impatience as the younger concluded, and addressed the moderator.

> "Moderator," he said, "a motion was some time ago made 'to dismiss the overtures,' *and I insist the first thing to be done is to consider of this.* We may then judge of the propriety of the recommendation and resolutions proposed by the reverend Principal; *but I desire that we may first proceed to dismiss the overtures.*"

He might have been more tolerant of the concessions of Principal Hill. They were not intended to do either him or his cause any harm. Is the reader acquainted with Voltaire's story of the two Roman Catholic missionaries who quarrelled at Pekin? A Jansenist and Jesuit, both brimful of zeal for Mother Church and the conversion of the Chinese, and both equally hostile, the one to the heresies of Jansenius, and the other to the policy of Loyola, had met in their rounds within the precincts of the Celestial Court. The Jesuit denounced the five propositions, and asserted the doctrines of Habert. The Jansenist also denounced the five propositions, and repeated the sarcasms of Pascal. They became angry and loud, and cuffed and scratched, and tore one another's beards, and the noise of the fray reached the ears of the emperor. "Clap up these French Bonzes in prison," said the great-grandchild of the sun, — "clap them up instantly in prison: could they not have staid and quarrelled in their own country?" — "And how long, sire, shall we keep them there?" asked a mandarin in attendance. "Till they have fully agreed," said the emperor. "Alas, sire!" replied the mandarin, who knew the sort of persons with whom he had to deal, — "alas, sire! in that case you condemn them to prison for life, *for they will never agree.*" Is the reader prepared to find the hinging point of the joke of Voltaire converted into a serious argument against missions by Principal Hill? Such, however, was the case. It had been stated by Dr. Erskine that there were various sects engaged in the societies, in whose welfare, deeming all points of inferior moment lost in the importance of the general cause, he felt so warm an interest. It had been asserted further, on the same principle, in the address of the Edinburgh Society, — a document characterized by the reverend Principal as breathing only "*a spirit of conceit,*" and fitted merely to excite feelings of "*compassion bordering on contempt,*" — that they sought not to "export the shibboleth of a party." The sectarian was to be sunk in the Christian. He had found, withal, in the society's regulations, that "every missionary to be ordained, after being approved of by the society, should be remitted for ordination to the particular religious connection to which he belonged." His reflections on these several points we give in the words of the *report:*

"Alas!" he exclaimed, "is this the whole extent of the liberality so much professed? Is this the sense in which '*the shibboleth of a party*' is disclaimed? What can be more palpably plain than that this remission of the approved missionaries for ordination to the particular sect to which they belong (and we find that all sects are invited to join in the undertaking), is, in fact, sending out '*the shibboleth of a party*' in its strictest sense — is sending out men warm with the deep impression of party, and is enlisting them in hostile bands against each other on the very eve of departure. How soon their polemical controversies may burst forth I know not; but when they do burst forth, *wretched must be the state of the half-converted heathen whose spiritual darkness shall only have given place to light rendered horrible by the shapeless phantoms of gloomy doubt and degrading superstition.* On account of the missionaries themselves, too, when these controversies shall have appeared, the societies at home may too late be led to deplore their hazardous and rash attempts — may too late discover that, *besides sowing misery where they promised happiness, missionaries have gone to fight, not merely by argument, but even* — THOUGHT FULL OF HORROR! — TO FIGHT BY CUTTING ONE ANOTHER'S THROATS IN THE BATTLES OF RELIGION ON A FOREIGN SHORE! If the societies recoil with horror from such an *anticipated*, let them be careful in due time to prevent this *realized*, consequence."

What, compared to this, was the ingenious fiction of Voltaire! The reverend Principal, as second minister of St. Andrew's, was of course a member of the Synod of Fife — one of the two synods from which the overtures under discussion had been sent to the Assembly. Why omit, as it turned out he had done, opposing the transmission of the Fife overture in the synod? Why not crush the snake in the egg? The reasons why, as stated by himself, are sufficiently characteristic. The overture, as originally drawn up, bore a preamble recommendatory of missionary societies. It stated "that a desirable spirit had of late appeared to pervade a numerous body of our fellow-Christians, in various parts of this island, for propagating the religion of Jesus Christ." We again return to the report:

"Such, sir," said the reverend Principal, "was originally the substance of the preamble to this overture, and I declared, on hearing it, what I have already repeated, that should any such preamble have appeared in the overture, *I should have strenuously opposed and divided the synod upon it.* As it pleased the gentleman who proposed it, however, to leave out *this highly objectionable clause*, I saw no reason for refusing my assent to it as it at present stands. The overture seemed to have a pious object in view; *and, if not promising to be useful, seemed at least to promise to be innocent, in its effects.* In its present form the Assembly may take it up or not, just as they think proper. It is clothed in expressions so general and vague, — IT RECOMMENDS AN OBJECT SO TRULY CHRISTIAN and warranted by Scripture prophecy, yet so great and comprehensive in its aspect, involving so many perplexing considerations, and promising such uncertain consequences, — THAT I AM INCLINED TO THINK THE ASSEMBLY are not called on to consider it, but MIGHT SIMPLY DISMISS IT AT ONCE, as wanting a specific object."

Great truths are laid open at times by the merest accidents; and one of these, stuck in, evidently all involuntarily, amid the tortuous syllogisms of the reverend Principal, we find in the passage just quoted. The Fife overture "RECOMMENDED AN OBJECT SO TRULY CHRISTIAN, THAT HE WAS INCLINED TO THINK THE ASSEMBLY MIGHT DISMISS IT AT ONCE." If the one leader originated in this debate a saying which might well be adopted as the watchword of his party, we think the other was no less successful in behalf of his.

But the reverend Principal was not equally open throughout. Too frequently are the deliberations of public bodies degraded by a mean spirit of trick. Wisdom and honesty to decide regarding the fair, the good, the prudent, are what the exigency demands; but some influential leader rises, and substitutes cunning instead. His object is not to secure, but prevent, the adoption of the proper course; and this object he pursues by means which, consorting entirely with the character of what he intends, are just and honorable in but the same degree as those employed by the gamester when he loads his dice. A complete list of the various stratagems resorted to in such cases would be a long one — longer by far than Bacon's catalogue of the "wares of the cunning man." Hints for half a volume could have been picked up at the last General Assembly from the speeches of some four or five Moderate elders alone. Nor, as we have already shown, did the debate on missions lack its quota of trick on the same side. One notable stratagem we have described as virtually deciding the fate of the two overtures, by binding them together. Mr. Hamilton resorted to another, when, in the hope of blackening the character of his opponents, and thus creating a prejudice against both them and their cause, he charged them with dishonestly appropriating to the support of their missionary schemes money collected for the poor. Dr. Hill was more ingenious; not only, he asserted, were missionary societies not good, but even those who most strenuously defended them seemed fully aware of the fact. We again quote:

"My reverend father, Dr. Erskine," he said, "has only touched their surface with delicacy and tenderness; *for his sagacity and discernment must have led him to perceive that they would not bear a more critical inspection.* Nay, he even has gone so far as to say that he approves of all the societies which have been formed, 'more or less,' — *a confession which seems equivalent to his owning that he does not approve entirely of any.*"

The hit was only indifferently successful. Dr. Erskine at once characterized the inference of the Principal as unwarranted. He had not veiled, he said, through feelings of delicacy or tenderness, as had been insinuated, any disapproval of the missionary societies of the country; for he did not disapprove of them, but very much the reverse. If he had spoken obscurely regarding them, it was unwittingly, not from design; and some portion of obscurity, in a speech wholly unstudied, might, he hoped, be excused. In a second stratagem, of a still worse character, Principal Hill was entirely successful.

The war of the first French Revolution was raging at the period of the debate, and the democratic principles caught by the people of Britain, as if by infection, from their volatile neighbors, were now undergoing a course of gradual absorption, overmastered by the intensely national spirit which both the reverses and triumphs of the conflict served to awaken. Still, however, the pest had not been altogether extirpated. "Our neighbor's house was in flames, and it was well," according to Burke, "that the engines should occasionally play on our own." Only two years had elapsed since the trials of Muir, Palmer, and Gerald had taken place; and Braxfield had not yet ceased reiterating his somewhat brutal joke, that our democrats "would a' be muckle the better o' being hanged." Even several years later, the present Lord President of the Court of Session, then Lord Advocate, could officially intimate to the sheriff of Banffshire that a farmer of that county, who had dismissed his servant for neglecting his work in attending a volunteer review, should be "stigmatized and punished by the scorn and contempt of all respectable men;" and instruct, further, "that on the first Frenchman landing in Scotland he [the farmer] should be immediately apprehended as a suspected person;" and that in the event of his property being destroyed by either the enemy or the king's troops, "care should be taken to prevent his receiving any compensation for the loss." The temper of the time was one of fear and suspicion; minds of fully the ordinary strength seemed unhinged by the terror of revolution; and, to excite their rage and hatred against any newly established popular society, it seemed but necessary to hint that there might possibly be something democratic in its character or tendencies. There were not a few of this conspiracy-dreaded class present at the time in the Assembly, mostly gentlemen of the law; and the reverend Principal thus proceeded to enlist their fears full against the missionary cause. The stratagem had at least the merit of being consummately ingenious, and, as we have already said, and shall afterwards show, it was entirely successful.

"Besides the considerations," he said, "which lead us to augur unfavorably of these societies from the circumstances I have enumerated, there is one argument, drawn from a consideration of a much more important nature in itself, *because threatening much more awful and extreme effects than even these, not, indeed, to the heathen or the missionaries, but to this country, to society at large.* The political aspect of the times, marked with the turbulent and seditious attempts of the evil designing or the deluded against our happy constitution, — against the order of everything we possess and hold dear to us, whether as citizens or as men, — renders it incumbent on me to state, that I observe with serious regret not only many of the striking outlines, but even many of the most obnoxious expressions, or expressions similar to those which have been held with affected triumph in the lately suppressed popular assemblies."

The Principal goes on to render the assertion as plausible as possible, by quotations from the regulations and preliminary address of the society over which the venerable Dr. Erskine presided. His art in twisting a meaning seems to have been very considerable indeed.

"In the letter I have so often referred to," continued the Principal, "it is said, 'They [Christians] perceive that their strength has been impaired by division; that the most zealous exertions of particular denominations have only had a partial and temporary effect; and that by union alone one obvious cause of failure may be completely removed. They wish, therefore, to make a grand, unanimous effort; to combine the wisdom, the prayers, the influence, and the wealth of all their brethren in all parts of the nation, and even to produce a general movement of the Church upon earth!' Again, 'While we rejoice in these associations as proofs that the desire to propagate the gospel is at present very generally excited, we beg leave strongly to recommend united exertions; and we submit to all such societies in Scotland, whether it will not be better to coöperate than to act alone. Let us join all our resources, and proceed with vigor. From harmonious beginnings at home we may perhaps be enabled to go on to an enlarged concurrence with similar societies

at a distance, and in our day to revive something of the liberal spirit of primitive times, when the multitude of them that believed were of one heart and of one soul.' And yet again, 'The society shall be willing to correspond with all societies and individuals who may have the same grand object in view, and shall either act by themselves or coöperate with others, as circumstances shall determine.'"

When ever before were there more terrible proofs of conspiracy adduced! and was not Principal Hill quite justified in alleging that these quotations were "*fully sufficient, without any addition or much comment, to warrant*" him "*in calling those societies highly dangerous, in their tendency, to the good order of society at large?*" True, it seemed a rather unlucky circumstance for his case, that men such as Dr. Erskine were their leading members. But then, with "new members," he said, "new views would be introduced; nor was it unreasonable to dread that their common fund should be perverted from its original channel, and be made the means, along with the other obnoxious circumstances mentioned, *of stirring up temporal strife, instead of promoting spiritual peace.*"

PART FIFTH.

We are told by Plutarch, of the Romans who besieged Syracuse, that after they had seen a few dozen of their galleys pitched into the air from the ends of huge beams, and a few hundreds of their legionaries crushed into the earth by immense rocks, they became so sadly afraid of the master magician who defended the city, that if they only spied a small cord or piece of wood above the walls, they straightway took to their heels, crying out that "Archimedes was going to let fly some terrible engine at them." A somewhat similar terror seems to have possessed the more strenuous supporters of the Pitt and Dundas policy *in our own* country, for a few years before and after the period of the debate on missions; and it was to this feeling of fear and suspicion, as we have said, that Principal Hill deemed it wisdom to appeal. At the distance of nearly half a century, when men's minds have cooled down, it strikes one with astonishment to see how very minute the cord sometimes was, and how very slender the beam, that filled men of at least ordinary good sense with dread and suspicion. Scarce an institution could be established, on however limited a scale, whether economic, educational, or religious, that some one or other did not decry as a revolutionary engine. Some became mortally afraid of benefit societies, some of prayer-meetings, some of Sunday schools. Masonic fraternities were deemed hotbeds of sedition everywhere: even parish schools came to be suspected. A country magistrate of the period, naturally a benevolent man, but rabid in his dread of revolution, was presiding on one occasion, in one of our northern towns, on a trial of some score of ragged urchins, who, in sacking a piece of planting of its rowans, had broken a few of the young trees. He had gone through the case with great good humor; there was nothing revolutionary in it. In proposing, however, that the parents of the culprits should become bound for their behavior in the future, he was seconded by a brother magistrate of the town, who remarked, half in joke, that they had better also bind the young fellows themselves, so far as a promise could bind them; and who, aware of their literary qualifications, actually wrote out for them a declaration of non-aggression for the time coming, which he asked them to sign. Glad of the opportunity of showing they could write, they came forward one by one, and adhibited their names, each succeeding boy in a style more clerkly than the boy that had gone before. The country magistrate stood aghast, for he saw conspiracy and sedition in the accomplishment. "What! what! what!" he exclaimed, his temper giving way for the first time during the course of the trial, "all these ragamuffins *able to write*! This must be put an instant stop to! In a few years hence we shall see them all hung for high treason."

One of the most extreme cases illustrative of the spirit of the time was perhaps that of the late Rev. Mr. Lapslie, of Campsie,—a gentleman who first introduced himself to terms of familiar intimacy with the unfortunate and not over-prudent Muir, of Huntshill, by the professed liberality of his political principles, and who, animated by his detestation of democracy and his hope of a pension, volunteered afterwards his evidence against him, but whose testimony, from the utterly infamous nature of his conduct, could not be received. The history of this man would exhibit Moderatism in its worst and most extreme phase. It may be deemed unfair, indeed, to select the atrocities of one individual as the characteristics of a party. If, however, that individual was *followed* by his party; if, in cases of acquittal for scandalous crimes, in which no merely secular court of the period would or could have concurred, they suffered him to act as their leader; if his worst peculiarities were but exaggerations of their own; if, instead of branding his conduct and casting him out of their society, they were content to regard him as a useful and active partisan; if, in short, they homologated his actings by making them to no very limited extent their own,—they must be content that he should be regarded as at least an extreme specimen of their class. For several years after entering on his charge, Mr. Lapslie bore the common Moderate character. He was known to be no bigot. He appeared occasionally in the boxes of the Glasgow theatre, and had, it was said, a happy knack of rendering himself agreeable at the tables of men in the upper ranks. On the determination of government to crush the revolutionary spirit among the people by a series of state prosecutions, the incumbent of Campsie sprung up at once into notoriety, and volunteered, as we have said, his testimony against Muir. He had been over-zealous, however, for the full accomplishment of what he had purposed. He had attended the sheriffs in their rounds, collecting evidence. He had even hinted to some of the witnesses, by way of refreshing their memories, that "berths might be provided for them under government." When the trial came on, his testimony was objected to, on the score that he was a party deeply interested in the case; and, to his surprise and signal mortification, the objection was sustained by the public prosecutor. Muir, in addressing the jury empanelled to try him, solemnly pledged himself that, if acquitted, he, in turn, would become Mr. Lapslie's prosecutor, and prove against him, by a cloud of witnesses, practices — nay, crimes — which he at that stage forbore to characterize. Though thus rejected as a witness, however, the minister was not altogether disappointed. His services, though not very honorable, had been at least very zealously tendered: they had attracted the notice of Pitt; and a pension was granted him almost immediately after the trial, which, considerably more than thirty years subsequent, his widow continued to enjoy. On the introduction of the militia act, so unpopular in Scotland, Mr. Lapslie exerted himself to give it effect in his own parish of Campsie with such hearty good-will, that some of his parishioners, to show their gratitude and respect, set fire to his outhouses in the night-time, and burnt them to the ground. He distinguished himself above all his fellows by his active hostility to Sunday schools and home and foreign missions, "believing them, in common with many other members of the Church," says a writer of the present day, who has sketched an outline of his biography, "to be deeply tainted with democracy." The accusers of our Saviour charged him with rebellion against Cæsar; we question whether there were any of them more in earnest than Mr. Lapslie. The latest notice of this singular divine which we have yet seen is to be found in "Peter's Letters to his Kinsfolk." We there find him drawn as a gray-headed old man, addressing the General Assembly in strains the most impassioned: "tearing his waistcoat open, baring his breast as if he had scars to show; bellowing, sobbing, weeping;" and finally sitting down, "trembling all to his finger-ends, like an exhausted Pythoness." What was it that had moved the old man, and why did he rave, and weep, and shake his gray locks? He had been engaged, soul, body, and spirit, in the defence of a Moderate clergyman accused of "illicit intercourse with his housekeeper," and who fared none the worse in consequence of having his case tried at a period when it was impossible, in the General Assembly, to convict Moderate ministers of crime.

We have been indulging in an episode; but it is one which serves to illustrate the temper of the time, and enables us to add to our series of sketches an additional portrait. Moderatism has often pointed to its men of science and literature — its poets, philosophers, and historians; the memory of such long outlives that of their humbler contemporaries. But it is well to remember that it was not of literature and science that the staple of the party was composed. It is well to enter into an examination of its coarser ingredients; to know somewhat not only of the gifted leaders who contended against the cause of missions and Sunday schools, but also of the humbler men-at-arms who fought under them with a zeal and heartiness in no respect inferior to their own. The deep cloud of moral and spiritual death which for a century brooded over our country, withering every blossom of hope and promise, had its upper sunlit folds of purple and gold, to catch and charm the eye of the distant spectator; but to know it in its true character, it was necessary to descend to where its lower volumes brooded over the blighted surface, and there to acquaint one's self with its sulphureous stench, its mildew-dispensing damps, its chills, and its darkness.

Some such introduction, too, is necessary to enable the reader either to enter fully into the character of Principal Hill's stratagem, or rightly to appreciate the spirit of the very singular political speech which it elicited. The speaker was a young advocate named David Boyle, ruling elder for the burgh of Irvine. We are inclined to hold that he could have been animated by no real zeal against missions; that it was his head, not his heart, which was at fault. A bit of cord hung over the wall; a piece of wood had appeared; the wily Principal had called out, "A revolutionary engine! a revolutionary engine!" There were certainly many playing off at the time; and the zealous advocate, infected by the general terror, had taken the representation too readily on trust. We insert his speech entire:

"I rise, Moderator, impressed with a sense of the *alarming and dangerous tendency of the measures proposed in the overtures on your table, — overtures which I cannot too strongly, which the House cannot too strongly, oppose, and which, I trust, all the loyal and well-affected members will be unanimous in opposing.* If, however, I should stand single with the two reverend Doctors and the gentleman who made the motion, I should this night go down to divide the House. Sir, numerous societies of people are at all times alarming; but at this time particularly so, whatever be the professions on which they are formed, or the pretexts they hold out to the world. The general professed object of the present societies is, indeed, good, and at a proper season would merit our countenance; *but there is nothing besides this general object at all good about them; all the other circumstances respecting them are bad; for I am free to assert — and I will maintain it in the face of any member of this Assembly — that all the societies which have of late years existed in this country have been more or less connected with politics.* Yes, sir, I do say that the associations of the people formed in various parts of the kingdom to petition for the abolition of the slave-trade, however good their design, and whether or not immediately arising from politics, did, at any rate, lay the foundation of the political societies which have since disturbed the peace and tranquillity of the country, and have cost so much trouble and difficulty to be suppressed. Still, however, the people meet under the pretext of spreading Christianity among the heathen. Observe, sir, they are *affiliated*, they have a *common object*, they *correspond with each other*, they *look for assistance from foreign countries*, in the very language of many of the seditious societies. Above all, it is to be marked, they have a *common fund*. Where is the security that the money of this fund will not, as the reverend Principal said, be used for very different purposes from the professed ones? *If any man says that the societies have not this connection and tendency, he says the thing that is not.* It now, therefore, becomes us as much as possible to discourage numerous societies, for whatever purposes; *for, be the object what it may, they are all equally bad.* And as for those missionary societies, I do aver, that since it is to be apprehended that their funds may be in time, *nay, certainly will be, turned against the constitution,* so it is the bounden duty of this House to give the overtures recommending them *our most serious disapprobation, and our immediate, most decisive opposition.*"

Very extraordinary, surely, regarded as the production of a man still living! It has so much of the true rust of antiquity about it, that to associate it with the present age by a link so unequivocal as the continued working-day world existence of the speaker, does violence in no small degree to the imagination. But it must have originated, as we have said, wholly in misconception and mistake, and should be regarded rather as an effect of the disreputable stratagem of Principal Hill, operating on a mind blinded by its fears and open to suspicion on only one side, than as the result of spontaneous conviction. We are pretty sure that the speaker, rendered wiser by the additional experience of forty-five years, would now be the very first to repudiate the sentiments which it expresses. He would deal by them as Knox and Luther dealt by the idolatrous tenets which in the days of their extreme youth they had deemed it their duty to hold. A remark, however, which seems naturally to grow out of the subject may not be deemed either irreverent or ill-timed; and we shall introduce it by an anecdote.

It is recorded of the celebrated Lord Monboddo, that, when the great Douglas case was brought for judgment before the Court of Session, he descended from the bench, and, taking his place beside the clerk, there delivered his opinion. What could have moved him? for he assigned no reason for the step. He simply rose from beside his brethren, and came down. Men of correct moral sentiment had but to consult their feelings in order to discover his lordship's motives. It was remembered that, previous to his elevation, he had been counsel in the case for one of the parties. It was known that, in common with all engaged in it, he had felt an intense interest in the issue, of which he could not divest himself, now that he was counsel no longer. And so it was at once inferred that, feeling himself rather a party than a judge, he had descended from the judge's seat, determined that, since he had now, in virtue of his office, to record judgment in the case, he should do so on the counsel's level, and, as it were, under protest of his own conscience. Believing his decision to be entirely just, he was yet sensible of an undercurrent of prejudice powerful enough to warp his better judgment. He took this mode of showing that he *was* sensible of it; and though it might, doubtless, have been better for him to have declined giving an opinion in the case at all, it must be confessed that, since he *did* give it, it was well it should have been under circumstances so marked.

Lord Monboddo carried his prejudices with him from the bar to the bench; and he felt that he did. Are the majority of our Lords of Session in the present day men of stronger minds than Monboddo, or possessed of a more complete control over their predilections and their antipathies? If the question cannot be answered otherwise than in the negative, is it possible to forget that in the present struggle not a few of our Lords of Session are as certainly parties in one character as they are judges in another? We do not refer to the controversy in its more obvious aspect—as a collision between two courts. In that aspect the Lords of Session may indeed be described as parties, and their decisions as decisions in favor of their own court. But we refer to it in a more emphatic sense — as a controversy between two great principles, Moderatism and Evangelism, and to the well-known fact, that the greater part of the men who now, in the character of judges, record their decisions against the latter principle, have zealously contended against it as partisans in the character of ruling elders. They have passed hot from their debates in the General Assembly to their seats in the Court of Session, and their findings in one character agree entirely with their votes in another. We are far from impugning their motives in either capacity. We doubt not they have been thoroughly conscientious; as much so when contending on unequal terms with Andrew Thomson, and made to feel that he was not only an abler man, but also a better lawyer, than most of themselves, as when pronouncing judgment in the Auchterarder case; as much so when opposing themselves to the overtures on missions, as when granting interdicts against preaching the gospel and administering the sacraments at the instance of the clergymen of Strathbogie. We doubt not they have decided conscientiously. We doubt not that Monboddo decided conscientiously in the Douglas case; but Monboddo could himself fear, that, though he judged honestly, there were yet disturbing circumstances that might lead him to judge erroneously: and we are convinced the public would think none the worse of the majority of the Lords of Session were they to manifest in some slight degree a corresponding fear.

The remarks of Mr. Boyle called up Dr. Erskine, unwilling as he was, he said, again to encroach on the time of the Assembly. He could not understand why all associations of the people, however diverse the purposes for which they had been established, should be treated thus with equal severity; or on what principle *proper* should be confounded with *improper* objects, from their merely possessing the common circumstance of being pursued, with a view to their accomplishment, by bodies, not individuals. What was there in the mere circumstance of union, of force enough to convert good into evil? He had yet to learn that societies formed in the cause of humanity tended to render the minds of men turbulent and seditious; or that the quiet of the state could be in any degree endangered by deliberations on the best possible means of Christianizing the heathen, or by discussions regarding the more promising fields of missionary exertion. Good government had nothing to dread from religion; irreligion, on the other hand, was the worst foe it had to combat. He proceeded to say, in language which we have already quoted, that he acknowledged, and gloried in acknowledging, himself a member of the Slave Abolition Society; that in no degree, however, on that account, was he the less attached to the constitution under which he lived. He believed he had given at least as many proofs of his regard for the peace of the land as the gentlemen opposite; and he was prepared, he trusted, in his humble sphere, to make as many and as great sacrifices to preserve it inviolate. He had no wish, he said, to see the people becoming disputatious politicians; for he had seen their loose political speculations serving but to waste and dissipate their minds, and thus doing them harm without producing any counterbalance of good. Nor was he at all partial to the late democratic societies; some of them served only to show him how a few cunning men may lead multitudes astray. The pretended analogy, however, between these lately suppressed political associations and the lately established missionary societies was by much too far strained to be just. The one class had followed the other in the order of time; but was there the slightest attempt to show that in this succession there was aught akin to the relation of cause and effect? Exactly the reverse was the case; and, to convince themselves thoroughly that it was so, they had but to examine into the nature of the ingredients of which the associations and societies were respectively composed. He was very sure, for his own part, that he saw none of their violent political reformers stepping forward to take part in the missionary cause. He was equally sure that those who exerted themselves in it most were men remarkable for their simplicity and purity of life, and from whom no good government could have any cause of alarm. Dr. Erskine sat down, and did not again mingle in the debate. The event determined that he should take no peculiar interest in missions as a minister of the Church of Scotland; but not the less on that account did he labor in their behalf as a minister of the Church of Christ; and his last work on earth, as we have already intimated, was the preparation of a pamphlet — one of a series — suited to draw the attention of the country to the good which they were the means of producing abroad. His remark with regard to the fact that he saw none of the more violent political reformers taking part in the missionary cause is a shrewd one. We have heard Chartist sermons in our time, and have described the divinity of the class as a sort of Moderatism possessed, — as composed of the commonplaces of a tame and inefficient morality, that never made any one more moral, shaken into uncouth activity by the eccentric energies of the revolutionary spirit. One of their preachers we heard descant on missions. What particular view did he take of them? or what is the opinion formed regarding them by the lay theologians of Chartism? Exactly the Moderate view, as recorded in the debate of 1796. The preacher denounced them as singularly absurd; nay, more, he deemed it little better than a crime to waste the resources of the country in benefiting foreigners, when there was so much to be done in our own country. "Charity, child, charity!" said Mrs. Tabitha Bramble, in entering her protest against the benevolent donation of her brother, honest Matthew, — "Charity begins at home; these twenty pounds would have bought me a complete set of silks, head-dress, pinners, and ——." — "Missions!" said the Chartist orator, — "missions! — why, half the money expended on missions would win us the charter."

The debate hastened to its conclusion. The Rev. Messrs. Johnstone, of Crossmichael, and Shepherd, of

Muirkirk, together with a Mr. Dickson, ruling elder for the Presbytery of Biggar, spoke in favor of the overtures. Dr. William Taylor, of Glasgow, and the Rev. Robert Knox, of Larbert, were strenuous against them. Dr. Taylor urged the old argument: there was a great deal still to be *done* at home, — all the more, he said, in consequence of the much that had lately been *undone* by the writings of Paine. He urged, therefore, that they should determinedly oppose themselves to the *Age of Reason* and the overtures, and offer up prayers for the spread of the gospel. Knox, a gentleman who had been settled in his parish by the military, was content to denounce the indelicacy shown by members friendly to the missionary cause, in taking it somehow for granted that there was more of conscience in supporting than in opposing it. The Assembly divided; and, in a house of one hundred and two members, the overtures were dismissed by a majority of fourteen.

The deposition of the Strathbogie clergymen was carried, in a house of three hundred and forty-seven, by a majority of ninety-seven. At least twice the number that voted in the Assembly of 1796, on both sides, attended the last extraordinary meeting of Commission, to record their resolutions on one side. The fact is no unimportant one. It shows that the languor and indifferency of the middle period of the Church's history is gone; that not only the policy, but also the strength and energy, of her earlier time has been revived. Nor has the deepening interest been restricted to members of Assembly, or even to the Church's office-bearers. The heart of the people has been stirred. Dr. M'Crie asked, some eight or ten years ago, in reference to the widely-spread apathy which prevailed even then among the people regarding the counsels of the Church, "Where were the fervent supplications for the countenance and direction of Heaven in the deliberations of the Assembly, which were wont to resound of old from the most distant glens and mountains of Scotland?" We can now reply to the query in other terms than the Doctor did then. Many a prayer-meeting was held in the thousand parishes of Scotland on the night of the Great Meeting in Edinburgh, and there ascended many a fervent petition from the truly excellent of the country in behalf of their endangered Church. In one northern semi-Highland parish, that reclines to the south under the evening shadow of the huge Ben-wevis, three several meetings of the "men" of the district,—hoary-headed patriarchs, on the extreme edge of life,—attended by numbers of the young, the fruit of a recent revival, were held on that night, and the time of prayer was prolonged from the fall of evening to the break of day. Our opponents may think very meanly of zeal of this character assuming thus the form of earnest prayer; but they must be profoundly ignorant if they think meanly of it as an element of strength and determination.

The overtures on missions were negatived mainly on the argument—we employ the words of the Rev. Mr. Hamilton—that it was "improper and absurd to propagate the gospel abroad while there remained a single individual at home without the means of religious knowledge." Only two years after, in direct violation of the Barrier Act, an overture originating with the Moderate party, which incapacitated presbyteries from sanctioning the erection of chapels of ease, passed into a law. Moderatism could command majorities in the Assembly, but not in all the presbyteries of the Church; and to the Assembly, therefore, by this act, was reserved the exclusive right of erecting chapels. What was the object of the measure? "To prevent," says a Church historian of the present day [Dr. Hetherington], "the erection of chapels of ease in any dangerous place where Evangelism was already strong," and to discourage the system of Church extension generally. The party would not give the gospel to the heathen because there was much to do at home; and they then discovered that they could not give it to the people at home because it interfered with their policy. But the Moderatism of the present day has nothing in common, say men such as the Rev. Mr. Robertson, of Ellon, with the Moderatism of forty years ago. Men of such respectable calibre might show just a little more sense by selecting positions just a little more tenable. The point is capable of demonstration, in even an arithmetical form. The statistics of missionary exertion in connection with the schemes of the Church establish the disputed identity of the party, and the fixed character of its tenets. What principle is it that, when it dare no longer oppose itself to foreign missions, contents itself with doing nothing in their behalf? The same Moderatism which so powerfully exerted itself against missions in the past. What principle was operative in the atrocity of Marnoch? The same Moderatism whose forced settlements in the last century desolated our national Establishment, and robbed her of one-third of her people. What principle in the present day do we find loudest in denouncing the erection of our *quoad sacra* parishes? That same Moderatism which set itself so insidiously at an earlier period to prevent the erection of chapels of ease. What principle demanded of the State, on a late occasion, in terms which could not be misunderstood, the ejection from the Church of all among its ministers who took part with the people? The same Moderatism which so ruthlessly secured in the past the ejection of Gillespie and the Erskines. But we feel ourselves engaged in an idle task. The point in reality is not a disputed one.

THE

RIGHTS OF THE CHRISTIAN PEOPLE.

THE TWO PARTIES IN THE CHURCH OF SCOTLAND.

THE following formed the leading article in the first number of "The Witness," which was published on the 15th of January, 1840. The succeeding papers are compiled from subsequent numbers of that journal. — ED.

We enter upon our labors at a period emphatically momentous, — at the commencement, it is probable, of one of those important eras, never forgotten by a country, which influence for ages the condition and character of the people, and from which the events of their future history take color and form. We enter, too, at a time when, with few exceptions, our Scottish contemporaries in the same field — unable, it would seem, to lead, and unwilling to follow — neither guide the opinions of the great bulk of their countrymen, nor echo their sentiments. Strange as it may seem, it is a certain fact, which in the nature of things must be every day becoming more and more obvious, that on one of the most important questions ever agitated in Scotland the people and the newspaper press have taken opposite sides.

A few simple remarks on the point at issue may show, more conclusively than any direct avowal, the part which we ourselves deem it our duty to take. There are parties which continue to bear their first names long after they have abandoned their original principles; and the historian, in tracing their progress, has to regulate his definitions by his dates. There are parties, on the contrary, which remain unchanged for ages. The followers of Wesley are in every respect in the present day what they were when their extraordinary leader first organized their society. There is, on the other hand, a section of our Scotch Seceders who see nothing to fear from the counsels or the increase of Popery, and who can compliment the Gowdies and Simpsons of the time on the policy which drove Fisher and the Erskines out of the Church. But the remark is exemplified at least equally well by two antagonist bodies which for the last century and a half have composed the same corporation. The differences of the contending parties within the Church of Scotland arise solely from the circumstance that the one retains its original principles, and the other has given them up; nor is it at all improbable that it shall be decided by the issue of the present conflict whether the Church shall continue to unite its old character to its old name, or whether for the future it shall retain the name only.

The evidence which establishes the thorough identity of the popular party with the original Church will be found to lie very much on the surface. The hereditary sympathies and dislikes of the Scotch people are strikingly corroborative of the facts furnished by history. Dr. Cook is well-nigh as decided on the point as Dr. M'Crie. The Churchmen of Glasgow who lately commemorated the triumph of Presbyterianism in the days of Henderson, are at one with the Dean of Faculty. The satires of Burns, and the David Deans of the novelist, add weight to the testimony of the first Seceders. Now, it is obvious that the unchanged must possess a mighty advantage over the transmuted party, — the advantage of a well-defined and long-sustained character. They have been thoroughly known to the people of Scotland for the last three centuries. The Chalmerses and Gordons of the nineteenth century agree in their theology and their views of Church government with the Witherspoons and Dr. Erskines of the eighteenth; these again with the Hendersons and Rutherfords of the seventeenth; and these with the Knoxes and Melvilles of the sixteenth. But we find no such consistency in their opponents. Their sentiments have ever agreed with those of the age; nor have they differed more in many respects from the first fathers of our Church than from their immediate predecessors on the unpopular side. Dr. Bryce is not at one in his religious beliefs with Dr. M'Gill, of Ayr, however closely he may resemble him in his views of Church polity; nor does Mr. Pirie approximate, in more than his dread of such irregularities as the revival at Kilsyth, and his abhorrence of the popular voice, to the eulogist of Gibbon and Hume. The minority who oppose the veto in 1840 differ from the majority who first declared in 1784 that they no longer regarded patronage as a grievance; for, while the one, in accordance with the skepticism of the age, would fain have abrogated the Confession of Faith itself, the other restrict their hostility to our books of discipline only; nor, in passing upwards, can we entirely identify the antagonists of Gillespie and the Erskines with the Churchmen who in a former age could so easily accommodate their conscience to the demands of Charles at the Restoration. Some few general features the party have all along retained. They have ever been favorably regarded by the men who derive their religion from the statute-book, and have ever secured to themselves the jealous dislike of our Christian people. Nor will it appear a mere coincidence, when we consider how naturally the same opinions and sentiments propagate themselves for ages in the same locality, that, with but one solitary exception, the predecessors of the seven suspended ministers, who have so promptly accommodated themselves to the encroachments of the Court of Session, should have yielded an obedience equally prompt to the unhappy act which overturned Presbyterianism in Scotland, and led to the longest and bloodiest persecution ever endured by the Scottish Church. It is, however, of the popular party alone that the experience of the country has been continuous and uniform, and respecting which the testimony of any one age may serve for that of all the others. In seasons of tranquillity it has ever constituted that portion of the Reformed Church in Scotland which has given to the character of the people the stamp and impress of a pure Christianity; in the day of trouble and persecution it has constituted the whole of it. There is a marked difference between the fixed essential stamina of the human frame and those flying humors which add mightily to its bulk at one period, and enter into the composition of no part of it at another.

Here, then, on a distinction as obvious as it is important, we take our stand. The cause of the unchanged party in the Church is that of the Church itself; it is that of the people of Scotland, and the people know it; it was the cause of their fathers, and the fathers of the Reformation; it is the cause of a pure, efficient, unmodified Christianity. And the cause opposed to it is exactly the reverse of all this. We appeal to the people, to history, to the New Testament. We appeal to even our opponents. We urge them to say whether, in the expressive language of Dr. M'Crie, the cry which now echoes throughout the country be not the identical "cry which has not ceased to be heard in Scotland for nearly three hundred years"? We request of them sincerely to consider their present position, as illustrated and determined by the history of the Church. Among what party (in the pages of Calderwood and Wodrow, for instance) do they recognize their types and representatives, and in what place and attitude do they find the types and representatives of the body to which they are opposed? History is more than usually clear and definite on the point: it is one of those as to which the testimony of the present age regarding the past anticipates that of the future regarding the present. It would be no overbold matter to class the John Frosts of our own times with the Jack Cades of the time of Henry VI., or to compare the part taken by the Mayor of Newport in the late riots to that taken by the Mayor of London in the disturbance of Wat Tyler. There are general similarities of conduct and circumstances which occur to every one, and which constitute the simpler parallelisms of history. But there are also cases that are more than parallel, and circumstances that are more than similar. It was identically the same, not a similar Christianity, which was denounced by the Sanhedrim, and which suffered in the ten persecutions. It was identically the same Protestantism for which John Huss endured martyrdom on the continent, and George Wishart in our own country. It was identically the same Presbyterianism for which Melville died in exile, and Guthrie on the scaffold. Is there no such well-marked identity of principle between the Churchmen on whom the fires of Middleton and Lauderdale fell heaviest, and the Churchmen exposed in the present conflict to the still more merciless exactions of the Court of Session? And would not such of our bitter opponents as profess a high respect for the fathers of our Church do well to remember, that what has already occurred may possibly occur again, and that there once flourished a very respectable party, who, when busied in persecuting the prophets of their own times, were engaged also in building tombs to the memory of the prophets slain by their fathers?

THE TWIN PRESBYTERIES OF STRATHBOGIE.

Some of our readers will be perhaps surprised to learn that there are now two presbyteries in Strathbogie,—the one recognized by the Church of Scotland as one of her duly constituted inferior courts; the other consisting of seven suspended ministers, recognized by no Church whatever. It was at one time supposed that secessions from the Scottish Church and the reign of Moderation would have come to an end together. But there is no mind sagacious enough to calculate on all the possibilities. The schism, too, seems to be spreading, and the members of this newly-erected presbytery are actively engaged in adding to their number one Mr. Edwards, an accomplished gentleman, who understands syntax, preaches a church empty, rivals Horsley in Biblical criticism, and is not less a Christian than any of the seven ministers themselves. Addison tells of a worthy author who wrote a large book to prove that generals without armies cannot achieve great victories. It is to be hoped that, for the good of learning, the argument still survives, and that it may possibly apply to clergymen, *quoad civilia*, when suspended by the Church and deserted by the people.

The presbytery met at Keith on Wednesday last. All the members attended, — the seven suspended ministers and all, — and the meeting was constituted by prayer. The seven insisted that their names should be entered in the sederunt by the clerk, as members of court. Their proposal was, of course, negatived, on the obvious plea, that so long as the act of suspension remains in force, they can have no status in the presbytery, or any Church court whatever. Mr. Mearns, the clerk, however, a son of Dr. Mearns of Aberdeen, and a person of similar views with themselves, engrossed their names in defiance of the legitimately constituted members. He was, in consequence, suspended, and the Rev. Mr. Bell, one of the preachers appointed by the Commission, chosen in his place. But the suspended clerk, like the suspended clergymen, held himself none the less in office for the suspension, and refused to deliver up the records. A scene of confusion ensued. Mr. Bell, the newly-chosen clerk of the presbytery, commenced reading a minute of their proceedings; Mr. Mearns, at the suggestion of Mr. Allardyce, began reading at the same time, and at the pitch of his voice, the minute of the previous meeting, rescinded by sentence of the Commission. The legitimate members carried, that whatever might be attempted by the pretended clerk should be held null and void. It was urged on the other side by Mr. Allardyce, one of the disqualified seven, that, in terms of the rescinded minute, the presbytery should proceed to take Mr. Edwards, the rejected of Marnoch, on his trials. The moderator, Mr. Dewar, of course refused either to recognize the mover as a member of court, or the minute as a document on which to found. It was modestly proposed by Mr. Allardyce, in turn, that Mr. Dewar should be forthwith removed for contumacy from the moderator's chair; and, five of the remaining six acquiescing in the proposal, it was pronounced that the moderator was removed, and that Mr. Cruickshank, of Glass, was appointed moderator in his place. Mr. Allardyce next suggested that, to avoid further interruption, the *presbytery* should retire into another room, and proceed to business. And accordingly the seven *suspended* ministers, with their *disqualified* clerk, left the place of meeting for an adjoining apartment, to take the *rejected* presentee on his trials, in terms of the *rescinded* minute. The *bona fide* presbytery remained to transact the real business which had brought them together. They were waited upon in the course of the meeting by a deputation from Huntly, with a largely signed petition from the inhabitants, respecting the building and constitution of a new church. The petition was read in the usual form, and ordered to be laid on the table until next meeting.

Suspended, disqualified, rejected, rescinded,—all these are English words, and bear very definite meanings. The *Presbytery of the Seven*—a phrase, by the by, that sounds very like the *Council of the Ten*—proceeded to business like their brethren; and they began, not by framing a confession of faith, or by drawing up a testimony, but by taking Mr. Edwards on his trials. They were not compelled to do it, one of them remarked; they were not forced into it by hornings and captions; and it had been said in high quarters that they might not be quite so precipitate. But the doctrine was a scandalous doctrine; they would listen to no delay. It was their duty to take Mr. Edwards on his trials, and they were resolved to do their duty. Mr. Edwards accordingly proceeded to deliver the exercises prescribed to him. One of these was a discourse on the text in Peter, "By which also he went and preached unto the spirits in prison." His views on the passage are not stated, and we have no means of knowing whether he remarked that there are discourses not unfrequently preached by the *spirits in prison* themselves. The other exercise was a piece of Latinity, termed an exegesis.

The meeting, at an early stage, was interrupted by the Rev. Mr. Robertson, of Gartly. He had been sent, he stated, as a deputation from the presbytery, in consequence of a report which had reached them that seven individuals, *calling themselves the Presbytery of Strathbogie*, were proceeding with the trials of Mr. Edwards, and he now wished to know whether the report was true. "*We* are the presbytery," said one, "and sent no such deputation." — "No reply should be given," exclaimed half a dozen others. "If we be interrupted in this way," remarked a member, bolder than the rest, "I shall move that the person interrupting us be taken into custody." Mr. Robertson left the room, and the seven proceeded to pass judgment on the exercises of Mr. Edwards. It is wonderful how genius may lie hid; but it breaks forth at last. Mr. Cruickshank, of Glass, has discovered that this hitherto neglected man is elegant in his Latin and profound in his English, and that he beats Bishop Horsley all to sticks in Biblical criticism; Mr. Cruickshank, of Mortlach, is equally decided; Mr. Masson was astonished at the research displayed in the one discourse, and the first-rate character of the other; Mr. Thomson was struck with the rich scriptural illustration; Mr. Cowie saw the difficulty and the triumph, — the defeat of Horsley, and the manly integrity of the Latin; Mr. Walker saw it too; and Mr. Allardyce, though he had not caught the whole of the more classical discourse, — not, of course, from any deafness, like that of the monk, in his *Latin* ear, — was quite of the general opinion. "It is sweet," says the old poet, "to be praised by those whom all men agree in praising." The seven suspended ministers are rich in classical literature, and deeply read in Horsley. The Bishop, however, has written one sentence, not heretical, which perhaps Mr. Edwards has not yet surpassed: it refers to religion, and we press it on their notice. "There is an incurable ignorance," says the divine, "which is ignorant even of its own want of knowledge." There is a sentence, too, in the classics which we think they would also do well to remember. "When the gods devote men to destruction, they first take away their senses."

And it is thus that these weak and misguided men are setting themselves up in senseless but bitter and dangerous hostility to the best interests of the Church of Scotland, and acquiring for themselves a prominent, but surely no enviable, place in her history. It would be a vain matter to argue the point with them; it is not argument they need. It would be equally idle, but for an opposite cause, to reason the matter with the Christian people of Scotland. But the case is a striking one: it shows how much, and in what degree, the *spiritual* character may be derived from a secular court; and how much and in what degree secular acquirements qualify for a spiritual office. It is not enough that a few obscure country clergymen find no flaw in a man's literature; it is not enough that they do not discover, or perhaps seek to discover, any very gross blemish in his reputation. There is an all-important change, regarding which our Saviour hath declared, with the solemnity of an oath, that the man on whom it hath not passed "shall in no way enter the kingdom of heaven;" and without this *great* qualification no other can be of any avail. Much has been written on the force of sympathy, — much, doubtless, that is fanciful and idle. But there is a sympathy to which our Lord refers that is not fanciful, — the sympathy through which "the sheep know the voice of the good shepherd, and follow him." This sympathy the people of Marnoch have felt and can appreciate; but they have not felt it with regard to the rejected presentee.

THE TWO STUDENTS.

There is a learned lawyer of the present day remarkable for his long speeches, — for an ability of writing with much ease what cannot be read without great difficulty, — and for the secularity of his views in ecclesiastical matters. This learned gentleman has written a book on the Church question, in which he discusses, among other points, the essential qualifications of a young licentiate. And so complete has he rendered the list, as to omit only a single point of fitness, — that one, however, the essential point emphatically described by our Saviour as "the one thing needful." He describes the difficulty with which the theological student has often to contend, the long term of privation, the immense labor, the many years of study, the great sacrifices in early life. He states that a parochial charge is the sole object for which all that he accomplishes is accomplished, or that he endures is endured. He states, too, that the remuneration is not proportionally great, — that the scanty income attached to parochial charges leaves, after all, only a life of struggle, care, and anxiety to the incumbent. He shows, besides, how inexpressibly hard it would be — how very unfeeling and very cruel — to suffer the effects of popular prejudice to disappoint the poor scholar of his scanty and inadequate meed, after his long years of endurance and exertion.

About fourteen years ago we formed a very slight

acquaintance with a student of divinity, who came from a remote part of the country to teach a school in a village on the eastern coast of Scotland. He was a young man of very respectable ability, and very considerable acquirement. He was a person, too, of more than common determination, and in setting himself to school, and in passing through college, he had to contend with all the difficulties incident to a humble station and very limited means. He was naturally of a metaphysical turn, and had carried away, when attending the moral philosophy class at college, the second prize of the year. Little more can be added, however, on the favorable side. There was a substratum of strong animal propensity in the character; some of the higher sentiments were miserably deficient; his metaphysical cast of mind had merely enabled him to master the subtleties of Hume, without enabling him to discover their unsolidity; and he had no practical acquaintance with religion. He had determined on being a clergyman from motives of exactly the same kind which lead students in the other walks to make choice of physic or of law. Things are always judged of by comparison, and the meed which may seem scanty and inadequate to a wealthy lawyer in extensive practice is deemed an object worth struggling for by men who, as mechanics or laborers, would have had to work hard for not much more than one-tenth the same amount of remuneration.

The student of divinity fared but hardly in the village. His school was tolerably well attended; it was seen that he was a good linguist and a respectable mathematician, and that his pupils improved under him. By and by, however, it was seen also that he was not at all the sort of person a student of theology ought to be. He was naturally cautious, and it was difficult to bring any direct charge home against him; and yet there was a general conviction in the village that he was not particularly sober, and not very strictly honest; and a report had gone abroad which, though it referred to something of a scandalous nature regarding him, was yet deemed not at all scandalous in itself. It was bad, but then it was true. There were religious men in the village,—he had formed no close intimacies with them; there were persons of an equivocal character in it,—they ranked among his most intimate acquaintance. He contracted debts which he seemed unwilling to pay. On one occasion he was summoned into court for the rent of a hall in which he taught his school; and he rendered to the magistrate, in his defence, eighteen ingenious, semi-metaphysical reasons against paying any rent at all. But the one simple argument of the pursuer—and it amounted to little more than the "Pay what thou owest" of the parable—proved an overmatch for the eighteen. In short, all who knew him had come to think highly of his ingenuity, and marvellously little of his principles, when his struggles in attending the classes both at college and the divinity hall came to a close, and he was taken on his trials by the presbytery of the district, to receive the finishing qualification through which immoral men are transformed, by virtue of a license, into teachers of morality, and men of no religion into disseminators of religious truth.

The clergyman of the parish in which the village is situated is a conscientious and devout man. A majority of his brethren in the presbytery are of the same character; and they determined, if possible, to keep the schoolmaster out of the Church. They tried him on Latin and Greek, on theology and the mathematics; but the schoolmaster was quite as accomplished a scholar as most of themselves. They tried to substantiate against him charges of whose justice they were all morally convinced; but the schoolmaster had been cautious, and they found them, one by one, vanish in their grasp. Difficulties were thrown in the way, and objections raised, but the perseverance of the probationer wore them down one after another; and the presbytery were at length comp
licentiate of the Church of Sc

there was no change produced by the license, except that the schoolmaster now and then read a clever discourse in the pulpit of a Moderate minister. He lived as before; never paid his debts when he could avoid paying them; got drunk occasionally with men who, as there is honor even among thieves, never betrayed him; and set his trust for the future in the law of patronage and the kindness of a Highland cousin. The fatal veto act of 1838 passed the General Assembly, and the poor licentiate was ruined. Ministers, such as the suspended seven, might have recommended him; the patrons of Mr. Clark or of Mr. Edwards might have presented him; there was no presbytery in the Church which, under the old system, could have possibly avoided ordaining him; but the people disliked and suspected him, and the people would not have him. In short, the poor licentiate was a broken man. It is scarcely necessary to add, as it does not bear essentially on the end we propose, that, losing heart and hope, he soon afterwards fell into open immorality, and quitted the kingdom.

At the time when we knew a little of the unlucky student, we were intimately acquainted with a student of a very opposite character. He had received an ordinary Scotch education, and had commenced business as a shopkeeper in the same village in which the other taught his school. He was a shrewd, vigorous-minded young man, invincibly honest, and, withal, diligent and careful; and he began to save money. His mind, however, became the subject of a very remarkable change. He began to feel that what he had been accustomed to regard as the truly important business of life is really but of minor importance after all, and that there is a "better part" to be first sought after, of incomparably greater interest and magnitude. Those doctrines of the New Testament virtually rejected by a considerable party in the Church as mysterious and peculiar continually filled his mind, — the fall and the restoration of man, the efficacy of prayer, the felt *influences* of the Spirit, the inexhaustible merits of the atonement. His heart was powerfully impressed, and he became anxiously desirous that the hearts of others might be impressed also. He thought he could tell forcibly what he had felt so warmly; and, after long and serious thought, and long and earnest prayer, — after he had taken the advice of all his better friends, and had carefully examined whether the guiding motive was really pure, and whether he was not confounding strong inclination for the necessary ability, — he shut up his shop, and entered the university as a student.

Wilberforce was a very different sort of person from the Dean of Faculty. The refined and elevated spirit of the one could appreciate those influences of the unseen world which come breathing upon the heart, awakening all its aspirations after the spiritually good, strengthening its desires for the truly useful, enabling it to forget self and every petty concern, and to set before it, as the prime object, the glory of God and the salvation of souls. The other is a cautious calculator on the amount of the ecclesiastical fee — the Joseph Hume of the Church's temporalities. No man can better balance the half-charms of the stipend, and the half-comforts of the manse, against the years laboriously spent, and the privations patiently endured, in striving to secure them. The one deplores a licentiate ruined in his prospects through the rejection of the people, and sent to spend a life of obscurity in bitterness and misery. "I do not," says the other, in writing of Dr. Carey, "I do not know a finer instance of the moral sublime than that a poor cobbler working in his stall should conceive the idea of converting the Hindus to Christianity."

But we must not lose sight of our friend the student. We wish some one would tell us how it is that the Moderates arrogate to themselves so much of the mind and accomplishment of the Church. It may be mere modesty asserting its right; but the present controversy at least does not promise to show that they are more than second best in either intellect or learning. The conscientious student wrought hard. He gained no prizes the first year, for he had started from a point far in the rear of all his competitors; but he was soon abreast of the front rank, and in the mathematical class of the second year he was declared, after a hard contest, the first man. He gained several other prizes besides; and, whatever might be thought of his religion, no one could well despise his learning. The little money he had saved as a shopkeeper failed him ere he had got half through his course. But, though as little presumptuous as any man, he believed in a superintending Providence, and that if he was really needed in the Church some unseen path would open for him as he went. And a path did open. He received unsolicited employment as a tutor in a respectable family, and soon after an appointment, equally unsought, to a parish school. He at length finished his preparatory course. He was naturally of a retiring disposition. He had no influential friends; he was acquainted with no patron; he did not set himself to court popularity. There seemed to be no way of access for him into the Church. He was confident, however, that he would find something to do somewhere; something in Sierra Leone, or Tahiti, or New Holland, if not at home; and so he did not feel very anxious. By and by, however, the people came to take an interest in him; they began to find out somehow that he was very much in earnest, and very much in duty; that he was on exceedingly good terms with a number of pious, old, poor people, who had only their Christianity to recommend them; that he was charitable to the utmost of his very limited means; and that, when sickness or distress visited a poor family in his neighborhood, he was sure to visit it too. In short, the result was, that not only did the people begin to like him, but it was the best people who liked him best. A vacancy occurred in a remote Highland parish, under the patronage of the Crown; off *went* a petition to Lord John Russell; down came a presentation from his lordship; not one of the parishioners so much as dreamed of the veto; and the friendless student is now a useful and respected minister of the Church of Scotland, and a zealous advocate of the popular right. He is, in short, one of what a smart contemporary calls the wild clergy.

We have drawn two portraits, so faithful in every trait, so little indebted to fancy, that in at least one district of country there are hundreds, nay thousands, who will be able at the first glance to write a name under each. They represent the two opposite classes of our theological students, — we grant, not fairly; — the one is a high specimen, the other falls somewhat below the average. But in the grand distinguishing principle, in the all-essential difference of motive, the representation is complete. The one class enter the Church earnestly solicitous for the high honor of being made fellow-workers with Christ; the other, that they may become gentlemen of from two to three hundred a year. The one class come frankly forward as the friends and advocates of the non-intrusion principle; the other discover that it is a principle denounced by the law, subversive of the Establishment, and most unfavorably regarded by "many of the *best* and *wisest* ministers of the Church."

THE PRESENTATION TO DAVIOT.

We paid our first visit to Daviot about twelve years ago, — late in the summer of 1828. It was on a communion Sabbath, and we went to attend sermon in the parish church. The parish is situated, as most of our readers are aware, in the Highlands of Inverness-shire, about six or seven miles to the south of Inverness. There rises a lofty rectilinear ridge directly over the town, composed of the old red sandstone of the district upheaved against the loftier primary regions; a dark line of mountains appears beyond; and in toiling up the long ascent, which passes from fertility and cultivation to a widely-spread sterility, the stranger supposes that he is quitting the inhabited part of the country altogether for the upper wilds. About five miles from the town, however, he gains the top of the ridge, and finds that a wide moory valley, traversed by a river, and mottled here and there with a few groups of cottages and a few patches of corn, intervenes between him and the hills. This long, wide valley comprises the greater part of the parish of Daviot, and the church, a handsome little edifice, occupies the northern bank of the river. We had no difficulty in finding our way. The scattered hamlets had poured forth their little groups of grave, church-going Highlanders; and the long, wearisome ascent seemed dotted with passengers to the top. We found the churchyard filled to the gate with the Gaelic congregation, and the wooden tent which served as a pulpit rising in the midst. The entire scene was characteristic of the border districts of the Highlands. There was a large admixture of the Lowland garb, especially among the females; but the plaids and the bright tartans carried it over the shop-furnished cloths and calicoes of the south; and an eye accustomed to the peculiarities of the Celtic form and countenance could scarce have mistaken the grave but keen-eyed descendants of the old clan Chattan, which, from time immemorial, had occupied this part of the country, for an assemblage of their Saxon neighbors of the plains. There was an air of deep seriousness spread over the whole. The clergyman who preached from the tent, himself a Highlander, was a devout, good man, of the popular school, and the attention of the Highlanders was riveted to the discourse. We may remark, in passing, that the Highland preacher who addresses Highlanders possesses a mighty advantage, in his language, over the Lowland preacher who addresses a rural Lowland population in English. The English language is unquestionably a noble instrument in the hand of a master; but few preachers, and certainly fewer congregations, acquire nearly the same mastery over it that even ordinary Highland preachers and congregations possess over the Gaelic. Almost every individual, in the one case, is acquainted with the whole vocabulary,—and a very expressive vocabulary it is, for at least narrative, description, and sentiment; in the other case, the acquaintance is limited, among the great bulk of the people, to a narrow round of ordinary terms. If there be no fatal defect on the part of the preacher, a Highland congregation is invariably an attentive one; and rarely have we seen Highlanders more seriously attentive anywhere than in the churchyard of Daviot on this communion Sabbath.

The minister of the parish (the late Mr. M'Phail) preached inside the church to an English congregation of about two hundred. He was a devout and excellent man—a man of very considerable wit, too. Mr. M'Phail's discourse, like that of the Gaelic preacher outside, was a very impressive one, and the congregation were deeply attentive. We were struck, however, accustomed as we were to the state of matters in the north, with the small proportion which the communicants of the parish bore to its general population. The number of females at the communion table considerably exceeded that of the males, as is commonly the case where communicants are not numerous, but the whole taken together were disproportionately few. And yet we could not avoid the conclusion, notwithstanding,—a conclusion which we have since had repeated opportunities of verifying,—that the people of Daviot are a serious and moral people, patient of religious instruction, and warmly attached, like all the rest of their countrymen, to the doctrines of the Evangelical school. They can understand and value the religion fitted by Deity to the wants and wishes of the human heart.

The parish is under the patronage of the Crown. When the good Mr. M'Phail was on his death-bed the people came to understand that interest had been made in high quarters to preëngage Lord John Russell, if possible, in favor of a certain young gentleman, who would have deemed two hundred a year and a free house a very comfortable settlement. It was not quite the time they could have chosen for themselves for urging anything of a counteractive tendency with his lordship; but they had no choice, just as a Christian army, when attacked by an enemy on the Sabbath, can have none; and so they united to petition Lord John that the appointment might be left open. His lordship cordially acquiesced: he went even further, and stated that any clergyman whom they agreed in recommending would be given to the parish. Mr. M'Phail died, and rather more than two-thirds of the adult male parishioners united in petitioning the Crown for the Rev. Mr. Cook, one of the clergymen of Inverness, — a gentleman, be it remarked, already settled as a minister in a town which, from its size and population, is known all over the country as the capital of the Highlands. The parish of Daviot is very extensive, — we believe, from eighteen to twenty miles in length; and yet, in little more than twenty-four hours all the signatures were adhibited to the petition — surely, proof enough of itself that any charge of canvassing the parishioners, which might be preferred against Mr. Cook or his friends, could not possibly be just. The people of a district twenty miles in extent, when exceedingly anxious to sign a petition, may contrive to do so in a very short time; but to canvass such a parish, in order to render people willing who were not willing before, cannot be done quite so much in a hurry. It was one of the objections to Bayes, in the "Rehearsal," that, for the sake of probability, he should not have brought about his great changes so very suddenly. Now, on the allegation that the parishioners had been canvassed, — an allegation unsupported, of course, by any inquiry, for inquiry might have led to very inconvenient results, — the prayer of the petition was refused. We attach no blame to Lord John Russell. He has been somewhat imprudent in believing too rashly, and that is just all.

A presentation to the parish was issued, through his lordship, in behalf of a young man favored by his friends, but whom rather more than two-thirds of the people have resolved not to receive or acknowledge as their minister. They could only reject him, however, through their representatives the communicants, seven of whom also declared against him — as nearly as may be the same proportion of this class as of the other. The poor people were very much in earnest. The day approached on which the seven were to exercise their privilege of the veto before the presbytery. Their fellow-parishioners were anxiously solicitous that they might be able to give an independent and resolutive "No" on the occasion, both in their own behalf and in theirs, without the fear of laird or factor before them, and urged them, therefore, to say whether any of them were in arrears with their rent, that they might instantly, by joint contribution, discharge them from the obligation. The evening preceding the meeting of presbytery arrived, and on that evening the seven communicants were interdicted by the Court of Session from exercising their right. It is unnecessary to comment on either the cruelty or the unprecedented nature of such a proceeding. We may instance, however, one of the dishonorable sophisms which our opponents employ in this case, as a pretty fair specimen of the whole. Instead of opposing in their statements the majority of the seven communicants to the minority of the three, and the majority of rather more than two-thirds of the parish to the minority of rather less than one-third of it, they oppose the *majority* of the one-third to the minority of the *seven*. The *argument*, it must be confessed, is worthy of the cause. We may state, too, a fact which illustrates the tone of feeling on the opposite side. The people of the parish of Daviot are far from wealthy. Highlanders on small sterile farms rarely save money; and there has been very little laid by by the people of this moorland district. In the true Presbyterian spirit, however, they have declared their willingness to lay down their hardly-earned pounds by tens and twelves apiece, rather than submit to the intrusion of a minister who, in their conscience, they believe unsuited to edify them. Such is the spirit which our Dr. Bryces and our John Hopes would trample into the very dust; but by Him who commended the poor widow and her humble offering it may be very differently regarded.

THE COMMUNICANTS OF THE NORTH COUNTRY.

In the preceding articles the Disruption controversy is illustrated in its immediate bearing on the rights of the Christian people invaded by patronage. In that which follows — the second point at issue — the possession of an independent spiritual jurisdiction by the Christian Church comes into view. The majority of the Strathbogie presbytery had been suspended by their ecclesiastical superiors; the minority had been empowered to exercise all presbyterial functions; and ministers had been appointed to conduct public worship in the parishes of the former. The majority applied to the Court of Session for an interdict to arrest all action of the ecclesiastical authority in the matter, and the decision of the Court was favorable to their claim. — Ed.

In the belief that the Church in her present struggle can have no better friend than the simple truth, we presented the reader in a recent number with an outline of the Daviot case, and a slight, but, we trust, faithful, sketch of the character of the parishioners. The poor Highlanders of Daviot are not unworthy the protection of the Scottish Church, though the number among them in full communion with her are so disproportionately few. But why are these not more numerous, since the general morals of the people seem so good? We crave the tolerance of the reader should we take what may seem a circuitous route in answering this question.

Civilization did not travel through Scotland with railway speed three centuries ago. There are still very considerable differences between different districts of the country. The same fastnesses which kept out the Romans and the English of old, still keep out improvement and the arts; and the Scotchman desirous to acquaint himself with the manners and usages which prevailed in the days of his great-grandfather, and curious to pass, as it were, from the present century to the middle of the century before the last, has but to transport himself to the western Highlands of Ross-shire, or to some of the remoter islands which lie beyond. About the period of the Union even the Lowland districts of the north of Scotland were fully a hundred years behind the Lowland districts of the south; they were inhabited by a wilder and more turbulent race, and were, with the exception of a few insulated localities, Presbyterian only in name. The framework of the Scottish Church had been erected in them, but the spirit was wanting.

Much, however, about the time rendered remarkable by the revival at Cambuslang and Kilsyth, a widely-extended district in the northern portion of the kingdom became the scene of a similar change. The popular mind suddenly awoke to the importance of religion; the inhabitants of almost entire villages were converted; prayer-meetings were established; clergymen became deeply fervent and instant in duty; and the morals of a considerable portion of the people rose at once, from the comparatively abject state which obtains in half-civilized communities, to the high Christian level. It is a fact well known to persons acquainted with the history of parties in the Church for the last eighty years, that no inconsiderable portion of the

Evangelical minority in our assemblies was drawn from this northern district; and that, at a period when Moderation was either extending its paralyzing influences over the people of the south, or wholly estranging them from the churches in which their fathers had worshipped, ministers of a very different theology, and of a very opposite character, were scattering the good seed liberally in this highly-favored northern province, and that the blessing of God largely accompanied their labors.

The effects of the change were all the more marked from the state of manners and morals prevalent at the time it took place. There is a mighty difference between civilization and barbarism; and Christianity contrasts much more strongly with the one than with the other. There was indisputably an all-essential difference between an Ebenezer Erskine or a Thomas Bateman before and after their conversion, but by no means so cognizable a difference as between the New Zealand warriors described by the missionary Williams before and after the same important change had passed upon them. The Scottish divine and the English physician were both respectable members of society when practically unacquainted with the truth. But not even the miracle wrought by our Saviour on the wild man who lived solitary among the tombs was more marked in its effects than the conversion of the two New Zealand chiefs, as recorded by the missionary. Previous to the change which transformed them into gentle and singularly compassionate-hearted men, the fierce and remorseless murderers and cannibals had never spared sex nor age, — had never fought with an enemy whom they had not subdued, — nor had they ever subdued a poor wretch whom they had not destroyed. Now, the change in our northern districts was one of striking contrast, on the same principle. It took place among a rude people. There were cases tried at the time by the hereditary barons on the court hills; the town of Tain executed a Strathcharan freebooter on the borough gallows, several years after; and cattle-lifting was common in all the districts, in at least the more immediate neighborhood of the Highlands. On one occasion the parish of Nigg — a parish in the eastern district of Ross, and one of the centres of the revival — was swept, in a single night, of all its cattle by a band of caterans from the west. The clergyman, Mr. Balfour, a brave as well as a good and eminently useful man, immediately set himself at the head of his parishioners, pursued after the freebooters, overtook them in a wild Highland glen, fought them, beat them, and brought back the cattle.

We have remarked that this northern district was a full century behind the Lowland districts of the south in general civilization. It is a rather striking fact, too, that the religion of the revival of this period resembled, in some of its accidental accompaniments, the religion of the south in the previous century. Christianity is ever the same, but it acts at different times on very different materials; and, though the greater effects are invariably identical, its minor traits occasionally differ with the character of the people on whom it operates. There are anecdotes related of the Pedens, Camerons, and Cargills, of the days of Charles II., that one hesitates either to receive or to reject, in at least their full extent; there are anecdotes of an almost identical character told of the later worthies of the northern districts. Stories are still preserved of a Donald Roy, of Nigg, — one of the first elders of the parish after the reëstablishment of Presbytery at the Revolution, — which, if inserted in the tracts of Peter Walker, or the older editions of the "Scots Worthies," would be found to amalgamate so entirely with the more characteristic anecdotes of these works, that the nicest judgment could not distinguish betwixt them. And Donald was only one of a class.

There were prayer-meetings, as we have said, established very generally over the district at this period. There were also meetings of a somewhat different character, and which resembled much more the meetings of an earlier age in the history of the Scottish Church than the contemporary meetings of the same period in the south. In the twelfth chapter of the First Book of Discipline we find it laid down, that in every town where there were "schools and repaire of learned men, a certain day in every week should be appointed for the exercise of what St. Paul calls prophesying." The chapter recommends that meetings be held for the edification of the Church, "by the interpretation of Scripture," and that at these meetings not only should lay elders be invited to communicate their views of particular passages for the benefit of the whole, but also ordinary members of the Church, if qualified by grace and nature for the duty. Now, meetings of exactly this primitive character were established in the north at the time of the revival; and in several districts of the country they still continue to be held.

A text of Scripture is proposed as an exercise at the opening of the meeting; and, in the manner prescribed in the First Book of Discipline, the individuals who take part in it rise in succession, either to propound their views of the passage, or to adduce from their own peculiar experience facts illustrative of its truth. We have listened with wonder to the extempore addresses delivered at some of these meetings by untaught men, — men from remote upland districts, who had derived their sole knowledge of religion from meditation and the Bible. Their simple truthfulness and earnest fervor; their exhibition of the workings of the human heart under the opposing influences of good and evil; their views of the effects of the renovating principle on the one hand, and the original depravity, acted upon by temptation, on the other; their enumeration of the various stages through which the pilgrim has to pass, and the changes effected in his views and opinions, — all these, in at least the choicer passages, have powerfully reminded us of Bunyan — the unapproachable Shakspeare of Christian literature. The individuals who take part in these meetings are emphatically termed "*the men.*" Though generally elders of the Church, they are not invariably so. Death is fast wearing them out. We have seen in one parish church, in the north, the elders' pew filled with them from end to end,—all worthies of the right stamp, who would have joyfully betaken themselves to the hill-side in the present quarrel; but their honored heads are all low to-day.

Now, there are three points to which we would recall the attention of the reader. The striking contrast between the manners and morals of the people in this district when Christianity was first introduced among them with power and effect, and the very opposite state of manners and morals induced by its influence, is the first of these. It is a curious fact, that the striking nature of this contrast, though all that remains of it be now merely traditional, has still a very marked influence on the people. It affects till this day the popular estimate of the religious character. But, unluckily, the good Protestant recollection of it is associated with a somewhat Popish feeling; and the high respect for the eminent Christians of a century ago is perhaps not sufficiently tempered by a recollection of the only ground on which, eminent as they were, they could have stood in the presence of Deity. Not merely is the pious ancestor raised high on a pedestal over the descendant, but that very pedestal proves also a stumbling-block to the descendant. We need only advert to the second point, as corresponding in character to the first. Nothing easier than to anticipate the effects on people so predisposed, of those sentiments of awe and veneration necessarily inspired by the belief that the more eminent Christians of the district had received, in their close walk with God, like the Pedens and Cargills of a former age, gifts and powers of an extraordinary character, through which they were at times enabled to triumph signally over the invisible enemies of another world, and at times to discern afar off the form and color of events while yet enveloped in the uncertain obscurity of the future.

The peculiar character and constitution of what we may term the meetings of *the men* is the third point to which we would direct the attention of the reader. With much, doubtless, that is excellent in them, they operate in the track of the traditional recollections adverted to. They raise, if we may so express ourselves, the standard of Christian qualification, by bringing before the great body of the people the peculiar experiences of singularly devoted and highly meditative natures as tests for trying men's spirits, and through which the believer is to judge whether he has in reality received of the Spirit of truth. Now, the great bulk of the population anywhere cannot form too lofty ideas of Christian morality or Christian privilege, nor is the estimate formed by the people of the north more than adequately high. But there is a mixture of error in it, inasmuch as it bears at least as direct reference to experiences of devout natures in an advanced stage of the Christian pilgrimage, to gifts very rarely bestowed, and to attainments not often made, as to the infinite merits of the full atonement and the free grace of that adorable Being through whom the believer can alone be rendered worthy. The effects on gloomy and melancholy natures — the Little Faiths, the Feebles, and the Ready-to-Halts, of the Church — have been in some instances very sad. There have been men in these northern districts thoroughly awakened to a clear perception of the realities of the unseen world, and whose lives were "hid with Christ in God," who have yet walked in darkness all their days, anxious and doubtful, and who could never command the necessary confidence to approach the communion table. The great bulk of the people stand afar off, impressed with feelings like those which held back the Israelites of old from the Mount, — not, be it remarked, because they are indifferent, or deem lightly of the privilege, but because they esteem themselves not worthy. And hence it is that communicants in this northern district are so few.* We are acquainted with men who would lay down their lives for the Scottish Church, and who have ranged themselves, in the present conflict, on the old Presbyterian side with all the earnest determination of her first fathers, who have not yet entered into full communion with her, and probably never will.

Now, on the whole, this state of matters is much to be regretted. It is by no means so bad a state as prevails in some of the southern and midland parishes of Scotland, where the lax morality and imperfect theology of the Moderate school has thrown open the communion table to people of all characters — to persons who live loosely, and believe they know not what, among the rest. Still, however, it is bad. It substitutes, to a certain degree, the standard of what we may term a traditional Christianity for the Christianity of the New Testament. It excludes serious and good men from sharing in a great privilege, of which they will never be able to render themselves deserving, but which has been purchased for them notwithstanding. It renders the cause of the Church less strong in her present position, in the districts in which it obtains, much as she is loved and venerated among their people. Finally, it lays her open, in cases like that of Daviot, to the plausible though unprincipled and unsolid objections of designing enemies, who can neither be made to feel nor understand the vast difference which exists between callous and dead consciences indifferent to the truth, and consciences scrupulously tender and anxiously awake,— between the practical infidel, who will not eat of the children's bread just because he has no appetite for it, and the timid Christian, who, while he longs after it, is yet restrained by a sense of his own unworthiness, and lives on in unhappiness without partaking of it.

SPIRITUAL INDEPENDENCE THE DISTINCTIVE PRIVILEGE OF THE CHURCH OF SCOTLAND.

We speak with all due respect when we say that, had our ancestors been content that our Church should have been based on the same foundation with the sister Establishment, they might have saved themselves many a harassing struggle, and many a severe and long-protracted pang. Three succeeding generations of our countrymen might have lived and died in peace. There would have been no imperative call to the battle-field; no need to brave the dungeon and the scaffold; no necessity, when broken and discomfited in the contest, to retire, as unsubdued in spirit as at first, into the wilder recesses of the country, and, in the midst of privation, suffering, and death, to cherish the indomitable resolution of maintaining in unbroken integrity the spiritual independence of the Church. We respect the English Establishment, with its long list of great and good men; but we are not to place on the same level the dearly-purchased privileges of our own.

It is surely well, since the struggle threatens to be a protracted one, to be preparing ourselves for it — "to be marking our bulwarks, and looking well to our walls." There are strong grounds of hope, and great cause for thankfulness. It is in no new quarrel that the Church and the people of Scotland are now engaged; the testimony of the past bears direct upon the present and the future; and we not only know that it is a righteous quarrel, from the principles which it involves, and because it was so especially the cause of the righteous in former times, but because the same unchangeable One who so especially favored it of old is in the same gracious manner especially favoring it now. We have evidence in our favor of the highest kind, and grounds of comfort on which it is even a duty to build. Nor are the minor considerations to be overlooked. We have read the history of Scotland to very little purpose if we are mistaken in deeming firmness one of the main characteristics of the people. It is the history of a determined handful, maintaining their place and name among the nations more on the strength of this quality than on even that of their valor itself. It was their firmness which gave effect to their valor, and enabled them to reap the fruits of it. It was this quality which of old, when English enterprise was so successful in Ireland and France, imparted so different and so disastrous a character and issue to English enterprise in Scotland. We see it paramount in the protracted struggle of our ancestors in the thirteenth century; we catch a glimpse of it at even an earlier period, when the Dane and the Vikingr ravished our coasts; we read it legibly inscribed in the remains of the first and second wall with which the Roman belied his proud vaunt of conquest; we see it standing out in high relief, and encircled with a halo of moral glory, in the troublous times of Knox and Wishart; we see it fixed in one unaltered attitude during the whole of the succeeding century, unmoved from its place by the utmost rigor of fierce and remorseless persecution; we see it, though miserably misdirected and mistaken, in the one striking historical incident of the century that followed, — in the enterprise of the handful of half-disciplined men who fought their way into the centre of the sister kingdom, and bore down before them the best troops of England again and again. Nor has the character changed in the least; nor is it forgotten to what country the soldiers belonged who, in one of the earlier battles of the last war, scattered in the charge the invincibles of Napoleon, and against whom, in its latest and bloodiest fight, the pride and strength of France was thrice disastrously broken, and which preserved entire to the last its own iron wall. There is surely ground of hope that in this quarrel, so emphatically Scotch, so peculiarly popular, so hallowed by all the old associations, so honored in the testimonies of departed worthies, so thoroughly identified with spiritual religion, so eminently favored with the countenance of Deity,—surely there is ground of hope that in this quarrel the grand national characteristic will not fail. Our Church has already spoken, and spoken by her greatest man; and not only did we feel the sense of sacredness and the high obligation of duty which the pledge involved, but we felt also, when the irrepressible plaudits arose around Chalmers, that it was a Scotchman who had spoken, and that it was Scotchmen who approved. We repeat his emphatic words: "Be it known, then, to all men, that we will not retrace a single footstep. We will make no concession to the Court of Session; and that not because of the disgrace, but because of the gross and grievous dereliction of principle which we would thereby incur. They may by force eject us out of our place, but they never will force us to surrender our principles: and if the honorable Court should again so far mistake its functions as to repeat or renew its inroads, I trust they will again meet the reception they have already gotten,—'To whom we gave place by subjection, no, not for an hour, no, not by a hair-breadth.'" It was more than Chalmers who spoke in these sentences; they are instinct with the genius of the Scottish Church,—they embody the main characteristic of the Scottish people.

THE "GRASPING AMBITION" OF THE NON-INTRUSIONISTS.

We have just seen in a Liberal London newspaper—favorable to the cause of dissent in the degree in which dissent is political, and wholly indifferent to it in the degree in which it is religious—a smart paragraph on the Church question. It reiterates the charge of clerical ambition and usurpation first preferred against the ministers of our Church, in the present struggle, by the Dean of Faculty, and then idly bandied among his party, until caught up by the Voluntaries in the manner in which drowning men clutch at straws. But miserably unsuited does it seem to serve their purpose. Our London contemporary "has repeatedly stated," he says, "that the great object of the clerical non-intrusionists is to grasp the whole patronage of the Church of Scotland." He adds further, that "the usurpers will ultimately be defeated;" and then concludes, hardly two sentences after, by asserting that the balance in favor of the non-intrusionists (the ambitious and usurping clergymen, be it remembered) was secured "*by the burgh elders elected to the General Assembly under the Municipal Reform Bill.* Well has it been remarked that error is ever inconsistent. It is not in the nature of things that good argument should favor a bad cause, or that what is true should militate against which is right.

It is no very difficult matter to say how a man such as the Dean of Faculty should be led, through a confusion of ideas natural to his party on religious subjects, half to believe his own charge. He, of course, sees that the great principle for which the Church is contending cannot exist without mightily strengthening one of our two ecclesiastical parties, and ultimately wearing out the other. He sees that if the majority carry their measure, they must become an immensely more preponderating majority. He sees, further, that they must of course possess some measure of power as such; not quite the sort of power possessed by his friends of old, but still a species of power; and seeing this, and reasoning in part from his own feelings, and in part from a pretty close acquaintance with the governing motives of his party, he concludes that this modicum of power is the main object of the struggle, and, in accordance perhaps with the professional license, describes it as the only object. All this is easily understood. It is equally obvious that in every struggle which terminates decisively, the conquering party becomes the more powerful one. When Christianity rose over paganism, Christians became in consequence more powerful; when Protestantism rose over Popery, Protestants became in consequence more powerful; when Presbyterianism rose over Prelacy, Presbyterians became in consequence more powerful; and there were no doubt respectable, gross-minded pagan, and popish, and prelatic gentlemen in those days, who, like the Dean of Faculty in our own times, would have looked to the inevitable power as the actual prize secured by those struggles, and as therefore the main object of the conquering parties. All this, we repeat, is easily understood; and it may be understood at least equally easily from the instances adduced, that a mere consequence arising out of any measure may be an essentially different thing from the great end proposed by that measure. It was no thirst of power that Christianized the world; it was no thirst of power that reformed the Church.

It is well to consider further the mode in which the non-intrusion principle can alone add to the power of the rising party, by adding, of course, to their number. It can add to their power only through the medium of the people. They are popular; the people love them, and they detest their opponents. The non-intrusion principle, if fairly established, would be simply a power conferred on the people of rejecting the men whom they hate. The power of the popular party in the Church would be a mere consequence, therefore, of the exertion of this power on the part of the people. If the party ceased to be popular, they would inevitably cease to be powerful, just in the way that their unpopular opponents are ceasing to be powerful. And this, then, is the kind of usurpation and grasping ambition with which they are charged! They love the people, and the people love them. They are striving to protect the people from the objects of their hate, by extending to them an ability of protecting themselves; and they are therefore called ambitious, and usurpers.

The Tyrant of the Cheronese
Was freedom's best and dearest friend.

But what is the particular kind of power which their popularly acquired majorities is to secure to them? Power to get churches for their sons and nephews? No! The people have been vetoing the sons and nephews of very worthy men, because, though they liked the worthy men themselves, they did not like their sons and nephews. What sort of power, then? Power of a far nobler and widely different character, — power to put down the men who used to force their sons and nephews into churches against the will and the interests of the people, — power to overrule the counsels of the hirelings who partook of the people's patrimony, but who wrought not for the people's good, — power to labor more and more effectually for the benefit of the people, — power, through their hold of the affections of the people, to spread anew the blessings of Christianity among the masses broken loose from its sacred and humanizing influences, — power to stem, for the good of the people, the demoralizing flood of infidelity which is threatening to bear them down, as it has borne down the millions of other countries, — power adequately to extend to the people, as of old, the blessings of religion and the light of learning.

The popularity of the party now happily dominant in the Church constitutes more than their strength; it is founded on a principle which renders it also their most powerful recommendation. It was not by flattering the people that men such as Knox and Melville became the trusted and beloved leaders of the people. They led them on the same high principle through which the discourses of our Saviour were so eminently popular, and through which crowds were attracted by the preaching of the apostles, wherever they went. God, in his wisdom and goodness, has fitted the glad tidings of salvation which he reveals to the human nature which he has made. The common people listen gladly to the gospel now, as of old, even when they close not with its offers; and the men who preach it in sincerity and truth partake of its popularity; and hence their influence with the congregations whom they address. Nor has this body of men — the Evangelical ministers of our country, the true representatives and descendants of our elder worthies — ever deceived the people of Scotland. What was the object of their long-protracted struggles in the past? Solely and exclusively the glory of God and the good of the people. The history of Rome furnishes us with one example of a poor patriotic man quitting his plough to lead the armies of his country, and, after he had fought her battles and defeated her enemies, returning a poor man to his plough again. The history of the Scottish Church abounds in such examples; the biographies of all her better ministers repeat the story of Fabricius. Who has not heard of the Herculean labors of Knox, and Melville, and Calderwood, and Bruce, and Henderson, and Guthrie, and those of their noble-minded coadjutors and associates, the other saints and martyrs of our Church? Where are the patrimonies which they bequeathed to their children, or what the amount of the riches which they hoarded? What was Knox's share of the forfeited Church lands? Just Fabricius's share of the spoils. Manfully did he struggle for these with a grasping and selfish aristocracy, but it was exclusively on the people's behalf. However great the opportunities of accumulation possessed by these men, they all died poor, many of them in utter destitution; but their wealth abideth notwithstanding, and an assembled world will hear of it at the last day. We have but to look, too, at the constitution which they framed for our Church to be convinced that they nourished in their poverty and self-denial no priestly feeling of exclusiveness; that their struggles were no Jesuitical struggles for the advancement of their order; that all which they did and suffered was truly and unequivocally for the cause of God and the people. With a liberality unmatched, save in the times of the apostles, they provided that the layman and his minister should sit together in their ecclesiastical courts armed with exactly the same authority, and gave to the people at large the power of choosing both. The Presbyterians of Scotland knowing this, and knowing, too, that the kindred spirits who represent these worthies in the present day are influenced by no lower motives than those by which they were animated, and that they pursue objects not merely similar, but identical, are not to be deceived by the palpably unjust charges of either hireling pleaders or prostitute scribes, who, mean-spirited and selfish themselves, have no heart to appreciate virtues removed not only beyond their practice, but even beyond their conception. That body are surely worthy of all trust who were never yet found to deceive.

POPULAR ESTIMATE OF THE TWO PARTIES.

"Rejection without reasons." How is it that the two great parties in the Church have come to differ so entirely on a point like this? — that the one party are so much disposed to trust to the people, and the other so determined to place no confidence in them, unless they cannot possibly help it? The question is a very simple one, but the reply involves some rather important principles.

It is a striking fact, but not the less a certain one, that the men most generally beloved and respected by the Presbyterians of Scotland, and the men most thoroughly disliked and despised by them, have been members of the same profession, and have belonged to the same body. The political field north of the Tweed has hitherto been singularly barren in patriotism. We have a few names which belong to our earlier struggles with England that are worth remembering, and that we are not at all likely soon to forget; but the Scottish politicians of the after ages are of a very questionable character indeed. Contrast our history in this respect with that of England. Where are our Hampdens, our Seldens, our Russells, our Algernon Sidneys, — where even our gallant and generous spirits, noble and disinterested on a basis of romance, — our Sir Philip Sidneys and Sir Walter Raleighs? Scotland reckons no such names among those of her statesmen of the last three centuries. The soil has been unfavorable to patriotism; the people, in consequence, down to a recent date, had no political existence. We have had great abundance of crafty politicians, — Mortons, and Maitlands, and Middletons, — men bent on the aggrandizement of themselves and their families, and as faithful to their masters as their natures allowed; but we have had no patriots, if, indeed, we do not except Fletcher, of Salton; and so much was he a republican of the old school, that he would only have set free one-half the people, and made the other half slaves. Certain it is, however, that Scotland has her revered and honored names notwithstanding, — names in no respect inferior to those of England, and now, after the lapse of centuries, much better known to the people. For every Englishman who knows anything of Hampden, we will find at least twenty Scotchmen who love and venerate the memory of Knox. All the true patriots of our country — the men who stood out disinterestedly in the cause of the people, and elevated them by their labors in the moral and intellectual scale — have been either ministers of the Church, or persons who had caught from them the truly liberal spirit which genuine Christianity never fails to infuse. Who was it that first addressed his "beloved brethren" the "commonality," at a time when they were sunk in the slavery of vassalage, and told them of a high spiritual level on which, as immortal creatures for whom Christ had died, they were no whit inferior to their masters? Who was it that assured them that, "albeit God had ordained distinction and difference in the administration of civil policies betwixt kings and subjects, rulers and common people, yet in the hope of the life to come he had made all equal"? Who but the greatest and the noblest of our patriots, — the man whose large-minded educational schemes are still half a century ahead of our age, — who shared his principles and maxims of political liberty with his friend, the elegant and masculine-minded Buchanan, — "principles and maxims," says Sir James Mackintosh, "delivered with a precision and enforced with an energy which no former age has equalled, and no succeeding age has surpassed," and the liberality of whose ecclesiastical polity our better Churchmen are even now striving at a distance to approach? There is little wonder that the people of Scotland should continue to cherish and venerate the memory of Knox.

Our great reformer is the true type and representative of the popular party, — the Christian patriots of Scotland. It is no difficult or uninteresting matter to trace the line through our country's history, from the days of Mary downwards. There is, in truth, not much else on which the eye can rest with pleasure. Unquestionably the author of the "Scots Worthies" gave his book the right name. The men whose biographies he relates were emphatically the worthies of Scotland; and the popularity of the work shows how decidedly the great bulk of the population have acquiesced in the propriety of the title. Nor is the popularity of the party less shown by the history of our Church in the last century than by that of the century which went before. Who but the Erskines and their followers could have led away from the Established Church five hundred congregations of Scottish Presbyterians warmly attached to the Church of their fathers? We have been much impressed by the abiding character of the memory and influence of ministers of the true stamp in our country districts. There are individuals of no other class so long remembered by the people of Scotland; striking passages from their oral discourses, only once delivered, sometimes survive the men themselves for two whole generations.

Even in our larger towns, where the population are more in a state of flux, half a century hardly succeeds in effacing the cherished recollection of an eminent minister. Dr. Balfour, of Glasgow, is better remembered in that city than any other man connected with the place who died so many years ago; and we question whether the recollection of Dr. Andrew Thomson is not more deeply impressed on the mind of the Edinburgh people, members of the Church, than that of any other citizen whose career of eminence and usefulness terminated within the present century. There does not exist a tenderer or more enduring tie among all the various relationships which knit together the human family, than that which binds the gospel minister to his people.

It is not less certain, however, that there is a very considerable portion of our Scottish clergy less popular, and regarded more generally with jealous dislike, than any other class in the country; nor is it any hatred of the order through which they suffer, for it is identically the same portion of the people who most venerate their brethren that most dislike them. In nine cases out of ten the minister of a country parish is either the man most loved and respected in it, or the man least cared for, and against whom the strongest prejudice is entertained. Half the witticisms of the country have been made at the expense of the cloth; and it will invariably be found that the more secular-minded the clergy of a district become, the more readily will these be picked up and repeated. The mere fact of their existence shows nothing. Shimei cursed David; the dragoons of the times of Charles II. were merry at the expense of the men whom they persecuted and murdered. Moderatism in Strathbogie has been profane in bad rhyme in attempting to be smart on some of the most revered ministers of our Church; and an Edinburgh artist, who has humor enough to make capital caricatures, and wisdom enough not to publish his creed, has been following in the same track. But in all these, and in similar instances, the joke meets with no response in the public mind. Very different is the case, however, when it affects a degraded and earthly-minded clergy. There is a disposition to receive and repeat. Dr. Johnson, with all his high respect for the English Church, could yet solemnly assure Boswell, in one of his serious moods, that he had scarce ever met with a pious clergyman. The time (that of the reign of Moderatism in our own country) was unquestionably a time of spiritual death in the sister Establishment. And it is well to remember that this was also the time when clergymen were the subjects of ridicule among every class of the English people, high and low, and the butts of almost every company. It was the atrocities of the French Revolution that first secured some little degree of respect for the cloth in the upper walks of society, by showing that even the husk of religion, the mere empty shell, could not be safely slighted. Christian clergymen cannot occupy with comfort a middle place; they cannot rest in the mere mediocrity of their station as gentlemen of from three to four hundred a year; and we accept it as one of the many proofs of the excellence of religion that such is the case. Even the men who do not profess to believe in Christianity at all, tacitly confess how highly they estimate its value, by the severity of their animadversions on unfaithful clergymen, and the high standard of morality and extensive usefulness by which they try them. No one ever expects morals of a high tone, or usefulness of a signal character, from the priests of a false religion. Their duties are comprised in a miserable round of absurd rites and ceremonies; and if they do no positive mischief, — if they be content with simply doing nothing, — we think they do well. But members of a Christian ministry are tried by another standard.

Hence one great cause of the unpopularity of the body now the minority in the Church. But there are other causes besides. The Moderate school is singularly unfavorable to the production of popular talent in the ministry.

It has unquestionably produced some very able men. Robertson was only inferior to his friend and contemporary Hume; and the sermons of Blair, though occasionally heavy, are nearly as finished pieces of composition as the Loungers and Mirrors of M'Kenzie. But though such men, when they exerted themselves, could no doubt be listened to from the pulpit with a good deal of intellectual gratification, the preachers of this school, regarded as a body, have been miserably tame and inefficient. In truth, Scotland does not produce talent enough, even were the whole of it engaged in the Church, to fill her thousand pulpits with Moderate ministers of but middling interest as preachers; and ordinary men are totally unsuited to make an impression. What is there within the reach of such? The commonplaces of morality dressed up in the merest commonplaces of language, — the gum-flowers of false rhetoric all fashioned after one tame pattern, — the offensive pulings of a sickly sentimentality; really there is little to wonder at in finding the churches where such ministers preach deserted by more than half their people, and the rest fallen fast asleep. Are our readers acquainted, however, with the case of men of even this stamp awakened in the middle of their indifference to a pervading sense of the importance of the one thing needful? — of men of ordinary powers who preached inefficiently for years, and then became converts to the truth? We are acquainted with cases of this kind. We are convinced, too, that there are few districts in Scotland in which our readers have not either known or heard of such, and have not been struck, like ourselves, by the degree of popular talent which the change seemed at once to communicate. No doubt a great deal must have depended, as it always does in such cases, on the new tone of earnestness imparted to the preacher. Men who wish to affect others must first be affected themselves. Much must have depended, too, on the whole mind being brought into play, — not the intellectual part merely, but the affections and the sentiments also. The grand difference, however, must have consisted in the newly-acquired anxiety to communicate the revealed truths of God, instead of the mere cogitations of the speaker. The change substituted the scheme of salvation, in all its infinite wisdom, for the *jejune* reflections and tame, inefficient moralizings of an ordinary man. Boston and Willison were by no means superior men to Blair and Logan, and certainly far inferior writers: why are they in such high repute among the people of Scotland, and the others left to the admiration of Moderate ministers and their supporters? Simply from their being what the more fashionable divines were not — faithful interpreters of the mind of God.

Hence one of the most gratifying circumstances connected with the popularity of the dominant party. It is not a popularity unworthily acquired. It does not even result from the gratitude of the people for important services rendered to them in the past, though this, no doubt, has its influence. It arises chiefly from the nice adaptation which exists between the popular mind and the truths of revelation, and the natural attachment which obtains between the faithful preacher and his flock. And hence, too, the importance of what we may term the shibboleth of the party, "rejection without reasons," and the dreaded abhorrence with which the Moderate section regard it. They have translated the phrase aright in its bearing on themselves, and find that it embodies exactly the same meaning with the handwriting on the wall.

THE EARL OF ABERDEEN'S BILL.

The Earl of Aberdeen brought forward, on Tuesday last, his long-expected bill on the Church question. Cowper tells us of men who "do nothing with a deal of skill." His lordship has been doing nearly as much without the skill. He proposes to reënact an already existing law, which has certainly not been suffered to fall into desuetude, and to do for the Church what he confesses the Church, in even her present circumstances, can do for herself. In one important respect, however, the proposed measure is better than if it had not been so bad. It will, no doubt, satisfy Dr. Cook and his friends, for it does not contain a single clause which might not have emanated from the Doctor himself. Dr. Muir would perhaps have framed a somewhat more liberal measure, though he, too, will soon be able to accommodate himself to its peculiarities, just as he learned to accommodate himself to the policy of Dr. Cook. But no individual who voted with Dr. Chalmers can consistently acquiesce in the bill introduced by the Earl of Aberdeen. It will satisfy all the friends of unrestricted patronage and the old system, but it will not have the effect of dividing the friends of a still older and immensely better system. It will satisfy the class who never yet satisfied the people; but the people and their friends it will not satisfy, nor will it have the effect, we trust, of breaking down the majorities of the latter.

"The people have at present the right," says the Dean of Faculty, in his pamphlet,—"and that they should have it is most fitting,—of submitting every ground of objection, of whatever kind, which they may entertain against the individual, to the clergymen of the presbytery." The Earl of Aberdeen, in his outline of the proposed bill, says nearly the same thing, only he says it in more words. The patron presents to the vacant parish; and the licentiate, his choice, appears before the presbytery, who appoint him to preach in the parish church to the people. The people then meet; and if the regular communicants have objections to urge of any kind, the presbytery receive these, either in writing or otherwise. They next sit and decide upon them. If they are held to be insufficient, the settlement proceeds, and the presentee is intruded upon the people; but if the presbytery deem them of sufficient force, he is set aside, and the patron presents another. And such are the main provisions of the bill introduced by the Earl of Aberdeen. What measure of protection does it furnish which did not exist under the old system? It adds, perhaps, in some slight degree, to the power of our Church courts; and yet that power was certainly very considerable before. We find it stated by the Dean of Faculty, that he is aware of no limit either to the nature of the inquiries, or to the strictness of the examinations, to which presbyteries may subject licentiates. The Church may reject, he asserts, on any ground whatever. It has unlimited authority to set aside, — unlimited authority to choose. Now, if this view of the matter be correct, the Earl of Aberdeen, as we have said, is merely reënacting an existing law; he is virtually doing nothing, and doing it at a considerable expense. But, granting that it is not strictly correct, — granting that some little additional power is conferred on our Church courts, — what are the Presbyterian people of Scotland to gain in consequence? What benefits did they derive from the power vested in our Church courts for the greater part of the last century, or in what degree would they have profited had that power been rendered a very little greater? It was a power in almost every instance employed either against themselves or against the true types and representatives of the original Church, — the pious and devoted ministers whom they most loved and honored. Popular privileges are essentially different things from powers conferred on Church courts; and we would just request our readers to mark how ready the very men who are most forward in calumniating our better ministers, and in raising against them the cry of clerical ambition and clerical usurpation, are to extend to them, notwithstanding, those very powers which they unjustly accuse them of coveting, and how sedulously they would withhold every shadow of popular privilege. They profess to dread the encroachments of the clergy, but it is only to conceal how bitterly they dislike all interference on the part of the people.

It is scarce necessary to pass over the various statements of the Earl of Aberdeen. He quotes the First Book of Discipline after exactly the same fashion as Messrs. Paul and Pirie, and proves, to the satisfaction of his peers, that the scheme of planting vacant parishes laid down by Knox — a scheme of free election, be it remembered — was less popular than the one embodied in the veto act. The Upper House was, of course, no place in which his lordship had any chance of being set right on the point. To the theology of the question there is no reference. The seven suspended ministers are respectable; nor do legislators, like his lordship, often look higher. Men who are too virtuous to be punished as immoral are quite suited to teach religious truth; and to urge that there is a very opposite doctrine in the Bible would of course be fanatical. And yet it does seem but common sense to draw a distinction between negative and positive character; nor does it appear very absurd to assert that men amenable to no law may be totally devoid of religion. Let us suppose his lordship's bill in its present form enacted into statute and acquiesced in by a majority of the Church. What would be the probable, nay, the inevitable, consequences? The Presbyterian people of the country have been thoroughly aroused on the agitated question, and aroused as a body. At no time were they indifferent to the principle which it involves, and very keenly could they feel, and very promptly could they act upon it. In what cases have the military been employed against the peasantry of Scotland since the rebellion of 1745, except in cases of forced settlements? Or in what other cases have handfuls of poor laboring men extended their hours of labor, and lived still more hardly than before, that they might raise their fifties and hundreds of pounds, — at first, to contend hopelessly in our courts of law against the intrusion of ministers whom in their conscience they believed not suited to edify them; and latterly, to build chapels for themselves, and support clergymen of their own choosing, to whose ministrations they could trust? Never did they cease to feel on the subject; but hitherto they have been aroused to act or resist merely in detail,—aroused by parishes at a time. They are now aroused in a body; and tremendous will be the revulsion of feeling if they find they have been deceived, and see the ministers in whom they trusted deserting them. We would say to our clergymen, therefore, only give up the true non-intrusion principles embodied in the veto act, and you will soon find how fatal an error it was ever to have agitated them. Had you contented yourselves with the provisions of the old system, and suffered Dr. Cook or Dr. Muir to direct your councils, you might probably have continued to exist as an Establishment for thirty years: retreat from the advanced position which you have taken up, and you will be down in one-third of the time. You will find in the supposed case the descent of a falling Church regulated by the laws which accelerate the descent of other falling bodies, and fearfully increasing its rapidity in the succeeding periods. Nor will the Earl of Aberdeen be able to protect or support you. He will be wholly unable to protect or support himself. Yield to his counsels, and timorously retreat,—give up the cause of the people,—and *you* will go down first, and he will follow you. Continue to occupy the Thermopylæ in which you have taken up your position, and both may be saved. Your place is not a new one to the venerated ministers and elders of the much-loved Church of our fathers; but never, perhaps, at any period, did so much depend on their decision as now depends on yours.

Supposing, however, that there should be no revulsion of feeling on the part of the people,—supposing that they should at once sit down under the disappointment as quietly and passively as if all their present excitement was merely simulated,—how would Lord Aberdeen's measure operate in their behalf? We all know the kind of acquirements which enabled the intrusionists of the last and the present century to pass through the sort of vestibule formed by presbyteries into the body of the Church: a little tolerable Latin, and a little somewhat less tolerable Greek; the general smattering of learning which enables clever young men to write indifferent sense in middling bad English, and justifies their high opinion of themselves; and, withal, that acquaintance with theology which implies a sort of half-knowledge of doctrines which they do not like, and which they cannot understand. Add to all this a degree of character which no police court in the kingdom would be able to impugn, and we have before us the qualifications of an accomplished licentiate prepared for ordination, an ornament to his order, and fitted, according to the estimate of Moderate presbyteries, to carry away the palm from Horsley. The people could neither love nor respect such a man, and by the more serious among them the less would he be loved and respected. Who that truly believes in the New Testament can think without concern of such a clergyman in connection with a parishioner anxiously awakened to inquire, with the jailer, "What shall I do to be saved?"—or without horror of him, associated with terrors awakened on a death-bed,—terrors regarding a future state of being, of which he knows nothing, and for which he cares as little? He is presented, however, by the patron; and these feelings on the part of the people, through which he is rendered unacceptable to them, are not permitted, by his lordship's provision, to weigh as anything. There is not a more definite assertion in his whole speech than that the mere unacceptableness of a presentee should be held no disqualification. The people must render their reasons. To affirm that in their consciences they believe the presentee unsuited to edify them, is not stating a reason; it is merely expressing a belief,—merely emitting such a declaration as the one required by the veto act. But, even permitting it to stand as a reason, what weight would the suspended ministers of Strathbogie attach to it if urged by the parishioners of Marnoch against Mr. Edwards? or into what else would it resolve itself, if carried before the higher courts, than into mere unacceptableness? The "sheep know the voice of the good shepherd, and him they follow;" but they will not follow a stranger. Why? Because, believing him to be a stranger, he is unacceptable to them. Even supposing our Church courts disposed at the present time to receive as legitimate almost any objections, and to act upon them, what guarantee have the people that this spirit is to continue? "Good is ever strongest at its beginning," says Bacon; "evil ever strongest in continuance." The one exists only through unceasing effort; the other gathers strength and grows up of itself. We remark, further, that we could not think very highly of even the honesty of men who, when deciding cases on unconfessed and disallowed grounds, could yet hypocritically urge that they decided them on grounds of an entirely different kind. If unacceptableness is not to be recognized as a legitimate cause of rejection, we would ill like to see it made an actual cause, and some unsolid and paltry shadow of objection employed to screen it, meanwhile, as a sort of stalking-horse. Let the Church of Scotland walk in unsullied integrity, as becomes her character,—her motives and her actions alike open to the eye of day.

No one could have anticipated, when she took up her present position, the length to which matters were to be carried against her. Doubts were perhaps entertained whether her hold of the secularities might not possibly be loosened by an enforcement of the principle of the veto; but could even the shrewdest have imagined that she was to be inhibited from preaching the gospel? It was perhaps deemed possible that the civil power might attempt pouncing on her temporalities, but it was not deemed possible that the civil power would attempt jostling her aside from her own proper place among things spiritual. She has been exposed to unlooked-for trouble. The tempest has been unexpectedly severe; and mariners are sometimes content in such circumstances to return for shelter to the port which they have quitted. But what might be safety to them would be destruction to her. The heavily freighted and laboring vessel of the Church must not return. There is security in the haven to which she is bound. On the open sea, too, there is comparative safety, let the storm rage as it may; but inevitable shipwreck awaits her if she turn her prow towards the shore which she has left.

THE SCOTCH PEOPLE AND THE PRESBYTERIAN CHURCH.

The people of Scotland have had many compliments paid them, — some on the score of intelligence, some on the score of conduct; and that portion of them on whom, according to Wordsworth, "the Church has laid the strong hand of her purity," has been ever held to comprise, in the true, not the aristocratic sense of the term, their "better classes." The numerous body of whom the Cottar of Burns and the Peddler of "The Excursion" may be regarded as samples and specimens, are invariably to be found in communion with either the Established Church, or some one or other of the several branches of Evangelical Dissenters which have sprung from her. Who ever heard of an intelligent Scotch Papist rising from among the people? or where are even the Burnses and Tannahills that represent the Scottish peasants and artisans of Episcopacy? The national type is decidedly Presbyterian in its intelligence, and still more decidedly so in its worth and its religion; and if we but strike off the Presbyterian catechumens and communicants of the country from the general mass, — the men either in full communion with the Church or her auxiliaries, or in the course of preparation for such a union, — we leave behind merely a *caput mortuum* of inert ignorance and superstition, or of fierce and reckless, and, in most instances, quite as ignorant infidelity. The class to which the Church is at present struggling to extend those privileges which so many of her saints and martyrs contended to secure to them, includes, in at least the proportion of nineteen twentieths, the worth, the religion, and the intelligence of the country.

On an estimate such as this have the non-intrusionists of the Church founded the measure for the integrity of which they are now called to suffer and resist. Were the estimate different, the measure would also be different. Cases may easily be imagined in which the popular voice would be a very improper element in the choice or rejection of a Christian minister. An entire people may sink into infidelity, as was the case with the French people during the first Revolution; or they may lie sunk in a state of gross and savage paganism, as is the case at present with the great bulk of the inhabitants of New Zealand. Consult the choice of the one class — the more civilized one — regarding religion or its teachers, and they trick out for themselves a painted prostitute in the spangled gauds of the opera-house, and, after dignifying her with the name of the Goddess of Reason, they prostrate themselves before her in simulated worship; or, more fantastic and more horrid still, they exhume the mouldering remains of the perished apostles of infidelity, and burn incense before the insensate and ghastly skulls. Consult the choice of the other class, and they seek out for themselves their native priests to assist them in their human sacrifices. In both these instances Christianity is compelled to act on a different principle, — the principle on which the apostles acted, — not within the Church, but in their efforts to extend the Church. The missionary principle is the only one which applies to the exigencies of such cases, and the people are not asked to choose their teachers, but entreated to listen to the teachers which have been sent to them. It is only when a Christian body have been formed into a Church, as was the case when Knox drew up his First Book of Discipline, that the principle now contended for can come into operation; and it is in the well-founded belief that our parochial communicants form such a body,—that all of them are members of the Church of Scotland,—that very many of them are members of the Church of Christ,—that they have a deeper stake in the appointment of their ministers than ministers themselves can possibly possess in their collective character,—that it is a duty demanded of them individually to "try the spirits, whether they be of God,"—that to this solemn injunction they are qualified to conform by Him who has laid it upon them;—it is, we assert, in this belief that our Church courts are now struggling to secure to the Christian people a directing voice in the appointment of their pastors. If they but believed, on the contrary, that these very people were "a brute insensate herd," an "irresponsible, unreasonable" mob, they would never once think of introducing among them such a principle. They contend for their privileges, as those of a Christian people in full communion with a Christian Church.

To the great bulk of our readers all this will seem sufficiently plain and obvious. They have all heard, and many of them have known from experience, of the general intelligence of the Presbyterian people of Scotland. Rarely do very superior men rise from among very ignorant masses. It was a Scotch ploughman that described the "Cottar's Saturday Night;" it was a Scotch shepherd that produced the "Queen's Wake;" it was a Scotch stone-cutter that wrote the "Lives of the British Painters, Sculptors, and Architects;" it was a Scotch weaver that bequeathed to America its "Ornithology;" it was a Scotch mechanician who invented the steam-engine; it was a Scotch herd-boy who first explored the hitherto misunderstood phenomena of the phases of the moon; it was a Scotch mason who planned the great Caledonian Canal, and threw the bridge over the Menai. Now, from no "brute herd" could such men have arisen. The classes that look down upon the people as irrational have not yet produced better samples. Our readers are also aware of the religious character of our better Presbyterian people. They are aware, too, that though Milton rightly describes hypocrisy as the "vice which walks unseen," it is not the less true that there is a religious sympathy which draws the good together, and through whose revulsions and antipathies unconverted and secular-minded men are very soon discovered to be such. They are aware, in short, that pious laymen are as thoroughly qualified to choose out for themselves pious, religious teachers, or to detect those who are not so, as the general imperfection and infirmity of judgment which cling to our fallen nature, and which insinuate their mixture of error into all human affairs, allow us to predicate of qualification in any case.

MODERATISM POPULAR, WHERE AND WHY.

There is a smart paragraph taking the round of our Scotch newspapers, descriptive of a recent settlement in a northern parish. A vacancy occurred, through the death of the incumbent, and the parishioners were presented by the patron with a leet of four, two of whom were Moderates, and two of the opposite party. Means, it is stated, were taken by some of the friends of the latter to influence their choice. The Moderates were men of a genial temperament, and the people were told so. One of them, it was urged, was fond of fiddling. "He will be the more useful at weddings," said the people. Nor has he any abhorrence, it was added, of whisky punch. "Nor we either," said the people; "we will go all the oftener to see him." In short, Moderatism triumphed on the principle alluded to by the poet, that "laymen have leave to dance if parsons play." The "fiddling priest" was preferred by a sweeping majority; and the fact is adduced by our contemporaries, either to show that Evangelism is struggling to emancipate the people to its own hurt, or that, in some cases at least, parishes choose well. We take the story as we find it, with certainly no proof that it is true, but as certainly with no suspicion that it is false; for we have seen quite enough of Scotland and its people to know that there are tracts of country in which incidents of the same nature might readily enough occur. We are acquainted with at least one district in the far north in which it had become a popular saying, at a time when smuggling was more common than it is at present, "Give us but a good-natured exciseman, and it matters little whether you give us a minister or no."

One of the great evils of Moderatism is its tendency to extirpate religion altogether. It is no doubt a bad state of matters when dissent is rendered inevitable in a religious parish by the tyranny of a forced settlement; and it is surely grievous to see the better people of the Church forced reluctantly, by congregations at a time, beyond her pale. But there may be a much worse state of matters than this. It is better that there should be religion in a parish, however harshly or cruelly it may be dealt with, than that there should be none; and there are parishes in Scotland, though the number fortunately is not great, where, through the indifference and the irreligion of the people, there can be no forced settlements and no dissent. We resided for some time in a parish of this character about sixteen years ago. It lies to the south of Edinburgh; and the parishioners, who were numerous at the time, were divided, by the accumulation of capital in the hands of a few, and the prevalence of the large farm system, into two extreme classes, — a class on the low level of the common laborer, which constituted the great bulk of the population, and a class, comprising some thirty or forty individuals and their families, who occupied a place in society rather higher than the middle one. Moderatism had been entrenched in the parish pulpit for well-nigh a century, and Moderatism in its most respectable form. It had neither lived grossly nor taught heresy. It had done no mischief; it had done merely nothing; and, instead of perverting, it had only suppressed the truth. The incumbent, at the period to which we refer, was an indolent, elderly, respectable man, rather dull than otherwise, who, having labored in his youth, had a sermon for every Sabbath in the year, and a few additional, and who very properly asserted in them all, and challenged scrutiny, that it was well to be virtuous, and not so well to be vicious, and that fanaticism was a sore evil. The upper class deemed him a sensible man, and heard his one sermon once a week; the lower had ceased attending church altogether; and in scarce any other district of Scotland have we found a less intelligent or a more irreligious people. The respectable among them — for there are differences among all classes — passed the greater half of the Sabbath in their beds, rose to dinner, and, if the evening was fine, went sauntering about the fields; with the less respectable, Sabbath was a day of drunkenness and dissipation. It was impossible that a forced settlement could have taken place in the parish: there was not religion enough in it to suggest objections or nourish dissent. The people would have well-nigh as soon thought of challenging the right of one of their proprietors to his lands as the right of a presentee to his glebe and stipend; and had their choice been consulted in his nomination, a turn for fiddling and good fellowship would have been powerful recommendations. It affords us much pleasure to add, that a different state of matters is beginning to obtain in this forlorn parish from what obtained in it sixteen years ago. There is less immorality and less ignorance and apathy, and the poor people have learned to rise earlier on Sabbath, and to attend church. The old and highly respectable Moderate, after drawling through his last discourse, was succeeded by a clergyman who preaches Jesus Christ and him crucified;

and the class to whom the gospel was preached of old have gone to hear him. There could be such a thing as a forced settlement in the parish now, and a Secession chapel as a consequence.

The apathy and indifference to religion which obtain in only a few districts in Scotland are very extensively spread over the sister kingdom, and dissent, in consequence, does not very often originate in the Church from what we may term an internal principle. The hereditary Dissenter, fixed in one locality, withdraws occasionally a few individuals from out the inert mass, or, as in the days of Whitefield and Wesley, the itinerating Dissenter succeeds in founding, though rarely, a meeting-house among them on the missionary principle. We have been informed, however, by a person intimately acquainted with the subject, that the main, though, as we have said, a not very active cause of dissent in England (for there are at present no very active causes in operation) originates within, not without, the pale of the Church, and in exactly the same way in which, as we have shown, it sometimes originates in Scotland. An evangelical Churchman of the Scott or Newton stamp is appointed to a charge; the inert masses are aroused by those powerfully impressive doctrines of the gospel, fitted by Deity himself to agitate and awaken, and which, through the accompanying influence of the Spirit, render men wise unto salvation; a church-going and religious people are trained up under his ministry; and, after performing his work of usefulness, he is summoned to his reward, and passes away. A stranger succeeds him, whose voice the sheep do not know, and whom therefore they will not follow, — perhaps, according to Cowper, "a cassocked huntsman and a fiddling priest," — at least a person who, like our old pastor in the southern parish, neither knows the gospel nor cares for it, and who tells his poor hearers that it is good to be good, and bad to be bad, and wise to eschew fanaticism. Dissent is the inevitable consequence of such an appointment in such a parish; but who does not see that the cause is a mixed one, and that the Evangelism of the one preacher has as certainly led to it as the Moderatism of the other? Puseyism contends for what it terms the apostolic succession; and, as the question is mixed up with religion, men of sense try to avoid smiling at its amazing absurdity, except when they are not seen. But there is a real apostolic succession to which it is well to attend, and the neglect of which is injurious to the Church of England now, and has inflicted incalculable injury on the Church of Scotland in the past. The true apostolic succession was kept up when Thomas Scott succeeded John Newton; but it would have been woefully broken had he been succeeded by the Rev. Titus Oates or the Rev. Dr. Dodd. Nor would the imposition of the Bishop's hands have mended the matter in the least. Is our own Church in no danger of breaking the apostolic succession in a certain district, should the ministrations of the Commission's ministers come to be superseded there? The people two years ago might have chosen a minister for his skill in fiddling; but they would choose and reject on very different principles now.

There is a sufficiently obvious inference which we draw from the fact furnished us by our contemporaries. The best argument against slavery is deduced from the degradation of character which slavery induces. It brutalizes those whom it oppresses, and renders them unfit for liberty; but, so far from seeking for its apology in the abuses of slavery, and so far from arguing that it should be tolerated or maintained because it is so execrable as to affect not only the physical, but also the mental condition of men, we contend that it is those very abuses, and those most mischievous effects, which render it so intolerable. Did it affect only the bodies of the unfortunates subjected to it, the abolitionist would be less the benefactor of his species, and more on a level with the class whose benevolent exertions are restricted to the prevention of mere animal suffering. Now, it is with Moderatism as with slavery. The one first treats men as if they were unfit for liberty, and then renders them in reality unfit for it; the other first treats them as if they were unfit to exercise any influence in the appointment of their spiritual teachers, and then renders them unfit for it, by weaning out the religious feeling from among them, and the knowledge of religious truth. But where, in either case, does the remedy lie? In destroying the power of the slaveholder, and emancipating the slave; in removing the prop on which Moderatism has leant, and without which it must ultimately fall. In the one case we emancipate a slave unfit for freedom. Yes, but he will never be fitted for it in slavery. Set him free, and, as happened to the king of Babylon of old, the beast's heart will leave him, and the heart of the man return. In the other case we extend a privilege to people, some of whom are unfitted to exercise it aright. True; we are reminded of that by the very men who rendered them unfit. But the privilege is in very bad hands already. An unrestricted patronage gives ten inefficient Moderates to the Church, to darken the popular mind and paralyze the popular judgment, for every one that the people will give to it; and, though a few mistakes will be made in those hapless parishes in which Moderatism has been longest encamped, the truth will be gradually spreading around them; nor is it likely that they can long continue to reverse the miracle in Goshen, by remaining insulated districts of darkness walled by light.

THE EARL OF ABERDEEN *versus* THE PEOPLE OF SCOTLAND.

The Earl of Aberdeen has determined to press the second reading of his bill. The Church of Scotland has had many enemies to contend with, — the priest, the prelate, and the dragoon; Moderatism, Voluntaryism, the

Court of Session, and the author of an unreadable pamphlet. And yet it is the Church of Scotland still. We trust it is also destined to survive his lordship's measure. The reader has heard of an eagle "struck at and killed" by a "mousing owl," but such prodigies do not happen every day; and we can hope that that Church of Christ, and the people, which outlived a century and a half of fierce persecution and the bitter hostility of five succeeding monarchs, — two of them at least skilful in playing on double meanings, and one of them remarkable for making long speeches and unreadable books, — may also outlive the assaults of a diplomatist skilful in concealing his intentions by carefully selecting his words, and of a special pleader, always more successful in making his addresses long than his meaning plain. It will be foul shame and dishonor to the people of Scotland if they suffer the Church of their fathers to sink beneath men of a lower grade than even the subsidiary tools of the enemies and persecutors who arrayed themselves against her of old. Our ancestors would have little recked the enmity of Rothes and Mackenzie, had not the craft of the one and the sophistry of the other been backed by the malignant despotism of Charles.

It were well that the Presbyterian people of Scotland should consider how deeply their interests are involved in the present struggle. We address ourselves to them as one of themselves, — simply as one of the humbler people, come out a single step in advance in this quarrel to speak for the rest. We say, therefore, both for them and ourselves, that we have no other stake of equal importance and value with our stake in the Church. Toryism in its first elements, and regarded simply as feeling, does not, and cannot, constitute the politics of the common people; there are, alas! few among them easy enough in their present position and circumstances to have no desire of change; and what can be more natural than that men in the lower walks of society should solace themselves, amid obscurity and toil, with the well-grounded belief — a belief sanctioned alike by reason and revelation — that they are in no degree an inferior race of creatures to the men set in authority above them; that their minds, in many instances, are of no lower order, and that most certainly their immortal souls are of no lower value? And hence a natural Whiggism, which must ever exist in the lower levels, whether the name exists or no. We are not political in making the remark; we speak with no reference to party; we state merely a fact. In this whiggish feeling the politics of the people have their origin. The laboring man snatches at every semblance of reform, for reform promises to better his condition. But the experience of eight years has shown how little mere statesmanship can do for the masses. The men who labored twelve hours per day before the Reform Bill passed, labor twelve hours still; taxation does not press less heavily on the poor now than it did then; nor are the sufferings of the country less, nor has its crime diminished. Goldsmith was quite in the right when he asserted that little of the misery endured by mankind can be cured by either kings or laws. We would be unworthy of freedom were we to assert that there is no difference between the slave and the freeman, however sunk in poverty the freeman may be. There is a wide difference. The freeman may, and he often does, toil harder, and he may, and he often does, endure more. We ourselves have toiled as hard as any slave in the colonies, and for well-nigh as little — food and raiment. But in the midst of toil and of poverty the mind of the freeman grows, the intellect ripens, and the sentiments expand; whereas the mind of the slave shrivels and decays. It is chiefly with reference to the better part of man that the poor mechanics and laborers of Scotland are more advantageously circumstanced in the present day than the vassals of Poland or the serfs of Russia. In addressing ourselves to this class — the "men of handicraft and hard labor" — we say it is incomparably of more advantage that you should have a voice in the nomination of your parish minister, than of the men who represent in Parliament the districts to which you belong. Members of Parliament can do very little for you, and you are now beginning to discover that such is the case. Ministers, if truly men of God, can do a great deal. We speak to the experience of such of our humbler countrymen as believe in sincerity the truths which the Scriptures reveal. We say, freedom is valuable to you, not because you fare better in consequence of freedom, nor yet because you toil less: such is not the fact; — you do not fare better, — you do not toil less: it is valuable to you from the independence of mind which it cherishes. Slavery has meannesses and vices inseparable from it, from which you are exempted; and your circumstances, though narrow, need be accompanied by none of that narrowness of intellect almost associated with slavery. And if such be the case, — if your advantages be chiefly advantages of mind, — shall we deem lightly of what relates to the better portion of the mind, and which involves its concerns for eternity? You are not creatures of this world only. The God who, in his great munificence, bestowed upon you immortal souls, has revealed unto you their priceless value, and the only way, through the blood of a Redeemer, in which your salvation can be secured. And one of the chief means which he has appointed for bringing you into that only way is the preaching of his word. Of how much importance is it, then, that the word be faithfully preached to you!

Now, under the influence of the system espoused by the Earl of Aberdeen, and which his measure has been framed to reëstablish, the people need not expect that the gospel will be faithfully preached to them. They have but to remember the past, in order to enable them to judge, in this respect, of the future. They have but to look at the class of clergymen by whom his lordship's measure is so zealously advocated, in order to conceive what sort of a Church the body would form of themselves. The ultimate fate of the Earl of Aberdeen's bill will decide whether the patrimony of the Church is in reality to constitute, as was originally intended, the patrimony of the people, or whether, for somewhat less than half a generation, and ere it be thrown into the general fund, it is to be appropriated to the support of a corporation of time-serving clergymen, — a class of public stipendiaries of all others the most useless, and which the dictates of a wise economy would select first for suppression, in a course of financial reform. In what degree would Scotland be the better of a thousand empty churches, in which men ignorant of the gospel would, with their lifeless ministrations, desecrate the Sabbath for hire? It is impossible, in the nature of things, that the ministers of any religious establishment can be merely a harmless race. They must rank among either the benefactors or the enemies of a country; they must be as blessings or as curses to it. Our Saviour himself has declared that there can be no neutrality where religion is concerned, and that those who are not for him are against him. Nor need we appeal to history to show that the mere priest — the mere creature of patronage, the mere tool of power — has been ever an enemy of the general welfare and of popular improvement. The Church of Scotland must be either a great benefit or a great evil to the people; it must be — what Knox and the first fathers of the Reformation intended — a dispenser of benefits, moral and intellectual, — a nurse of knowledge, of virtue, and religion; or it must bear as a nightmare on the energies of the country, until at length the popular indignation gather strength and shake it off. It is well that the people of Scotland should know that these alternatives are involved in the adoption or rejection of the Earl of Aberdeen's bill. The future history of the Church cannot resemble its history in the past century. It must inevitably either sink into a lower depth of inefficiency, or rise into a more general and extended usefulness; and it is well that the people of Scotland should consider how necessary a result this must prove of the fate of his lordship's bill.

In the last century the two antagonist parties of the Church were spread over her parishes like the wheat and the tares in the one field. An inefficient and time-serving clergy were in many instances the near neighbors of ministers conscientiously faithful and eminently useful. The policy of our ecclesiastical courts was unequivocally bad, because our majorities were so; but in many a parish and in many a district were the true objects of the Church accomplished, and the true interests of the people pursued, through the influence of a devout and diligent minority. But there are two causes which must effectually operate in preventing any return to such a state of things in the future. The old Presbyterian party in the Church have taught the patrons and the patronage-assertors of Scotland — men such as the Earl of Aberdeen — a lesson which they will not soon forget. They have taught them that so essentially popular is Presbyterianism in its original integrity, that it is impossible for it to acquire power without directly militating against the abuse of unrestricted patronage; and their influence, therefore, will be exercised in carefully excluding it. What more natural than that for the future the patron should present to the people's hurt, — not to his own? or that he should introduce exclusively into the Church members of the party whose very existence is bound up in patronage, and who, with the instinct of self-preservation, would compass sea and land to preserve it in its unbroken malignity? But the second cause craves more serious thought, as it regards a more urgent danger. What is to become of our present majority? England saw two thousand of her Presbyterian clergy ejected from their livings and their churches in one day, and there were several hundreds of surely our best ministers ousted about the same time from the parishes of Scotland. Are our countrymen of the present age prepared for witnessing a similar exercise of power on the part of either the Court of Session or the House of Lords? Are they prepared to give up the men whose sole crime it is that they have stood up to assert in the people's behalf, agreeably to our original standards, that no minister be "obtruded into any church contrary to the will of the congregation"? Are they prepared to give up the Church itself? For what is the Church, apart from its better ministers, but a piece of dead framework of importance to the hirelings who derive from it a provision for themselves and their families, but of no value whatever to the people? Or do they think that our more devout and more excellent clergymen, in the face of their solemn professions, will learn to accommodate their consciences to the provisions of Lord Aberdeen's bill, and proceed forthwith, in union with the Dr. Cooks and Dr. Bryces of the Church, to force the Youngs and Edwardses of Auchterarder and Marnoch on the reclaiming people? Assuredly the poor man's main stake is involved in this quarrel. It would be the duty and the interest of the people of Scotland heartily to oppose his lordship did he merely set himself to rescind the Reform Bill. It has not done much for the poorer people. Legislation can neither lighten their toils, nor make them happier under them; but at least some of the moral effects of the bill have been good. It has brought public opinion to bear against many abuses. It brought it to bear on the abolition of the slave-trade, and led to a great act of national justice in the final emancipation of the slave. But were the Earl of Aberdeen to blot the Reform Bill out of the statute-book, he would inflict but a slight and trivial injury on the people of Scotland, compared with the injury which he now contemplates.

That people possess a power in the present day which they did not possess in the days of Sir George Mackenzie, nor yet in the days of Bolingbroke. We are told that, shortly after the Union, the Scotch representatives found themselves entirely lost among the Commons of England, who opposed them in every national question, in the proportion of nearly ten to one. But they soon discovered a remedy. The English were divided into two great and nearly equally balanced parties; and though the forty-five Scots formed a very poor minority of themselves, they found that whatever side they chose to range themselves upon became straightway the majority. They discovered that they could adjust the scales, though they could not outweigh even the lightest of them; and they became influential in consequence. Parties in the present day are more equally balanced than they were in the days of Queen Anne; and it were well for Scotchmen to consider whether it be not their duty to give that prominence to the interests of their country now which their ancestors did a hundred and twenty years ago. Questions of the first magnitude should always have the first place assigned to them; and it is of immensely more importance to even the Conservative Presbyterians of Scotland that the Earl of Aberdeen's measure should be defeated, than that the Earl of Aberdeen should form the member of a new cabinet. Our contemporary the *Globe* has a pertinent remark on the subject: "We have not a particle of doubt," says this able paper, "in affirming that the spiritual independence of the Scottish Church, and the efficiency of the will of the Scottish people, are things the fate of which politicians have not to determine, and which determine the fate of politicians."

DEBATE IN THE EDINBURGH PRESBYTERY ON LORD ABERDEEN'S BILL.

In the debate which Mr. Miller described in the following article, the bill by which Lord Aberdeen had essayed to terminate the agitation in the Church of Scotland fell under the logic and sarcasm of Dr. Cunningham. His lordship saw fit to withdraw his measure. — Ed.

The present struggle threatens to be a protracted one. But there is no lack of symptoms on the part of both the friends and the opponents of the popular principle, which indicate the final result. Our readers will find a full report in our columns of the proceedings of the Edinburgh Presbytery at its meeting of Wednesday last. The chief business of the meeting arose out of the present position of the Church in connection with the attempt of the Earl of Aberdeen to convert into law the mischievous absurdities of the Dean of Faculty [Hope]; and the decision arrived at by the presbytery, by an overpowering majority, and after a discussion of six hours, was to petition Parliament against his lordship's bill, as directly subversive of the spiritual independence of the Church, and wholly at variance with the genius of Presbytery. No report, however literal, can convey an adequate idea of a debate so animated and interesting as that which took place on this occasion. There is a vast difference between a series of speeches spread over a few closely-printed columns, and a spirit-stirring *viva voce* discussion; but our report must be very defective indeed if it does not convey the impression of strength contending with weakness, and show that there was much feebleness and much timidity on the one side, and much courage and great power on the other. The cause, backed by the decision of our law courts, and by a considerable portion of the wealth and a large proportion of the aristocracy of the country, must ultimately go down, for there is no heart and no strength in it.

We fain wish we could give our readers at a distance some such idea of the late meeting of presbytery as we ourselves have had an opportunity of forming. The Presbytery of Edinburgh is the most ancient in the kingdom. It may be regarded as the nucleus of the Scottish Church. According to Knox, "before that there was any public face of the true religion in this realm, it had pleased God to illuminate the hearts of many private persons, who, straightway quitting the idolatry of Papistry, began to assemble themselves together." They elected out of their number good and judicious men, such as "God by his grace" had best qualified for their elders and teachers; and from this small beginning, principally within the town of Edinburgh, arose the Presbyterian Church of Scotland. There is nothing to mark the antiquity of the presbytery in the hall in which they assemble. It is a modern erection, lighted from above, with a few portraits suspended on the walls, and a bust or two placed on brackets. There is a gallery for strangers, of limits all too scanty on occasions such as that of Wednesday last, and the members occupy the area below. From a front seat, which we were fortunate enough to secure, we could overlook the whole. The parties, instead of being ranged on opposite sides, were mixed up together, and apparently for a very excellent reason — the non-intrusionists were all too numerous, and their opponents too few. The original Presbyterians bid fair to fill all their own house, as at first; and if Moderatism insists on retaining its own side, it must proceed forthwith, as in the days of Gillespie, to eject and expel.

Some of the better known names in the presbytery are borne by men of very striking appearance. Dr. Muir is an eminently handsome man — thin, gentlemanly, dignified, tastefully dressed, with a well-formed head of moderate size, such as a phrenologist would expect to find on the shoulders of a person rather of fine taste than of comprehensive genius. We would have deemed him quite in his proper place in the Upper House of Parliament, either as a lord spiritual or lay. Dr. Gordon is also a strikingly handsome man, but with a much more remarkable development of head. It is a head of the Melancthon type, — high, erect, with an overpowering superstructure of sentiment on a narrow base of propensity, and a forehead rising, as in the case of Shakspeare and Sir Walter Scott, to the top of the coronal region. Combe, in one of his phrenological works, give a print of a similar head, and states that among the heads of many thousand criminals which he has examined, he had in no instance found a resembling development. If, however, the Earl of Aberdeen carry his measure, prisons will be quite the place to find them in, and the phrenologist will require to modify his statement by a note. Among the figures of the younger members of the court, that of Mr. Guthrie is one of the most striking. He is an erect, lathy, muscular man, of rather more than six feet two inches, who would evidently not have been idle at Drumclog, and who, if employed at all, could not be employed other than formidably. Though apparently under forty, the hair is slightly touched with gray, and the features, though beyond comparison more handsome than those of his ancestor the martyr, bear decidedly a similar cast and expression. The appearance and figure of Mr. Cunningham is scarcely less striking than that of his friend Mr. Guthrie. He is tall, but not so tall, though rather above than below six feet, and powerfully built. His head is apparently of the largest size, — of the *nemo me impune lacessit* calibre; and the temperament is of that firm bilious cast which gives to size its fullest effect.

Mr. Cunningham commenced the debate in a speech of tremendous power. The elements were various: a clear logic, at once severely nice and popular; an unhesitating readiness of language, select and forcible, and well fitted to express every minuter shade of meaning, but plain, and devoid of figure; above all, an extent of erudition, and an acquaintance with Church history, that, in every instance in which the argument turned on a matter of fact, seemed to render opposition hopeless. But what gave peculiar emphasis to the whole was what we shall venture to term the propelling power of the mind, — that animal energy which seems to act the part of the moving power in the mechanism of intellect, — which gives force to action and depth to the tones of the voice, and impresses the hearer with an idea of immense momentum. There were parts of Mr. Cunningham's speech in which he reminded us of

Andrew Melville when he put down bishops Barlow and Bancraft, and shook the lawn sleeves of the latter; and we could not help wishing that, by any possibility, circumstances should be so ordered as to afford him an opportunity of trying conclusions face to face with the Earl of Aberdeen. His powers of sarcasm are great, and of a peculiar character. He first places some important fact or argument in so clear a light that there remains no possibility of arriving at more than one conclusion regarding it. He then sets in close juxtaposition to it the absurd inference or crooked misstatement of an antagonist, and bestows upon his ignorance or his absurdity the plain and simple name. White is always white with Mr. Cunningham, and black black, and he finds no shade of gray in either. His confidence in matter of fact, based on an extent of erudition recognized by all, tells with a crippling effect on his opponents. He referred, during his speech, to the often-repeated sophism denying the non-intrusion of the early reformers — Knox, Calvin, and Beza. What, he asked, do the Earls of Aberdeen and Dalhousie know of the opinions of these men? This much, and no more. Lord Medwyn inserted in his speech on the Auchterarder case a few partial and garbled extracts from the writings of Calvin and Beza, which, in their broken and unconnected state, seemed to bear a meaning at variance with the principles which the men in reality held. Mr. Robertson, of Ellon, quoted the passages at second-hand, not omitting even the errors of his lordship's printer. The Earls of Dalhousie and Aberdeen quoted them at third-hand from Mr. Robertson. And such is the entire extent of their lordships' information on the subject, and such the amount of their authority. He then proceeded to show what the views of the reformers on non-intrusion really were;—that they all held, with the ancient fathers, the doctrine for which the Church is now contending. "There is no member of this presbytery," he added, "who will question the fact." And he was quite in the right; no member did question it.

He offered to prove, further, that Dr. Muir, on the agitated question, holds exactly the principles of Cardinal Bellarmine; and the Doctor took particular care not to demand the proof.

Mr. Cunningham was followed by the Lord Provost of Edinburgh, — a gentleman who has been a reformer all his life long, and who evidently feels that, in the present struggle, he is occupying exactly his old ground. He was listened to with much respect. His remarks were characterized by a vein of sound good sense and much gentlemanly feeling. Dr. Muir then rose to express his approbation of the Earl of Aberdeen's bill.

How, we asked, when listening to the powerful logic of Mr. Cunningham, will Dr. Muir contrive to find answers to arguments such as these? We might have spared ourselves the query. Dr. Muir did not attempt finding answers to them. He spoke as if no one had spoken before him. He reiterated all his old assertions, and assured the meeting that he was thoroughly conscientious and quite in earnest. Pascal could mortify his senses by shutting his casement on a delightful prospect. Dr. Muir restrains the reasoning faculty in the same way out of a sense of duty, and eschews argument as a gross temptation. When convicted of an absurdity, he talks of persecution, and clings to an exposed misstatement with the devotedness of a faithful nature true to a friend in distress. He carries on every occasion all his facts and all his opinions home with him. Nothing adds to their number, — nothing diminishes them; and when the day of battle comes, he brings them out with him again. His troops fight none the worse for being killed; they rise, all gory, like Falstaff's opponents, and fight by the hour; his antagonists complain, with Macbeth, that his dead men come to "push them from their stools."

He was followed by Mr. Penny — a smart gentleman, who is tedious with very marked effect — on the same side, and succeeds, when he is particularly pathetic, in making his audience gay. He was liberal in tendering to the presbytery the benefit of his law, and generously advised them to submit to the Court of Session, without cherishing the remotest expectation of being paid for his advice. He excels, too, in divinity. His speech gradually rose into a sermon; and when he came to the most serious part of it, the gallery laughed. He was succeeded, in reply, by the Rev. Mr. Begg, of Liberton.

Of all the gentlemen whom the caricaturists have failed in rendering ridiculous, Mr. Begg has escaped best. Some of the others are striking likenesses. There is no likeness in the case of Mr. Begg. There is no exaggeration of feature or figure for the artist to catch, and so he has caught none. He is a young, good-looking man, rather above the middle size, with a well-developed forehead, — frank, vigorous, and energetic. His brief speech contained one or two pointed hits, which told with excellent effect, and a historical statement of much importance in its bearing on the Earl of Aberdeen's bill.

He was succeeded by the Rev. Mr. M'Farlane. We are admirers of the good sense and poetical feeling, but not of the style, of Harvey; whereas the Rev. Mr. M'Farlane seems to admire only his style. He rounds his sentences after the same model, and leaves out only the poetry and the good sense. His flowers are all sun-flowers. Pliny speaks of an orator who used to set his periods to music: we are convinced that, if Mr. M'Farlane were well watched, he would be found modulating *his* periods by the full symphonies of the Jewsharp. All feel, however, that when delivered in public they want their necessary and original accompaniment; and we think the reverend gentleman should benefit by the hint. A respectable and sensible man, a Seceder, sat beside us. "Ah," he exclaimed, with a groan, "a weak brother!" The Rev. Mr. Bennie followed, in a sparkling, witty speech, that at once awakened the gallery, and cost the moderator a considerable amount of trouble. All was extempore: there was not one idea which did not bear reference to some previous remark from the opposite side, and yet every sentence had the point of an epigram. The labored dullnesses of an inane and feeble mind have rarely been more pointedly contrasted with the spontaneous felicities of a mind singularly ingenuous and fertile than on this occasion. Drs. Clason and Gordon followed in addresses, brief, but of great moral weight, and conceived in an admirable spirit; and the whole was wound up by Mr. Cunningham.

Nothing more tended to the spread of the Reformation than the public disputations between the reformers and their opponents. There was breadth of principle and force of argument on the one side, united to generous feeling and conscious integrity; and merely sophistry, meanness, misstatement, and the disreputable shifts of a petty ingenuity, on the other. On every occasion on which they met, the better cause prevailed; and the people saw and felt that it did. Good argument is always popular argument. If Dr. Muir and his friends really wish well to the people of Scotland, they could still hold by their peculiar opinions, and yet be of great service to them. All that is necessary is to grant their opponents such opportunities of meeting with them in the various parishes of the country as they afforded them at the meeting of the Edinburgh Presbytery on Wednesday last.

REVIVAL IN ALNESS.

The Moderate and Evangelical parties, differing in their views of Church government, differed also, throughout the whole course of their history, in their cast of sentiment touching the religious life. The one, pushing the supernatural element in Christianity gently into the background, and seeking no more, by way of realizing the Christian character, than a general observance of moral precept, a polite tranquillity of feeling, and a cultured elegance and propriety, recoiled in timorous suspicion from all religious emotion, sudden in occurrence and transcendent in degree. The other, throwing the supernatural element into commanding prominence, explicitly declaring the exertion of Divine and creative energy indispensable in the formation of Christian character, regarded every agitation of the popular mind arising from a religious cause with that deep, reverent, and sympathizing interest which befitted a direct manifestation of Divine power. This, like every other distinction between the parties, was vividly apprehended and profoundly understood by Mr. Miller. It is brought out in the following article. "Dr. Muir's Declaration," to which reference is made, can be easily imagined as a manifesto on the part of certain of the Moderate leaders. — Ed.

We extract the following interesting notice of one of the recent revivals in Ross-shire, from the *Inverness Courier* of Wednesday last. It comes from the pen of a correspondent of that paper, — a person who seems to have witnessed what he describes in no light or irreverent spirit; and we have been favored with several private letters on the subject from the same part of the country, which corroborate his statements:

"The great religious movements which are taking place in various quarters of this county are drawing a large share of attention; and a short account of what has occurred in the parish of Alness may not be uninteresting to some of your readers.

"The usual fast-day preparatory to the celebration of the Lord's Supper was held on Thursday, the 30th ultimo; but nothing remarkable was observed on that day. The first symptoms of anything like an awakening made their appearance on the Friday evening, when, under the ministrations of that faithful and self-denying servant of God, the Rev. Mr. Macdonald, of Ferintosh, a considerable number were brought under concern, and made to cry out, beneath the stings of an awakened conscience, 'What must we do to be saved?' During the sermon which completed the duties of the sacramental Sabbath, the movements in the congregation, which had been begun on the Friday evening, were increased to a much greater extent. Then, but more especially on the services of the following day

(Monday), one could not cast his eyes around in any direction among the thousands collected on the occasion, without witnessing in almost every half dozen of hearers one, if not more, deeply moved,—some sobbing audibly; others, evidently by the greatest effort, restraining themselves from bursting out aloud; while many, utterly unable to command their emotions, gave vent in loud screams to their agonized feelings. Nor was this confined to any age or sex. The young and the aged, the gray-headed man and the child of tender years, might everywhere be observed deeply affected; and we conceive we are within the mark when we say, that on this occasion many hundreds were brought under serious impressions; for there is scarcely a family in the district but has one, two, or more of its members under deep convictions. It was truly a heart-stirring sight; and we could wish that those who make a mock of such scenes could have looked upon it. Insensible to every good and holy feeling must he have been who could have beheld it with cold indifference.

"When witnessing or hearing of such events, one is irresistibly led to ask, Is this the work of the Spirit of God? Though time alone can give a *perfectly* satisfactory answer to this question, yet there are circumstances attending this particular work which tend to show that it is indeed genuine, and not spurious. This revival has followed the means which the word of God teaches to employ. Prayer-meetings have for some time been established through the parish by the faithful and zealous clergyman, Mr. Flyter, who has now had the satisfaction of seeing his labors blessed and his supplications answered. There was nothing in the instrument which could lead us to attribute the result to him. He is well known to all who heard him; and his style of preaching is as familiar to most of them as is that of their own clergymen; and he has been often known to proclaim the thunders of Sinai with as much, if not with greater force, on previous occasions. Indeed, the terrors of the law and the consolations of the gospel were, as they ever ought to be, blended together."

We passed a few days during the summers of the last two years in the scene of the revival. It is a semi-Highland district of considerable extent, bordered by the Frith of Cromarty on the south, and ascending, towards the north, from a richly variegated and comparatively populous level, into a mountainous and thinly-inhabited tract of country. The whole forms a portion of what has been termed the land of the Monroes, — a clan described by Buchanan as one of the most warlike in Scotland, and which, unlike most of our Highland clans, embraced, at an early period, the doctrines of the Reformation. The name has since been widely spread. It gave to Gustavus Adolphus some of his bravest general officers, and to the United States of America one of their best presidents. But though now considerably mixed with other names, through the breaking up of the feudal system, it still abounds in the district. The people in general are a simple, but not unintelligent race, and warmly attached, through the associations of nearly three centuries, to the Church of Scotland. There is a hollow still shown among the hills, where their ancestors used to meet for religious worship during the persecution of Charles II. Their minister of that period had been amongst the faithful few who, in the northern portion of the kingdom, had chosen rather to quit their livings than outrage their consciences; and, despite the utmost efforts of the Bishop of Ross, — as thorough an Erastian as Dr. Bryce himself, — he succeeded in finding protection among his people for nearly thirteen years after the term of his ejectment. In the year 1675, says Wodrow, he celebrated the communion on the borders of his parish, amid an immense concourse; and "so plentiful was the effusion of the Spirit, that the oldest Christians present never witnessed the like." Among many others, says the historian, one poor man, who had gone to hear him merely out of curiosity, was so affected, that when some of his neighbors blamed him for his temerity, and told him that the bishop would punish him for it by taking away his horse and cow, he assured them that in such a cause he was content to lose not merely all his worldly goods, but his head also. Eventually, however, the good minister fell into the hands of his enemies, and, after wearing out many years, amid squalor and wretchedness, in a dungeon of the Bass, he was released but to die — a victim to the cruel hardships to which he had been subjected. The parish at a later period, under the ministry of the author of an admirable Treatise on Justification, well known to theologians (Mr. Fraser, of Alness), was the scene of a second revival. It took place sometime about the middle of the last century; nor had its effects wholly disappeared at the time of our last visit. The district had still its race of patriarchal worthies, though every year was lessening their number, for the greater part of them had reached the extreme verge of life. There was, besides, a hereditary respect and reverence among the people in general for the beliefs and the services of religion. They remembered their fathers — the lives which they had lived, and the hope in which they had died; and the recollection had its legitimate influence. It has been common with skeptics of a low order — men who absurdly borrowed their analogies more from the principles of human jurisprudence than from the inevitable laws of nature — to challenge the great truth of revelation, so often exemplified in the history of nations and of families, that the iniquities of the ancestors are visited on the descendants. And yet we see in a thousand instances that, from the very nature of things (another name for the will of Deity), the law must as certainly exist as the law of gravitation itself. The corresponding truth embodied in the same commandment, that blessings and mercies are conferred on thousands among the posterity of the faithful and the devoted, has been less marked and seldomer challenged; but it is, like the other, a truth often confirmed by experience, and in no cases more frequently than in cases of revivals. Where the Divine fire has been kindled of old, it seems ever readiest, though often after long intervals, to ascend anew; and the cause, so far as such things can be accounted for on understood principles, seems to be the one just hinted at in the case of the parishioners of Alness. There survive in such localities fond and respectful recollections of the worth of the departed, associated with what we may term a traditional belief in the excellence of Christianity; and thus the mind is kept more open to receive as good what their ancestors proved and testified to be emphatically so.

We visited Alness, on the last occasion, early in the May of 1839, when the excellent clergyman of the parish was on the eve of setting out for the General Assembly. The Auchterarder case had been just decided in the House of Lords, and the present difficulties of the Church were very generally anticipated by the graver parishioners. There was a deep interest excited in this remote district. Dr. M'Crie, in writing of the General Assembly seven years ago, laments the indifference with which its meetings had come to be regarded by the people, compared with the deep interest which their fathers had felt in them. "Where," he asks, "is the general anxiety of the country, and where the fervent supplications for the countenance and direction of Heaven, in the deliberations of the Assembly, which were wont to resound from the most distant glens and mountains of Scotland?" We could have instanced at least one district. The "*men*" of Alness, at the time of our visit, were holding their prayer-meetings in behalf of the Church; and we need hardly say on which side their minister came to register his vote. Moderatism has disturbed the country with its forced settlements, but it never yet excited the spleen of a newspaper press by its revivals, and it always flourishes most where there are no prayer-meetings to perplex its operations.

We perceive the minister of an adjacent parish has affixed his name to Dr. Muir's declaration,—a circumstance which has enabled his parishioners fully to understand it. This gentleman has been now about four and twenty years in the enjoyment of the temporalities of the cure. When obtruded upon the parish, it contained no Dissenters. The people, like their neighbors, were marked by their church-going habits; and the church, a roomy and commodious building, was filled every Sunday from gable to gable.

About one per cent. of the parishioners attend it now. Within the last few years a meeting-house has sprung up in its neighborhood. Some of the younger people during the time of divine service wander into the fields; the rest, who have not quitted the Church, travel far to attend the ministrations of the clergymen of other parishes. The whole congregation did not comprise twenty persons when we heard sermon under the intrusionist about a twelvemonth ago, and of these nearly one-half had fallen asleep ere the middle of the service. And such, as instanced in Alness and this unfortunate parish, are the comparative merits and comparative popularity of the two parties in the Church. Would Sir Robert Peel and the Earl of Aberdeen deem it a stroke of profound statesmanship to pass a measure which would have the effect of ejecting from their charges men such as the minister of Alness, and of setting men such as his neighbor in their place? And yet there is scarce a Presbyterian in Scotland so ignorant as not to know that such would be the effect of the bill which the one so unwillingly relinquished, and which the other would have supported so readily.

The Rev. Mr. M'Donald, of Ferintosh, whose labors have been so signally honored in the recent revivals in Ross-shire, has been long known and esteemed in that part of the country as one of the soundest and most zealous divines in the Church. How marvellously have times changed within the last twenty years! Little more than that period has elapsed since this gentleman was summoned to the bar of the General Assembly for preaching, in the Strathbogie and Aberdeen districts, exactly the same doctrines which have been rendered so powerful to alarm and awaken within the last few months in Tarbat, Tain, and Alness. He had been guilty of preaching the gospel where, in these days, the gospel was very rarely heard. Dr. Mearns, of Aberdeen, another of Dr. Muir's supporters, took the lead among his assailants; but, notwithstanding all the energy and zeal of the party, the case unaccountably broke down, and

Mr. M'Donald was discharged unharmed. His assailants, however, contrived to legislate on the subject by way of prevention, and embodied their decision in the shape of a declaration, denouncing it as "irregular and unconstitutional for a minister of the Church to perform divine service in the meeting-house of a Dissenter, or, during his journeys from place to place, in the open air, in other parishes than his own." We find a masterly review of the whole case, by Dr. Andrew Thomson, in the "Christian Instructor" for 1819; and rarely has irreligion and intolerance, when masquerading under the forms of an ecclesiastical decision, been more powerfully exposed. The Doctor had to battle in the minority in these days, and to endure many a defeat; but his labors were not in vain. He did not influence his opponents, for that would have required something more than argument,—something on their part as well as on his,—candor, perhaps, and Christian principle; but the country listened to him; and so extensive and so marked has been the change, that the very individual whom he then defended against the wrath of the Presbytery of Strathbogie was empowered by the Church last spring to do in that district what he then narrowly escaped being thrust out of the Church for doing. Mr. M'Donald, of Ferintosh, was one of the ministers lately deputed by the Commission to preach in Strathbogie.

There is much comfort in the reflection, that in the time of the Church's difficulties her adorable Head should be thus manifesting himself in her favor. It will matter little who may be among her enemies if he rank among her friends. The Book of Providence contains many difficult passages; but there are others of which the meaning seems comparatively obvious; and of these not a few refer to periods of revival in the Church. The time of the second Reformation was one of these. The purpose of mercy at that period extended to more than individuals,—it embraced the entire Church. There was a season of severe and protracted trial at hand; and the infusion of new vigor gave earnest that the "strength was to be according to the need," and that she was to survive the struggle, and ultimately to triumph in it. Had she been destined to extinction, her vigor would not have been increased. Another very remarkable period of revival occurred in the west of Scotland shortly after the time of the Secession. The Church had sunk into a state of miserable depression. Her strength seemed passing wholly from her to the body of devout and venerable men whom the high-handed majorities that constituted at once her weakness and her shame had thrust beyond her pale; her people were joining them in thousands; and it seemed as if the mere *caput mortuum* that remained behind could not long continue to exist. The breath of public opinion in less than half an age would have acquired strength enough to sweep it away; for, though an Establishment has existed in Ireland without the people for centuries, it could not exist in Scotland without them for half a century. The characters of the two nations are essentially different. At this crisis, however, the separation to a considerable degree was staid. The revival at Cambuslang, Kilsyth, Kirkintilloch, and Muthill, took place. There was thus proof vouchsafed that, though many of God's people had left the Church, God himself had not left it; and, in consequence, thousands who would have otherwise gone over to the Secession remained in her communion. Chatham, as quoted by Junius, could speak of infusing a new portion of health into the constitution of the country, to enable it to bear its infirmities. There was thus a new portion of health infused into the Church, and she was enabled to bear the infirmities under which she would otherwise have sunk, until a day when, with invigorated powers, she has begun to shake them off. The history of the future can alone read the legitimate comment on the economy of Providence in the present revivals; but who can doubt that they are tokens of mercy? They read a lesson to religious Dissenters which they would do well to ponder in connection with the advice given by Gamaliel to the Jewish Council. If God be for us, assuredly they should not be against us.

CONSERVATISM ON REVIVALS.

"My friend Smart," said Johnson, "used to show the disturbance of his mind by falling upon his knees and saying his prayers in the street. He was deemed mad, sir; and yet, rationally speaking, it is much greater madness not to pray at all, than to pray as poor Smart did; though I am afraid there are so many who do not pray, that, through the generality of the neglect, people never think of calling their understandings in question." Now, what was strong sound sense in the days of Johnson is very excellent sense still. If a man look exclusively to the approbation of his neighbors, it is very unsafe for him to deviate from the ordinary course, and quite as much so to rise above the common level of conduct as to sink beneath it. There is a mediocrity of virtue which it is dangerous to exceed, and a subdued style of religion, "content to dwell in decencies forever," to which men who are often loudest in their praise of toleration extend their tolerance exclusively. The Judaism of Gamaliel would have been esteemed by this class as the well-regulated religion of a man of sense; the overpowering convictions of Paul, after his journey to Damascus, they would have denounced as fanaticism. They deem the form of Christianity which can exist independently of conversion a much better thing than the Christianity which conversion must precede; and regard the man whom the sense of an awful futurity never moved as a wiser person than the man whom it moves so deeply that he proves unable to conceal his feelings.

Now, to the unrecked madness of this class — the class whose number, according to Johnson, prevents people from calling their understandings in question — does the recent work of revival in Scotland owe the opposition which it has received, and the contumely which has been heaped upon it. The myriads of which the class is composed have been startled from their propriety by discovering that the principle which was potent enough to overpower the jailer of old, and to compel him to cry aloud in anguish and uncertainty, should have lost none of its energy since, and that it operates on the human mind now after exactly the same fashion that it operated then. An attenuated and shrivelled form of Christianity had become one of the decencies of society, and men took praise to themselves for treating it with good manners. Religion had sunk into a respectable mediocrity, and had become, therefore, a fit subject for being not only tolerated, but recommended, by the class who would have extended neither recommendation nor tolerance to its Author. We remarked on a former occasion that the natural principle of admiring or enduring only the mediocrity of virtue was exemplified on Calvary with a peculiar force and emphasis, of which the history of the universe can afford no other instance, by showing that it was as fatal to rise infinitely above as to sink greatly below the medium and average line. The world could tolerate neither our Saviour nor the two thieves, and it therefore crucified both him and them. And Christianity in Scotland no sooner begins to resemble its Master, than the men who tolerated, and even admired it in its state of tame and inefficient mediocrity, turn round to spit and revile, and, in short, to treat it exactly as they would have treated Him. We speak, of course, of only its more respectable enemies, the mediocritists, — the men who, though they would have crucified our Saviour, would have crucified the thieves also. We do not speak of the men who, like some of our contemporaries, would have accomplished only half the work, by suffering the malefactors to escape.

Among the more respectable class we rank a Liverpool

conservative journal, to which our attention has just been called,—a strenuous advocate of Protestantism in Ireland, and of Church extension on the Episcopalian basis. This paper collects its facts from the *Aberdeen Herald*, and decides unhesitatingly, on the evidence furnished, that the "proceedings" at Rosskeen must have been at least "unseemly, if not blasphemous;" and expresses a wish that the leaders in the Church should exert themselves "to prevent, or at least restrain, such outbreakings of ignorant fanaticism." Now, with the *Aberdeen Herald* we have no controversy. We believe the ingenious editor advocates the substitution of a knowledge qualification for the existing property qualification,—unquestionably in the sincere and honest hope of furnishing the country with a more liberal and efficient constituency. We understand, too, that he excludes all religious knowledge from his scheme, in the natural and not very blamable fear of being himself deprived of the franchise through the exercise of his own test. Some of the remarks of the Liverpool conservative, however, we shall take the liberty of examining:

"We cherish the most sincere regard for the Church of Scotland, and wish to see her shine in the pure and chastening light of other and worthier days; but it is impossible to witness such proceedings without experiencing feelings of the deepest regret and alarm. We should not perhaps have noticed this affair at Rosskeen at all, had we not been aware that any apology founded upon the obscurity of the place cannot be offered or pleaded by the Church; for it is not many months since our attention was drawn to similar scenes in the vicinity of Glasgow, which several otherwise estimable clergymen of the Establishment endeavored to justify. We allude to the fanatical follies perpetrated at Kilsyth, and defended by the Rev. Mr. Burns and other ministers, who ought to know better, and entertain more elevated views of religion."

Now, this passage was written by a gentleman who professes to believe in the thirty-nine articles, who denounces the anti-scriptural policy of the present ministry, deprecates the spread of Popery, laments over the decline of Protestantism in Ireland, and advocates the extension of the English Church. It is fraught with instruction. It is because the conservatives who can think and write in this manner are so numerous that the party are so inefficient, and that they so utterly belie their name. Why is it that Protestantism in the Episcopalian Church of Ireland should have seen, during a century and a half, the Roman Catholic population of the country doubling and quadrupling around it, without any corresponding increase in the limited number of its own adherents, — that, in brief, on this unhappy arena practical error should have proved a stronger principle than ostensible and theoretic truth? Simply because the practical error had a principle of vitality in it, — that it was a vigorous and powerful superstition, — and that the nominal faith opposed to it wanted life and vigor. Dead forms of truth cannot contend with living principles, be the principles as base or erroneous as they may. Living Socialism is an overmatch for dead Christianity. Now, one of the grand errors of what we have termed the mediocritists in religion — a class that still hold nineteen-twentieths of the patronages of the Church, and who have long overlaid its energies both in England and our own country — arises from their ignorance of this important, though surely simple, fact. They established a dead Protestantism in Ireland, and yet calculated on its strength as living truth. They patronized an inefficient Moderatism in Scotland as a rational and modified form of Christianity, and held that, as it was in the main a very excellent and sensible thing, with no fanaticism in it, the masses would straightway submit their passions to its government. And now, a numerous body of the same class, though with, we trust, a mixture of good and wise men among them, are employed in extending their Church — trusting, doubtless, through a religion which eschews revivals, to absorb dissent and annihilate Chartism. Would that they were more intimately acquainted with the laws which regulate antagonist forces, and knew better how to calculate on their respective degrees of power! There is more strength in Chartism alone, weak and disreputable as it is, than in all the modified Christianity in England that scoffs at revivals. The man who writes as above of the work of revival in Ross-shire, — a work in which Episcopalians such as John Newton and Thomas Scott, or Archbishops Usher and Leighton, would have rejoiced to join, — can write as follows, and in the same column, of religious education:

"The Church appears to have thrown off the lethargy which temporizing and undecided legislation had brought upon her, and to have set herself to work, as far at least as this extensive diocese is concerned, for the regeneration of our deluded population, in right good earnest. There can be no doubt whatever on the minds of any persons who have given attention to the subject, that the instruction of the middle classes on religious principles has been lamentably neglected, or that dissent and infidelity have labored to sow their tares in ground predisposed to receive and nurture their vicious qualities. To this, in a great measure, may be ascribed the prevalence, in the present day, of Chartism, Socialism, Radicalism, and the other delusions of which the merely scientifically tutored is so frequently made the victim."

There is a moral chemistry in the ecclesiastical questions agitated in Scotland in the present day that is fast decomposing the old elements of party. How completely, for instance, does our first extract neutralize the effect of the second. Dugald Dalgetty was of opinion that "Protestantism" was a very respectable watchword when pay was good and quarters comfortable; but the confession betrayed the mercenary. Now, on a similar principle, the Conservative who wishes to render "religious education" an effective watchword for political purposes in Scotland, should avoid sneering at religious revivals. We find our contemporary mightily prefers the policy of Dr. Bryce in Church matters to the policy of Dr. Chalmers. His idea of religion seems to be, that it is a principle at once very pliant and very powerful, — a something for the Court of Session to control at will, but able to control everything else, however potent, — a moving power, that, like steam, can overthrow mountains, and yet be turned off by a stop-cock, — a Samson, feeble and irresistible by turns, that can be bound with green withes at one time, and set loose to rout an embattled host at another. A word in his ear. If the stop-cock be able to turn it off, the mountain will never be levelled by it. If the green withes bind it, the Philistines have nothing to fear from it. The religion represented by the Moderatism of Scotland is a principle which would yield readily to the Court of Session; but there does not exist a single antagonist power to which it would not yield as readily. It is a principle destined, not to control, but to be controlled.

We have oftener than once expressed our thorough confidence in the work of revival in Ross-shire. We are acquainted with the ministers engaged in it, the style and manner of their preaching, and the doctrines which have been rendered effectual in its production; and we are assured a time is yet coming when many of its present enemies will be content to speak of it in a different tone. There is a numerous class who can more than tolerate religion in its reflection, though they may hate it heartily in its real presence, — who can admire it when it becomes the theme of poetry, or is embodied in a classic literature, but not before, — who deem family worship a very excellent thing in the stanzas of the "Cottar's Saturday Night," and Christianity a noble principle in the pages of Cowper. Now, to such men religion appears good in its reflex influences, though not in itself; and to such the scene of the revival will present appearances in the future more in accordance with their taste and fancy than those which it exhibits at present. The effects of a similar revival in the district, which took place in the early half of the last century, were felt in it for more than eighty years after.

There were few dwellings, however humble, in which, regularly as the day rose and set, family worship was not kept; and in the course of an evening walk the voice of psalms might be heard from almost every hamlet. There was a higher tone of morals among the inhabitants than in many localities at least as generally favored; more content, too, with not less privation; — no Chartism, no Socialism, no infidelity. The people, in short, were what the statesmen termed a "well-conditioned people." Effects such as these should render even the utilitarian tolerant of revivals; and why not also the *litterateur?* They have to wait only a very little.

THE OUTRAGE AT MARNOCH.

The instalment of Mr. Edwards in the temporalities of Marnoch took place on Thursday last, and proved the occasion of a scene without precedent in the history of the Church of Scotland. On many former occasions have the forms of religion been prostituted to serve very vile purposes. On many occasions has the disguise of profession proved all too flimsy to cover the meanness of the objects which it has been assumed to conceal. But on no former occasion has the prostitution been equally public, or the utter inadequacy of the disguise rendered palpable in the same degree to a circle equally extensive. To the profanation at Marnoch the eyes of an entire community have been directed, and the consequences which it involves affect the religious interests of a whole kingdom.

A heavy snow-storm had burst out on the preceding Wednesday; and on the morning of Thursday the country round Marnoch was deeply enveloped in snow. Huge wreaths of drift had choked up every road and pathway, and the stream which sweeps past the manse and church-yard was toiling, brown and swollen, through the half-melted accumulations that in some places arched it over from bank to bank, and in others had sunk undermined into the torrent. It was no day for journeying pleasantly, or even safely; but the interest of the people of the neighboring parishes had been deeply excited in behalf of their poor neighbors, and hundreds might be seen wending over the heights in all directions in lines of six or eight,—some robust man in each party breaking a way through the snow for the rest. Before eleven o'clock a crowd had gathered round the church, sufficient almost to have filled it twice over. There were individuals present from Keith, from Huntly, from Banff, from Portsoy;—all the parishes for miles round had sent out their spectators; and, assuredly, the spectacle which on that occasion they witnessed will never be effaced from their memories. Mr. Edwards and his friends arrived before noon; and, after commencing the business of the day, with singular appropriateness, by breaking into the manse through a window, they moved on to the church. In a few seconds the building was crowded almost to suffocation. The parishioners ranged themselves in the body of the edifice; the strangers occupied the galleries, and clustered in dense masses outside the windows and doors; a few Edinburgh lawyers were seated in a pew in the centre; and—curiously enough—the reporter of an Intrusion newspaper in the pulpit. One of the suspended clergymen opened the proceedings by prayer; and the words took the form of an address to Deity, but they were listened to merely as the necessary adjuncts of an act of outrageous injustice and oppression; and yet, strange as it may seem, the attention of the audience proved all the more deep in consequence of the estimate. Every phrase employed seemed to gather new meaning from its utter inappropriateness; and, impressed through the force of contrast, the dead commonplaces of a lifeless devotion seemed starting into frightful activity through the influence of a spirit of possession. When the form was over, and the gentleman had sat down, an elder of the parish rose, and demanded of him, for himself and his fellow-parishioners, by what authority he and his brethren had met there. Mark the reply! "By the authority," he said, "of the National Church, and in the name of the Lord Jesus Christ!" A shudder ran through the meeting. It was again demanded of the suspended clergymen, on the part of the people, in whose name, and in what capacity, they had met there; and the gentleman who had opened by prayer reiterated his assertion, and with similar effect as before. It was demanded of them whether their appearance was sanctioned by the authority of the General Assembly, or made in direct opposition to that authority; and the question met with no reply. The people declined to sist themselves at the bar of what they could not regard as a court either civil or ecclesiastical, and read, by their agent, a solemn protest to that effect, in which, deprecating the great wickedness and tyranny about to be inflicted upon them, and the gross mockery of justice and desecration of religion which its forms involved, they stated that, before a competent and lawful presbytery, they were prepared to prove objections to the life, qualifications, and doctrine of the obnoxious presentee, sufficient not only to preclude his admission into the Church, but even to justify his deposition if previously admitted. But what weight could be allowed to statements such as these by men whose very appearance in that place was a trespass? The protest was read; and the people, gathering up their Bibles from the pews, rose in a body, and quitted the church. There were old gray-headed men among them, who had worshipped within its walls for more than half a century,— men, too, in the vigorous prime of manhood,—others just entering on the stage of active life. All rose, and all went away,—many of them in tears. It was the church in which, Sabbath after Sabbath, their fathers had met to worship; it had formed the centre of many a solemn association, many a sacred attraction; and they were now quitting it forever. Even the "buyers and sellers in the house of God"—the men to whom persecution is business—seemed awed and impressed for the time. "Will they all go?" they were heard to whisper. Yes, all went; the pews were emptied from gable to gable. The sacred and the civil may be mixed up and confounded in idea by courts and individuals; but it has been ordained by God himself that their natures should keep them apart. No secular power on earth can impose a *minister* on a people. The control of judges and magistrates affect, as in this remarkable case, the temporalities only. The experiment has been tried; and our readers may see the case of conflicting jurisdictions virtually decided by the extent and degree to which the Court of Session can give a clergyman to the parishioners of Marnoch. And it is well to remember that to secure a result so disastrous—to verify the same ruinous experiment on an immensely larger scale—has the Earl of Aberdeen been struggling to legislate for the people of Scotland.

The parishioners, after quitting the church, held a brief but impressive meeting in a hollow at the foot of the hill on which the edifice has been erected. The day was still dreary, and the snow lay thick and white around them. And in that snowy hollow, oppressed by a sense of the grievous outrage to which they had been subjected, but more in grief than in anger, they expressed their settled determination never, by word or act, to recognize as their minister the man to whom the patrimony of their church had been adjudged, and to adhere to one another in all their future efforts for obtaining redress of the wrong; and then, separating in silence, they returned by different routes to their respective homes. The church meanwhile had become a scene of tumult and confusion. The strangers outside had rushed into the body of the building when the parishioners had quitted it, and had begun to express their sense of the sacredness of the service by shouts and hisses, and the flinging of missiles. Assuredly the secular party may read their future fortunes in the incident, should the same wretched success attend them in the present struggle on a large scale that has attended them in the parish of Marnoch. Miserable, in such an event, would their fate prove: the surges of popular indignation would rise and overwhelm them; and who, among the millions of the empire, would raise an arm in their defence? A magistrate entered the church in the midst of the tumult,—a man much respected in the district,—and succeeded in restoring order. He had no sympathy with the representatives of the civil court in the profanation in which they were engaged. No one could be more hostile to the settlement of Edwards; and hence, in no small degree, through his influence with the people on that account, his ability of protecting the miserable objects of their hatred and contempt. An incident at this stage brought out very strikingly how entirely the parishioners had left the church. An individual present complained to the magistrate, who is himself a parishioner, that the Marnoch people had taken as active a part in the riot as any of the rest. He was asked, in turn, where these Marnoch people were, and succeeded in pointing out a young man in one of the galleries,—the only parishioner present,—who stated, when questioned, that he had taken no part whatever in the disturbance, and was only there because he could not get out through the crowd. There was a passage immediately cleared for him; and thus, ere the actual work of intrusion began, the last parishioner present was enabled to leave the church.

In these circumstances the ordination proceeded. The bellman of a neighboring parish officiated as precentor; there were prayers repeated, in which God was named, that the stipend of Marnoch might be appropriated to the support of Edwards; and the preacher argued, in his discourse, that the men through whose agency he was thrust upon the people should be accounted ministers of Christ! Never, surely, on any former occasion, did arguments tell with more wretched effect. Ministers of Christ! It was unnecessary to ask from whom they had derived their authority; the business of the day read a too unequivocal comment on the question, and answered it too surely. Mr. Edwards stood up in that crowded assembly. He declared, with all the solemnity of an oath, that he would subject himself to the superior judicatories of the Church, and seek earnestly to maintain her unity and peace, whatsoever troubles or persecutions might arise. He affirmed, in the hearing of all, that zeal for the honor of God, love to Jesus Christ, and desire of saving souls, had been his great motives and chief inducements to enter into the functions of the holy ministry, and not worldly designs or interests of any kind. He asserted that he had used no undue methods, either of himself or through others, in procuring his call to the parish. What call? He promised, too, that, through Divine grace, he would perform among the people all the duties of a faithful minister of the gospel. Every eye was turned upon him, and there was no longer any disposition evinced to hiss or hoot. Even the more volatile portion of the audience were tamed into sobriety and seriousness for the time. A deep shudder again ran through the assembly. The mummery proceeded. There were hands laid upon his head; and he became a minister of Christ in the sense understood by the men through whom his vocation was conferred. It is customary for an acceptable minister on such occasions to receive the hearty welcome of his people at one of the doors of the church. But no such welcome awaited on Mr. Edwards. Mr. Peterkin, of Edinburgh, the legal agent of the suspended clergy, wished him much joy; Mr. Robertson, of the *Aberdeen Constitutional*, and Mr. Adam, of the *Aberdeen Herald*, shook hands with him as they hurried past to assert the popularity of Intrusion; a captain of police in attendance took his arm to escort him through the crowd; and, as he turned his back on the desecrated edifice, the assembled hundreds hissed him from the door. And such are the more striking particulars of an event destined to occupy a prominent place in the history of the Church of Scotland.

It is unnecessary to offer a single remark on the subject. The lessons which it inculcates almost every one may read. Religion is the business of time for eternity; and without an all-pervading conviction of its importance, and a deep-seated belief in the reality of its objects, life passes unblessed by its influences, and death comes uncheered by its hopes. It comprises the arts of living well and of dying safely; and it lives and breathes in an element of faith. But not only must there be an all-pervading belief in its objects, but also in the honesty, sincerity, spirituality of its messengers. They must be regarded as *sent;* and it is with this vital element of belief that the civil or the secular cannot interfere. Where is there a power on earth that can inspire the people of Marnoch with confidence in the character of the man who must henceforth walk in shame and dishonor among them, and bear, as if in scorn, the name of their pastor? Through what form or process are the dying to be led to long for his presence at their bedsides, or to wish for an interest in his prayers? Through what influences are men awakened to anxiety for their spiritual state to be brought to ask counsel or guidance of him? Can the civil court stretch out its arm in the matter, and be as God between this man and the people? It has already done its utmost, and the deplorable scene of Thursday last has been the result. The country, we reiterate, may see in the case of Marnoch the true power of the Court of Session in the spiritual field. It may see, besides, the fate which awaits the Christian people and the National Church, if the secular element prevail in this eventful and surely most important struggle.

SUPPLEMENTARY NOTES OF THE SETTLEMENT AT MARNOCH.

Chesterfield has exemplified his ideas of indecency somewhat whimsically, by remarking that, though there may be nothing improper in dancing in a ball-room, it would be decidedly indecent to dance at church. He was in the right at least in referring to the church for the illustration. What would pass without remark in a place less solemn becomes coarse and indecent there. What would be simply business in a lawyer's office strikes as a gross impertinence in the house of prayer; and an air which might grace the jockeyism of Newmarket, would shock, when exhibited in the pulpit or the elder's pew, as impious and profane. The appearance of some of the suspended clergymen on the morning of the settlement seems to have happily exemplified the remark of Chesterfield. None of our readers can have forgotten the striking picture drawn by Chalmers of the "coarse and contemptuous clergymen, booted and spurred for riding commissions," who assisted in perpetrating the forced settlements of the last century, — men now gone down to dishonored graves, whose memories rot unburied in the recollection of the country, and whom even their successors in principle and policy deem it prudent to denounce and disown. Archbishop Beaton in his steel harness was comparatively respectable: he was a bold, though not an honest man. The booted and spurred clergymen drawn by Chalmers were as despicable as they were wicked. Now, it is curious to observe how closely the perpetrators of the forced settlement at Marnoch resembled, in externals at least, the abettors of forced settlements in the last age. They entered the church apparently in high spirits, — one dangling a thick, short riding-whip, another sporting a stout stick, excellently fitted for a market brawl. All had the air of men wonderfully well pleased, and quite aware that they were on the eve of doing something clever. Whips and sticks were laid on the pew before them, intermixed in grotesque confusion with sparsely written documents tied up in tape — decisions of court and opinions of counsel. Bibles somehow they seemed to have forgotten, or, perhaps, rather left designedly behind them, as mere bundles of *ex parte* documents on the other side. And there they sat, all looking smart, and waiting very knowingly till the people should sist themselves at their bar. Among them was Mr. Edwards, encircled by gentlemen of the law who hold by the theology of the Court of Session, and kindly regarded, too, by gentlemen of the press chiefly remarkable for holding by no theology at all. Like the young man sent by the sons of Eli with a flesh-fork to desecrate the sacrifice of the people, and to make men "abhor the offering of the Lord," he had come to take by force what without force the people would never have yielded him. The business of the morning went on. During the reading of the solemn and well-judged protest of the congregation, there were nods, and winks, and half-suppressed chuckles, among the party. The joke was by no means apparent. A man thoroughly convinced that the hundreds around him had all been born to immortality, and had all souls to be lost or saved, could hardly afford being merry on any such occasion; but it was certainly no conviction of the importance of man's destiny that had brought the party there. As for the joke, all our readers know that to occupy the chair of the scorner requires neither the perception of wit nor the peculiar inventive power in which wit originates. Men of wonderfully little sense or humor can sneer and make merry at whatever involves eternal interests, or concerns the cause of God.

Their merriment, however, received a check. A man may repeat a lie, it has been said, until at last he actually brings himself to believe it. Now, among the Intrusionists present there were not a few who had done more in the cause than barely work for their fee by drawing up papers and making speeches, — men who had busied themselves, into the bargain, in asserting in newspapers and magazines the popularity of their principles, and that the movement in the country was confined almost exclusively to a few clerical agitators. When, however, the people rose and left the church in a body, they were undeceived, and looked somewhat crest-fallen. Mr. Peterkin found that the author who writes *Columns for the Kirk* in the *Observer* had deceived him. Another legal gentleman present began to discover that he had been not a little misled by the statements in "Blackwood." The people are of some importance, after all; and we question whether a thousand Court-of-Session Mr. Edwardses, in the thousand manses of Scotland, would compose a Church that would come quite up to the idea of even the Lord President, or whether he would deem the body and members in such a case more than worthy of their secular and only head. The people all went away: the Intrusionists remained behind, chop-fallen and blank. The fate of the Earl of Aberdeen's intended measure was sealed by that act. His lordship has read it aright. It has taught him that there are things which lie beyond the reach of diplomacy; that he has misrepresented and calumniated the best and most revered men of his country to little purpose; and that it is one thing to lend a diminished and still sinking influence to the party under whose sway religion has ever sickened and pined away, and quite another to legislate for the people of Scotland. The tumult began, and the fears of the Intrusionists seem to have been very marked and very edifying. The disturbers are represented as merely a few thoughtless lads in the gallery, who took, unwarrantably enough, to the flinging of snow-pellets and the making of noises. Men of fortitude have borne as much without wincing; and the men of the court had brought both whips and sticks with them, on the principle, apparently, that made the Copper Captain gird himself with a long sword; but, too meek to fight, and not quite prepared for martyrdom, they sat cowering and shivering in the pew, staring at one another with pale and piteous faces, miserably afraid to remain where they were, but by far too frightened to rise and go away. The missiles flew thick and fast. The editor of the *Constitutional* seems to have taken a snowball, in his imminent terror, for a piece of flying seat; and a bit of a wandering cigar, which, if it came lighted, must have very much resembled a bombshell, seems to have struck utter astonishment to the inmost soul of the editor of the *Herald*. Both gentlemen, with the rest of the party, doubtless wished themselves at home. The noises continued, enlivened by an occasional snowball; business stuck fast, — so did the Intrusionists; and, as the afternoon began to close in, a shade of deeper anxiety and terror lengthened their faces, as they surmised the possibility of being left in the dark to the tender mercies of the urchins in the gallery. We are no advocates of violence or outrage; but we justify neither when we remark, that the party may estimate the weight of their religious character, and the degree of moral force which they possess, from this event. They but experienced the reflex influence of their own character coming back to them from the people. Our former remarks on this part of the subject have, we are happy to find, given great offence to the *Aberdeen Herald*, which has produced an article on the subject, chiefly remarkable — and we are serious when we say so — for the editor thanking God. Johnson expressed his pleasure on one occasion that his publisher should have grace enough to thank God for anything. We are far from sure in this case, however, that the unhappy northern editor, instead of breathing a prayer, is not mouthing an oath.

To proceed. Hope was well-nigh gone from the party, when a magistrate and an officer of police appeared. The snowballs and the noises ceased. Mr. Walker, of Huntly, who had borne up wonderfully in the time of terror, grew nervous at the sudden reverse; and forgetting, in his confusion of idea, that he was the Court of Session's minister, began to issue orders to the magistrate, instead of waiting to receive orders from him. His advisers, however, soon set him right. The magistrate, well knowing his place and his new powers, dictated to the officiating clergyman the length of his sermon; and he also, knowing his place, made it as short as he was bidden. There were some very remarkable passages in the discourse. It was seriously stated by the clergyman that the obnoxious presentee had "long set his heart on becoming minister of the parish; that the firmness with which he had pursued his object plainly showed him to be a man who could be daunted by no common difficulties, or turned aside by no considerations of labor or anxiety;" and that the "same firmness, perseverance, and zeal," which in this instance had rendered his aim successful, would now be directed in furthering, through extraordinary exertion, the spiritual interests of the people. It must be confessed the argument is singularly wide in its scope. If there be aught of solidity in it, then has the Church most to hope from her bitterest, keenest, most inveterate enemies. What may not Christianity owe to the activity of Robert Owen, or the zeal of the Jesuits? There must have been much of good to expect, on this principle, from the infidelity which in Paine, Hume, and Voltaire, so powerfully assailed religion with the pen. There must have been as much to expect from the Bonners, Beatons, Claverhouses, that pursued her with fire and the sword. Nay, if we are to ground our hopes exclusively on qualities such as firmness, perseverance, activity, and zeal, without taking into account the objects which they are exerted to secure, where shall we find created being more hopeful than that terrible Spirit of untiring energy, who, devoid of hope, defeated, miserable, and open to the eye of Omnipotence, never once slacks in his zeal or relinquishes his purpose? Another passage of the gentleman's discourse was more striking still. He alluded to the guilt of pastors who warn not the people. "The minister," he said, "who neglecteth to do this is not the people's pastor, but a *hireling, who careth not for the flock, but for the wages,—who scatters the flock, and drives them away from the fold;* and great is his guilt, and great will be his condemnation. He is an unjust steward; and woe will be to such a pastor." What wonder that the audience should have shuddered to hear truths so solemn delivered in circumstances that read upon them so striking a comment! The preacher finished his discourse; and, coming down from the pulpit, heard Mr. Edwards take upon him vows of equal solemnity, and then constituted him minister to Peter Taylor of Foggie-loan.

The parish of Marnoch is one of the most populous country parishes in the north of Scotland. The parishioners are a sober and industrious race of people, who have hitherto led quiet and peaceable lives, undisturbed by political agitation. But they are far from being an ignorant or unintelligent race. They partake largely, on the contrary, in the characteristic shrewdness of their better countrymen, and share deeply in the old Scottish predilection for theological study. Of one theological work no fewer than sixty copies have been sold in the parish; a Sabbath-school library, lately established among them, already contains two hundred and fifty volumes; and so deeply are they interested in the cause of the Church, that petitions in her behalf, asserting her spiritual independence, have received five hundred signatures among them in the course of a single day. There are men in the parish who have missed scarce a meeting of presbytery or synod since the proceedings which have obtruded Edwards upon them began,—one tradesman, in particular, whose interest in the case had led him to travel, mostly on foot, from church court to church court, not less than a thousand miles. And these people, under the reign of Moderatism, would have been lost to the Church. But we live in a better time. The guilt and folly of forced settlements attach no longer to our ecclesiastical courts. The minion of the Court of Session may fatten on the temporalities of Marnoch, but he forms no part of the Church of Scotland. It is he, not the people, who is severed from her communion.

SKETCHES OF THE GENERAL ASSEMBLY OF 1841.

PART FIRST. — OPENING OF THE ASSEMBLY.

THE General Assembly of the Church commenced its sittings on Thursday last. Perhaps on no former occasion was the preliminary pageant marked by a degree of splendor equally great. Royalty put on all its robes in the person of its representative, and summoned together all its attendants. The civic magistrate was there with his mace, the soldier with his sword; there was much show and glitter, — pages, and lackeys, and guards, and a long line of coaches, — antique insignia, that the same mental faculty to which we owe the metaphor and the allegory had devised ages ago, to symbolize the functions and authority of office; robes and liveries of uncouth splendor, — heirlooms of the same early period, and whose fantastic gayety, like the richly-tinted lichens of some ancient obelisk or mighty oak, seemed indicative of the vast antiquity of the institutions to which they had so long been attached; above all, immense multitudes of spectators thronging the streets far as the eye could reach, and which, forming of themselves by far the most imposing part of the spectacle, served also to show that the love of such pageantries lies all too firmly imbedded in man's nature for the utilitarian or the economist to dislodge or eradicate. Such were the components of the pageant; and the natural effect of the whole was to lead men's minds into the past. It was scarce possible to cast the eye along the glittering lines of bayonets stretching away in long perspective, or to mark the flashing sabres of the dragoons, without calling to recollection that both had been far differently employed for more than a century, and that Presbyterianism is now the established religion of Scotland, not because the state preferred it, but because, in opposition to kings and courts, backed by the civil magistrate and the military, the people preferred it, and held by it in distress and persecution, until at length, in the good providence of God, the oppressors were removed from their high places, to wear out life in beggary and exile, and what was so emphatically the national religion became perforce the recognized religion of the state. The mind wandered from the pageant of Thursday, with all its liveried pomp and solemn glitter, to a scene of lonely heaths, where, amid the graves of their slaughtered kindred, a persecuted people worshipped God agreeably to the dictates of conscience enlightened by his word, and where the mountain echoes, ever and anon awakened by shouts of mingled rage and exultation, or the patter of the deadly musket, told too surely that the murderous men-hunters were abroad.

The tone of the Assembly, as indicated by its first meeting, gave evidence that the privileges purchased at so mighty a cost by the ancestors will not readily be relinquished by their descendants. It is difficult to catch the traits of expression — if we may so speak — of a great assemblage animated by some powerful feeling. The preliminary pageant outside, like the fringe or the foldings of a robe, presented a comparatively easy subject for the pencil; one could have cut a model of it out of tin or pasteboard. The expression of the meeting within — resembling rather the features animated by the mind — can be less adequately described. Nothing, however, could be more obvious than what the expression conveyed. It bore, in all its traits, the stamp of earnestness and deep interest. The densely occupied galleries, with their "overbellying crowds," and where scarce an additional spectator could have found standing-room; the fixity of posture, with the general movement at every pause, both so indicative of fixity of attention; the universal "hush, hush," when the slightest noise in some over-crowded corner threatened to rob the audience of but a fragment of the debate; the oneness of direction in every face; the forward attitude; the hand raised to the ear,—all served to show how thoroughly men are beginning to appreciate the importance of our great ecclesiastical struggle. The well-filled area, too, thronged at so early a stage by well-nigh all the members of Assembly; the jealous and watchful care evinced at every step of the proceedings, lest a single hair's breadth should be inadvertently yielded up; the uncompromising character of the majority, growing in numbers and stern resolution as the opposition in high places thickens and darkens over them; the excitement, increasing as the debate proceeds, until at length the interest grows all too painful, and the hour of dismissal comes as a felt relief to even the most eager,—such were some of the more strongly-marked circumstances indicative of the temper of the Assembly, and by far too prominent to escape the notice of even the least observant. It is a significant fact that, in its first vote,—a vote involving the main principles of the contest in their most practical form,—the Assembly should have declared its determined adherence to its principles by a majority of two hundred and fifteen to a minority of eighty-five; for such, in the division pressed on Thursday, has been the overpowering majority against the motion of Dr. Cook that the commissions from what he termed the *minority* of the Presbytery of Strathbogie should not be received. We may remark in the passing that the negative character of his motion—the unwillingness it implied of presenting in a positive form the claims of the deposed—is not without its meaning. When the wild beast droops the eye it meditates a retreat; and there is evidently a drooping of the eye here. The intense interest felt in the proceedings of this Assembly — an interest which, for the present at least, seems to swallow up the consideration of all other concerns — bears reference, doubtless, to the important struggle in which the Church is engaged, and on the issue of which so much depends; but we cannot avoid the conclusion that there is another important cause in operation. The skeleton Assemblies of half a century ago — Assemblies composed of mere handfuls of members, and which but half excited the half-fledged curiosity of a few listless idlers, who came to yawn in the galleries, or to mark peculiarities of elocution or diversities of style — owed their unpopularity, not exclusively to the essentially unpopular character of Moderatism, but also to the skepticism of the age. A wide-spread indifferency affected all the churches of Europe. The desires and wishes of men restricted to the present scene of things expatiated so exclusively in the political field, — a miserable Eden, surely, possessed of no tree of life, and into which death and sin had entered, — that they sought none other; and, save to a chosen few, those hopes which, founding on the immortality of the soul and the revealed will of God, look far into the future, seemed mere hallucinations of a past state of things, whose unsolid character the intelligence of a practical age had at length succeeded in demonstrating. The case seems different now. The reaction in favor of belief has begun powerfully to operate in both false and true churches. Popery is evidently rising. Protestantism seems fast quitting the neutral ground it had so long occupied, by two opposite outlets, and aggregating its divided forces on opposite sides, — here advancing towards its original type, there precipitating itself full on Rome. The felt reference to the spiritual nature and future state of man exerts, as of old, its influence on human affairs. Ecclesiastical questions promise to be no longer subordinate to merely political ones; and the General Assembly of the Church of Scotland is felt, in consequence of this change, even by worldly men, to represent one of the greatest interests of the kingdom. It is only fifteen years since Canning, in his place in Parliament, predicted that the first war in Europe would be a war of opinion. It was of political opinion he spoke. He had watched the accumulation, and marked the evident direction, of that power which has since produced the revolutions of France and Belgium, and extended the franchise over Britain and Ireland. But the present is, above all others, a time of sudden change. The tide whose rise he marked has since fallen, leaving no inconsiderable mass of impurity and corruption behind it; and the current is now setting in full in an opposite direction. The political war is past, and the next great conflict of the world will be in all probability a conflict, not of secular, but of religious opinion.

It would be well to be prepared for it. There is no class of arguments which worldly men set aside with a feeling so ineffably contemptuous as the class derived from prophecy. There has been, no doubt, abuse in this province, as in all others; but it is the only province in which the sober and proper use has been denied in consequence. We shall venture to refer to it, notwithstanding the virtual prohibition. Many of our more judicious interpreters of prophecy are much in error if the Church be not entering, in the present time, on a period of protracted conflict, in which, though she may have to long often and vehemently for peace as a blessing, she shall have to contend for the right as a duty; nay, to struggle, perchance, for very existence. If such is to be the event, it would be surely well for "him that believeth not to make haste." If there is to be no "discharge in this war," let us look well to the posts in which the providence of God has placed us, and exert ourselves, in his strength, that they be maintained. Let us not desert them. Better to be in his battle than in quiet elsewhere. The evening will at length come, and we shall lay us down and be at rest. It is scarce possible to take a cool survey of the various stages of the present conflict, without being struck by a remarkable peculiarity in its character. Cowley, in one of his graver pindarics,—"The Ode to Destiny,"—describes a game of chess, in which the various figures seem to move of themselves along the board, with apparently no hand to guide them. He sees skilful and unlucky moves. A *pawn* rises to the top, and "becomes another thing and name." A *knight*, "that does bold wonders in the fray," amazes him with its success. He approves the gaining, censures the losing party,—admires their better moves, condemns the false and unfortunate ones. But the moves are not *theirs*. He raises his eyes from the board, and sees two shadowy figures bending over it, and propelling the pieces along the squares. And such, he exclaims, is the game of life.

> "With man, alas! no otherwise it proves,—
> An unseen hand makes all the moves:
> And some are great, and some are small,
> Some climb to good, some from good fortune fall;
> Some wise men, and some fools, we call,—
> Figures, alas! of speech, for Destiny plays us all."

Destiny is not the word: the Scriptures, and, from these, the Confessions and Catechisms of our Church, furnish us with a better. With this emendation, however, we have been often reminded of Cowley's seemingly extravagant fiction, during the course of the present controversy. "An unseen hand makes all the moves." The game has got very palpably beyond human management. But the event is in the hands of God. We cannot see it; we cannot see even the nearer moves; we can see only our duty. We can but see that in this quarrel we must assert the Headship of Christ and the rights of his people. And certainly, though the shore be dim and distant, the compass is true.

PART SECOND.—THE MODERATES.

We attempted in our last a brief—we are afraid rather inadequate—description of the opening ceremonies of the General Assembly, and the aspect of its first meeting. There are few things more tiresome than a speech from some nameless member at the close of a long debate, in which the superior men of the meeting or Assembly have already taken part, and of which the important and leading points have been fairly exhausted. And as articles on the merits of the questions discussed might seem, in connection with the very ample report given in our paper, but mere supernumerary speeches,—speeches of the kind which exercise, not the judgment, but the patience, and make men clamorous for the vote without in the least affecting it,—we shall rather attempt conveying to our readers some idea of the appearance of the Assembly, and of its leading men, than venture to solicit their attention to the subjects with which the Assembly has had to deal. It is not in the nature of the mind to be contented with the mere names of men, or the mere dry details of events. The imagination, even where least active, is ever engaged in drawing scenes and portraits; and hence the widely-spread popularity of that style of composition in which Bunyan and Scott were such masters,—the style in which narrative, reflection, and dialogue are blent, and relieved by description. It is, of all other styles, the best suited to satisfy, if we may so express ourselves, the cravings of the entire mind.

We stand fronting the Lord High Commissioner, a robust, handsome man of forty-nine, in a military uniform, and see the moderator seated immediately below, and the table of the House in front laden with books and papers. There are one or two men in lawyers' gowns beside it, with large bunches of gray horse-hair on the outsides of their head, and high notions of the Court of Session within. In the cases in which the countenance is smooth and youthful, there is to an unaccustomed eye something singularly ludicrous in a disguise so uncouth. It must, no doubt, have been deemed impressive some two or three centuries ago; but few in the present day will maintain that the horse's hair might not have been left in the horse's tail, and yet the learned gentlemen have looked none the less wise. A few leading men surround the table. The antagonist parties are ranged fronting each other, on the seats that rise on the opposite sides, or mingle together on those in front. Mark how very thin the ranks of Moderatism have become. They occupy merely a few of the nearer seats, forming, as it were, but a front lining to the wide vacuity behind. The party seems melting away, like icebergs in summer. There is, on the contrary, a dense, compact square on the opposite side, that stretches far under the gallery, and which is visibly adding to its numbers year after year. We restrict our sketches at present to the decaying party. Whatever else may be affirmed regarding them, it cannot be denied that they wear in general a very comfortable air. If it be persecution that is thinning their numbers, it must be of a kind under which the individual thrives, though the corporation perishes. In nine cases out of ten, they are, in the language of Wordsworth, "rosy men, right fair to see."

Observe, first, that elderly man seated at the foot of the table. The face, a strongly-marked one, seems indicative of shrewdness and self-possession. The features are somewhat of the Roman cast, except that the nose droops more over the upper lip than in the Roman type, and the cheeks are more pendulous and square, rather militating in their expression — which seems to speak of the languor and relaxation of advanced life — against the general cast of the countenance. The forehead is well and equally developed, but by no means very striking. The same remark applies to the coronal region, which is bald. There is no surplus amount of sentiment, if phrenology speak true, and certainly no marked defect. The head is rather a large one, but by no means of the largest calibre. He is rising to speak, and the general hush shows that the Assembly deem him a man deserving of being attentively listened to. Mark his figure: it is compact, well built, and of the middle size. Age has in no degree exaggerated the rather handsome outline; but we may discover its effects on the figure notwithstanding. He stands with equal weight on both legs, and the effect is that appearance of stiffness incident to advanced years, which painters remark as inevitable to the attitude. When standing, too, he uses a slender staff. There is nothing particularly emphatic in his mode of speaking. Nature never intended that he should be a great orator; the necessary depth of feeling and vigor of imagination were denied, and he seems to have known it; but shrewdness, self-possession, and good sense were given; and, availing himself of these to the full extent, he has rendered himself eminently skilful as a debater. He is thoroughly a man of business. Some of our readers must have already recognized in our description Dr. George Cook, ostensibly, if not in reality, the leader of the Moderate party, and unquestionably one of their ablest men.

The reputation of Dr. Cook is a mere shadow beyond the precincts of our ecclesiastical courts. So far from being a European reputation, it is not even a British one. He is the author of a very sensible History of the Scottish Church, which people do not read in Scotland, and which is not known elsewhere; and of a very respectable biography of Principal Hill, which gathers dust undisturbed in the shelves of our public libraries. The works of great authors make them a name; but in the case of Dr. Cook the process is reversed, — it is his celebrity as a Church leader that has made a name for his works. His historical volumes appeared at nearly the same time with the "Life of Knox," by Dr. M'Crie, and both works traverse nearly the same ground, and discuss the same principles. What have been their respective histories as literary undertakings, or what the comparative amount of influence which they have exerted on opinion? It is wholly unnecessary to answer the question; it is quite enough to ask it. The great historical genius has reared a monument to the fame of his country conspicuous over Europe, and whose pregnant record has been translated into well-nigh all her tongues. The man of respectable general talent who set himself to write history is himself a sort of finger-post, visible in a narrow area, by which we contrive to find out his work. The same character of obscure respectability attaches to his labors as Professor of Moral Philosophy in the University of St. Andrews. Is the fact questioned? If ill-founded, it can surely be easily met. What truths has he discovered? What new system has he invented? What old one has he invigorated? What fresh impulse has he given to the study of his science? What striking figure even, or happy illustration, has he originated? Who quotes his remarks? Who asserts his originality? There is but one answer — "None!" Dr. Cook is simply a man of good sense, conversant with tangibilities, — things that can be seen and handled, — but singularly ill-fitted to calculate regarding the invisible elements of power by which the tangible and the material are moved and governed. He is eminently a matter-of-fact man; but the balance by which he weighs is a balance of only one scale, and he overloads it with the temporal and the secular. Few men stand more in need of knowing, as a first principle, that the invisible may be without body, and yet not without weight.

Now, mark, beside the Doctor, a man of a very different appearance, — in stature not exceeding the middle size, but otherwise of such large proportions that they might serve a robust man of six feet. We read of ships of the line cut down to frigates, and of frigates cut down to gunboats. Here is a very large man cut down to the middle size; and, as if still further to exaggerate the figure, there is a considerable degree of obesity besides. Hence a very marked uncouthness of outline, with which the gestures correspond. But it is an uncouthness in which there is nothing ludicrous: it is an uncouthness associated evidently with power, as in the case of Churchill and Gibbon, or in the still better known case of Dr. Johnson. Mark the head. It is of large capacity,—one of the largest in the Assembly, perhaps, and of formidable development. The region of propensity is so ample that it gives to the back part of the head a semi-spherical form. The forehead is broad and perpendicular, but low, and partially hidden by a profusion of strong black hair, largely tinged with gray. The development of the coronal region is well-nigh concealed from the same cause; but, judging from the general flatness, it is inferior to that of either the posterior or anterior portions of the head. The features are not handsome; but, in their rudely-blocked massiveness, there are evident indications of coarse vigor. He speaks, and the voice seems as uncommon as the appearance of the man. There is a mixture of very deep and very shrill tones, and the effect is heightened still further by a strong northern accent; but it rings powerfully on the ear, and, in even the remoter galleries, not a single tone is lost. That man might address in the open air some eight or ten thousand persons. He is the very beau ideal of a vigorous democrat,—a popular leader, born for a time of tumults and commotions. Dr. Johnson threatened on one occasion to raise a mob; and no one acquainted with his indomitable force of character can doubt that Dr. Johnson could have done it, and that the mob would have looked up to him as their leader. The man we describe—if there be truth in natural signs, or if nature has written her mark with no wilful intention to deceive—could lead, and head a mob too. But where is conjecture carrying us? That uncouth, powerful-looking man, so fitted apparently for leading the masses broke loose, is the great friend and *confidant*, and, so far at least as argument and statement are concerned, the grand caterer, — flapper, as Gulliver would perhaps say, — of the tory Earls of Dalhousie, Haddington, and Aberdeen. If nature intended him for a popular leader, never surely was there an individual more sadly misplaced. We have before us the redoubtable Mr. Robertson, of Ellon, — the second name, and first man, of his party.

Mr. Robertson is a good illustration of what can be accomplished by sheer force of character. He is eminent in no one department of literature or science. His mind is as little elegant as his person. His style is cumbrous and heavy, unenlightened by fancy, or uninformed by philosophical principle. His range of fact is exceedingly narrow; his learning not above the average of country clergymen. He set himself to promulgate to the world, in a bulky pamphlet, the views on Non-Intrusion entertained by the early reformers; and, omitting entirely the previous step of first acquainting himself with what he professed to communicate, he drew his knowledge, as he wrote, from the speeches of the Lords of Session in the Auchterarder case, copying, all unwittingly, in his extracts, the very blunders of the printer as part of the text. He pronounced on the judgment of Calvin at a time when he only knew Calvin in the quotation of Lord Medwyn. And yet, though thus superficial and unaccomplished, with no name beyond the Scottish Church or the present controversy, Mr. Robertson is undoubtedly the natural head of his party, — the leader of the forlorn hope of Moderatism. He has character, courage, momentum, and unyielding firmness.

Observe, next, that elderly and yet active, young-looking man in the front seat. He is of the middle size, slightly but well made, and, for a Scotchman, singularly mercurial in all his motions. There is nothing remarkable in the form of the head or forehead, and the size certainly does not exceed the average, if, indeed, it does not fall much below it. The features would be handsome were it not for that singularly disagreeable *Voltaire-like* expression, —

quite enough of itself to mar the beauty of an Apollo. There is a fidgetiness about the figure, an apparent inability of sitting still, a sort of uneasy-conscience activity. The head jerks from the right to the left, and from the left to the right again. Never was there a more inveterate whisperer, or a more persevering smiler of smiles. Let fortune frown as it may, that man has always a smile in store, — we should perhaps rather say a silent laugh; but he would be a miserable physiognomist who could mistake his smiles for those of enjoyment or triumph. "These things are my diversion," said Pope to Richardson, pointing with a ghastly grin to one of the pamphlets with which he was ceaselessly annoyed. "These things are but my diversion." — "May Heaven preserve me!" ejaculated Richardson, as he quitted the room, "from diversion such as has been this day the lot of Pope." The smiles of the figure before us become contorted at times, like those witnessed by the guidsire of Wandering Willie amid the ghastly revellers in "Red-Gauntlet," when his very nails became blue with horror, and the marrow was chilled in his bones. The mercurial, smart, oldish-young man has risen to speak. His voice is clear, — so is his style; but, unlike the other two speakers, he succeeds in but a very faint degree indeed in attracting the attention of the House. There is a deplorable want of weight about him, both morally and intellectually; and the audience seem but to listen occasionally, to pick up from him extreme notions, obsolete for nearly the last quarter of a century, but curious as illustrative of the Moderatism of the last age. We have before us a Moderate of the extreme school, — a man true in all respects to the old character of his party, — Dr. James Bryce, of Calcutta.

There are amusing points about the Doctor's character; and of all the Church's opponents, he is perhaps the man whom the Church could worst afford to lose. The opposition of the others, however determined, is modified in its ostensible object, if not in its intensity, by the pressure from without. The Doctor's opposition is the unchanged opposition of the year 1796, so famous in the annals of the Church for its debate on missions. We have now before us the first literary production of Dr. Bryce, in the form of a volume of 380 pages,—a prize essay, entitled a "Sketch of British India." It was written to maintain that "to attempt diffusing Christianity in India by means of missionaries (we employ the Doctor's own words), would be a work not only fruitless in the issue, but dangerous to the peace and prosperity of that country, and ultimately fatal to the British empire in the East." This prize essay proved the foundation of the Doctor's fortunes. No danger to the interests of British commerce in Hindustan could be apprehended from a man holding such rational views; and so Dr. Bryce was sent out by the East India Company to represent Scottish Presbyterianism in Calcutta, and to eschew missions. Has the Doctor been since converted to other views? Why not, then, give the public at least one pamphlet that will read, in the form of a "true and faithful narrative of the conversion of the Rev. Dr. James Bryce"? It would form, surely, a very curious work in itself, and an interesting addition to Dr. Crichton's two-volume list of converts besides. Cowper speaks of his letters as the mere "shavings" of his mind,—things planed off and cast away. Few minds of the present day cast off more shavings than that of Dr. Bryce; but it is a mere deal-mind to the back. He published his prize essay in Scotland: it saw the light, and died. He preached newspaper paragraphs in India: they not only died themselves, but were well-nigh the means of killing others. He printed sermons, and accused Dr. Andrew Thomson of making money by reviewing them. Do any of our readers know anything of the sermons of Dr. Bryce? And now he is casting off shavings as lustily as ever on the Church question. The number, however, is no doubt exaggerated. Almost all the more absurdly Erastian pamphlets, which cannot be read even by the men who try, are attributed to the pen of Dr. Bryce.

The more notable men of the party are soon exhausted. Observe, a little to the Doctor's right, that tall, thin man, with the singularly grave cast of countenance, and the very long neck and face. We have described Mr. Robertson, of Ellon, as a large man cut down to the middle size. Here, on the contrary, we have a man of the middle size stretched out to a stature of some four or five inches more than nature seemed to have intended. It would appear, too, as if the elongating process had been restricted chiefly to the neck, face, and head. Has the reader ever marked how figures seem to lengthen when viewed through a pane roughened by the bulb on which the glass had been formed? The appearance may convey some idea, though an exaggerated one, of what we describe. That rather peculiar-looking man is Dr. Hill, Professor of Theology in the University of Glasgow, — the gentleman preferred by the Senatus to Dr. Chalmers. We need hardly add that he is a grave mediocritist, a solemn enunciator of commonplaces, a man who never originated a great thought, and who never sported with a small one. Shall we describe any of the others? That rather good-looking man, with the gray head, brown whiskers, straight nose, fresh complexion, and very sharp facial angle, is Mr. Bisset, of Bourtie, who bids Church extensionists peruse his pamphlet, and pause; and the adust, robust, middle-aged, less handsome man beside him is Mr. Paull, of Tullynessle, whose surname begins with the same letter as that of Mr. Pirie, of Dyce. They are both decidedly the most influential men in their respective Sessions, and, like the man in the play, have been speaking prose all their lives long.

PART THIRD. — THE EVANGELICALS.

The better-known men of the minority we exhausted in our last; we now turn to the vastly more numerous body on the left of the moderator — the party who represent in the Assembly the great majority of the members and elders of the Church of Scotland, and, with but a very few exceptions, all its lay members. In one respect they differ strikingly in their appearance, as a body, from their antagonists. There are among them many aged and venerable men, — quite as many, at least, as on the opposite side. But their proportion of men in early or middle life is greater in a very marked degree. Slight as the circumstance may seem, it is in reality an important one. It indicates the tendencies of the age and the history of the parties, and whispers of a principle of death and diminution on the one side, and of vitality and increase on the other. The same remark applied in this country, in the times of the Reformation, to those two antagonist parties of which the one held by the obsolete superstition, and the other by the revived faith. Few conversions take place late in life. It has been stated by Dr. M'Crie that the conversion of the elder Argyle, when a very old man, was an extraordinary instance, and that it stands almost alone in the history of the Scottish Reformation. Pfizier, in his "Biography of Luther," remarks, in a similar style, that it was chiefly the young, or at least men who had not passed the term of middle age, who ranged themselves on the side of the restored Christianity, and fought the battles of Protestantism.

The moderator of the Assembly has just risen to mark the rise of a member of court. There is a peculiar dignity in the manner and appearance of Dr. Gordon, and a noble and manly beauty in the countenance. His stature does not exceed the middle size, and yet the figure so fills the eye that he appears tall. The complexion is fresh and clear, but the face is thin, and the hair bears its marked tinge of bright silver. The forehead is of extraordinary height — quite as tall and erect as even that in the more idealized portraits of Shakspeare; and, though the breadth is less, it is quite as finely rounded a-top. "A forehead of that type," said the late Dr. Spurzheim, when in Edinburgh a good many years since, "is one of perhaps the least common which nature produces." There is not in the whole Church a more exquisitely elegant or truly noble mind than that of Dr. Gordon, or one whose courage, with all his gentleness of disposition, would mount higher in a time of extremity.

Now, mark that elderly gentleman standing at the end of one of the middle seats, against the crimson-covered barrier which fences off the Lord High Commissioner's portion of the house from the central portion assigned to members of Assembly. He has risen, not to speak, but merely for change of posture, for the debate has been protracted, and he has been patiently waiting it out, to record his vote with the evangelical party in the cause of discipline and reform. He is a man rather above the middle stature, well made, and, though plainly, very neatly dressed. Age has silvered his hair, and there is a slight stoop of the shoulders; but the vigor of the figure is left unimpaired; and the silent though emphatic testimony of the countenance, the compression of mouth indicative of firmness, the cast of sober thought which dwells in the singularly significant lines of the forehead, the deeply contemplative expression of eye, all indicate an intellect in its prime. The complexion is pale, but healthy. Observe the form of head. The silvery hair clusters round the forehead; but causality, rising full, broad, and high, from an ample base formed by largely developed knowing organs, stands out like a tower, shading the locks, as it were, to either side, and strongly catches the light on its rounded upper line, as in the portraits of Burke and Franklin. We have before us a man of more than European reputation, — a man whose name, pronounced in any part of the world in which letters are cultivated or science is known, would at once ensure recognition and respect. No writer of the present age unites a higher degree of literary ability to exact science; no writer of our own country unites them in a degree equally high. The Earl of Aberdeen, true to his character as a diplomatist, and indifferent apparently to character of any other kind, could describe the evangelical party as composed of men low in accomplishment and intellect compared with their opponents. Spoke his lordship the truth? We stake the intellect and accomplishment of that one man, not merely against those of any individual on the opposite side, but against the intellect and accomplishment of the whole opposite side put together; appealing confidently to the country for its verdict in the case, and yet confining our statement of the merits to the bare pronunciation of a name. That man, with the nobly philosophic forehead, and (to quote from his own description of Sir Isaac Newton) "the fine head of hair, as white as silver, without baldness," is Sir David Brewster.

The part taken by Sir David in the present struggle is suited to tell powerfully on ingenuous minds in behalf of the Church. When the collision between the civil and ecclesiastical courts took place, he had not made up his mind on the problem which it involved. He saw too clearly, however, not to see that the question was no indifferent one, or one in which he could remain neutral, but that, as a subject of the realm, and a member and office-bearer in the Church, it would be imperative on him to act some determinate part regarding it. He accordingly set himself carefully to examine. He read, and studied, and brought to bear upon the subject the same powers of patient investigation which had rendered him so eminently successful in the field of scientific inquiry. What has been the result? It is only necessary to mark the position he has taken up in order to ascertain the conclusion at which he has arrived. But there were, perhaps, disturbing influences that interfered with the process. Will it be deemed a disturbing influence that Sir David was born a reformer; that throughout life he has been the determined opponent of sinecurists, who profess to teach, and do nothing, and uncompromisingly hostile to every immorality in the class who set themselves to acquire a smattering of theology, in order that they may become qualified, in the sense of Dr. Cook, to teach it again for a bit of bread?

The moderator again rises. A loud, ruffing noise has broken out in the galleries. At least two-thirds of the members of Assembly have joined in it, and the business of the court is interrupted. A very distinguished member has just entered. He is a man well stricken in years. His pace is slow, and his locks, like those of the two gentlemen just described, are bathed in silver,—"the lyart haffets wearing thin and bare." His person is large and massy, though his stature does not perhaps exceed five feet nine or five feet ten inches; and there is no tendency to obesity. He is very plainly dressed. The complexion is pale, the face large, and the features uncommonly firm and massy. There is an inexplicable, mysterious, undescribable something in the expression, that inspires awe and respect. And mark the head. It would be saying marvellously little were we but to say that there is not such another head in the house,—we may add, not such another head in Edinburgh, in Scotland, Britain, Europe. The breadth across the forehead is what the phrenologists term not simply large, but enormous. The length, too, in profile, is so very great, that the bulky heads around seem but of moderate size. The front portion, however, from the ear to the forehead, is considerably massier in proportion than the posterior region, and stands up more conspicuously; and there is a noble development a-top. He has seated himself a few feet to the moderator's left. The grave, deep expression seems as fixed as the features to which they impart so solemn a character. But he is evidently following the speaker—one of the most powerful in the house—with much interest; and all at once the countenance is lighted up in a manner as difficult to describe as the expression which has just disappeared. We can compare it to but the sudden lighting up of an alabaster vase, or to an instantaneous gleam of sunshine. The expression slowly changes, until it has passed into the more habitual one; and he rises to address the Assembly. All at once every individual present has grown a zealous conservator of the peace; but for half a moment the "hush, hush," is too general, and makes more noise than it allays.

The speech has the disadvantage of being read, not spoken, and read at first with several stops and interruptions, and in a rather low though audible tone. But there is an intense attention already excited, despite the apparent disadvantages. As the speaker proceeds, the voice rises, strengthens, deepens, till it seems to roll in thunder through the house. There is energetic action, confined chiefly, however, to the right arm and shoulder. The earnestness is overpowering. Even the dullest hearer, firing as he listens, feels himself carried along by the o'er-mastering force of an eloquence whose components can scarce be analyzed, but which is at once power of character, of argument, and of illustration, — an irresistible sincerity, that, through a magic sympathy, makes others sincere too, at least for the time, — and a vehement poetry, that seems but to pass through the imagination that it may assail and overpower the heart. Eloquence has been compared to a stream; but here the comparison seems inadequate. We must have overbearing ponderosity and heat as well as resistless rapidity. We must have weight as well as motion. If we illustrate by a stream at all, it must be by a stream of dense, molten lava pouring down the steep side of a mountain, and floating away on its surface rock and stones, and entire buildings. "There is no man," said Jeffrey of the present speaker, "that so enables me to form a conception of the oratory of Demosthenes." Need we name the far-known leader of the Scottish Church, Dr. Thomas Chalmers, "the greatest of living Scotsmen," or attempt drawing the character of a man more extensively known than perhaps any other of the present age, and destined to grow upon posterity?

Mark, in the same corner of the house, but several seat-breadths further away from the moderator, a person of a very different appearance. He is below the middle stature, and, though turned of thirty by perhaps five or six years, seems at this distance, from the smallness of his features and figure, some years younger. His person is well formed, his features good, and the expression seems indicative of great activity and energy. The forehead is very remarkable. We are by no means sure of the truth of phrenology in its minuter details; but nature does certainly seem to set her mark on the foreheads of men of extraordinary capacity. In the man before us, the part immediately above the eyes — the seat, it is alleged, of the knowing organs — is in exact proportion to the face below; but the upper part swells out in the region of causality and comparison, especially in the former, so that it projects at either side, and forms a broad bar across. There is perhaps scarce a head in the kingdom in which the reflective organs are more amply developed; and the mind consorts well in this instance with the material indications. They mark decidedly one of the ablest men in the Church, — a man fitted for every walk of literature, — whether power or elegance of intellect, just taste, or nice discrimination, be the qualities required. It is curious to remark how unwilling people generally are to believe that a person by much too short for a grenadier may yet be a great man. It is at least equally curious to note the delight which nature seems to take in iterating and reiterating the fact. A very large proportion of the intellect of the age just passing away was lodged with men who fell short of the middle size. Napoleon was scarcely five feet six inches in height, and so very slim in early life as to be well-nigh lost in his boots and his uniform. Byron was no taller. Lord Jeffrey is not so tall. Campbell and Moore are still shorter than Jeffrey; and Wilberforce was a less man than any of them. The same remark has been made of the great minds of England who flourished about the middle of the seventeenth century. One very remarkable instance we may perhaps exhibit to the reader in a new aspect. In the August of 1790, some workmen, engaged in repairing the church of St. Giles, Cripplegate, found under the floor of the chancel an old coffin, which, as shown by the sexton's register, had rested there undisturbed for a hundred and sixteen years. For a grown person it was a very small one. Its length did not exceed five feet ten inches, and it measured only sixteen inches across at the broadest part. The body almost invariably stretches after death, so that the bodies of females of the middle stature require coffins of at least equal length; and the breadth, even outside, did not fully come up to the average breadth of shoulder in adults. Whose remains rested in that wasted old coffin? Those of a man the most truly masculine in his cast of mind, and the most gigantic in intellect, which Britain, or the world, ever produced, — the defender of the rights of the people of England; as a scholar, first among the learned of Europe; as a poet, not only more sublime than any other uninspired writer, but, as has been justly said, more fertile in true sublimities than all other uninspired writers put together. The small old coffin disinterred from out the chancel of St. Giles contained the remains of that John Milton who died at his house in Bunhill Fields in the winter of 1674, — the all-powerful controversialist who, in the cause of the people, crushed the learned Salmasius full in the view of Europe, — the poet who produced the "Paradise Lost." But we find we have exhausted our space for the present, ere we have finished or named our portrait.

PART FOURTH. — THE EVANGELICALS.

We resume our half-finished portrait. The gentleman whose appearance was sketched in our last has risen to address the Assembly, and a general "hush" runs along the galleries, like that which greeted the speaker previously described. The voice is clear and well modulated; the action simple. The arm is stretched out at an angle raised a very little above the horizontal; but, as the speaker warms, the angle rises. Mark, first, the wonderful flow of language. Of all the members of Assembly, that member has perhaps the readiest command of English; and his spoken style the most nearly approaches to a written one. The words pour in a continuous stream, fitting themselves, with a singular flexibility, to every object which they encircle in their course; insinuating themselves, if we may so speak, into the innermost intricacies of every thought; sweeping, with a steady certainty, along the lines of every distinction, however nicely drawn; and, while thus exquisitely true to the mental processes whose findings they signify, modulating themselves, as if by some such natural law as that which gives regularity and beauty to the crystal, into the combinations which best satisfy the ear, and accord most truly with the rules of composition as an art. Language is a noble instrument, though there be but few who can awaken all its tones. There is something very different in the extempore power here exhibited, from that, slowly exerted through complete mastery over language, shown by our more accomplished writers, — something so different that it is a comparatively rare matter to find the same individual possessed of both. The language of Fox, so fluent and powerful in debate, trickled but slowly, and not very gracefully, from his pen. The written style of Chatham was loose, redundant, and not overladen with meaning. And both Dryden and Addison, on the other hand, and, we may add, our own countryman, Adam Smith, though great masters of English as authors, — men thoroughly acquainted with every nicety and elegancy of the tongue, — could scarce find words enough, when they spoke, to express their commonest ideas. But some few happy geniuses have been masters of language in both departments, and have spoken and written with equal power and facility; and we have one of these in the speaker before us. Cowper could remark to his friend John Newton, in a half-sad, half-sportive vein, that the world was singularly unwilling to admit any style to be good which recommended Christianity; and most of the writings of this gentleman labor under this disadvantage. But the man who ventures to deny them the praise of great vigor and great elegance, would himself require to stand on higher literary ground than that occupied by any enemy of the Cross in the present day.

The subject of the speech is a question of heresy. These have been numerous charges preferred against the pannel, all of them very serious, — all referring to beliefs within whose sphere of operation the offers of the gospel must have been rendered of non-effect; but they have been submitted to the court in a detached and separate form, and we feel disposed to wonder how any one mind could have fallen into error on so many different points. Mark how the speaker grapples with the subject, — how he traces the various branches of heresy to one common root, — demonstrating to the conviction of all that they form parts of a coherent system, — a system as coherent as that of Robert Owen, or Hume, or Hobbes; and that the pannel, having once laid down his erroneous first principles, must have been as miserable a logician as a divine had he not derived from them all the various inductions of error which form the counts of the indictment. And, this point firmly established, mark now how the speaker brings the various counts to the standard of God's word. Mark how irresistibly complete in every case the demonstration of the errors, and yet how very brief the statement. We need hardly add that this singularly able and accomplished man is the gentleman whom the Earl of Aberdeen would have so fain recommended to the Calton Jail, — the Rev. Mr. Candlish, of St. George's.

But who is that tall and very strongly-built man in the same corner of the house? — so strongly built, that we are scarce aware his stature considerably exceeds six feet, except when we see men of the ordinary size beside him. He is large-limbed, broad-shouldered, deep-chested, and his very large head is covered by dark-brown hair, as thickly curled as that of the Hercules Farnese. His complexion is pale, indicating perhaps a sedentary life and studious habits; the nose is slightly aquiline, the compression of the lips speaks of firmness; but the general expression is one of mildness and tranquillity, and he seems marked by a peculiar quietness of manner. A speaker on the opposite side has been making some very strong statements, and the gentleman we describe has been marking a few jottings, in the course of the speech, in a small memorandum-book. His employment has been matter of remark in the galleries. There has been a good deal of whispering among the audience, and the whisperers invariably turn their eyes in his direction; and some of the more disadvantageously placed among them stand up on tip-toe to catch a glimpse of him. He rises, for the other speaker has sat down, and comes forward to the open space beside the table of the house. One-half the spectators in the galleries and the area behind rise too, — rather, it would seem, in consequence of some sympathetic influence than from any exertion of the will; but the cry of "seats, seats!" brings them all down again, and silence is instantly restored. The speech opens with a few vigorous, compact, logical sentences, enunciated in a tone of subdued power, but peculiarly indicative of firmness and resolution. The style is less flexible than that of the former speaker described, and, though the sentences roll on without pause or interruption, less copious; but there is an even more concentrated strength, and the precision is at least equally great. Mark how the words arrange themselves into sentences, which could be punctuated more readily than those now flowing from our pen, — so very distinct are the members, and so very defined the meaning. Mark, too, the strictly logical sequence of the thoughts, the clearness and order of the propositions, and how the inevitable and undeniable conclusions, condensed into the concluding members of single sentences, give more than epigrammatic point to the style. The amount of meaning thrown at times into a short, compact antithesis is altogether amazing. The speaker warms as he proceeds. The voice heightens; and such is the force and energy of the tones, that the arguments seem projected, missile-like, against his opponent. There is corresponding action. The right fist, firmly clenched, is raised every two seconds to the shoulder, and then aimed with tremendous force in the direction of the floor. We are reminded of the "iron man of iron mould" in the allegory, who went about with his huge flail, beating out the grains of truth from the chaff and stubble of falsehood. How palpable every incongruity in the reasonings of his antagonist has been rendered! how thoroughly have the misstatements been exposed! how completely have the sophisms been frittered to pieces! And now, after every flaw in their structure has been pointed out, they are held up, as it were, at arm's length, to the derision of all. So entire is the exposure, so very finished the demolition, that, without the employment of a single ludicrous idea, the effect is that of the most caustic ridicule. An expression of blank helplessness falls on almost every countenance on the opposite side of the house. These arguments cannot be met, these statements cannot be gainsayed; and they know it. The speaker has finished, and the individual who has encountered so tremendous an overthrow rises; but he rises like William of Deloraine, when, dizzy, blind, and haggard, he staggered into the lists "a ghastly and half-naked man." He has concluded, in his confusion, that some reply is essential; but his thoughts are scattered; and so, after saying nothing in a few sentences, he sits down again. Who is this right stout man-at-arms who has wrought such signal confusion in the array of the opposition? Our readers are, we doubt not, prepared to furnish the name, — Mr. William Cunningham, of Edinburgh.

Turn next to that gentleman a few paces away. His stature rises a very little above the middle size; but his person, though well proportioned, is rather delicate than robust. There is something very gentlemanly in the whole appearance. An air of openness and courtesy pervades the countenance; the complexion is fresh; the features are small; the nose straight and sharp, but not prominent; the forehead well developed. He is a man evidently not turned of forty, and yet the head is bald, showing a fine fulness in the region of sentiment. He rises to address the Assembly, and a deep attention is instantly excited. His voice, though clear, is not strong; but the silence, from this circumstance, is just all the more deep. And mark the classic beauty of the language, and how very nicely the words fit the ideas which they are employed to express. There is a singular acuteness of intellect exhibited, a minuteness of information — especially regarding the territorial lines of demarcation between the civil and the ecclesiastical — that renders cavil hopeless, and a staid sobriety of judgment that solicits and ensures confidence. Few men so completely possess the art of making facts tell by placing them in a light so clear that the just inference becomes inevitable; and they thus come to serve the purposes of both fact and argument too. There is a refreshing manliness of spirit in the whole tone, and a nobleness of aspiration after the good, the just, the fair, the honorable, which even the men who differ from him most, if in any degree men of candor and right feeling, cannot but recognize and esteem. A gleam of imagination occasionally lights up the simple elegance of his style, and he concludes in a vein of chaste and graceful poetry. That speaker is Alexander Dunlop, — a man authoritatively quoted in our civil courts in questions of ecclesiastical polity, and well and honorably known in the present momentous struggle as a powerful champion on the side of the Church, and a shrewd and sagacious leader.

The Church of Scotland has hereditary claims on Mr. Dunlop. Her cause is a family one — a sort of heir-loom. One of his ancestors — the well-known Principal Carstairs, the friend and adviser of William of Orange — was subjected, for her sake, in the persecution of the seventeenth century, to the thumbkins, and bore the torture without shrinking. An ancestor in the male line, now known as the elder Dunlop, to distinguish him from his descendant, was the editor of that admirable Collection of Confessions of Faith, Catechisms, and Books of Order and Discipline, of public authority in the Church, published early in the last century, and now recognized as so valuable that it sells for some four or five times the original price. The cause of the Church is thus a hereditary cause to this gentleman, — a circumstance which must no doubt have had its predisposing influence; but it does surely bear on the present collision, that the lawyer who was deemed of highest authority in Scotch ecclesiastical law ere the conflict began, — a man whose opinions and facts on ecclesiastical questions have been quoted by pleaders as decisive, and sustained by judges as just, — should have so determinedly and unhesitatingly taken up his position on the side of the Church. The special pleaders who now most strenuously oppose him were in the habit, scarce three years ago, of quoting him as an authority. We do not know a better illustration than Mr. Dunlop of Bacon's remark, "A man young in years may be yet old in hours, if he has lost no time." Commentators on law rarely pass into authorities during their lives, and are not often referred to in court by their contemporaries; and yet we have learned that Mr. Dunlop was little turned of thirty when his work on "Parochial Law" came to be regarded as of standard authority.

Mark, now, that gentleman in the seat under the gallery. He is of the middle size, and well but not strongly made. His complexion is of a transparent paleness, that speaks perhaps of severe study, perhaps of delicate health, — very possibly of both. His features are regular; the nose is of the straight Grecian form; the forehead is of large capacity, and very amply developed in the region of causality. There is a cast of abstraction in the expression. His age approaches fifty, and yet, though pale and thin, we might well deem him some ten years younger, from the transparency of the complexion, and the smooth, unwrinkled character of the skin. We have before us Dr. David Welsh, the friend and biographer of the great metaphysician Dr. Thomas Brown, and one of the most acutely philosophic intellects of Scotland in the present day. His biography of his friend, independently of its merits regarded as a well-written narrative of the incidents and events which marked the life of an extraordinary man, is one of the finest pieces of metaphysical criticism which the present century has produced. Dr. Welsh stands very high as a professor of Church History,—a professorship which, in the last age, when there were many to assail the Church, and few to defend her, was held to require less talent than any of the others, but which has now come to be differently regarded. In no department of history is a profound philosophy more indispensably necessary; in no department has intellectual power, added to Christian principle, a more promising field of usefulness. How much has Dr. M'Crie accomplished as an ecclesiastical historian! and how immense the influence which his writings exercise on public opinion! The professor of Church History has to meet with antagonists such as Hume and Gibbon. Moderatism in the last age could cultivate the friendship of these men, and yet hold, even when complimenting their philosophy and their literature, that men of the most ordinary capacity were qualified to counteract the poison which they were assiduously spreading in the historical track. Another opinion prevails now; and so Dr. Welsh is Professor of Church History in the University of Edinburgh. His testimony on the side of the Church in the present struggle we deem very valuable. It bears on the same point with that of Mr. Dunlop, but it rests on its own independent grounds. Their separate evidence has the merit of being at once distinct in basis and uniform in bearing. We have in the one the highest authority in Scotch ecclesiastical law, in the other the highest authority in Scotch ecclesiastical history.

PART FIFTH. — THE EVANGELICALS.

We resume our sketches. A gentleman of a very striking figure has just entered the court, — evidently a member of some note, for there runs along the gallery a hurried whisper, and we may here and there see an extended finger pointing him out to a stranger. He is an erect, muscular, lathy man, some six or seven inches above the ordinary stature. His height, at the lowest estimate, cannot fall short of six feet two inches; and the mould into which his large frame has been cast, "the square-turned joints and length of limb," indicate mingled strength and activity. He is standing manfully in the breach, in the present conflict, in behalf of the Church, and has to encounter many an assailant; but were the breach not a figurative, but an actual and material one, — such a breach as the cannon of Napoleon made in the walls of Jean d'Acre, — and were that gentleman's well-pointed arguments converted into a good half-pike, there are very many ingenious men in the opposition who would entertain serious objections against joining issue with him on the question of its practicability. The countenance is marked by the lines of resolution and firmness. The complexion is dark, indicating what phrenologists term the bilious temperament, and the facial angle unusually full, approaching more nearly to an angle of ninety than is at all common in even the Circassian type of head. The head appears large for the body, large as that is; and, when seen in profile, such is the length from the ear to the forehead, that the line of the face forms almost a square with the line a-top. Though not yet turned of forty, the thick strong hair, originally coal black, is tinged with gray, and, with the deep lines of the countenance joined to the dark complexion, speaks apparently of a period of life more advanced. He has risen to speak. Mark the clearness and power of the tones. They already reverberate through the house, though pitched apparently on a much lower key than that to which they are capable of ascending. Some of his remarks have provoked the anger of the opposition, and there rises a confused Babel-like hubbub of sound, loud enough to drown any two ordinary voices. Not that of the speaker, however. Mark how it also rises higher and higher as the confusion swells; and we can still hear it ringing over all, "loud as a trumpet with a silver sound." The clamor subsides, and the speaker proceeds. The ideas are as clear as the tones in which they are conveyed, and there is much readiness of wit, and great lucidity of statement; but the chief element of the speaker's power is his felt sincerity. There is a thorough, straightforward honesty of purpose about him, joined to an unfeigned, earnest zeal for the great first principles from which he derives all his deductions, that, without disarming the hostility of his opponent, at least robs it of much of its bitterness. He can say severe things at times — very severe things — of Moderatism, with its dead, inefficient form of Christianity, — a body without life, and in which the fermentation of putridity has long since begun. He can say still severer things of the aristocracy, — of the self-seeking and exclusive spirit which led them of old to grasp what should have been in reality the patrimony of the people, the educational and ecclesiastical funds of the country, through which schools and churches should have been erected and endowed; and very severe things of their mean and narrow-sighted policy in the present day. But there is "nought set down in malice." All arises from an honest conviction, unembittered by a single grain of the *odium theologicum*, when he assails what he knows to be but a shadowy and unsubstantial semblance of religion, and, undisturbed by one particle of democratic jealousy, when he denounces, as alike wicked and foolish, the course pursued by the great body of the titled and high-born of our country. Mark his dress. He is no clergyman; and, were he to come to count descents with the gentlemen on the opposite side who are so very forward in maintaining the cause and asserting the dignity of certain noble lords,—quite as forward as if they were their footmen, and engaged in battling, as in duty bound, for the honor of their livery,—it would be found that of these noble earls—for of their supporters and apologists we say nothing—not a few would deem their genealogies mightily improved could they but claim relationship with some of his progenitors. We have before us Mr. Maitland Makgill Crichton, of Rankeillor,—a gentleman one of whose ancestors in the male line was the friend of Knox, and a fellow-worker with him in the cause of the Reformation,—who can show, ranged among his family portraits, the portraits of that General Leslie who led the armies of the Covenant, and who is the undoubted representative in the present day of the ancient Lords of Crichton and Fendraught, though he has not yet asserted the title.

It is singularly gratifying to meet with the good old Church names still enrolled on the side of the Church. The two vocables "Argyll" and "Aberdeen" express, when associated with the historical recollections proper to each, the whole controversy. It is particularly interesting, too, to find names that had well-nigh disappeared for the greater part of two centuries coming again into view, fixed, as it were, in exactly the same places as of old,—just as the fixed stars appear, when the night falls, in the very position in which they had been seen when the night fell last. We see in the list of the eldership the name of Brodie of Lethen, and that of another younger scion of the family. Presbytery, in our northern districts, had very few asserters during the persecutions of the seventeenth century; but its few it had, — men who could both dare and suffer for its sake; and among these the Brodies of Lethen take a prominent place. We have now before us a very scarce old work, the "Diary of Alexander Brodie, of Brodie," one of the Senators of the College of Justice of 1650, a staunch Covenanter, and a man of deep and fervent piety. We find in his notes frequent mention of his neighbor and relative, Brodie of Lethen, a person of a similar stamp. The time was one of great trouble and perplexity, — the winter of 1654. Glencairn and his Highlanders were in possession of the open country. The season was singularly severe; for the sea had risen further on the land than for forty years before, and the Findhorn was coming down red from the hills, so high in flood as to be unfordable for several days, and the Highlanders could not get across to wreak their vengeance on Lethen. But at length they came, and burnt every house to the ground, with all the corn stored up from the previous autumn for the sustenance of the family and its dependents. When the enemy departed, the inmates, scattered for the time, again met. They met, in that dreary season, amid the blackened and wasted walls, when every streamlet was swollen into a river, and the winds howled amid the roofless and darkened turrets; but with what intent? We employ the simple language of the diary, "To come under a new, firm, inviolable covenant with God, that they should be his, and he should be theirs." The vows of each are recorded. "Old *Lethen*," says the diary, "renewed his acknowledgments, and prayed the Lord for a willing, honest heart; and desired to give up himself and his wealth, family, children, wife, and his own life, to the Lord, that he might be glorified in them, and that his life might not be in himself and to the world, but *to*, *in*, and *for* the Lord." His son, the heir of the house, was equally decided. "He professed his willingness to consecrate himself and his to God, and that, as long as he had a house or family, it should be the Lord's,

He alone should be worshipped in it; and he should have no God but Him." Now, we do think it well that the old Presbyterian party should reckon among its adherents so many of the old Presbyterian names.

But we digress. Mark that elderly man beside the table. He is of the middle stature, but stoops slightly. His complexion is pale, inclining to sallow; the head, though not large, — at least not of the largest size, — is well proportioned; and we may mark it in its full development, especially in the regions of intellect and sentiment, for it is very bald. Has the reader ever seen Holbein's portrait of Erasmus, or a faithful print of it? Mark, then, that countenance: the form of the nose, the compression of the thin lips, the acute and watchful expression of the eyes, the very complexion even, is that of the elegant and subtile-minded scholar of the age of Luther, whom no shade of distinction ever escaped, and who, if not always powerful, was at least always ingenious. He rises to speak, in reply to a spruce lawyer on the opposite side. The voice is not strong, — we at first hear very imperfectly, — but, though not strong, it is clear; and as the speaker warms, the tones heighten. He is evidently cutting the nerves of his opponent's logic, not with a weighty weapon, but with a sharp one. The process has a considerable degree of quietness about it; but the stroke is reiterated, and the nerves divide. We have before us Dr. Patrick Macfarlan, of Greenock.

It has been often remarked that the two grand parties of the British legislature — its whigs and its tories (we employ the words in their old meaning) — are alike necessary in preserving the balance of the state. With but the one party the wheels of government would revolve too rapidly; with but the other, they would either stick fast or slide backwards; with both united, there is at once force enough to propel, and *vis inertiæ* enough to counteract any overplus energy in the moving power. And hence slow but well regulated motion. Now, we can imagine two such parties in a Church blessed with a representative government like ours, of which, somewhat in the manner described, the one would be of signal use to the other,—parties opposed to a considerable degree in ecclesiastical polity, but thoroughly at one in their views of doctrines and duties. These are certainly not the parties which divide it at present. It would be too much to have in the Church a single minister who did not preach the gospel; nor could any good, but, on the contrary, much evil result from his being there. And in the ranks of Moderatism, how many are there by whom the gospel is not preached, and to whom it is not known! But in the array of their opponents it is easy to discover the elements of two parties which might coexist in the Church for good,—one of them as a regulating influence, the other as an impelling force. We recognize in Dr. Macfarlan one of these personified; and, of course, employ the word in its best sense when we say that in matters ecclesiastical he represents the tory. The Doctor, some thirty years ago, was a sound Non-Intrusionist, friendly to a modified patronage. He has seen since that time nearly all his party shooting ahead of him; but what the Doctor was thirty years ago the Doctor is still. He is just a sound Non-Intrusionist, friendly to a modified patronage. Did the reader ever see on the banks of a navigable river a beacon fixed in the foreground, and the vessels sweeping past?

Now, mark that strongly-featured man a few benches away. He is barely of the middle size, and stoutly made. The nose has an almost Socratic degree of concavity in its outline;—indeed, the whole profile more nearly resembles that of Socrates, as shown in cameos and busts, than it does any other known profile to whom we could compare it. The expression of the lower part of the face indicates a man who, if once engaged in battling in a good cause, would fight long and doggedly ere he gave up the contest. The head is also marked by the Socratic outline in a singularly striking degree; the forehead is erect, broad, high, and the coronal region of immense development. He rises to speak. His voice, though not finely modulated, is powerful; his style of language plain, energetic, and full of point, — such a style as Cobbet used to write, and which, when employed as a medium for the conveyance of thoughts of large volume, is perhaps of all kinds of style the most influential. He is evidently a master of reason; and there runs through the lighter portions of his speech a vein of homely, racy humor, very quiet, but very effective. That speaker is Andrew Gray, of Perth, one of the vigorous and original minds which the demands of the present struggle have called from comparative obscurity into the controversial arena, full in the view of the country. Mr. Gray's admirable pamphlet, "The Present Conflict," took the lead, we believe, of all the publications of which the unhappy collision between the civil and ecclesiastical courts has been the occasion; and it must be regarded surely as no slight proof of the judgment of the man, that of all the positions he then took up, not one has since been abandoned. He marked out the *Torres Vedras* of the question, and the lines have not yet been forced.

But we find we must run hurriedly over a few of the remaining characters, indicating, as we pass, rather the subject of a portrait than attempting to draw one. That pale, thin, middle-sized man in black, with the prominent features and thoughtful air, is Mr. Charles J. Brown, of Edinburgh, — a man of an acute and nicely logical mind, and inferior as a theologian to perhaps no minister in the Church of Scotland. The gentleman beside him, with the snow-white hair, ample forehead, and dark eyebrows, is Dr. Thomas Brown, of Glasgow, — one of the most respected clergymen in the kingdom, — a man who succeeded Dr. Chalmers in one of his city charges, and yet preserved the congregation entire; and who, at an age not far removed from the threescore and ten, preserves all the intellectual freshness and vigor of his youth. The thin, handsome, erect, elderly man beside the moderator's chair, with the slender ebony cane in his hand, is Dr. Makellar, the moderator of last Assembly, — a gentleman chosen to the office from the general weight of his character, and the trust reposed in him by the Church, as one in whom, in times of difficulty and trial, the most thorough confidence could be placed. There is a very fair representation of the magistracy of the country on these benches. The Church, if in a state of rebellion, has certainly very singular abettors. That gentlemanly man in black, rather below the middle size, is Sir James Forrest, of Comiston, Lord Provost of Edinburgh. The taller man, a few seats away, is the ex-Provost of Glasgow. The eminently handsome, well-built man, of at least six feet, who has just taken his place in the front seat, is the Sheriff of Fife. The aristocracy have also their representatives; and well would it be for the country if the average character of the class stood as high in all that regards the truly good and honorable as in the sample which these benches furnish. The lawyers, too, muster strong; and so we deem it an interesting feature of the collision to find so many of these taking their stand with the Church, in determined opposition to the decisions of the civil court; — holding, as we do, that, were the case a fairly balanced one, the professional bias would have inclined them all the other way. Our readers cannot fail to remember that such was very strikingly the case in the collision which took place last year between the House of Commons and the Court of Queen's Bench. Almost all the lawyers of England declared on the side of the court.

But we have exhausted our space in passing over a few of the better known names of the party. The list contains many others which we might pronounce with but small chance of recognition on the part of the reader, — the names of humble laborers in the gospel, of whom the world knows little, but whose ministry God has blessed for the conversion of souls, and who, in their obscure, though surely not unimportant spheres of usefulness, are loved and honored as the instruments of much good. It would be a dark day for Scotland that would see them ejected from their charges, and strangers thrust into their places, — shepherds whose voices the flocks would not hear, and whose unblest footsteps they would fear to follow. Thus melancholy, however, must be the result, if the civil court succeed in maintaining its place within the territory which it has so unhappily invaded. The Church cannot recede. She has marshalled her front of defence on the last rood of ground which she can conscientiously occupy, either with respect to the spiritual welfare of her people or the honor of her Divine Master. There remains for her no back-ground space on which to form within the pale of the Establishment. She has already arrived at her last barrier.

SCOTTISH LAWYERS: THEIR TWO CLASSES.

SADDLETREE, in the "Heart of Mid-Lothian," is made to exclaim, in astonishment, "Who ever heard of a lawyer that would suffer for any one religion or other!" There may be humor in the joke, but certainly no truth. Some of the most eminently religious men which either this or the sister country ever produced have been distinguished members of the legal profession. Sir Matthew Hale, not more eminent for his unbending rectitude as a judge than for the profundity of his attainments as a lawyer, cultivated a close walk with God; and we know not in the whole round of English theology a more thoroughly spiritual composition than his discourse on the Knowledge of Christ Crucified. Among his contemporaries of the legal profession in our own country we reckon one of our martyrs, Archibald Johnstone, Lord Warriston. The early half of the following century had likewise its lawyers of eminent piety. The writings of Lord President Forbes show that the ablest jurist of his age or country was also one of its best and most devout men. His predecessor, Lord President Dundas, was also a man of personal piety. As the century advanced, however, that night of spiritual darkness which had sunk so gloomily over the Scottish Church involved the Scottish bar in a gloom at least equally deep, and still more palpably haunted by the gross and obscene shapes which come abroad at such seasons. There are writers of the present day who, though not at all particularly squeamish regarding what and how they describe, can do little more than hint at the grossnesses and debaucheries which had come to characterize our Scottish lawyers of this period. Lockhart, in his "Life of Burns," speaks of their "tavern scenes of audacious hilarity," and but insinuates the rest. Heron, who must have known of the matter from more than hearsay, attributes the ultimate ruin of the poor poet to the influence of their example. There still survive traditional anecdotes and *bon mots* of the class, that, like plague-spots on the walls of a building, serve to show how tainted the atmosphere must have been, and how deep the infection. We find inklings, too, to the same effect in the early life of Scott, — more than mere hints of great intemperance, joined to great profanity. The Faculty of this period, though it seems to have had marvellously few Christians, had, notwithstanding, its many elders; and, as might be anticipated, we discover a fierce extreme of opinion on religious subjects in almost every instance in which they registered their views in our church courts, — a bitterness of hostility to the gospel truly wonderful. In the famous debate on missions (1796), the clerical leaders of Moderatism were content merely, as in the case of Mr. Hamilton, of Gladsmuir, to denounce the gospel as something so immoral and bad, that, if communicated to the heathen, it could not fail of destroying their native virtue; or, as in the case of Principal Hill, to oppose the scheme of sending it out of the country, sheerly from a fear lest the missionaries, when they got beyond the reach of the law, should quarrel on points of speculative divinity, and cut one another's throats. The lawyers who mingled in the debate took higher ground; and it is a fact worth noticing, that at least one of these lawyers sits on the bench in the present day.[1] The divines only argued that missionary societies should not be encouraged because they were in the main mischievous and foolish. The lawyer who is now a magistrate proposed that they should be dealt with as bands of conspirators leagued against the state. We need hardly add that he forms one of the majority who have decided against the Church.

A change, however, came over the Scottish bar. The irreligion of the class had become well-nigh universal, when, to employ the language of the "Presbyterian Review," "through the influence of a revival, proceeding entirely from within, converts to Christianity were raised up from among the ranks of the careless, the worldly, and the infidel." Lawyers at least not inferior in talent and accomplishment to any of their contemporaries began to walk professedly by the light of revelation, and to illustrate, by the purity of their lives, the excellence of what they professed; and a return to the old beliefs heralded, in almost every instance, a return to the old Presbyterian views of Church government. The bar during the darker period had produced many advocates of popular rights, some of them eminently able men; but the rights they asserted were political, not religious; for while its earlier whigs had been cast, if we may so express ourselves, into the Scottish Presbyterian mould of their country, its whigs of the middle period had been mere irreligious Englishmen. The most zealous protester against the first act of intrusion perpetrated in Scotland under the infamous law of Bolingbroke was Duncan Forbes: his zeal was that of the whig grafted on the Christian. The pointed remonstrance directed against patronage by the General Assembly about the time of the Secession was drawn up by Lord President Dundas. And the authorship of the period, as connected with the bar, bore a similar stamp. Lord Dreg-

1 Lord President Boyle.

horn's pamphlet against patronage is one of perhaps the ablest which has yet appeared on the subject. Though no religious man himself, he had eminently pious relatives; and thus, while he, as it were, saw the question with his own eyes, he seems to have felt regarding it with *their* feelings. Another able pamphlet of the time, written in the same track, was the composition of a second lawyer, Crosbie, the Councillor Pleydell of "Guy Mannering,"— the acute, conscientious, warm-hearted Pleydell, who never thought other than justly, and whose feelings were ever as generous as his reasonings were sound. He, too, was a determined opponent of patronage. But when lawyers ceased to be religious, patronage ceased to be felt as a grievance, and their whiggism took exclusively a secular form. Whatever might be their ideas, too, regarding independence of every other kind, of spiritual independence they had none. It was not until the old beliefs were revived among them — the beliefs held by Forbes and Dundas, and for the maintenance of which Warriston had died — that the old principles came to be again asserted. And hence that most important portion of the Church party in the present struggle drawn from the ranks of the legal profession.

It would, however, be saying a great deal too little were we to say that, while this religious section of the Faculty are zealous in behalf of the Church, the portion whose character has undergone no change are merely indifferent to it. There is a bitter hostility evinced. The times in which a mechanic could fight for the honor of his craft are over, but not the times in which a lawyer can contend for the jurisdiction of his court. There is a tangibility, too, about the claims of the Court of Session, in the present instance, which, to a man conversant with the tangible only, seems to have peculiar force. They relate to the seen and temporal, — to things which are the objects of his own belief; whereas the things to which the claims of the antagonist court chiefly refer are but the objects of the beliefs of other men. There is a strange confounding, too (a common mistake among lawyers), of the *right* with what they deem the *enacted*. There is, withal, a blind, but too natural dislike of the spiritual element, which, having not seen, they yet hate. And hence the hostility of this class. They are by much more numerous than the other; but, in at least a moral and religious point of view, the hostility of the many weighs immensely less than the support and friendship of the few.

THE NEW POLICY: EVANGELICAL MODERATES.

"We have now but one safe course of tactics left us," said a shrewd divine of the unpopular party, a member of the General Assembly of last year,—"we have now but one safe course of tactics left us: we must unite evangelical preaching to the Moderate policy." He spoke to only a small knot of friends, but the remark has got abroad. Unimportant as it may seem, it is more pregnant with meaning than half the speeches of his party; and we are much mistaken if in the present juncture the Church has not more to fear from the course which it recommends than from the Protest of the Rev. Dr. James Bryce, late of Calcutta, or the Declaration of the Rev. Mr. James Grant, still of Leith.

None but a bigot will dare restrict the piety of Christendom to his own Church or his own party; but there is no bigotry in affirming that the piety of almost every Church and sect has its own peculiar type. The inoperative, mystic piety of Rome, as illustrated in Fenelon and Madame Guyon, was very dissimilar in aspect to the manly, active, spirit-stirring piety of the Puritanism of England, as illustrated in its Calamys, Baxters, and other worthies of the times of the Commonwealth. The piety of the Scoto-Episcopal type, as illustrated in Leighton, with its quiet tolerance of all impurity and all oppression, was assuredly a very different thing in appearance from the stern covenanting piety of Presbyterian Scotland, as illustrated in Melville and Henderson, with its noble declaration of eternal warfare against all abuse and all tyranny. The basis of Christian principle was the same in each. We have as little doubt of the vital Christianity of Madame Guyon as of that of Richard Baxter himself; and we believe Leighton to have been as sincerely pious as Henderson. But while the foundations were the same, the superstructures were different. In the language of the inspired volume, "hay and stubble," as certainly as "gold and silver," may be piled on the rock which human hand has not laid. The piety of every Christian Church has its own type; and the peculiar and well-marked type of the piety of Presbyterian Scotland is utterly at variance with the policy of Moderatism. If there be any one trait stamped more legibly on the character of the piety of our Church than another, it is the regard which she has ever manifested for the will of her Christian people in the formation of the pastoral tie. If any one great principle stand out prominently in her history as the main object of her severe and long-protracted contendings, it is the principle which imperatively demands that she take her spiritual law from only her spiritual Lord, and pay respect in all things which pertain to eternity only to Him by whom the "praises" of "eternity are inhabited." It will prove by no means very easy to reconcile, within the Scottish Church, Evangelical doctrine with Moderate policy. The associations of three centuries conspire to render the coalition a monstrous one. True, in a few extreme cases, such a coalition seems already to exist; but the Evangelism in these cases will be found to be either Evangelism in a deplorably false position, or Evangelism of a radically extrinsic type. In the belief, however, that the Church may be in some little danger at present from the policy recommended by the Moderate divine, we would fain call the attention of our readers to the consideration of the two classes of persons in whom the coalition which he proposed seems actually effected.

We would first remark, that a very minute portion of the Evangelism of the Scottish Establisnment is Evangelism of the Scoto-Episcopal type. We have our sighers after an "audible response" from the congregation, — men who would deem it no very great hardship to be compelled to *use the sign of the cross in baptism*, and who are such sticklers for the existence of a certain mysterious virtue in the rite of ordination, derived somehow, by descent ceremonial, from the times of the apostles, that the Puseyites of England openly challenge them, in their leading organs, as worthy brethren lucklessly misplaced. It is no marvel to find the Evangelism of such men dissociated from at least the non-intrusion doctrine. All such have in them the germ of the true priest. They must of necessity regard every clergyman, however secular in his personal character, as possessed of something sacred which the people want. He is at least an ordained brother; he is vested in the priestly office, and the priestly office is a high and holy thing; and if ordination be so good a matter in the individual, what must not multiplied ordinations be in the ecclesiastical court? What weight can the voice of a parish have, compared with the judgment of a presbytery, — the assent or non-assent of a mass of the profane, unordained *lay*, set off against the solemn decision of a sacred conglomeration of the ordained *ecclesiastical?* Hence, too, much of that monstrous tolerance of evil in the Church which is peculiar to the Evangelism of this type. Archbishop Leighton and Archbishop Sharpe were dignitaries of the same Church at the same time, — "*brothers in God.*" All that is sacred in ordination, according to the Puseyite code, could have been derived from Pope Alexander III., though foul with incest and red with murder, or from Cardinal Beaton, after he had let Mrs. Marion Ogilvy out through the castle postern. Is it from a consideration of this kind that some of our very few Scoto-Episcopal Presbyterians can open their pulpits, though they themselves preach only the gospel, to brethren who neither preach it themselves, nor yet know it, except through the instinct by which they hate it when preached by others! — or that they can make common cause in the present struggle with a party tolerant of all abuses, and infamous for all? They are a class from whom the people of Scotland have somewhat to fear, and nothing to hope. They gild, by their purity of character, the feculent grossness of their party, as the mountebanks of the last age used to gild their pills. They have the merit of doing their duty in their own parishes, and of pursuing a course of policy which goes far to secure that duty be not done in any other parish besides, — affecting all the time to confine their interest as ecclesiastics each to his own little sphere. We are of the opinion that the moral of Archbishop Leighton's life has never yet been fully read, and that it addresses itself powerfully to this class. Our readers must have heard of the happy reply attributed to him, when, ere his final decision in favor of Episcopacy, he was asked, in a phraseology common to the period, whether he did not "preach to the times?" — "When so many preach to the times," said Leighton, "surely one solitary divine may be forgiven should he preach for eternity." What was the result, as shown in the history of his life? In failing to preach to the times, — in failing, in other words, to assert the great principles for which Christ's people were then contending, and for which his father had suffered, — he failed also, palpably, utterly, lamentably, to preach for eternity. Except for his writings, — and these had no connection whatever with his unhappy choice, — never was there a more profitless life. His piety — and who can doubt its depth or fervency? — was neutralized by his position. He saw evil triumphing in his own party, and good depressed and persecuted in the antagonist one; and at length, quitting his office in despair, — for the fruits of all his labor had been but disappointment, and worse, — he retired into private life, and died in obscurity. His story has not yet been written with an eye to its true meaning.

So much for our Scottish Evangelism of the radically extrinsic type. Its Evangelism of an opposite kind, in a false position, though the amount be fortunately very small, — so small that our readers could run over all its representatives on fewer than half their fingers, — is a still more deplorable object. Its unseemly, and surely most unenviable and uneasy position, will be found to have originated entirely in some peculiarity of personal character. There is a class of peculiarities which arise from overweening conceit, and which are of all human frailties the most irresistibly ludicrous. Comedy has gleaned a rich harvest from among them in the past, and every age and every locality produce their fresh supply. There is a period of life — the period between boyhood and early youth, the adolescent stage of human existence — when it is natural for almost all to over-estimate themselves; and perhaps this is not less necessary than natural. The confidence felt is a moving power to urge the aspirant upward and onward in his toilsome career. But the ability of forming a juster estimate of himself comes as he proceeds. He feels that his powers have their limits; that there is much which he cannot perform at all, and much in which he is excelled by others; and, as years mature his understanding, and difficulties test his strength, he learns to think soberly and justly of himself. Such is the ordinary course. Minds there are, however, in which the overweening confidence of adolescence lasts all life long, — men of the ordinary stature, who mistake themselves somehow for giants, and who cannot be convinced, frame the argument as we may, that they are not looking down on all their fellows. It is a fact which we shall scarce need to prove to at least one-half our readers, that by much the greater part of the falsely placed Evangelism of the Church has been fixed in its miserable attitude by this ludicrous but not the less lamentable weakness; that the few men now opposed to the measures of their brethren, but who not many years ago, some of them not many months ago, were zealous beyond measure in a similar track, are men whose overweening conceit rendered them standing jests among the lighter spirits of their several districts, and for whose laughable vanities the graver class, who deemed them good but weak men, found it no easy matter to apologize.

Let us imagine a clergyman of no more than the ordinary calibre snugly placed in a country parish, — indolent but respectable, — remarkable for being emphatic in his commonplaces, and for having nothing else to be emphatic in, — zealous above all his brethren in his denunciations against patronage, and apt to be particularly severe on some of the best of them, just because *their* denunciations were less frequent and less loud than his own; — let us, we say, imagine such a person dreaming on his sofa that he was decidedly one of the first men, if not, indeed, the very first man, in the Church. Let us imagine him discovering that he had a very large head, and that it required a very large hat. Let us imagine him measuring and remeasuring, and, in short, finding out that he was a singularly great man, and then fully resolving on serving himself heir to Dr. Andrew Thomson in the leadership of the Church. Let us further imagine him throwing up his parish with this view, and accepting of a chapel in a large town. Of course, to a person like him the way to the first places in the Establishment could not be other than open. Let us imagine him taking every opportunity of speaking in the inferior church courts, — making long speeches on great questions because they were important, and long speeches on little questions because it was ingenious to show how much could be made out of them. Let us imagine him successful in rendering himself a very sad bore, and a very grievous hindrance to all manner of business, with no one to listen to his speeches or to reply to them, — with a drowsy moderator in front of him, and sleeping reporters behind. Let us then imagine him turning to the press, big as ever with his own importance, and magnanimously resolved on confounding the sleepers by an eloquent appeal to an impartial public. Let us imagine him well-nigh realizing the story of the Welsh curate in Joe Miller, who, in printing a sermon, requested the bookseller to throw off as many copies as there were families in the united kingdom; but, when urging on his publisher a second edition, let us imagine almost the whole of the first returning unsold. Finally, let us imagine him concluding that half the public and two-thirds of the Church had entered into a conspiracy to eclipse his bright genius, — thoroughly convinced as ever of his clear claim to the leadership, — jealous of Dr. Chalmers, — certain that our Grays, Cunninghams, Candlishes, and Dunlops, are but *vain*, light men, with hats immensely smaller than his own, — publishing a dull, bulky pamphlet, crammed with borrowed thoughts and original vituperation, in the hope of settling the present controversy and crushing his old friends, and, in short, making common cause with Moderatism, — and all this in the evangelical garb. Our draught may be but a mere fancy sketch; but if it be otherwise, has the Church any very great cause to regret the opposition of such a man?

Let us imagine yet another case. Let us conceive, if we can, a man vain to a proverb, equally convinced of his oratorical powers with the other, and of his natural right to be a leader in the Church. Let us imagine him ever involved, on the score of personal dignity, in controversies the most ludicrously small, — engaged, for instance, heart, soul, and spirit, in asserting, to the confusion of all and sundry, that his newly erected church should be called the *first* church of the town to which it belongs. Let us imagine him, confident of his own unparalleled powers, refusing his pulpit to a man such as Dr. Andrew Thomson. Our Saviour taught more than good manners when he instructed his followers to choose the humbler places when they sat at feasts; let us imagine the injunction reversed by the individual whose character we describe. While yet a young man, let us imagine him pressing himself forward, all unbidden, in our venerable Assembly, amid the aged fathers of the Church. Let us imagine him engaged in endless speeches that could not be listened to, and grown a thorough master of that particular species of fine speaking which rejoices in supernumerary adjectives. But though thus forward and vain, let us conceive of him also as a zealous assertor of the original principles of Scottish presbytery,—as going along with the Church in all her decisions,—as committing himself, in reported speeches and printed sermons, to all her principles,—as publicly recognizing her leaders as men of God,—as, in short, a foot-soldier in the very vanguard of the party, and only nothing more because, despite of his own estimate, nature had denied the necessary power. Imagine him either piqued to find it so, or that a dangerous crisis has at length come, and stealing meanly away by a side-path, of which, of the hundreds present, only one other individual could avail himself, and that one, by his own confession, not a member of the Evangelical party. But our sketch is not yet completed. Imagine the subject of it taking his place, not many months subsequent, at a political dinner, and rising, after one of the bitterest Intrusionists in Scotland, to denounce the very party for whom he had so long spoken and written, whose principles he had professed, and whose determinations he had defended, as a party with whom he had "no sympathy," and who were but urging the fall of the Establishment "*in the desperation of human pride.*" Was it not enough that he had saved himself? Surely a very little magnanimity might have enabled him to spurn the commonest trick of the renegade. This, too, may be but a fancy sketch; but if it be otherwise, we again ask, has the Church any very great cause to regret the opposition of such a man?

It is scarce necessary to remark in connection with such men, and especially the first, that it is one of the many advantages of our Presbyterian Church that every man finds his true level in it. We have our leading bishops, but they are all bishops of Heaven's making. It is through no indirect or unworthy influence that the ablest men take the first place in our Assemblies, and that character asserts its power there with all the force of a natural law. This, however, is not the point. We have described two classes who either already unite, or are on the eve of uniting, the doctrines of Evangelism to the Moderate policy. Their joint numbers would scarce amount to half a score; but much has been made of their characters in the present controversy, especially of those of the first class; and the Church's worst enemies have copiously quoted and enthusiastically cheered the pamphlets and speeches of the others. We would say to the people, Beware of all of the Moderate party who are on the eve of joining them.

MODERATISM: SOME OF ITS BETTER CLASSES.

Let us suppose a young man, brought up in all the deadness of Moderate principles from his very childhood, naturally quiet and amiable, and of a soft, retiring disposition. Let us suppose him marked out by his friends for the Church, just as they might have marked him out for physic or the law, and he himself, with little inclination one way or another, acquiescently pursuing the necessary studies. Let us suppose him at length settled in a parish, — respectable in acquirement, unexceptionable in conduct, and possessed, as a clergyman, of that sort of negative character which has formed a starting-point to thousands, — a starting-point, in their upward career, to some who have subsequently become at once props and ornaments of the Church, — a starting-point to others in their course downwards to a level of degradation too low to be reached by any except scandalous and unfaithful ministers. Let us imagine him at this stage with all his predilections in favor of the Moderate policy, the whole course of his education bearing full upon it, and himself as yet unqualified to understand anything higher, though, through the influence of a temper naturally quiet and retiring, little disposed to take a prominent part in church courts.

Let us next imagine a silent but very wonderful change taking place in his character. Let us imagine the breath of a living Spirit kindling up into light and heat the hitherto dead embers of his painfully gathered though but inadequately understood theology. "The wind bloweth as it listeth;" nor can we say why, in the stillness of the calm, the sudden breeze should rise at times in the recesses of some solitary valley, and heap together and carry upwards in its eddies the hitherto unseen and scattered foliage. Suppose, however, the change not restricted to the clergyman whom we describe. Let us imagine it also extended to many of his people,—a singular reformation taking place among them,—open immoralities suppressed, and an anxious concern awakened in hundreds together regarding the realities of the unseen world. Let us imagine their minister, thoroughly impressed and in earnest, entering on a course of duty very different from the skeleton round which he had at first proposed to himself,—no longer restricting himself to even Sabbath-day ministrations,—not even restricting himself to days at all, but atrociously guilty of the very abomination of his party,—preachings by night; guilty even, according to Rowland Hill, of being an instrument in the "conversion of souls at unseasonable hours." And yet we can imagine such a man, thus zealous and sincere, but thus retiring also in his habits, and little disposed to take an active part in church courts, remaining nominally, and for a brief transition period at least, in the ranks of Moderatism. His doctrines can be *no longer* the doctrines of his party; his policy, were he called on to act, could be quite as little their policy. It would be as impossible for him to obtrude a hireling, ignorant of God and religion, on a parish such as his own, as it would be for him to preach a gospel that had not Christ in it. But, though impelled to preach, he is not compelled to act. The prejudices of his education have still their hold of him; and so, nominally at least, he still ranks on the side of Moderatism. Would that the party had many such! In the first place, they might do it good; in the second, it is scarce possible, in the nature of things, that it could retain them long. It is not on one occasion only that Evangelism has drawn even her leaders from the ranks of the opposition. Henderson had but to be converted, and the timeserver and the intrusionist became the first man of Scotland in forwarding the work of the second Reformation.

There is another though less decided class whom it is also but justice to mention. The increase of Evangelism in the country has excited much bitter hostility and much determined opposition. There are both ministers and elders in the Church of Scotland, and especially the latter, whose entire exertions in their official capacity have been exertions against this principle and its workings. Were we to strike out of their catalogue of doings and sayings all they have done and said against missions, all they have spoken and written against revivals, all their canvassings and pamphleteering against church extension, all their efforts, secret and open, to secure the subjection of the spiritual to the secular power, all their severe and protracted labors to open our parishes to the intrusion of Youngs and Edwardses, and to show that it should be so, — were we to denude them of their deeds of this and a similar character, we would leave them nothing to connect them, even incidentally, with vital Christianity. The whole of their acts that have borne on religion in any way have been acts in the opposition. But the party has another and better class, — men brought up Moderates, and who still record their votes on the Moderate side,—who are by no means devoid of the feeling that the standard of duty is unequivocally an Evangelical standard. They are men in most instances pretty far advanced in life, by no means devoid of conscience, nor yet unimpressed by the truths of revelation; and who, after having preached Moderatism long enough to discover that it is but of very little use, have been groping doubtfully, and in much darkness and feebleness, after a "more excellent way." Instead of opposing the schemes of the Church, some of the class have done their little all to help them. They have been stirred up, partly through a growing seriousness, and partly by the example of some of their neighbors of the popular party, to more diligence than they were wont to exercise in their parochial labors; and if little fruit has been produced, there has been at least a desire awakened for its production. They at least respect Evangelism. "Be thankful," said one of the class, an aged and respectable man, to some young ministers, his co-presbyters,—"be thankful for the *time* in which you have come into the Church. When *we* entered it, there was less light and lower views of duty." Of this section of Moderatism we say just what we have said of the other, Would that it were a more numerous one! It is at least convinced of a truth, which men such as Dr. James Bryce will be slow to learn,—the truth that Evangelism is the vital principle of Presbytery,—that it could have no life without it as a Church, and no stability without it as an Establishment.

It is no matter of regret, we repeat, that Moderatism should have its better classes. The true matter of regret respecting it is, that the individuals of which those classes are composed should be so very few. The party has its statistics,—its unquestionable and unquestioned tabular exhibitions of character; and in these we unfortunately find its average modicum of usefulness fixed exceedingly low. Good character is a good thing, however; and though an over-large supply of it might render a schism in the party scarcely less inevitable, in the event of any ill-advised perseverance in the course chalked out by the protesters of the Commission, than that course would render inevitable a schism in the Church itself, still the party love to avail themselves of the respectability which it imparts. It is marvellous how often single names are referred to, and how the character of one is made to serve for a hundred. We have been reminded of the fact, we know not how often, by an old, and, we are afraid, not very pointed story, told us by an aged relative, some five and twenty years ago. At a time shortly after the old pious race of Scotch sailors described by Peter Walker had worn out, and long ere seamen's chapels and Methodism had done aught to raise a serious race in their stead, our sailors were a decidedly irreligious class. Honest old John Menzies, of Aberdeen, however, who lived at this time, was not only one of the bravest and most skilful seamen connected with the port, but also one of the most truly pious men of the city. Almost every one knew and respected John Menzies. A party of very decent women had met at Leith, and the conversation turned, among other things, on the irreligion of sailors. "Ah! poor fellows," said one of the women, "we should not judge over rashly; there are surely good men among them. For my own part, I can say that one of the very best men I know is a sailor."—"That, cummer, may well be," said another woman; "I also know a sailor who is the worthiest man alive."—"And I, too," said a third, "know a sailor who has very few equals." This, of course, looked remarkably well; three Christian sailors found on so slight a survey, it was hard to say how long the list might become. Unluckily, however, the women came to compare notes, and discovered, in consequence, that their three super-excellent sailors just resolved themselves into honest old John Menzies, of Aberdeen.

PRAYER: THE TRUE AND THE COUNTERFEIT.

"It has been long held by the people of Scotland, that prayers laboriously polished in the study ere repeated by rote in the pulpit,—fine addresses to Deity smoothed up with the same small care which sonneteers bestow on odes to their mistresses' eyebrows,—are in reality very poor sort of things." We said so a paper or two ago; but the justice of the reflection has been challenged. We hold that it has its foundation, not in prejudice, but in truth.

A Scotch Highlander, who served in the first disastrous war with the American colonies, was brought one evening before his commanding officer, charged with the capital offence of being in communication with the enemy. The charge could not well be preferred at a more dangerous time. Only a few weeks had passed since the execution of Major André; and the indignation of the British, exasperated almost to madness by the event, had not yet cooled down. There was, however, no direct proof against the Highlander. He had been seen in the gray of the twilight stealing from out a clump of underwood that bordered on one of the huge forests which at that period covered by much the greater part of the United Provinces, and which, in the immediate neighborhood of the British, swarmed with the troops of Washington. All the rest was mere inference and conjecture. The poor man's defence was summed up in a few words: he had stolen away from his fellows, he said, to spend an hour in private prayer. "Have you been in *the habit* of spending hours in private prayer?" sternly asked the officer, himself a Scotchman and a Presbyterian. The Highlander replied in the affirmative. "Then," said the other, drawing out his watch, "never in all your life had you more need of prayer than now; kneel down, sir, and pray aloud, that we may all hear you." The Highlander, in the expectation of instant death, knelt down. His prayer was that of one long acquainted with the appropriate language in which the Christian addresses his God. It breathed of imminent peril, and earnestly implored the divine interposition in the threatened danger, — the help of Him who, in times of extremity, is strong to deliver. It exhibited, in short, a man who, thoroughly conversant with the scheme of redemption, and fully impressed with the necessity of a personal interest in the advantages which it secures, had made the business of salvation the work of many a solitary hour, and had, in consequence, acquired much fluency in expressing all his various wants as they occurred, and his thoughts and wishes as they arose. "You may go, sir," said the officer, as he concluded: "you have, I dare say, not been in correspondence with the enemy to-night. His statement," he continued, addressing himself to the other officers, "is, I doubt not, perfectly correct. No one could have prayed so without a long apprenticeship; the fellows who have never attended drill always get on ill at review."

Now, we are of opinion that the commanding officer evinced very considerable shrewdness in this instance. We learn to make our common every-day language a ready medium of communicating all our various thoughts and feelings, *just because it is* our common every-day language, —just because, through constant habit, we come so intimately to associate the arbitrary signs with the ideas which they represent, that at length, ceasing to mark their distinct existence as signs, they become identical with the thoughts of which they were at first but the instruments. There is surely no fanaticism in arguing after this fashion; nor was the Scotch officer in any degree a fanatic, though he carried the principle a little further. He argued that the men with whom prayer is a habit acquire the language of prayer; and it was on this principle that he tested the suspected Highlander. The mechanic and the tradesman learn to wield their technicalities — so stiff and unmanageable to all but themselves — with as much ease as if they were the commonest vocables of the language. The vocabularies of chemistry and the mathematics, of geology and botany, however difficult and repulsive to others, never encumber the chemist or the mathematician, the geologist or the botanist; they serve, on the contrary, to impart clearness to their thinking and fluency to their reasonings. But no one ever mastered these vocabularies without much practice and study; and, in like manner, the closet has its vocabulary, which it also requires practice and study to master. In the every-day communications which the Christian holds with his God, there are other thoughts conveyed, and other feelings expressed, than those which he employs in his every-day converse with his fellows. The recesses of the internal man are laid open; the bias to evil, though manifested in but embryo imaginings and hidden moods, is confessed and deplored in language varied according to the character of the imagination or the complexion of the mood; there are implorations for assistance against enemies felt, though invisible, and the nature of whose ever-varying assaults is suggestive of the ever-varying petition. The circumstance, too, that it is God who is addressed, gives a peculiarity to the style. We walk erect in the presence of our fellows; and as it is the privilege of our species to walk erect, shame to the low and mean natures that do otherwise! But is there any one who can prostrate himself before his Maker in a humility too profound? All revelation, too, with its vast breadth of meaning,—that breadth which, the more we examine it, expands the more,—is composed of but the elements, the materials of prayer; and an intercourse with God for a thousand lifetimes united would not suffice to employ them all. Prayer is so mighty an instrument that no one ever thoroughly mastered all its keys. They sweep along the infinite scale of man's wants and of God's goodness. But, comparatively at least, this instrument has been mastered; it is mastered to a considerable degree by every converted man. He acquires the vocabulary of the closet as the proper language of the state of which he has become a free denizen, and his fellow-citizens recognize it as their common tongue. The Scotch officer was not altogether ignorant of it; and to the positive existence of such a language the anecdote of his experiment on the Highlander owes its point.

To the Christian possessed of the language of the closet we very decidedly oppose the mere Moderate, by whom that language has not been acquired. Nay, we go further. We affirm that the ability of recognizing this language through that sympathy which soul holds with soul, and that perception through which experience recognizes its kindred experience, are elements, and no unimportant ones, of the present controversy. We would deem a Christian people fully justified in rejecting every clergyman in whose prayers they did not recognize this language. We know there are good men who write their prayers. We are aware that Knox wrote prayers for the rude and untaught people of Scotland, whom it was his high and honorable vocation to civilize and instruct; but the language in which they were written was the heart-stirring language of the closet. They were altogether different from the things we censure, — those pieces of labored feebleness, whose polish is but the polish of baldness, — things that are not prayers, but the semblances of prayers, — not substance, but the reflections of substance, — the mere echoes of hearts that reverberate because they are hollow. And the difference can be well felt. It can be tried by the test of the Scotch officer. On grounds such as these we again repeat our remark, — we repeat, that "it has been long held by the people of Scotland," and held justly, "that prayers laboriously polished in the study ere repeated by rote in the pulpit, — fine addresses to Deity smoothed up with the same small care which sonneteers bestow on odes to their mistresses' eyebrows, — are in reality very poor sort of things, — mere embodiments, in most instances, of an inefficient world-hunting Moderatism, that *plays at sentence-making.*"

MR. ISAAC TAYLOR ON THE INDEPENDENCE OF THE CHURCH.

NOTHING proper to a Church and State system, says the celebrated author of "Ancient Christianity," in his work on "Spiritual Despotism," published some years since,—"*nothing proper to a Church and State system demands the subserviency of the Church to the State.*" Such is the decisive declaration of one who, himself from principle an Episcopalian, yet laments with the greatest earnestness over the "fatal surrender" which the Church of England has made to the State of her spiritual prerogative and independence,—a step which he regards as in a preëminent degree the source of those perilous circumstances by which she is surrounded. And in this we believe him to be not far from the truth. A Church may be subject to many corruptions, and may tolerate many abuses; but until she divests herself, as the Church of England has in great measure done, of the powers of government and the reins of discipline,—of her spiritual independence and freedom,—she possesses within herself that machinery, a due exercise of which may accomplish her purification and revival. Deprived of these powers, however, the well-spring of her vitality is poisoned; she floats a helmless, mastless hulk upon the waves, "at the merciment," to quote the words of Mr. Taylor, "of her foes and of her friends."

We are strongly of opinion, from the incidental expressions made use of by this deservedly esteemed writer in the work referred to, that, were his attention turned to the present contest of our Church with the civil despotism of the day, he would have no hesitation on which side to take his stand. He would hesitate not—as he presumes, with reference to the Church of England, that no "practical and impartial" man would hesitate—"to give his aid in restoring to the Established Church that INDEPEN-

DENCE and those vital functions which Christianity demands for her," and which the Scottish Reformers, in contradistinction to those of England, secured to us in a manner conformable to God's word, and which, they fondly imagined, would preserve us from further molestation. Thus he speaks of the English Establishment:—"Too long she has consented to be mocked with the empty forms of independence; and is now so placed that she must assert and regain her lost prerogatives, or fall lower still. The assembling of convocation effectively at her own discretion, and for the exercise of *substantial functions,—the unprompted election of her bishops*, and the annulling of lay encroachments upon ecclesiastical property [an evil that we also wish to see 'annulled'],—are obvious points of that Church reform which the course of events demands." How refreshing is it, in a Church which, with all her boasted emblazonries of rank and pretension, is trodden under foot by an iron despotism, to meet with one of such congenial sentiments with ourselves, who can proclaim aloud, with equal boldness and ability, her degraded and enslaved condition, and the means necessary to be adopted for reinstating her in that status which it behooves the Church of Christ to occupy! Mr. Taylor advocates an infusion of lay blood into the organic government of the Church,—the complete disenthralment from the bonds of state supremacy; and looks forward to the accomplishment of these reforms, along with a correction of the abuses of patronage,—such an amendment of the whole system "as would concede something to the people, and *absolutely exclude* the merchandise of souls,"—as fitted to acquire for the Establishment, what she is not now possessed of, the submissive and cordial reverence and regard of her people. He does not, indeed, acknowledge the scriptural right of the people to a direct voice in the appointment of their ministers. But the conclusion at which he arrives on this point from another source of evidence may have equal weight with those who make primitive practices and ancient fathers the "gods of their idolatry;" and it is, so far as it goes, very satisfactory, as coming from one who has made the history of the pristine churches a subject of deep and fruitful study, and whose predilections are all in favor of the hierarchical system of the Church of England. "In fact," he says, "though not to be traced in the canonic writings, the popular voice and suffrage in the election of the bishop unquestionably obtained a very early prevalance, and those who absolutely excluded the WILL of the people in the choice of their pastors, although not reproveable by the letter of Scripture, yet oppose one of the most ancient and universal of ecclesiastical usages."

In his summary of scriptural proofs concerning the different forms of Church government, we scarcely think that Mr. Taylor at all grapples with or meets the arguments and facts by which the system of Presbytery may be maintained from the word of God. He no doubt expresses in an able manner the incoherent and destructive nature of Congregationalism; but he seems chary of coming into too close collision with the advocates of Presbyterianism. We leave it, however, for our readers to judge how far he has in the following passage portrayed the leading characteristics of the two Establishments of this country. "If a choice were to be made between two actual forms of Presbyterianism and Episcopacy, whereof the first admits the laity to a just and apostolic place in the management and administration of the Church, while the second absolutely rejects all such influence, and at the same time retains for its bishops the baronial dignities and the secular splendor usurped by the insolent hierarchs of the middle ages, then, indeed, the balance would be one of a different sort; and, unless there were room to hope for a correction and reform of political prelacy, an honest and modest Christian mind would take refuge in the substantial benefits of Presbyterianism." We are inclined to believe that the writer has in these lines, perhaps altogether unwittingly, been trying his hand at portrait-painting; and that the contrast between the "counterfeit presentment of the two brothers" tells by no means against our northern Establishment.

DEFENCE ASSOCIATIONS.

It was natural, as the crisis of the conflict approached, that the Evangelical party throughout the parishes of Scotland should adopt such an organization as might enable them most effectively to promote their principles and vindicate their position. Hence arose the Defence Associations which figure in the following article. — Ed.

It was an important step, not for our country only, but for the whole human species, when our humbler countrymen of old, associating for mutual defence, surrounded a few mean villages with rude walls, and procured their Charters of Community from monarchs jealous of the proud barons, their oppressors. Our historians, especially the earlier ones, have dwelt almost exclusively on the hard-fought battles of our country, on the barbarous feuds of proud and haughty barons, the intrigues of courtiers, and the negotiations of statesmen. Our poets and romancers have revelled amid the uncouth splendor of courts that were but conning their first lessons in politeness, and have exhausted their power of narrative and description on the barbaric pomp of tournaments, and the spirit-stirring scenes of war and the chase. Transactions and events of an immensely more important character have been passed over undescribed. In tracing to its earliest origin the liberty of our country, we would pass over kings, barons, and knights, — all that has been permitted hitherto most to occupy the memory and fill the imagination, — and, descending from the castle and the palace, we would select, as the true benefactors of the present time, the denizens of a humbler sphere. We would pick out the rude mechanic plying his simple art in his humble cottage, behind the rampart of undressed stone which his own hands had assisted to rear,—his black jack of hammered iron, and his round head-piece suspended from the rafters above, — his sword crossed over his long bow, and his six-eln spear stretching athwart the wall. Burgher does not sound half so nobly as knight; but it is to the burgher, not to the knight, that we owe the liberty of the subject, the manumission of the vassal, the emancipation of the slave, humanizing commerce, equal laws, the arts of social life, and the first asylums and baiting-places of the Reformation. The association of the oppressed many against the grinding despotism of the powerful few has been peculiarly blessed in almost all the states of Europe, and nowhere more emphatically blessed than in our own country. Nay, had we to furnish appropriate emblems of the despotism over which, in their long struggle, the people ultimately triumphed, and of the liberty which they at length achieved, — if we could scarce find a fitter symbol of the one than some proud baronial castle, with its huge gray walls thinly sprinkled with iron-barred windows, its overhanging bartizans, its deep moat, its jealous drawbridge, its cruel dungeon hid deep from the air and the sun, its court of summary trial, and its grave-besprinkled mound of execution, — we could scarce devise a more appropriate representative of the other than some humble town, rudely but strongly walled round, its hardy inhabitants trained to arms, and bound by the most solemn engagements reciprocally to defend each other, its straw-covered council-house rising in the midst of its one irregular street, its narrow and crowded dwellings clamorous with the sounds of mechanic labor, a few armed burghers watching at its gate, and the sweeping declivity below thickly besprinkled with its minute and multitudinous patches of cultivation.

Now that a crisis has arisen in which it is necessary for the people of Scotland again to unite, as of old, it is well to consider the kind of arms which it is most their safety and interest to wield, and the class of enemies against which they would do well first to direct them. Our ancestors commenced operations by drawing closely together, and surrounding their humble dwellings with a wall. They would scarce have succeeded in obtaining their charters of community had they applied for them in the character of defenceless serfs. Their descendants must also draw closely together; but wall-building will scarcely avail them. It must be their work rather to demolish walls erected already.

Our Church Defence Associations may be made to subserve a very important purpose. We have had occasion to remark, oftener than once, that in many of our rural districts political opinion is still a serf bound to the soil. It is not men, in most of these, to whom the Reform Bill has actually extended the franchise; it is acres. It is not farmers, but groups of fields, estimated in the laird's rent-book at fifty pounds per annum, that enjoy the privilege of returning representatives to Parliament. The tenant is but the mouth-piece of his farm, and the proprietor his prompter. Now, without being particularly political, we must just say that this is not at all what should be. Opinion should *not* be a serf bound to the soil. It is men, not acres, who should enjoy the franchise. It is not according to the British constitution, either as it was or is, that a proprietor should possess as many votes as he possesses farms; and it is well to remember that, as for every privilege which man enjoys man shall have to give an account, the tenant, though he can transfer his vote to his landlord, cannot transfer to him his responsibility. It may be quite right, if he so will it, that he should vote with his landlord; but it is at least equally right that he should vote with him only because he wills it, and is convinced in his own mind that his determination is a good one. In a point of singular advantage for observation, we have been often astonished to see how implicitly even a rack-rented tenantry seemed to have taken it for granted that the vote was their proprietor's, not theirs. Regularly as term-day came round, the rent, to its last shilling, had to be produced; and, had bank-agents been as unaccommodating as the laird, almost every Martinmas might have witnessed its roups of live-stock and utensils; and yet, notwithstanding, every dissolution of Parliament saw the votes of an oppressed tenantry thirled to the manor-house. Our Church Defence Associations are admirably suited to correct this evil. There are many merely political questions on which it is difficult for plain men to form an opinion,—many, too, in which there is so equal a balance of right and wrong, that one might hesitate to encounter a contingent evil, however slight its character, in deciding either for or against them. But no true Presbyterian in Scotland, however little skilled in politics, will experience any difficulty in making up his mind on the Church question, in its bearing on scenes such as that of Culsalmond and Marnoch. Directed and impelled by our Defence Associations, we trust to see it insinuate its wedge between the Intrusionist landlord and the votes of his Non-Intrusionist tenants; and we are of opinion the attention of our friends cannot be too strongly directed to this point. The wealthy commoner who reckons fifty farms on his roll, and the farmer, his tenant, who rents, at fifty pounds per annum, one of the smallest of them, are placed politically on exactly the same level, and it is surely high time that both the proprietor and the farmer should begin to know it.

All other Scottish parties have been already drawn out into the political arena; they have been already tasked to their full strength, each against its antagonist party; nor has there been a means left untried by which the power of any one of them might be increased. But the Presbyterianism of the Church of Scotland has not yet been drawn out in its character as such. It has been lost amid *other* and lower parties; and, now that it is gathering to a head in its own proper form, it may be well conceived of as a new force marching into the heart of a lengthened fray. We have referred to a kind of political *vis inertiæ*. Mr. John Dunlop, in his masterly work on association, tells us, in illustrating this principle, that in 1789, when the whole existing state of society in France seemed ready to explode, and when the assembling of the States-General was commenced, the great body of the common people remained such careless spectators of the universal commotion and struggle which was impending, that few of them took the trouble of voting at the elections, and that where a thousand were expected to come forward, not perhaps fifty made their appearance. There has been more of this *vis inertiæ* among the Presbyterians of the Church of Scotland than perhaps any other body in the kingdom. But we have in the present controversy a force potent enough to overcome it; and it will, we trust, be a main object with our Church Defence Associations to bring this force to bear. The passive must be converted into the active throughout the country. The "grave livers" of Scotland have never been drawn out in any purely secular quarrel; nor has the country, in any of her popular struggles, presented a very imposing attitude without them. They have ever constituted her strength. The poet of Scotland who so truly described himself as "prompt to learn and wise to know," but whose wisdom and knowledge too little influenced his own unhappy career, could see clearly from what scenes the glory of his country arose, and in what class her strength mainly consisted. Too little serious himself, he could yet recognize in her humble men of devotion and prayer her "guard and ornament," her best wealth in her times of peace, and her encircling "wall of fire" in her day of trouble. We can trust that, with the Divine blessing, on which all must depend, our fast-forming associations will show that he did not overestimate their importance.

FORESHADOWINGS.

WHATEVER God in his wisdom may have designed as the termination of the existing troubles, it were well that for the present at least the Church and people of Scotland should be prepared for a time of extremity. Nor do we entertain any fear of inducing a timid feeling among the assertors of the present quarrel by referring to the imminence of the danger. Some of our readers will perhaps remember the remark of Burns on one of the criticisms of a friend, who suggested that he should strike out from his sublime address of the Bruce the alternative of the "gory bed," as impolitic in the circumstances. It tended to make death frightful, said the critic, and presented a discouraging and disagreeable image, which the skilful general would scarce venture to suggest to his troops on the eve of a great battle. Burns knew better. "It was the battle of Bannockburn," said the poet, "which they were going to fight; and the man who would have shrunk at the image of the 'gory bed' was no man fitted to fight there."

It is imperatively necessary that the country be thoroughly aroused. Its chance of escaping from the present imminent danger (if in such a matter we may speak of chance) will be in exact proportion to its sense of it. All must have remarked how very difficult it is to realize extraordinary events as things of probable occurrence in one's own times. We acquaint ourselves with matters in their ordinary course, — with the common, every-day affairs of life, —and give to our anticipations of the future, from an inherent law of our nature, the complexion of what we may term our average experience of the present. And hence the difficulty to which we refer. Occurrences similar to those more striking events of history which belong *to* experience in its extended sense, but not to our own individual experience, are almost never anticipated as probable; nay, even their very possibility is held doubtful. A sort of instinctive, unreasoning skepticism declares against them. Many of our readers must remember with what feelings, some fifteen or twenty years ago, they were in the habit of regarding the narratives of those terrible visitations of the plague which, as late as the middle half of the seventeenth century, used from time to time to thin the population of Britain. Visitations of so frightful a character were viewed as belonging exclusively to the past, — so exclusively, that their return seemed scarce possible. It seemed well-nigh as probable that the country should again see that John Milton who had to remove from his house in Bunhill Fields during the ravages of the pest, as the ravages of the pest itself; and sad stories of dead bodies dragged on hurdles to the nearest hillock, and thrown into hastily-scooped graves, — of whole hamlets left desolate, — of strange barriers arresting the progress of the disease in crowded cities, — barriers such as slender runnels of water or cross lanes, — of clouds of vapor standing up like erect walls over the infected districts, — of cottages burnt to the ground, for all their inmates had perished, and all within reeked with the rank steam of infection; — these and many such narratives seemed merely dreams of tradition, — not sober realities, but a sort of misty extravagances, which, however connected with the past, no one could associate with times so sober as the present. Southey, in one of his earlier prose writings, ventured to urge the probability of the return of such strange and terrible visitations, and the suggestion was regarded as wild and unnatural — as the somewhat *outré* stroke of a bold writer straining after effect. We have lived, however, to see cholera strike down a hundred millions of the human species; we have seen it, regulated by its own eccentric and inexplicable laws, ravaging our cities and villages, as if its districts had been assigned to it by the rule and the measuring line. Clouds of murky vapor have stood up for days and weeks together over our towns, as if the destruction that was pressing upon them had taken to itself a visible form; cottages have been again burnt to the ground for the same sad cause as of old; and, as the flames arose, we have seen their light flashing on the lonely graves of their perished inmates, — graves scooped out of wooded hillocks, far from churchyards and every accustomed place of sepulture, or on the skirts of mountain-streams, or the verge of solitary seashores. Events similar to those which we could scarce credit as possible in connection with our own country and our own time some eighteen or twenty years ago, are now registered in our experience as portions of our country's recent history. And it is well to remark that this sort of instinctive skepticism applies as certainly to signal atrocities perpetrated by men, as to extraordinary visitations in the providence of God. A repetition of the Irish massacre seems as impossible now as a visit from the pest appeared twenty years ago. Men are still slow to believe that our civil courts in the nineteenth century may be found as decidedly opposed to Christ, his cause and government, as they were in the seventeenth. The atrocities of forced settlements, though we see them occurring around us, still seem rather to belong to a former age than to the present time; and the latest era of persecution for conscience' sake continues to appear as if it had closed when William III. landed in Torbay. It were well for the country to be thoroughly aroused from the indifferency which this natural, though not the less irrational, skepticism induces. The revolutionary cycle seems fast revolving in Britain. In Scotland, at least, we now stand on the very brink of some of the more intolerable evils by which great convulsions are invariably preceded; and in a very few months, if the Presbyterianism of the country bestir not itself all the more vigorously, it shall have to witness, as of old, the disestablishment of the national *religion*, and the ejection from their charges of all its better pastors. There are more than the controversies of the seventeenth century reviving.

To the people in the present crisis we have but one advice: they must arouse, associate, prepare themselves. If they but stand still, it will be to witness the infliction of one of the widest spread desolations that ever yet visited their Church or country. There were only two hundred parish churches shut up on the first Sabbath of the winter of 1662, through the policy of Commissioner Middleton, backed by the tyranny of Charles. The policy of our Hopes and Aberdeens, backed by Sir Robert Peel, threatens to shut up at least twice that number, and to render the others of as little value to the community as the churches occupied by the curates during the disastrous reign of Prelacy. There can be no doubt that the people *will* be thoroughly roused; but it is all-important that they should be roused in time. It is all-important that they should be roused rather to prevent evil than to avenge it. They err egregiously who hold that one vigorous blow, through which the Evangelism of Scotland would be thrust beyond the pale of her Establishment, would restore quiet to the country. It would restore to it such quiet as the similar blow dealt to it by Middleton did, — a quiet compared with which all the popular ebullitions of either the present century or the last would be scarce worthy of being regarded as popular ebullitions at all. But it would be well, surely, for both the Church and her enemies that the experiment should not be made. The fight at present is on the breach. Better that it should be decided there than by blowing up the citadel at a later stage.

TRANSLATIONS INTO FACT.

PART FIRST.

AN act of Parliament is confessedly a dry-looking document; a collection of acts forms a dull, unreadable book. If we double the amount, the fatigue of perusal necessarily doubles; the density increases in due proportion as the volumes spread over the shelves, and reaches its acme as they multiply into a complete law library. A heavy atmosphere presses upon the dust that gathers over the folios of Themis, and its dense vapory folds reflect a mirage of only slumbrous images. The tall, weighty columns, each with its single broad margin patched over with notes, like a pond-edge studded with bogs; the sections and paragraphs doled out by the tale, as if the framers had been fearful, seemingly not without cause, of repeating the same provision twice,—here and there the blunder actually committed, notwithstanding the precaution,—here and there the opposite mistake of a provision running counter to the rest, turned, as it were, thwartways in the passage, as logs sometimes do when floated down a stream; the long, loose, unmusical sentences, that forget themselves, and run into paragraphs; the thick, dense words, that seem selected with the express design of eclipsing the meaning,—that at least, in many instances, serve admirably to effect the apparent purpose; the glimmering cross-lights of idea that meet the student at every turning, with all the perplexing bewilderment, but none of the picturesqueness, of cross-lights in an ancient building; the equable, slumbrous, Lethe-like rumble, rumble of the style; the general resemblance of every one leaf to every other,—of page to page, of section to section, of act to act; and then the enormous amount of the whole,—one fifty pages following another fifty pages,—the bookbinder interposing his fence of pasteboard and calf when we number the thousand,—then another thousand commencing,—then another, and another, and another,—and, after numbering the term of Methuselah's years twenty times told, the thousands as if still but beginning;—truly it seems no way wonderful that so many lawyers should be so little acquainted with law, or that they should find it so much easier a matter to listen to the decisions of the dozen arbitrary legislators of the Court of Session, than to plod through the acts of the hereditary and representative legislators of the two Houses of Parliament. It is easier to listen to decisions than to plod through acts; just as it is obviously easier to pick up the smattering of information which passes current in the gossip of the day, than to ground one's self thoroughly in the knowledge which is to be derived from books. "Gigantic geniuses, fit to grapple with whole libraries," are not geniuses of every-day production; but men qualified to collect news occur in crowds, go where we may; and hundreds of the class write "solicitor," "advocate," or "W. S." on their door-plates, and attend the Parliament House.

But if it be thus a heavy matter to read law as stored up in huge folios, it is far from being a heavy matter to read it as written on the face of a country. We pass from the sign to that which the sign represents. All is cold and obscure abstraction in the one; all is breathing, animated existence in the other. Let us take, by way of example, but a single act,—the act through which Commissioner Middleton overturned Presbyterianism in Scotland. It is merely a piece of bad, unideal prose in the statute-book; but what a deeply interesting though fearful tragedy of many scenes does it not appear amid the hills and fields, and in the towns and villages of our native country! Gibbets rise tall and black over assembled crowds; and we see in the hands of the public executioner gray-haired men of God, content rather to die than deny their Master. The churches of the land are silent, or re-echo only the mutterings of a debasing superstition. The voice of psalms mingles on the hills with the patter of musketry. There is cold, and hunger, and violent death, amid yonder rocks and moors, and in those solitary dens and caves. Thousands die on fields of battle, or are forced into exile, immured in dungeons, borne away to be sold as slaves in the colonies, perish in tempests chained to the sinking wreck, or welter under flood-mark, as the tide rises, tied down amid the ware and tangle of the shore. There is blood everywhere, as in the land of Egypt when Moses called up the first plague. Blood in council-chambers,—blood on the boots and the thumbkins,—blood on the ermine of the judge,—blood on the lawn of the bishop,—blood on the scaffold and the headsman's axe,—blood in the churchyard, where the debased criminal and the honored martyr are huddled together in a common grave,—blood beside the cottage wall, where the lonely widow watches the corpse of her murdered husband. The rising sun is reflected on pools of blood, that thicken amid the hills beside new-made graves; it sets upon blood freshly spilt on fields strewed with yet quivering carcasses; the Clyde flows sullenly along the arches of Bothwell, and the eddies are crimsoned with blood. There is blood everywhere; and the cry of the land rises to Heaven. How very terrible the reading of this iniquitous act, when we thus pass from the statute-books of the country to its history,—from the sign to the thing signified! We peruse the scene a little longer. An empty throne appears in the distance; a bigot king wanders, discrowned, in pitiable exile; and the last of his descendants perishes, in scorn and beggary, in a foreign land. Take, as another example, the scarce less iniquitous act of Queen Anne, and peruse it in a similar manner. A dense fog of indifferency and practical error creeps over the grand religious institution of the country, and in district after district its moral influence becomes more than neutralized; for, instead of ministering to the religious feelings of the people, it but serves to shock and outrage them. Not a few of our churches become scenes of violence and perjury; from not a few of our pulpits there are doctrines promulgated which souls cannot receive and live; and the better men of the country, unable to eject those who buy and sell, — those whose traffic, darker than that of the money-changers of old, is a traffic in men's souls, — quit in sorrow the place so grossly desecrated. One humble chapel rises after another amid their hamlets, where they worship in the purity and freedom with which their fathers worshipped. But the comparatively indifferent sink into yet deeper indifference. No man cares for their souls; for when did the hireling care for his flock? The evening and morning hymn is silenced in many a cottage. Immorality and improvidence come in like a flood. The Sabbath becomes a day of weariness, — fit preparation for its becoming a day of toil. The old spirit of honest independence evaporates; for, in a state of slavery to vice, the whole abject feelings of the slave are induced; the pauperism of the country multiplies a hundred-fold, and, fierce in its distress, threatens to play the footpad with our capitalists and proprietary. And when at length, after the lapse of a century, the spirit of a better time revives, it finds but a mutilated body to animate, — a body palsied in part, — shorn of not a few of its members, and bearing within, in, alas! no small amount, the seeds of corruption. We peruse exactly the same statute, in an abridged form, in the settlements of Marnoch and Culsalmond; and what honest man so dull as to miss its true meaning in digests so clear, pointed, and concise?

It is ever an important matter to be able thus to translate written laws, if we may so speak, into overt acts and their consequences. It is a higher ability in its perfection than that of the mere lawyer; it is the ability of the profound statesman and legislator. All men, however, possess it in some degree — even men who cannot so much as read written law; and it is to the general diffusion and exercise of this faculty that the Church, in the present controversy, owes the support of so preponderating a majority of the people. If lawyer-like misinterpretation of statutes, or the calumnies of seven-eighths of the public press, could have misled them, they would have been all on the other side. Mr. Robertson, of Ellon, would not have been plausible, nor the Earl of Aberdeen diplomatic, in vain; nor would almost all have seen fallacies deplorably palpable in the arguments of Dr. Cook, and in the utter lack of solidity in the motion of Dr. Muir. It was the general ability of translating into the tangibilities of action the misinterpretation and the calumnies, the plausibilities and the diplomacy, the arguments and the motion, that rallied her supporters round the Church. We are told by the lawyers, for instance, that spiritual independence in connection with the Establishment means just no more than that degree of independence which the Court of Session now chooses to allow her. We test the doctrine by the tangibilities of history, — action seen retrospectively, — and find that, if it be true, all the histories of our Church and country must be false. It must be entirely false that, in the long battle of the sixteenth and seventeenth centuries, the Church was ultimately victor; it must be false that the charter granted to her in 1592 is still unrepealed, — that there was a revolution settlement in her favor, or that an act for securing the independence of her government formed a basis of the treaty of union. And accordingly we find that, by a strange enough fiction of law, the unreality of all this is actually taken for granted by the assertors of the doctrine, and that, as if there had been no charter, no revolution settlement, no treaty of union, they argue that the Black Acts of 1584 are still in force, — acts which, according to even Principal Robertson, were repealed only eight years after their enactment. If this doctrine be true, these statutes are still the law of the Church, and all the rest of her history is a lie. And to what do the calumnies of the press amount when translated into events? What sort of light do the outrages at Marnoch and Culsalmond throw on the oft-repeated assertion, that it is clerical power, not popular right, for which the Church is contending? What clerical party, on the meanest and most grossly palpable of subterfuges, were content to increase their own power at the expense of the people there? And in what party, on the other hand, did the people recognize their best and most devoted friends?

A similar translation of the Earl of Aberdeen's bill at once fixes its character. If the bill be a desirable bill, then the dilemma, in which ministers of the gospel could do only one of two things, — either outrage their own conscience by pronouncing reasons of objection to be good which, from the very nature of things, they could not know to be either good or otherwise, or of outraging the consciences of congregations by subjecting them to forced settlements, — this, we say, if the bill be desirable, would be, of consequence, a desirable dilemma. We have read somewhere of the Code Napoleon, that in at least one important respect it differs materially from the statute-book of our own country. The bearing of our statutes on special cases is fixed by decisions; the laws of the Code, on the contrary, are illustrated by examples. Special cases are imagined beforehand; and it is the part of the magistrate to compare with these the cases which actually occur, and to decide accordingly. Examples conceived on a similar principle would be fatal accompaniments to the bill of Aberdeen. Nor are we quite sure that they would tell very decidedly in favor of the *liberum arbitrium.* There are cases, at least, in which even it would translate lamely enough into fact, — cases in which presbyteries and synods might be as free from the necessity of perpetrating forced settlements as Adam was free, ere the Fall, from all compulsion to sin, and in which their freedom might possibly be not better employed. At all events, in all human affairs the balance of justice wavers least when there are efficient checks to steady it. These, however, are but desultory remarks, and serve merely to introduce the subject which we sat down to illustrate. It is our purpose to attempt translating into fact one or two of the plausibilities of Mr. Robertson, of Ellon, one or two of the arguments of Dr. Cook, and, perhaps, one or two of the assertions of Dr. Muir; and to show that it has been chiefly through a tacit process of translation of the kind we describe that they have so utterly failed in impressing the religious portion of the community, or other than an inconsiderable portion of the Scottish public in general. We are told that *Candid* remarked with surprise, in the Court of El Dorado, that the *bon mots* of the king, even after they had been translated, still remained *bon mots.* The reverse of this will be found to be exactly the character of the principles which we intend translating into fact. They decompose, and become mephitic in the process, —

> "Woman to the waist, and fair,
> But ending foul in many a scaly fold."

PART SECOND.

Corporal Trim translated the fifth commandment into fact by settling on his aged parents the full half of his meagre pay as a soldier. Intrusion and non-intrusion, patronage and anti-patronage, are things equally capable of being translated into fact; nor is the process too difficult a one to be mastered by men well-nigh as humble as even the corporal himself. The tangibilities which these terms express bear upon all. The country may have its tens of thousands on whom a clergyman has never been intruded, and its hundreds of thousands who have never had an opportunity of exercising their choice in the selection of a clergyman for themselves; but it does not contain a single individual, to whom religion is anything, whether Churchman or Dissenter, who is not living in a certain felt relation to some one or other of the tangibilities of intrusion or non-intrusion, patronage or anti-patronage. We ourselves, for instance, have lived at different periods of our life in relation to them all,—now subjected to the evils of an unmitigated patronage, now participating in the limited privileges of a bare non-intrusion principle, now enjoying all the many signal advantages of free, uncontrolled choice. We have shared, in turn, in all that the Church is contending for, and in all she is contending against; and a piece of simple narrative, bearing on the circumstances of each case, may at once serve to illustrate our meaning, and to show not only how very important the principles of the present controversy are, but the secret also of the people's thorough understanding of them.

There are parishes in Scotland which contain areas of about twelve hundred square miles, and whose parish churches were some twenty years ago removed from the parish churches in their nearest neighborhood by a long day's journey. We resided in one of these for part of a twelvemonth, ere the government had given its supplementary chapels to the Highlands, and saw, for the first time, at the bottom of a little sandy bay that opened into the boisterous Atlantic, a Scottish parish church, between which and the nearer places of worship there stretched forty miles of wild sea-coast on the one hand, and fifty miles on the other. A stormy sea of barren hills occupied the interior; and the eye, in passing from the serrated peaks and gray, dizzy precipices of the higher grounds, encountered scarce anything more inviting on the lower than dark moors, and still darker morasses,—long, narrow plains at the bottom of retiring bays, overblown by sand,—and rock-skirted promontories studded with stone. It was no favorable locality for illustrating the excellence of the Voluntary principle. All the more respectable sort of people who can treat themselves on Sabbaths to a joint and a decent suit of broadcloth contrive also to treat themselves to a sermon; but—alas for the utterly poor!—nineteen-twentieths of the simple inhabitants of this wild district could treat themselves to neither Sabbath joints nor broadcloth. For at least one-third part of every year they had no meal, even, and scarce any potatoes; — their chance of provisions for the day depended almost exclusively on the uncertain fishing of the night; and they had to rest wholly for their religious provision on the National Establishment. Voluntaryism had done nothing for them, and could do nothing. But what had the Establishment done? It had given them a qualified minister, — a man who had been tried for a very gross crime by the General Assembly, but at a period when the General Assembly was the one court in Europe in which no such accusation was in any instance followed by conviction; and so, though all the parish held him guilty, he was still a qualified minister. He was naturally a dull man, of somewhat less than average intellect, based on a strong animal nature; and his pulpit ministrations were perhaps the most miserable things of the kind ever heard, — pieces of disjointed patchwork, badly read, borrowed in part without judgment, and, where original, written without care or thought. It was impossible to listen to them. Regarded in a religious light, they were desecrations of the Sabbath; in an intellectual, mere lullabies to set men asleep. The manse was one of the houses in the parish in which no family worship was kept, save for one week in the year, — the week in which the sacrament was dispensed, — and then, in order to appear as decent as possible in the eyes of one or two low-country ministers who usually came to assist on such occasions, the family were called together, and the form gone through. We saw in one instance an act of discipline performed in the parish. The minister had come home from his morning walk fierce with passion, — actually bellowing. His two elders were instantly sent for, to hold a session; and three boys were brought before them to undergo the censure of the Church. The little fellows had met their minister in his walk, and had deemed it excellent sport to remind him, somewhat too circumstantially, of the offence for which, a few years before, he had been tried by the General Assembly. And such was an average specimen of the respect entertained for him by his parishioners. We cannot give the darker shades of this picture; we shall not even hint at them. Be it enough to say, that such was the only clergyman in a tract of country considerably more than thirty miles square, and that we had no alternative, for some thirty Sabbaths together, but that of either attending *his* church, or of attending no church at all. To have heard sermon anywhere else would have involved a two-days' journey. Here, then, so far as we ourselves and ninety-nine hundredths of the poor parishioners were concerned, the worst tangibilities of intrusion were involved. Arguments translated into facts the most stubborn bore equally against the plausibilities of Voluntaryism on the one hand, and the sophisms of Moderatism on the other. The reservoir provided here at the public expense was but an accumulation of filth, breathing miasma and infection. Then, why care for its maintenance? say the Voluntaries. Because there was none other in the locality, and the people perished for thirst. Then, why now endanger its existence? say the Moderates. Because, existing as a mere tank of stagnant corruption, it mattered not to the surrounding country whether it existed or no; or, we should perhaps rather say, its existence, in the circumstances, was a positive evil. We exert ourselves, therefore, not to break down the reservoir, but to purify it, — to cleanse it from the feculent poison which has long reeked and festered in it, and to fill it with the pure and living stream, that all around may drink and be refreshed. This, however, is not quite what we intended to say. We set out by remarking that the country does not contain a single individual, to whom religion is anything, who is not living in a certain felt relation to the tangibilities of intrusion or non-intrusion; and we thus present the reader with one passage in our experience of the tangibilities of intrusion. Need we say that gladly would we have exercised the veto on the appointment of this Highland minister of the Moderate school, or that all his people would eagerly have joined with us? Of the latter, we may just remark, that they were a simple-hearted, inoffensive race of men, not indifferent to the blessings of the gospel, and not too unintelligent to distinguish it from its counterfeits.

We changed the scene for a district in the south of Scotland, not five miles from the Scottish capital. It would be worth while inquiring how it should almost always happen that the common country people in the neighborhood of large towns are less intelligent, not only than the common people of the towns themselves, but also than the common country people who reside in more sequestered localities. Such, however, in our individual experience at least, we have ever found to be the fact. We have seen shaded maps, on which, from the statistics of crime as furnished by the criminal courts of the several districts, a darker or lighter shade was given to particular localities. Here, where crime most abounded, the shade was intensely deep; there, where it was somewhat less frequent, a lighter tint spread over the provinces; yonder, where it was less frequent still, the tint was still lighter; and a faint twilight tinge indicated a yet lower degree of delinquency than characterized even the lowest of the other three. Could the comparative ignorance and intelligence of the several provinces of a country be marked out in a similar manner, we are convinced that well-nigh all our large towns would present the singular appearance of specks of comparative light, encircled, if we may so speak, by halos of darkness; and that a medium tint, here darker, there lighter, would spread over the country beyond. In the southern locality to which we had now removed we found ourselves within the very circle of one of these tenebrific halos. There was a stagnant vacancy of mind among the people, — a slumbrous lack of intelligence, — and at least as strongly-marked an indifference to religion as to all kinds of useful secular knowledge.

Carters, common laborers, and farm-servants formed the great bulk of the population, with a thin sprinkling of mechanics, petty dealers, and public-house keepers. Church-going among the carters and laborers seemed to have entirely worn out; the farm-servants were better but by a single degree; and, whatever one might have thought of religion itself, there was certainly little to afford pleasure in contemplating the more palpable effects of the want of it here. The men, dirty and unwashed, and in their week-day clothes, might be seen loitering about their hamlets every fair Sabbath morning, more especially about the public houses, to which, in the villages, according to the too faithful description of Cowper, almost every tenth step conducted the traveller. The Sabbath evening passed in brawling and coarse debauch. Not the Highland parish itself presented to the Voluntary a field more hopeless, though, of course, from an entirely different cause. In the southern locality there was money enough consumed on the taverner to have supported half a dozen clergymen; but while there existed a strong appetite for what the taverner had to give, there existed no appetite whatever for what the clergyman had to give. The supply was fitted to the demand, on the true Adam Smith principle, and there were no efforts made at the time to lessen the one kind of appetite, or to create the other. The parish had, of course, its *qualified* minister, — a respectable, indolent, not unsensible Moderate, within whose bounds of superintendence one could have lived for years not in the least in danger of his coming to the knowledge of the fact. We never saw him, though we resided a considerable part of two twelvemonths in his parish, except in the pulpit. There, however, we have heard him read, rather drowsily, a sort of essays called sermons, in which there was now and then a respectful allusion to Christianity as something very good, and neither nonsense nor heresy, but in which flat and unprofitable vacancy was occupied by but the uncertain echoes of ill-defined thought, and in which no

Saviour was offered to a perishing people, and no scheme of salvation unfolded to them through his blood. A respectable rural congregation — small, compared with the population of the parish, but not very small absolutely — dozed around him in the pews, or in waking fancy sowed their turnips or reaped their corn. In relation to ourselves, at least, the case was one of decided intrusion. We would have vetoed, if we could, this inoffensive Moderate, of whom nothing worse could be said than that he was of no manner of use; we would have vetoed him, and have taken very conscientiously, when we had done, the necessary declaration. In this southern district, however, less than a journey of two days sufficed to bring us out and home from other churches than the parish one. Dr. M'Crie preached within fewer than five miles of us; and so, quitting our state-provided minister, we became Dissenter for the time. One example more of a similar kind.

The Voluntary controversy had burst out in its first fury, and, with certainly no long-cherished prejudice in favor of Establishments to mislead us, — with very considerable experience, too, of the working of at least one Establishment, — we had quietly taken our side. We had gone to reside in a southern burgh, filled at the time with the buzz of politics and the din of controversy. Voluntaryism mustered strong, and an incipient Chartism still stronger; and, not particularly enamored of the spirit of either principle, we naturally sought the parish church in preference to any of the three chapels of the place. We had no previous knowledge of the party to which the clergyman belonged. We knew merely that he was a clergyman of the Establishment; and *establishment* at that period was the great watchword of the party to which we had attached ourselves. We found that he was a gentleman, — certainly not gross, and by no means either unaccomplished or uninformed. There was a considerable amount of elegance in his discourses. A laudable degree of care had been obviously bestowed on the composition.

The thinking, if neither bold nor original, had enough of vigor to solicit the attention of some of his more intelligent people, — almost all conservatives, — and his perorations, generally neat, bore always some complimentary reference to a Saviour, and to some inexplicable benefit which He had bestowed upon mankind. But what that benefit was, or how mankind might avail themselves of it, this respectable gentleman neither knew himself, nor could he tell it to others. His theology rose no higher than that of Blair; his ability of enforcing it was considerably lower; and had we been set to pick out in all literature, sacred and secular, the compositions which his discourses least resembled, we would have selected the Epistles of St. Paul. It was pity for him! He was generous and hospitable, though a little *imprudent*, perhaps; for he sometimes gave dinners on Sabbath, — a thing which no Moderate minister should do in these latter evil days, however much inclined. He could occasionally give his pulpit, too, to men of his own party so much more extreme than himself, that even his congregation — a sufficiently Moderate one — were accustomed to complain. The only sermon and prayers we ever heard from a clergyman confessedly not Unitarian in which even the name of Christ did not occur, we heard delivered from his pulpit, but not by himself. We continued to attend his church for nearly two months; but, beginning to find that establishments may be countenanced at too high a price, we left him for the time, and went over to the Voluntaries. Nor was the change, in this instance at least, very advantageous; but if the animating spirit was not superior, the form of words was at least more sound. We need scarce add, that our relation to this accomplished and highly qualified minister was the intrusion relation; that we would have vetoed him if we could, and taken the declaration. But it is high time to illustrate the opposite principle, — the non-intrusion one, as opposed to the anti-patronage principle on the one hand, and to the intrusionist principle on the other. A single instance may serve to translate it into fact. We have lived under the ministry of men whom we would not have chosen, and whom we could not have rejected.

A country parish far from towns, with a simple rural population considerably out of the way of the influence of our lighter periodical literature, and with the Shorter Catechism stereotyped on their general tone of thinking; — a good sincere man, of moderate ability, laboring among them in the ministry, walking conscientiously his round of duty, and useful and acceptable in that round, not so much from any intrinsic fitness in himself, as from his practical acquaintance with that scheme of salvation which He who adapts all his means to the accomplishment of his ends has thoroughly accommodated to the wants and wishes of the human heart. We have lived in such parishes, and under the ministry of such men. We have remarked, too, that such parishes, left to their free choice, would select for themselves such men. The higher order of minds would scarce fit them equally well; — a principle which applies in a similar degree to all literature and all philosophy. Between the loftier and the humbler minds there must exist an intermediate class; wanting which, the lowlier could receive no benefit from the loftier. Burke was unintelligible frequently in even the House of Commons; and until Colin Maclaurin brought down the "Principia" of Newton to the still high level of the previous flights of philosophy, men of no ordinary intellectual stature had to take its extraordinary merits on trust. It is on identically the same principle that in a simple country district the gospel would be more acceptable and more useful from a Boston than from a Butler. And hence the importance of permitting men, in such matters, both to judge and choose for themselves. The mind requires its particular fit as certainly as the body, and, when enlightened by Christian principle, takes its own measure best. What we meant to remark, however, was, that in such parishes we have felt ourselves living in relation to the tangibilities of the mere non-intrusion principle. Left to ourselves, we would have perhaps chosen men of a higher intellectual order, — men such as, in Edinburgh for instance, all, whether Churchmen or Dissenters, can virtually *choose* for themselves, in virtue of their living in relation to the tangibilities of the anti-patronage principle; but never surely would we have vetoed such men.

PART THIRD.

. John Knox might have been an English bishop had he willed it. It is matter of history that the offer of a diocese was made him at the special request of Edward VI., backed by his council; and, could honors and emoluments, and the favor of royalty, have biassed the reformer, Puseyism would now be looking up to him as one of her transmitters of the apostolic virtue. He would have formed a connecting link in the long electric chain through which she charges her surplice-coated vessels of the altar with the subtile and fiery fluid which already lights tapers there, and bids fair ere long to kindle up fagots. But Knox himself, in the supposed case, like all the better bishops, his contemporaries and friends, would have been utterly unconscious of what he conveyed. The tractors of the mesmerist take as much note of the planetary fluid which they are said to transmit, as he would have done of the apostolic ichor. We are told by Dr. M'Crie of the Latimers and Cranmers, his associates, that they were "strangers to those extravagant and illiberal notions which were afterwards adopted by the fond admirers of the hierarchy and liturgy. They would have laughed," says the historian, "at the man who would have seriously asserted that the ceremonies constituted any part of the 'beauty of holiness,' or that the imposition of the hands of a bishop was essential to the validity of ordination. They would not have owned that person as a Protestant who would have ventured to insinuate that where this was wanting there was no Christian ministry, no ordinances, no Church, and perhaps — no salvation." Nor are we left to guess at the opinions of Knox on the subject. In the concluding chapter of the "First Book of Discipline" — a work hastily drawn up, but of which the well-matured materials must have revolved as thought in the mind of the reformer for years — we are told that the Popish priesthood, "having received no lawful calling to the holy ministry, are utterly devoid of either power or authority to administer the sacraments of Christ." For it is "not the clipping of crowns," it is added, "nor the crossing of fingers, nor the blowing of those dumbe dogges called the bishops, nor yet the laying on of their hands, that maketh true ministers of Christ Jesus." What then? Certain it is that what Rome itself did not possess, Rome could not have conferred on others. But how are true ministers made? Hear the reformer himself. "By the Spirit of God, first of all, inwardly moving the heart to seek to enter into the holy calling for Christ's glory and the profite of his Kirk; thereafter by the nomination of the people, the examination and approval of the learned, and public admission by both the Church and the flock." Assuredly a more likely matter! — a better scheme, obviously, than the clipping or crossing process, the blowing of the "dumbe dogges," or the laying on of their hands. Knox lived three centuries ago; but we are quite content to stake his masculine understanding against that of Newman and Pusey united, giving them all the odds of the world's progress into the bargain.

Now, there are great truths embodied in this singularly pregnant sentence of the reformer, and very admirably do they translate into fact. They describe adequately the *qualified minister*, in the only rational definition of the term, — a man qualified to be useful in his high walk of duty, because called to it by God himself, chosen by the people, and admitted by the Church. We sketched in our last, as specimens of a numerous class, three several clergymen under whom we had been living at different times in the intrusion relation, and described them as all qualified ministers according to the Moderate definition. One of the statements of Dr. Cook, in the anti-patronage debate of last General Assembly, fully bears us out. The confessed leader of his party rose to say, that "absolute patronage had never been known in this country." There was laughter, as well there might be, from the opposite benches, and cries of "Marnoch!" "Marnoch!"—"Will the gentlemen hear but my explanation?" said the reverend Doctor, somewhat testily. "It will remove all ground for the merriment they have manifested. Can a patron go elsewhere but to a man who has affixed to him the stamp of the Church's approbation? No man can be brought into a living whom the Church has not solemnly and carefully examined, and declared fit for the work of the ministry." And to exactly the same effect is the doctrine maintained by Mr. Robertson, of Ellon. It is on this principle, he holds, that the late Presbytery of Strathbogie did right, not wrong, in giving the qualified minister Edwards to the parish of Marnoch. It is on this principle that, nicely conscientious, he cannot sustain mere dissent on the part of the people as an adequate ground for rejecting a presentee, and demands, therefore, tangible reasons of objection on which he may sit and judge. His entire hostility to the veto is founded on this principle,—the principle that all the licentiates and all the ministers of the Church must be held qualified, unless the contrary can be established; just as in the eye of the law all men must be held innocent of crime unless they can be proven guilty. And on nearly a similar basis did Dr. Muir found his motion in the General Assembly of 1839. The fundamental principle of the party involves, when translated into fact, either the great and palpable falsehood that all the ministers and all the licentiates of the Church of Scotland are qualified to edify the body of Christ, and, of necessity, not only members of that body themselves, but also peculiarly fitted for their calling by God himself; or the equally palpable falsehood that the Christian people have no other measure of duty, with respect to what and whom they hear, than the ability of church courts to detect delinquency and error. We draw bolt and bar every night, and set a guard in our streets, in the belief that there may be thieves and men of violence abroad. Fling open your doors, says Moderatism, and dismiss the watch. The millions of the country are all honest and inoffensive, except the few hapless individuals who have been convicted of crime in the High Court of Justiciary, and either thrust out of the world or banished the kingdom.

We have opposed the priest-making of Puseyism to the process through which, according to Knox, true ministers of Jesus Christ are made. The one is all sheer materialism, — "crossing," "clipping," "blowing," and the "laying on of hands." The very basis of the other is spiritual. But it is not all spiritual. It is in part spiritual, in part intellectual, and, if we may so express ourselves, negatively moral; and it will be found that it is the merely negatively moral and intellectual portions of it which Moderatism selects, and that the spiritual is altogether rejected. It approaches the Puseyite scheme to the nearest degree possible in the circumstances; but in one very important respect, each tried by its own standard, it falls materially below it.

"We cannot try men's hearts," said the old statesman, when passing judgment on the favorite of a friend who had been recommended as faithful, but rejected as incompetent, — "we cannot try men's hearts, but we can at least catechize their heads." Now, there is a provision in the scheme of Knox for the catechizing of the head. The approbation of learned ministers, appointed for the purpose of examination, is a *sine qua non* to admission. Character, too, in the negative sense, is held to be at least equally important. "It is to be observed," says the reformer, "that no person noted with publique infamie be either promoted to the regiment of the Church, or retained in ecclesiastical administration." And such, in the constituting of a true ministry, was the part given to church courts, in contradistinction to the part assigned in the same work in the first instance to the Spirit of God, and the part assigned to the people in the second. The Church, according to the Puseyite scheme, deals with the materialisms of ordination, reckoning on a necessarily accompanying virtue; the Scottish Church, in her courts, according to somewhat less than one-half the scheme of Knox, deals with matters equally tangible and evident, — matters of doctrine, acquirement, and, in the low judicial sense of the term, character. Dr. Pusey and his friends give us the evidence of our senses for the crossing, the blowing, and the laying on of hands. Dr. Cook and his friends, selecting one portion of the scheme of Knox, profess equally to give us the evidence of our senses for the literature, the theology, and, if we may so express ourselves, the lack of character positively bad. Both deal equally with tangibilities; but there is this striking difference between them: the tangibilities in the case of Puseyism, viewed in connection with its own ostensible beliefs, are fraught with a necessary virtue. In virtue of his baptism, the priest is a *regenerated* man; in virtue of his ordination, — we apologize to our readers for using such terms, but they are those of the party, — in virtue, we say, of his ordination, he is both qualified to *regenerate* others, that is, to baptize them, and to *feed their souls with the body of the Lord*, — that is, to administer to them the sacrament of the Supper. Moderatism is less consistent. It does not hold that baptism is regeneration; it does not hold that the sacrament of the Supper is the body of the Lord; it does not hold that any of those tangibilities on which it insists — literature, theology, or negative character — is what the sacraments are not — *conversion*. It holds — for in the circumstances it is impossible it should hold otherwise — it holds that a fully qualified and accomplished minister — one who, according to Dr. Cook, cannot, in the nature of things, be intruded, no, not into a Culsalmond or a Marnoch, seeing that the "Church has affixed to him the stamp of her approbation," and whom Mr. Robertson could not *conscientiously* reject in virtue of any rejection on the part of the people — may be, notwithstanding, an unconverted man, practically unacquainted with the gospel himself, and with neither wish nor will to urge the acceptance of it upon others.

But though such be the consistency of Moderatism, not such was the scheme, nor such the views, of Knox. Church courts were left to deal with facts and arguments, — to catechize the head and the life of the presentee. To the people a part at least equally important was assigned, and in which, resting as it did between God and their conscience, the Church too well knew her duty to interfere.

"Christ the Head of every man!" There is a duty, doubtless, which the Church owes to her adorable Head, and to the people her members. But in no degree does that duty supersede the duty which every individual member owes to Christ as *his* Head; and his responsibility for what and how he hears is a responsibility which he cannot roll over upon any Church. Churches, however false and detestable, are never to be summoned to the bar of judgment. Their portion is in this world exclusively. The tyrants of the Inquisition must be there, — the assassins of St. Bartholomew's day, — the bloodhounds of the Irish massacre, — the murderers of Hamilton, and Wishart, and Walter Mill, — the kindlers of the flames of Smithfield, — the iron-hearted persecutors of the Piedmontese, — all who in the cause of Rome pursued to the death the saints of the living God. But Rome herself will not be there. Her judgment shall be in this world. Long ere the great white throne shall be set, or the books opened, — ere the sea, and death, and hell, shall give up their dead, — must her place be void among the nations, — a dark and silent blank, where there shall no light shine and no voice be heard, and from which, for ages and centuries, shall the smoke of her burning ascend; while around and over shall the great voice of much people be heard, praising God "for his righteous judgments" in "avenging the blood of his servants at her hand." Nor will the Scottish Episcopal Church stand at that awful bar. Not Rome herself wears a redder surplice, nor do her hands smell more rankly of murder. But *her* portion will be assigned her in this present world also. One Church only shall abide the day of the Lord's coming, — that Church, of all climes and all ages, which shall comprise all saints, and the roll of whose members is the Book of Life. It is as individuals, each man apart, that all shall have to stand at the bar of final judgment; and hence the necessary recognition of the will of the people in all for which the people shall have to answer there. Hence, too, the solemn bearing of the doctrine of Christ's Headship on the existing controversy, not only, and not chiefly even, in its connection with the Scottish Church, but in its bearing on every one of the Church's members individually. To Christ, as his Head and King, must every man render an account of how and what he hears. And hence the peculiar fitness of the enlightened and truly Christian principle of Knox. Mark the close adaptation, the one to the other, of the two first qualifications which he lays down as essential to the character of the minister of Christ, and the formation of the pastoral tie. The first, in an especial manner, concerns the minister himself. It involves as its basis conversion to God, for without conversion qualification cannot exist; and then, further, "the Spirit of God inwardly moving the heart to seek to enter into the holy calling of the ministry, for Christ's glory and the profit of the Kirk." On this surely most important foundation rests the ordination formulas of both the English and the Scottish Church. Hence the solemn avowal of the candidate for orders in the one, that he judges himself "to be inwardly moved by the Holy Ghost to take the office upon him." Hence the not less solemn pledge of the licentiate in the other, that "zeal for the honor of God, love to Jesus Christ, and desire of saving souls, are his great motives and chief inducements in entering into the functions of the holy ministry, and not worldly designs and interests." But this is not enough. For the truth of this solemn oath there is but one man responsible,—he who takes it; whereas, the consequences and character of his ministry must inevitably affect more than himself;—the people have also their responsibility. If *he* must render an account of what and in what spirit he preaches, they also must render an account of what and in what spirit they hear. "Christ is the Head of every man." And so the people's turn comes next. It is the people who must nominate. By the light which God has vouchsafed, — by their sympathies, their experience, and their knowledge, as Christians,—by those deeply based, undefinable feelings through which the voice of the true Shepherd is distinguished from that of the stranger and the hireling,—through, in short, that entire capacity in Christ's people to which the command, "Beware of false teachers," is addressed by Christ himself,—must their views be regulated, their choice directed. It is they, the people, not presbyteries or synods, who are mainly interested in the matter. Life and death must tell of it. Throughout time the complexion of their spiritual being may depend upon it. Its effects, as it regards them, are to stretch onwards through eternity, and reach the dread bar of final judgment. And who, in a question so vital, shall dare interfere, and take the decision out of their hands, though all unable, in the impotence of presumption, to divest them of the attaching responsibility? Who are the prophets prepared to stand in this gap? Muirs, Cooks, and Robertsons? One tells us there can be no such thing as intrusion in the circumstances, seeing that all clergymen are alike qualified: "There is no man to whom a patron can go who has not affixed to him the stamp of the Church's approbation." Another assures us that his conscience interferes, and that he must be permitted, therefore, to decide for the Marnochs and Culsalmonds of the country, that Edwardses may be thrust into the one, and Middletons into the other. A third takes a still bolder flight. The wise, the good, the venerable of the country, assert the principle of Knox; and he coolly tells them that they are just "taking a forward step in the great march, the end of which would be, in Scotland, the dissemination of infidelity and misrule."

It is unnecessary to show how miserably these men fail in their duty, by thus absorbing that of the people into their own, — confounding, by something immensely worse than any mere confusion of idea, the examination of the Church with the privileges of the flock. Nor need we again refer to the nice and masterly precision with which Knox could line out the provinces of each. It would be no easy matter to exhaust our subject. It stretches along the entire line of the existing controversy. Every principle has its corresponding fact; every argument its answering illustration.

THE TWO CONFLICTS.

We have had occasion oftener than once to remark the great celerity of movement, if we may so speak, which characterizes the events of the present age. It would seem as if the locomotive and the railroad had been introduced into every department of human affairs, — as if the amount of change which sufficed in the past scheme of Providence for whole centuries had come to be compressed, under a different economy, within the limits of less than half a lifetime. Events thicken in these latter scenes of the great drama. There is a condensation of the *matter* as the volume draws to its close — the adoption of a closer and denser type. One seems almost justified in holding that the great machine of society is on the eve of being precipitated on some all-important crisis, and that the rapidity with which the wheels revolve marks the sudden abruptness of the descent.

Now, there is at least one advantage which should be derived from living in such a time. It furnishes opportunities which have a tendency, if well employed, of lengthening the term of one's *rational* existence. It provides reflection with the materials of extended observation, and enables us to weigh one class of events against another, not, as our fathers did, in two unequal scales, — the one furnished by personal experience, the other by the uncertainties of historical narrative, — but in the more equally adjusted balances of personal experience alone. A Scotchman of the times of Charles I. knew of only religious struggles. It was the one question of the age, whether all religious light was to pass to the people through the medium of Laud and his coadjutors, broken into a colored maze of deceptive splendor, in which every object put on a false and distorted appearance; or whether they should not look direct on that Sun of Revelation which, more emphatically than in the meaning of Solomon, "it is a good thing to behold," and whose bright yet sober effulgence is the untinted medium of truth. A century passed, and a sleepy expression of mediocre power and half-intelligence rested on the face of British society. The great religious struggle had been over for more than an age; and the denizens of the time, in summing up the portion of history which fell within the range of their own experience, could have told of little else than of the petty intrigues of corrupt and selfish statesmen, or of the conflicting claims of rival princes, — men by whom kingdoms, with their people, were regarded as but mere family properties, and wars as but a sort of lawsuits that determine their disposal. There passed half a century more, and all was changed. The masses were in motion; the great interests of classes and communities were agitated; and politics had become a desperate game, at which the people played deeply against their rulers, with happiness and freedom as the supposed stake, and at the close of which, falling into a true gambler's quarrel, they filled the earth with anarchy, violence, and blood. The series of these three great states of things, if we may so express ourselves, occupied two whole centuries. Individual experience stretched but a little way along the line. It could know, in its own proper character, of only one of the three conditions. Its borrowed recollections of a former state of things failed adequately to mingle with its observations of a present state. They were not *personal* recollections; there was substance on the one hand, mere shadow on the other. Men looked on a gray and silent past, through the darkened and colored glass of history, as merely curious inquirers; while on the living, bustling, tangible realities before them they gazed through the clear atmosphere of sentient existence, as earnest, excited, interested spectators.

Through that quickening of the wheels of Providence to which we advert, the case is essentially different now. Individual experience embraces the three distinct states; and men in the pride of middle manhood, who have not misused their experience, know at least a little of each. The intrigues of mere individuals form no inconsiderable portion of our country's history during the reign of George IV.; so much so, that from the trial of Caroline to the death of Canning there seems little that may not be referred to the petty manœuvring of diplomatists, or to the piques or partialities of the sovereign. With the times of William, however, a sterner element is introduced; the masses become the all-potent moving-power of the state engine, and for a time legislation serves but to index their wishes. A noiseless revolution then succeeds. There is a sudden shifting of scenes, a changing of actors, a thorough revival of principles, unseen, on at least the surface of affairs, since the times of the Charleses. The antagonist parties that at the Reformation shook all Europe with the violence of their conflict, rise in their most characteristic form, in the two great establishments of the empire; and, though the contest at its present stage may be regarded as but an affair of outposts, the war has already begun. Twenty years have thus repeated to us the lessons of two centuries.

We are afraid it will scarce be disputed that the great political movement of the country has terminated in disappointment among at least the masses. Chartism, however doubtful its evidence on other matters, testifies all too truly, by the very extent of its own existence, that the physical condition of the people has not been bettered. The election committees of the House of Commons demonstrate all too unequivocally that their moral character has not been improved. Nay, to state the case in negatives is to do it injustice. Indirectly, at least, the tone of our national morality has been greatly lowered. Whigs, Tories, Radicals, Chartists, are all alike in error, if ever before there sat a British Parliament based on so large an amount of bribery and corruption as the Parliament so lately called together under the provisions of the Reform Bill, and to secure the return of which nearly a million of the people registered their votes. Are our religious struggles to terminate in disappointment equally marked and lamentable? — to leave behind them, even though successfully maintained, no nobler trophies among our people than the pangs of an ever-accumulating physical distress, or the atrocities of an ever-sinking moral degradation? We have formed far other hopes; nor are there indications wanting which serve to show that in these hopes it is not irrational to indulge. The signal success which in the past year has attended the several schemes of the Church, during a season of great depression and distress, is of itself a sign of encouragement. In tones more significant than those of speech, it reminds the class who, on the plea of "lacking leisure to do good," are solicitous to cease from the present conflict, that He who decreed of old that the walls of Zion should be "built in troublous times," can build them in troublous times still.

It furnishes no incurious or uninstructive employment to run over the various features of the two great popular movements which have agitated Scotland during the last twelve years, — the political and the ecclesiastical. . They present themselves to us as a series of scenes; but we shall lack time even for bare enumeration. In the "Vision of Don Roderick," the dead stillness is broken by the blast of a trumpet, and straightway the giant Destiny arises, and, striking down with his iron mace the curtain of rock which interposes between him and the future, all in an instant becomes violence, commotion, and war. We have a similar recollection of the first beginnings of the great political movement. We stood, in a calm, still evening, early in the August of 1830, — only twelve years ago! — beside a half-deserted seaport in the north of Scotland. A fleet of fishing-boats, bound for the herring-bank, mottled the offing; a large French lugger lay moored beside the quay, with her huge brown sails drooping heavily from her masts in the calm. Groups of town's-people, mostly mechanics, sauntered along the shore, or rested in front of the lugger, looking curiously on the foreigners. The entire scene seemed representative of quiet industry enjoying a leisure hour amid the repose of nature. But "hark the twanging horn!" It was the post coming in. A few minutes elapsed, and then a newspaper, damp from the folds, was handed to one of the mechanics. How strangely exciting, how tremendously important, the tidings which it conveyed! "REVOLUTION IN FRANCE!" — three days' war in the streets of Paris! — the government overpowered! — the king dethroned! — the people signally victorious! Huzza! It was interesting to mark the sudden effect, — the instant hive-like buzz that arose among the congregating groups; the excitement among the French crew, none of whom could read English, but to whom, notwithstanding, the important newspaper was handed; the unnatural effect of their strange French pronunciation of the English words, as they hurried over them, made all the more strange and unnatural by the intense emphasis with which the words were accompanied, and which spoke so unequivocally of the overpowering anxiety to know what they conveyed.

It was the first blast of the trumpet that had blown, and the whole British people awoke. There ensued a period of unquiet agitation and sanguine hope, — agitation in which all among the laboring classes shared, and hope in which they all indulged. Scarce any one deemed himself so obscure but that some of the anticipated good might reach him. There was at least some indirect advantage to be derived to him; his labors were to be less, or his remuneration greater, or he was at least to walk more on a level with the aristocrats of the country. The future historian of this stirring period would require no slight skill adequately to represent the general expression of society, if we may so speak, during its high fever of excitement and expectation. Some of the earlier effects might be easily anticipated. There is scarce a village in Britain that cannot point out its wrecks of the Reform Bill, in the forms of broken-down and dissipated mechanics and bankrupt shopkeepers. Not that the Reform Bill was bad; we see it interposed by the providence of God at the present time as a bulwark between the Church of Scotland and the miserable politicians who would so fain crush and destroy her. But, if not bad in itself, it at least *led* to much that was bad. The village trader, whose predecessors in business had gone on quietly, adding pound to pound, and had risen, on their hard-earned and honest savings, to the enjoyment of the accompanying modicum of respect and influence, found a different way to rise, — a way which the accompanying municipal reform, no doubt good in itself also, threw more widely open to him than even the extension of the parliamentary franchise. Influence, respect, civic honors, and authority, were the rewards of his predecessors in business, if they but prospered in their calling. He, on the other hand, found a way to civic authority without prospering in his calling; nay, of which, if he availed himself, all hope of prospering in his calling might be rationally regarded as at an end. He, learned to canvass for votes on his own behalf, and rose to the dignity of a bailie. He learned to canvass for his friend the member, and enjoyed the unspeakable honor of handing the great man through the streets on the day of the election. He became eloquent on platforms, brilliant at public dinners, skilful in the framing of resolutions, happy in the drawing up of patriotic petitions; acquired, in short, the whole trick of public business, and, in nine cases out of ten, winded up his own by getting into the Gazette. A general unsettledness possessed the community, — the unsettledness of salient hope. In almost every village there were two great classes, — the solicitors and the solicited; and as the spirit of *Young Reform* was honest, enthusiastic, sincere, the soliciting class exerted themselves for the general good and their own individual glorification; while the class solicited were passively patriotic just for the general good alone. But the spirit of *Young Reform* became less honest as it grew older. Experience came to teach unwilling pupils that there lies but little within the reach of mere statesmanship. The over-toiled poor had to work as long and to fare as hardly as before. Periods of depression came on, as if there had been no extension of the franchise. The funded debt increased, as if the Reform Bill had never passed the Lords. Men became weary, too, of seeing a vulgar upstart aristocracy of cunning canvassers and adroit beggars of votes taking the places of the soldier and not worse burghal aristocracy, who had carried things all their own way under the ancient *regime*, and of finding that the new men, like the old, were getting places in the colonies for their sons, and places in the excise for their nephews, and the people meanwhile none the better. Chartism broke off, indignant, and set up for itself. A quieter and tamer class crept silently into the opposite scale, and solaced themselves, when registering their tory suffrages, by calling them *conservative*. Worst of all, franchise-holders began to consider by thousands whether, as they could do almost nothing for the country by *giving* their votes, they might not do just a little for themselves by *selling* them; and hence the election markets of the country, with their ticketed oaths and priced perjuries. The generous romance, the high-toned enthusiasm, of *Young Reform*, evaporated as he rose in years, until at length, changing his character altogether, he sunk into a worn-out and selfish truckler, devoid both of virtue and the belief in it; and thus what had been *Young Reform* became *Old Corruption*.

Nor has the great political fever been more favorable to the intellectual than to the moral character of our country. A few contemplative natures there are that need no other spur to quicken them in the pursuit of knowledge than just the love of it. But it is far otherwise with the great bulk of the species. In the average intellect attention never concentrates save under the influence of some serious belief. And hence the superficiality of a merely political people. They catch up shadows of opinions, impalpable and unreal as those thin films which, according to the old metaphysicians, bodies in the light are continually casting off, and which were regarded as the direct causes of vision. They are less the recipients of knowledge than the objects on which a kind of knowledge is reflected, — mere blank tablets, athwart which a periodical press throws, like a huge magic-lantern, its fantastic and ever-shifting images. The period of political excitement created no thinkers. There was not enough of earnestness left among the people, after the first delirium had passed, to give motion or direction to their thoughts. It was Christianity through which the popular mind in Scotland was originally developed; through Christianity alone can it be awakened anew. The distracting turmoil of secular politics, with the accompanying excitement, has ever served but to dissipate and weaken it.

From the ecclesiastical struggle we anticipate effects of a very different character from those produced by the political one; and certainly the first fruits are not of a kind suited to disappoint expectation. Both struggles might be represented, we have said, in a series of scenes; nor would the scenes characteristic of the ecclesiastical struggle form the less striking series of the two, — whether we choose to draw from the atrocities that impart to the resistance of the Church its character of stern necessity, or from the strange instances of discordant coalition exhibited in the motley array of her assailants, or from the courts in which bewigged and berobed law deals upon her its censures, in all the conscious bravery of horse-hair, white ribbon, and taffeta, and devoid only of moral weight; or, more pleasing surely, from the spectacle of earnest multitudes gathered together in her behalf, and prepared to assert her cause in its true character, as Scotland's old hereditary quarrel; or from the evening meeting in some rural hamlet, to which, from distant glens and solitary hill-sides, a devout and thoughtful people have gathered, to wear out the night in implorations to Heaven for her safety; or from scenes of family devotion in many a lonely cottage, in which her name and her cause are not forgotten when gray-haired patriarchs wrestle in prayer with their God.

Very much still remains to be done; but we accept as a token of good in her behalf the strengthening devotional feeling of the country, — the deeper tone of spirituality imparted to the ministrations of so many of her clergymen, — the great increase in the number of her prayer-meetings; nay, it is something, too, that Moderatism itself, provoked to unwonted diligence, should be attempting, with a hand stiffened by disuse, to trace out the line of duty. Instances are not wanting in which, awaking from its sleep of a century, it has half striven, in its bewilderment, to escape from its dreams of *effete* commonplace into the living realities of the gospel; and we have high authority for saying that it is well Christ should be preached, even though preached out of contention. There is much implied in that marked increase which has taken place, during the course of the last twelvemonth, in the funds of the various schemes of the Church, and to which we have already referred. It conclusively proves that the controversy in which she is entangled has had no narrowing or secularizing effect on the minds of the classes most engaged in it; that its tendencies are of a directly opposite character; and that, amid harassments and perplexities at home, there has been more thought of our countrymen abroad destitute of the means of religious instruction,—of the poor benighted Hindu, of the long-lost house of Israel, of the young among ourselves growing up in ignorance, and of the old and middle-aged passing on in darkness to their graves,—than at periods when the peace among us was unbroken, and all our narratives of persecution belonged exclusively to the past. Nor are there proofs wanting that the effects of the struggle are good intellectually. Our *litterateurs* need be in no fear of seeing the country thrown back into a state of barbarism. It was in times such as the present that the humble peasantry of Scotland learned to foil at their own weapons the most skilful controversialists of the persecuting Church, and left their death-testimonies to posterity, to bear witness alike to the indomitable firmness and integrity with which they maintained their principles, and to the high degree of intelligence which they had learned to exert in the defence of them. "The severities to which he had been subjected," says Sir James Mackintosh, "had led Bunyan to revolve in his own mind the principles of religious freedom, until he had acquired the ability of baffling, in the conflict of argument, the most acute and learned among his persecutors." There is an important principle involved in the remark. It exhibits the necessity which stimulates to thought and invention, arising direct out of religious belief acted on by persecution, — a principle the efficacy of which may be soon tested in Scotland, as of old. Meanwhile there is a degree of interest excited, which has already operated favorably on the popular mind. Men are falling back upon the past, with all its earnest feeling and deep thinking, who were content hitherto to skim over the cold superficialities of the present. The Reformation is recognized once more as super-eminently the great event of modern history; and there is more read and known regarding it than at any other period for the last hundred years. It is a fact of some importance that our ecclesiastical histories have become the most popular and salable books of the time.

"I have ever been an enemy to religious strife," said Lord Dunfermline, in allusion to the existing controversy, when throwing his entire weight into the opposite scale, — "I have ever been an enemy to religious strife." His lordship had gained a great deal by the political "strife," then well-nigh at its close, — influence, title, broad lands, and solid guineas; whereas by the "religious strife" he could expect to gain nothing. Besides, its cross movements had thrown him out in his calculations, and converted the last political act of his life into a somewhat ludicrous blunder. And so, as the singularly charitable advocate of the grossnesses of intrusion, and the singularly liberal detester of the just rights of Christian men, he looked very magnanimous, and denounced "religious strife." We have attempted placing the two strifes before our readers in some of their more palpable effects. Both were alike ordered by the Disposer of all things, and their time and their bounds set, with no reference, surely, to the antipathies or predilections of churchmen or politicians. Peace and war come alike from God. But it seems no difficult matter to say which of the two seems the nobler and more hopeful battle, or in which it is most a privilege to be called to contend.

TENDENCIES.

PART FIRST.

One finds but little difficulty in estimating the tendencies of a bygone time in the page of history. The events stand out in a clear light, portable in bulk, and arranged in due order. We see in what they have begun and in what they have terminated; and arrive, with scarce an effort, at our conclusions regarding their general scope and bearing. But it is far otherwise with the tendencies of a present age. It is no such easy matter to estimate *their* strength and direction. We are too deeply interested in the passing events to appreciate them justly, or we are interested in them too slightly, and our indifferency has equally the effect of setting our judgments at fault. They bulk large or small in our minds, less in agreement with their own true proportions than in accordance with the medium of predilection or prejudice through which we survey them. We are too much among them, and too near them, to see them as they really are, or to mark the direction in which they are bearing us in their course. The current of tendency in the past, as exhibited in history, is a clear, transparent stream, that sparkles in the sunshine. As involved in the occurrences of the present, it is a turbid and sullen tide, with a sombrous curtain of cloud resting over it and on either hand, and with thick darkness before. The voyager finds it a comparatively easy matter to trace his course on the chart. The observations are already taken to his hand on the graduated margin, and carried carefully across by the reticulated lines; and the ocean he is crossing must be a wide ocean indeed if he does not see the land which he has left a very few inches astern of him, and the land to which he is going a very few inches ahead. But it is a quite different matter to trace his course over the broad and living sea, with its tossing waves and its perplexing currents, when the distant horizon sinks all around him over a trackless waste of waters, and he knows that far beyond the line of that wide circle, where sky and sea seem to meet, the waste spreads on, and on, and on, for hundreds and thousands of miles. And when all is dark with sleet and rime, and his bark is staggering onward before the tempest; when wild uproar and giddy tumult reign below, and gloom and thick cloud darken the heavens above; when no star looks out from amid the rack by night, and no sun shines through the thick fog by day; when, amid the restless welter of the deck, he has lashed his pilot to the helm, and stationed his forlorn watch in *the top*,—he must be content to confess a lack of knowledge as certainly as a lack of power, and that he is in no degree less able to control the irresistible waves and winds that are driving him involuntarily on, than to say where they have brought him, or to what untried scenes of terror or peril they are hurrying him away.

But however difficult it may be to estimate the true tendencies of a present age, it is all-important that they *should* be estimated; just as it is all-important to the voyager in the storm that he should know where he is, and to what coast he is driving. And it is peculiarly important in an age like the present, when the powers of good and evil seem as if mustering their forces for some signal struggle.

We are told by chivalrous old Barbour, in his "Acts and Achievements of the Bruce," that when

> "Sir Aymer and Johne of Lorne,
> Chasit the kinge with hounde and horne,"

the pursuing body despatched five of their lightest and most active men to overtake the hard-pressed warrior, then in full view, and to detain and hold him at bay until the coming up of the rest. And overtake and bring him to bay they did. But ere the main force of Lorne and Sir Aymer could reach the green holm in which he had turned on his pursuers, the sward was cumbered by five bleeding and mutilated corpses, and the formidable fugitive had again shot far ahead. The Church of Scotland has not fared so well. The Voluntary controversy overtook her in her course during the dominancy of a whig ministry, and had unquestionably strength enough to keep her at bay during a time which she could have employed, had she not been so entangled, as peculiarly opportune and favorable for securing her safety. Placed in an eminently popular position, and warmly supported by her lay members, who felt that her quarrel was in reality theirs, she had to deal with a government whose only mode of estimating the importance of religion was by determining the votes that it could command, and to whom, with more than the emphasis of the old proverb, "the voice of the people was the voice of God." The religious element, in its character as such, never entered into their calculations. If the popular power of Scotch Voluntaryism mustered as twenty, and the popular power of the Scotch Establishment as twenty-one, they would just have subtracted the lesser from the larger sum, and have given the Church the benefit of the balance. Every vote against her was regarded as a positive deduction from the justice of her claims. And it was under a government of this character that the Voluntary controversy broke out, to divide the popular forces of the country, and to place our rulers for the time in the circumstances of the ass between the two bundles of hay. Let political Voluntaries assert what they may, the controversy is now dead — dead as any of the five hapless pursuers of the Bruce, who, like evangelic Dissent in this instance, were so active to their own hurt. But it is all too apparent that, ere it sunk into utter weakness and died, it accomplished its work. It entangled and detained the Church at a time when otherwise she would have been employed in making secure her safety through the popular influences; and, when thus entangled and kept at bay, other enemies came up.

The same change of ministry[1] which had the effect of placing an already sinking Voluntaryism *hors de combat* had the effect of placing a much elated and sanguine Moderatism in what Moderatism itself deemed a position of great strength. It saw full before it a scene of triumph, — the return of the days of its old majorities, and of its high-handed and much-loved policy; and all that seemed necessary to secure almost instant victory was just one bold stroke. Hence the unceasing exertions of Moderate influence with the conservative government to baffle all attempts at even an indifferently fair adjustment of the controversy. The Church, in her course towards safety, — a course that had now become much more dubious and uncertain than before, and which promised, humanly speaking, much fewer chances of escape, — had to contend with an enemy formidable mainly from the entanglement and delay that it occasioned. Moderatism had most certainly no intention of bringing down the Establishment. It is well aware how very miserably it would fare without it. We give our present Lord Justice-Clerk [Hope] full credit for attachment to the Scottish Establishment, and believe that, had he to choose between two great evils, he would rather see it Evangelistic than Puseyite. At this most important result, however, has the Church now arrived, and the question has assumed a new aspect in consequence. It is a point virtually decided by the resolutions of the late Convocation, that the existing controversy shall be either settled on fair, non-intrusion principles, or that the Establishment of Scotland shall not be a Presbyterian Establishment. The second enemy that has entangled and kept the Church at bay promises soon to sink into a state of as great powerlessness as her first enemy. But it, too, may have accomplished its work. The great apostasy has been meanwhile rising into strength in England, and asserting

1 The accession of the Conservatives to power in 1841.

its place as the master principle of that kingdom. It was powerless at the time when Voluntaryism contended with our Church. When Moderatism contended with her, its joints were still unknit, its muscles undeveloped, its strength rather prospective than actual. But it is an immensely stronger principle now. The Church has been detained and entangled in her course by antagonists much indeed her inferiors in prowess; but ere she has succeeded in fully mastering them, it would seem as if the main body of the enemy had come up. How strange if, in the revolutions of those cloud-enveloped and mysteriously-complicated wheels of Providence which the prophet in vision saw, the efforts of Voluntaries, many of them truly Christian men, and the active hostility of Moderates, men at least hostile to superstition and to the dogmas of the "malignant Church," should turn out to be but mere diversions, made all blindly and unwittingly in favor of the great apostasy!

There can be at least little rational doubt that Puseyism will now exert an influence on the adjustment of our Scottish Church question which at an earlier period it could not have exerted. When Voluntaryism began its opposition, Puseyism had no existence; when Moderatism began its opposition, Puseyism was comparatively weak. Nay, independently of both, the Church, in her present position, had she been but prepared to take it up, might have very possibly compelled a fair and liberal settlement from Conservatism when Sir Robert Peel entered upon office, or from Liberalism ere Lord Melbourne quitted it. Neither of these statesmen, left to themselves, could have contemplated for a moment the disestablishment of the national religion of Scotland, with all the long train of evils which such an event must of necessity draw along with it, as a thing to be permitted in any circumstances. But a new party has become strong in the political field, that, through the disturbing influence of an element of religious belief, will be wholly incapable of estimating these evils aright. We say an element of religious belief. It is common to all sincere religionists, whether their creed be a true or a false one, to "hope against hope," — to hope at least against probability, — to shut their eyes to what seem the teachings of experience in cases in which these teachings run counter to some promise of their religion, and to open them to the promise only. We believe, as Christians, for instance, that the knowledge of the Lord shall one day cover the whole earth. Why? Do we find grounds for any such belief in either the present state of things or in the world's past history? Very slight grounds indeed. If we see true churches springing up in one part of the globe, do we not see them dying out in another? Tahiti and the Sandwich Islands have their Christianity. Yes; but what has become of the Seven Churches of Asia? America has had her revivals. Yes; but how much of the living religion of the Reformation is now to be found on the Continent of Europe? We do not found our belief in the ultimate triumph of our religion on the evidence of history, or on a survey of the present prospects of society. We have a much better foundation; we ground it on the promise of our God. And, let the probabilities run as they may, it is a belief which we shall therefore continue to hold fast. Now false, like true churches, have their beliefs, firmly held after this fashion, which run counter to the probabilities; nor can there be elements that more disturb calculations, or that lead to the perpetration of greater follies and crimes. Puseyism indulges in them; nor has there been any lack of indication regarding the points on which they are concentrated. There is not one of our readers more thoroughly based in the belief that China, or Hindustan, or the Persian empire, shall be one day Christian, than Puseyism is grounded in the belief that Scotland shall be one day Puseyite. It is formidable, in a crisis like the present, to have to come in contact with such a principle. The rational weighers of probabilities are easily dealt with; not so the blind hopers against hope. Men of expediency, such as Sir Robert Peel, — men less in danger of believing anything they don't see than of doubting when they ought to believe, — will find no difficulty, as we have said, in at least estimating the circumstances in which our country is at present placed. Sir Robert, two years ago, would have acted in due accordance with such an estimate. But it is at least questionable whether the expediency party which he represents is powerful enough to act upon it now. The hopers against hope — the bigots who "believe because it is impossible" — muster strong in the rear of our statesmen of mere expediency. Their influence to disturb, disarrange, disappoint, is great, and will, we doubt not, be vigorously exerted. We have to expect, in consequence, we are afraid, much wilful misrepresentation, much intentional misapprehension, much exaggeration of our claims as unreasonable and absurd, much insinuation that our designs are selfish and dishonest; delays ingeniously spun out to wear us down; perhaps a bill meanly equivocal in phrase, framed intentionally to palter in a double sense; perhaps no bill at all.

If such be the state and apparent tendency of things, what course ought the Church to pursue? Is it at once her interest and her duty vigorously to persevere in forming her congregational associations, and in securing everywhere the adherence of her people? Her better consolations and encouragements are to be derived from the highest of all sources; but there can be no harm in remembering, besides, that if there be powerful principles opposed to her, the principles for which she has to contend have been, ever since the Reformation at least, by much the strongest in Scotland. "It matters not," says Carlyle, in his quaint but striking manner, — "it matters not though a thing be a small thing; if it be a true thing it will grow." Cromwell and Napoleon were once puny infants. But there was a principle of life in them, and of undeveloped power; and so they both grew up to be very great men. Rather more than a century ago, Moderatism cast out of the Church of Scotland four clergymen. A small matter, it may be thought. Yes; small in much the same way that the infant Cromwell and the infant Napoleon were small. The transaction involved one of the principles of our present controversy. The thing was a small thing in itself, but then it embodied a great and true principle, and so the small thing grew. And in the present day, the four rejected clergymen are represented by five hundred clergymen and by five hundred thousand people. If the worst comes to the worst with the Church of Scotland, she bids fair to begin her course, not as a small, but as a very great thing, — to begin with the five hundred ministers and the five hundred thousand people. And to the life-imparting, growth-securing principle of the Secession, she adds another master-principle whose strength has also been amply tested in Scotland. The contendings of the Secession in the last century involved mainly the non-intrusion principle. The contendings of our Presbyterian fathers in the previous century involved, mainly, the great doctrine that Christ is the only Head of the Church, and that, in the things which pertain to his kingdom, she owns no king or lord but him. And in our present struggle both these principles of strength are united. We have glanced, however, at but a small portion of our subject; it is of great extent, and as important as extensive; and we shall embrace an early opportunity of returning to it.

PART SECOND.

It is a widely-spread belief of the present time, and certainly one of its not less striking characteristics, that the men of the passing generation are to be the spectators of a series of stranger changes and more remarkable revolutions than have been witnessed in almost any former period of the world's history. We say, widely spread. It is a belief that professes to be founded on Scripture, and has, in consequence, one set of limits in the far-diffused infidelity of the masses. Nay, more, it professes to be founded on an interpretation of Scripture exclusively Protestant, and has thus another set of limits in the superstitions of Puseyism and Popery, that still further restrict its area. But outside these lines of boundary, inevitable in the present state of Christendom, — outside of infidelity on the one hand, and of Popery and Puseyism on the other, — it may well be described as a belief extensively diffused. There is scarce a country in the world in which Protestantism exists as a living faith, from America to Australia, and from Australia to Great Britain, in which it does not exist. There is scarce a Protestant body, from the Episcopalian to the Independent, from the Baptist to the Presbyterian, in which it has not its zealous assertors. It may be found in minds of almost every calibre, — in union, in some instances, with great doctrinal extravagances, and active, ill-regulated imaginations, — united, in others, to codes of belief soundly orthodox, and to great general sobriety and strength of judgment. The extent to which it prevails renders it one of perhaps the more remarkable traits of the religious world in the present day. Beliefs of a somewhat similar character have spread not less widely at other times. A belief that the end of the world was close at hand had immense influence in stirring up our ancient barons and their retainers to engage in the earlier crusades; but it was the belief of a barbarous and uninformed age, alike remarkable for the credulity of a superstitious laity and the pious frauds of an unprincipled priesthood. A belief obtained very generally among Papists early in the latter half of the seventeenth century, that the year 1666 was to be marked by some great religious revolution and the coming of Antichrist; and, through a curious coincidence, the Jews pretended, says *Voltaire*, that their Messiah was to come this year, — a delusion which led in part to the temporary success of that singular impostor Sabbatei Levi; while in England, says Burnet, "an opinion did run through the nation" that this year was to usher in the day of judgment. But the belief, thus various in its character, and which is said to have originated in a vulgar misapprehension of the mystic number in the Apocalypse 666, was restricted, like the other, to the superstitious and the ignorant. It is a peculiarity of the existing belief, that it is entertained by all our more eminent expounders of prophecy in the present time, and that the writings of well-nigh all the more judicious expounders of the past bear upon it also. The Medes, Tillingasts, and Flemings of the seventeenth century point direct in the same line with the Keiths, Brooks, and Bickersteths of our own.

The fact is unquestionably a curious, and surely not unimportant one, in its character as a fact. It was curious, even as a fact, that a belief should have prevailed throughout the world, in the days of Augustus Cæsar, that some very great personage was just about to appear upon earth; nor was the importance of the belief lessened in the least through the mistakes and misapprehensions to which, in some instances, it led. It was no doubt sufficiently absurd in Virgil to imagine he had found the wonderful child for whom the whole world was waiting, and under whose reign "the serpent's brood shall die," in the obscure Salonius, the infant son of Pollio. It was scarce less absurd in Tacitus, in the following century, to hold that he had discovered the king "who was to come forth of Judea, and reign over the whole earth," in the Emperor Vespasian. But perversions and misconceptions such as these militated in no degree against the general basis of reality in which the belief itself was founded. It *had* its foundations in truth, however wrapped up in the empty and untangible obscurities of Sybilline prediction, or mixed with the gross and palpable delusions of an impure idolatry, or misdirected by the active but blind ingenuity of philosophic historians or accomplished poets. And the incident of the eastern sages, as recorded in Matthew, shows us that it was a belief through which, employed aright, the Saviour might be found, even by men outside the pale of Judea. This general belief of the period, so curiously handed down to us in pagan literature, was in reality a warning in Providence to the whole world that the King of the world was coming.

Now, we speak advisedly when we say, that not since that time was there any belief founded in prophecy at once so widely spread and entertained by men of such general solidity of understanding as the belief of the present age, to which we refer. It has no doubt been exhibited, like the other, in many a various phase of absurdity and delusion. All our readers must have heard of Lady Hester Stanhope, who died, a few years since, amid the upper wilds of Lebanon, in the full expectation that she was to be visited there by the Saviour in person, and who kept in her stable a horse on which he might ride. They must be acquainted, also, with the extravagances, in the same line, of the followers of Campbell and Irvine. They may have differed widely, too, from the peculiar views of the variously-composed body known as the "Personal Reign Men" of the present day, and perhaps thought of the class with a sort of tacit reference to the "Fifth Monarchy Men" of the times of the Commonwealth. We question, however, whether it would be in any degree more wise to slight the belief in which these extravagances have originated now, than it would have been wise to have slighted the belief in which the extravagances of Virgil, and not a few of his contemporaries, originated in the reign of Augustus Cæsar. The belief which furnished the Roman poet with but the occasion of a mean compliment to the reign of a cunning usurper, led to far higher results in the case of the eastern sages; the belief which, operating on the crazed imagination of a Lady Stanhope, terminated in but an insane folly, may be a very different thing indeed in the mind of a

Dr. Keith; and we think there can be at least no harm in urging on our readers an examination into the extent to which it in reality prevails, and of the data on which it professes to be founded. There is at least nothing fanatical in the advice. It can be in no degree irrational to devote one's self humbly and prayerfully to the careful study of that portion of Scripture regarding which Christ himself has so emphatically said, "Behold, I come quickly: blessed is he that keepeth" *in mind* "the sayings of the prophecy of this book." There is but one book in the whole Bible to which the blessing *particularly* refers. It is the book on which this belief of the religious world professes to be specially based, — the belief that the present remarkable pause among the kingdoms of Europe is but a pause preceding some great hurricane, in which the very foundations of society may be unfixed, — that the sixth vial is now in the course of being poured out on the vast river Euphrates, to dry up its failing waters in the sight of peoples and nations that have peace given them meanwhile, as if to enable them the more carefully to mark the sign, — and that, when that sign shall be accomplished, there shall burst forth upon them a storm like that which the prophet saw in the cave, when "a great and strong wind rent the mountains, and brake in pieces the rocks, before the Lord."

The inquirer, in the course of his search, and especially when setting himself to examine rather the extent and varieties of the belief than the grounds of it, will scarce fail of finding many curious passages, — some of them, no doubt, very extravagant, some of them eminently striking; and the following passage among the rest: "When the beast of Rev. xiii. 1 is described," says a writer of the present year, "*he has upon his ten horns ten crowns;* but when the beast of Rev. xvii. 3 is represented as carrying the woman, he still has ten horns, *but he has not a crown upon any horn.*" And who, ask our readers, can be the writer of this wildly democratic, this fiercely revolutionary passage,—this passage that in reality outdoes, in its quietness, the loudest treason of the most ostentatious Chartism? No democrat, no revolutionist, we assure them. It was written in a quiet English vicarage, by a beneficed clergyman,—a man who, believing, indeed, that the present age will not pass before all the ten horns of the beast shall want their crowns, has yet evidently no other interest in the democratic spirit than that which he takes in it as one of the signs of the times. That such passages should be written and published by such men, must be regarded as one of the signs of the times also, and, we are of opinion, one of not the least significant. The phase which it presents may be well deemed extreme; but, as one of the many phases exhibited by a widely-extended belief, remarkable, in all its multitudinous aspects, for its unity of general scope and direction, we deem it not without its degree of startling interest.

But, in speculating on the effects of the disestablishment of the religion of Scotland, let us deal with the probabilities of the event as if no such belief existed. It is of signal importance, at a time like the present, that a conviction so widely spread should be carefully examined. If found to be solid, it may greatly influence conduct; but it must not be permitted to influence calculation. There can, however, be no harm in referring to the somewhat shrewd circumstance, that the calculations and the belief fill with revolution exactly the same period of time. He must know exceedingly little of the history of either Presbyterian Scotland or of revolution in general, who believes that our vexatious Church controversy is to sink at once into quiet whenever some five hundred ministers and some five hundred thousand people shall have quitted the Establishment. It is only then, properly speaking, that the war is to begin. Revolutions go commonly, like twin stars, by pairs. There is first a comparatively quiet revolution, and then a much more noisy one; and the civil courts have succeeded in accomplishing only the quieter of the two. They have succeeded in revolutionizing the constitution of the Church of Scotland; and when they shall have disestablished her, the work, so far as it is theirs, shall be complete. But the other revolution is still altogether future. The revolution of Charles I. was pretty nearly accomplished when John Hampden had been made to suffer fine and imprisonment in England, and the service-book of Laud had been introduced into the High Church of Edinburgh. But then came the counter-revolution, and it was not fully accomplished until a discrowned head, melancholy of visage, and with locks prematurely gray, had dropped with hollow sound on the scaffold at White-hall. The revolution of James was well-nigh complete when the refractory bishops had been sent to the Tower; the counter-revolution was not completed until after William had landed at Torbay. Charles the Tenth brought *his* revolution to a close when he had revoked and disannulled the constitution of France; but it took three days longer, and a considerable amount of hard fighting besides, to bring to a close the revolution that followed. Such, in short, is the general history of revolution. Such, we are certain, has been its invariable history in Scotland in connection with the Presbyterianism of the country. The war, we repeat, instead of drawing near a close, is but on the eve of beginning.

It will be carried on under one set of circumstances in our country districts, and under another set in our large towns. Democracy has its strongholds in the one, Conservatism in the other; and in the more democratic localities will the war be hottest at first. All the churches of Aberdeen connected with the Establishment will fall vacant in one day. With these, four-fifths of the churches of Glasgow, four-fifths of the churches of Edinburgh, and, in short, in nearly corresponding proportions, the churches of almost all the other large towns and cities of Scotland. Nor is it merely ministers that these churches will lack; they will lack also congregations. Moderatism has spoken of its five hundred licentiates patriotically waiting on tiptoe to rush, each like an ancient Curtius, into the five hundred perilous breaches that are to be made on this occasion in the Establishment. But it has not yet said anything of five hundred waiting congregations. The gap made by the congregations must remain unfilled, like the gaps made by the Indian tomahawk in the cranium of Lieutenant Lesmahago. Now, it is a very simple fact, but a not unimportant one, that it is the congregations who pay the seat-rents; whereas the patriotic licentiates, instead of paying the rents, will be able only to benefit the community by receiving the stipends. It is also a fact, that in Glasgow, Paisley, Dundee, Aberdeen, and several of our other large towns, the magistrates receive the rents with one hand, and pay the stipends with the other; and we are afraid it would scarce fail to put the good men somewhat out, should the inveterate old habit be so broken upon through an inability of finding employment for the receiving hand, that they would have to restrict themselves to the use of the paying hand exclusively.

Out of the twenty-nine pulpits of Ross-shire, twenty would be left vacant; and to persons at all acquainted with the character of Scotch Highlanders in the present age it is quite unnecessary to say what would be the nature of the ferment which such an event would occasion. Our Highlanders are a patient people: they have, alas! been much trampled upon, and they have borne it quietly. But though a patient, they are not a weak people; nor are they unintelligent. They have got names, in their simple, expressive Gaelic, for the two parties in the Church. They describe the clergy of the one party as "the ministers who care for *their* souls," and those of the other as "the ministers who do not." They understand perfectly, too, the true nature of a religious Establisment. They regard it, not as a pension fund set apart for the sustenance of a useless clergy, but as a provision made for *their* benefit. It is but a few years since a party of them, ejected from their homes in the north of Scotland, left in quiet sadness their mountain hamlet, on their journey to the sea-port from which they were to take ship for America. They had been previously ground down by the exactions of a needy and rapacious landlord, until their lives had become ceaseless struggles between want and hard labor; and the feeling that binds Scotch Highlanders to their native soil had been in some degree weakened in consequence. But it *was* their native soil that they were leaving, and so they quitted it, as we have said, in silent sorrow. In their onward journey they passed the parish church. It was the one part of all the country that was theirs: it was their only property. It was the only thing that the landlord had not been able to tax, until, like the hard-earned fruits of their labors, it had become his own. It was *theirs*, and they were now leaving it forever. A host of recollections rushed upon them, at once tender and sacred; and there, beside the much-loved building, and amid the ashes of their fathers, they lifted up their voices and wept. And it is men such as these that the revolution of the civil courts is now on the eve of robbing of their only property. It would be utter madness to speak of resistance. They will not resist; their much-loved ministers have taught them better; but let these twenty churches be thrown vacant,—let all the evangelistic churches of the Highlands be thrown vacant,—and the cause of the aristocracy in Scotland will count weaker from the date of the event than it had hitherto done, by thirty thousand fighting men. Conservatism, too, may give up at least the northern Highlands as a political field whenever it pleases. One of the first effects of the revolution in country districts everywhere will be a thorough separation between the intrusion landlord and the non-intrusion tenant. The political feeling never attained to great strength among the rural population of Scotland. It is the proprietary and the *acres* of the country that have hitherto voted at elections. Landlords have been in the habit of bringing the representatives of their estates with them to the poll, and their estates have invariably turned out to be of the same mind with the landlords themselves. There is now a new element introduced, or, rather, an old element revived; and our proprietary would do well to take the measure of its strength. "All for the Church, and somewhat less for the state," was a leading principle of the old Scotch whig, as drawn by Belhaven in the days of the Union; and it will be found that the character still applies. But we are indicating, and that feebly, not so much the first beginnings of the war in our country and Highland districts, as the directions which these first beginnings are likely to take. We feel that we are only entering on our subject.

PART THIRD.

Is the reader acquainted with that singularly amusing and interesting work, the "Autobiography of Heinrich Stilling"? Heinrich, a German of the true type,—for to a simplicity so extreme that it imparted a dash of eccentricity to his character, he united great natural powers, and acquirements of no ordinary extent and variety, —had passed, in his eventful career, through many changes of station and employment. In early life he had wrought as a journeyman tailor in an obscure province. In his first stage of advance he had taught a village school. In the second, he had acted as a sort of mercantile clerk and agent. In the third, he had applied himself to the study of medicine, and practised with various success as a physician in a tenth-rate German town. In a fourth, he had added the practice of surgery to that of physic, and had learned to couch for the cataract. He had received, in a fifth, an appointment to a professorship of agriculture and commerce in a provincial academy. In a sixth, he had been transferred, first to one university, then to another of higher standing and celebrity, and distinguished himself by his lectures on the economical, financial, and statistical sciences. Continuing to practise gratuitously as an oculist, he acquired a degree of skill perhaps unequalled at the period over Europe, and became the honored instrument of restoring to their sight many hundreds of the blind. He rose high in fame as an author; did much, through the exercise of his very popular powers, to stem the flood of neologic rationalism, which, during the latter half of the last century, deluged the continent; asserted, in his writings, in opposition to the cold, inoperative Theism disseminated from France as a centre, that "God must and will be worshipped in his Son," and that "in Christ, and in Christ only, is the Father of men to be found." And, after a long and singularly useful life, he died, about thirty years ago, in the possession of the esteem of all good men, with a long list of honorary titles attached to his name, a popular and influential writer, a leading professor of the practical sciences, a doctor of philosophy and medicine, and private aulic councillor to the Grand Duke of Baden.

We refer to his strangely varied and surely not inglorious career for the sake of an illustration which it furnishes, in connection with one of the more striking peculiarities of his character. As he rose, step by step, in his course, he was ever in the habit of seriously inquiring of himself whether he had yet reached the proper place to which Providence in an especial manner, as he thought, had been guiding him from his youth up. He had all along felt himself gravitating, through the force of events, if we may so speak, towards some unknown vocation, the true destiny of his life, — as the sun, with all its planets, is said to gravitate towards an unseen and mysterious centre, hidden deep in the profound of space; and, believing that there awaited him some peculiar, specific work to perform, he was solicitously anxious at each stage to know whether he had yet entered on the exercise of it, or whether he might not continue to await the call of duty inviting him to some other sphere of action. There can be little doubt that he carried the feeling to an extreme more in accordance with the peculiar mysticism of the German than the sober common-sense of the British character; but the doubt need be quite as slight that, in the great majority of cases, men err on the opposite side, and err much more fatally than Stilling did. It is much to know one's real place and vocation, — so very much, that half the blunders and mishaps which occur in life, including all that is ridiculous in the classes that shoot above their proper mark, and almost all that is most pitiable among the classes that shoot beneath it, occur just in consequence of their not knowing their legitimate sphere and proper employments. They fail to appreciate their true destiny, and make shipwreck in consequence; just as those who failed to solve the enigmas of the Sphinx were destroyed by the monster as a penalty of their misapprehension.

But why so obvious a remark? It may be found not without its bearing, we are of opinion, on the present crisis of the Scottish Church. It may at least serve us to illustrate what we might be perhaps unable to make equally plain without it. The disestablished Church of Scotland bids fair to take up a place not occupied by any Church in Europe since the times of the Reformation; and it would be well that all sincerely interested in her welfare, and the work which in times past she has been honored to carry on, should not mistake it. We can imagine scarce anything more fitted to be fatal than a misapprehension of her true place — her proper employment; and it is impossible not to see that there may in some instances be considerable danger of such a misapprehension. The question which, with respect to himself, cost Heinrich Stilling so much grave thought and severe self-examination, should seriously engage every member of the Free Church of Scotland with respect to her. What, in the present great crisis, is her proper place? — what her true vocation? Of one thing we may be assured: the separating process of which her contest with the civil powers has been so remarkably the occasion, and which, in its various stages of involuntary classification, serves so strikingly to remind one of the testing trials of the bands of Gideon, bears reference to some very important end. We may be assured, further, that the work prepared for the parties which it divides will be in meet accordance with their respective characters.

Among the prose writings of the poet James Montgomery there is an exceedingly curious little piece, less known than most of his other writings, designated an "Apocryphal Chapter in the History of England," which purports to describe a state of matters induced by the total extinction of Christianity in the country. There are many curious incidents narrated in it; and one of the most curious is a sort of *missionary* enterprise, undertaken with the design of restoring the vanished faith, by the country's more prudent skeptics and more sagacious men of the world. So long as Christianity existed among them, we are told, they had been indifferent to it at best; some of them had made it the subject of not very respectful jokes, — some of them had openly contemned it; but, now that it was gone, they suddenly opened their eyes to the startling fact, that a vast and irresistible mass of depraved, reckless, hunger-bitten intelligence was preparing to bear down upon them and destroy them, and that the only barrier efficient to protect them in the circumstances was just the Christian *superstition*. That barrier, therefore, they had set themselves determinedly to reërect. They went out to preach, says the poet, in "market-places and town-halls, and on oratorio evenings at the theatres; but, alas! never having known much of the matter, and having cared less, — having the misfortune, too, of being pretty widely known, and of being conscious of it, — they drivelled so exquisitely, in their confusion, as to provoke at once the scorn and the wrath of the multitude, who presently silenced them with such missiles as were wont to be thrown on better men in the days of Whitefield and Wesley."

Now, the incident is of course a fictitious one; but it is not on that account without its large admixture of truth. It is true to nature, if not to fact; and the country will by and by have an opportunity, it is not improbable, of seeing many counterparts to it among the real occurrences of the time. The *residuary* Establishment will find it as necessary to exert itself in behalf of a nominal Evangelism, when the truth shall have left it, as it was found necessary by the skeptics of Montgomery's "Apocryphal Chapter" to exert themselves in the behalf of Christianity. Moderatism will find itself in circumstances in which, for the first time, its very existence shall have to depend on its ministerial exertions; and, for a season at least, violent exertions will be made. The dead body will be galvanized in all its limbs and features; and if the wild convulsions and contortions fail to resemble life, they will have at least the merit of being exceedingly like possession. But the impulse, though more than sufficiently energetic in the commencement, will not, and cannot, be permanent. The stone of Sisyphus will return to where it gravitates. It has been well and philosophically remarked, that no man ever changed his true character merely by determining to change it. There is something more than the sheer force of resolution required. And what is true of the individual is equally true of every body composed of individuals. Moderatism will set itself to work with, no doubt, a dogged determination of working hard and long. It will strive for a while to transmute into activity, by sheer dint of resolution, its native indolence of character. It will set itself to propel the ponderous axles and pinions of the Establishment by main strength; but that which should be the grand moving power of the machine it will assuredly neglect. It will merely set its shoulder to the master wheels. The sole moving power of any Church, whether established or disestablished, — the only moving power, indeed, that is of the slightest value, that is not rather mischievous than beneficial, — is that power which acts through converted ministers and office-bearers, with all the permanent efficacy of a fixed law. And as this moving power. Moderatism neither has nor wishes to have, its exertions must of necessity be both inoperative and short-lived. The remark refers mainly to Moderatism of the genuine type; for mainly to Moderatism will the throes and spasms of this period of convulsion be restricted. The Quietism of the residuary Establishment will walk softly, according to its nature, — then, as now, appalled rather than stimulated by the disruption. Its Rowism will continue to halt lamely, like a patient with an unset bone. Its Politico-Evangelism, as if palsy-struck for the time, will cower helplessly under the consciousness that when a religious ministry has lost its character, its zeal comes to be regarded as but the mere ebullitions of an offensive selfishness, and that to remain as quiet as possible is its true policy in the circumstances, seeing that the more thoroughly it may succeed in hiding itself, the better may it hope to fare.

Now, it would be much, we repeat, for the disestablished Church to know at such a time its true place and vocation. It will stand on high ground, and this not merely in the eyes of religious men all over the world, but also in the estimate of mere men of honor.

A clergyman, not a hundred miles from Edinburgh, who gave in his adherence to the resolutions of the Convocation, felt, since the late discussion in Parliament, that he had taken a step of doubtful prudence; and, sitting down all alone, with the glebe in his front and the manse in his rear, he resolved, in the first place, to let his signature in the fatal list stand for nothing, and to exert himself, in the second, whenever the opportunity should occur, in repealing the veto. Not quite satisfied, perhaps, with the resolution at which he had arrived, and naturally desirous of making up by the gratulations of others what was wanting in his own, he bethought himself of one of his neighbors, — an Intrusionist heritor, — much a Moderate and a man of the world, who had sturdily opposed him hitherto in all his movements on the side of the Church, but whom, in the main, he had found respectful and not unfriendly. I must just call on Mr. ——, he said, and tell him what I have at length determined on doing, and that we are much more likely to agree for the future than hitherto. And call on him he accordingly did. But, alas! there awaited the poor man none of the anticipated congratulations. The heritor, unluckily a gentleman, and acquainted with the code of honor, though ignorant of the constitution of the Scottish Church, heard him patiently avow his altered sentiments and resolutions, and then, seriously addressing him, "Mr. ——," he said, "hitherto I deemed you and your party in the wrong; but, though I opposed, I respected you; and, regarding you as honest in your convictions, I had pleasure in recognizing you as my minister. I must now beg leave to say that you have found means to change my opinion, and that I can attend your ministrations no longer."

We instance the story merely to show that there are points of a practical bearing in the existing contest which even mere men of the world can thoroughly appreciate. The man honest in acting up to his convictions, and who can make large sacrifices for the sake of principle, is deemed at least an honorable man by the numerous class ignorant of those higher motives which bear reference to an unseen world. With the members of this class, in spite of themselves, the disestablished Church must stand high, — a witness to the importance of truths little known or heeded, but which are destined, in these latter times, to grow upon the notice of the world, to constitute the great watchwords of its terminal struggle between the powers of good and of evil, and to receive their final confirmation at the last day from that adorable Sovereign of all, whose right equally it is to rule over the nations now, as to judge them then. With the men who in reality know the truth, whether at home or abroad, the position of the disestablished Church will be better appreciated. The testing-trial has been protracted and severe; the chaff and dust have been blowing off at every stage in the process. It will be a chosen and well-tried band that, at the last stage, now apparently so near, shall go forth from the Establishment, leaving behind them the residual culm and debris; and, let *party* assert what it may, the sacrifice ultimately will not be under-estimated. The religious feelings of the country will be on their side; nay, the very consciences of their opponents will be on their side also, in the degree at least in which these consciences are enlightened and awakened; and, as in other times, death-beds, despairing and unblest, shall yield an impressive testimony in their favor.

Now, it would be of vast importance for the Church to be fully conscious of all this. In her new circumstances she will be exposed to peculiar temptations and dangers; and there is nothing which, with the blessing of her Great Head, seems so suited to guard and strengthen her against these as a right apprehension of her true place and standing. It would be well for her to know where her strength lies; it would be well for her to know, also, in how many different ways it might be possible to make that strength less. The history of our Scottish seceders — so very pregnant a one, that we much regret it has not yet been written in a style worthy of it, and which we would fain recommend as a theme not unsuited to the pen of the ablest and most judicious writer of the party, Mr. M'Crie — is full of instruction to the Church in her present position. It reads its significant lessons also to the Church's opponents. What, however, we would specially advert to at present, in connection with it, is the important fact that the first seceders, goaded, no doubt, by that persecution which maketh even wise men mad, suffered themselves, in the latter stages of their struggle, to lose temper, and that, as a consequence of losing it, they lost also much of the power which their position would have otherwise secured to them. When thrust violently out of the Church, they carried with them the warm sympathies of all its better people. They had taken their stand on the old Presbyterian ground, and had maintained the ancient quarrel nobly, and in a right spirit. Though weak in the ecclesiastical courts, they were morally strong, for they had much of the strength of Scotland behind them, and the high-handed tyranny of Moderatism was exactly the sort of thing best fitted to strengthen them yet further. They failed, however, fully to realize the true nature and importance of their position. They quitted the Church under the irritation of defeat. They felt that they had been wrongously overborne and beat down, on ground on which, constitutionally, they had a right to stand; and we are much mistaken if their after mishaps and dissensions may not be traced mainly to their indulgence in this unhappy feeling. The same men who, during the series of persecutions to which they had been subjected in the church courts, had acted with uniform temper and judgment, lost all command of themselves when they came afterwards to discuss, in their free, independent synod, points of *not* the highest possible importance; and, after a series of the most deplorable and ill-judged wranglings, they broke up into separate parties, that refused to hold all communion with one another. This lesson, we repeat, is eminently instructive. There is much which ought to be guarded against in the irritation which persecution induces. And there is another danger to be avoided, against which it is possible the first seceders were not sufficiently watchful. It is perhaps natural for men who have suffered for conscience' sake to feel that they have, as it were, purchased a right, by their sacrifices, to maintain their peculiar opinions bluntly and uncompromisingly. The state induced is, for obvious reasons, unfavorable to a spirit of conciliation and concession, and hence, probably, in part at least, the unhappy differences of the first seceders. Men who had submitted to the loss of all rather than yield to even the supreme judicatories of the Church, felt afterwards very little inclination to yield to one another. Now, to enable the Free Church of Scotland rightly to profit by the teachings of history in this instructive case, there seem to be but two things necessary — a sedulous cultivation, through the appointed means, of the spirit of her Master, and a right appreciation of the high place which she seems destined to occupy.

The course of the Church is becoming plainer every day; but, like every other course which every other Church on earth has pursued, it is not quite devoid of its shoals and quicksands, on which the unwary might make shipwreck; and it may be found no unprofitable task to map out a few of the more formidable of these.

PART FOURTH.

It is of the nature of Protestant dissent in free states in which there exist established religions, to take its stand on the side of Liberalism. There are principles involved in its character and position that determine its political place, if we may so speak, with well-nigh the certainty of a fixed law; and it must be sufficiently obvious that if such be the tendency of dissent generally, the bias in the Free Church of Scotland cannot fail to be mightily strengthened by the peculiar circumstances of her situation.

In the first place, she must necessarily recognize her disestablishment as a consequence of a most unjustifiable revolution effected in the very vitalities of her constitution, through the aggression of the civil courts, seconded, in the narrowest spirit of partisanship, by the existing government. In the next place, it is impossible not to see that the persecuting influence will be brought to press hard upon her, especially in country districts, through the agency of the privileged classes, — the classes who possess the lands and inhabit the manor-houses of the country. It is obvious, too, that there are points at which the residuary Establishment, backed by the power of the secular courts and the state, will be made to abut against her with harassing and irritating effect. Questions will be necessarily arising between the skeleton Church and the national Church *de jure*, in which the powers that be will prove themselves no impartial adjudicators; and thus there bids fair to be induced among the adherents of the Free Church a spirit of disaffection with the order of things, through which they will be made to suffer. There are analogies, too, between the important spiritual rights for which they contend, and the secular claims asserted by Liberalism, which must exert, in some cases, a sort of fraternizing influence. The cause of religious liberty ever involves that of civil liberty also. For two whole centuries — from the times of the Reformation until the earthly principle, true to its original character, degenerated into mere license, — another name for tyranny, — and demanded not only emancipation from the rule of man, but unconditional release from the laws and government of God also — it went hand in hand with the spiritual principle. With the return of the old circumstances — circumstances in which the pressure of persecution will be again felt — the old coalition among the classes who suffer will be again formed. In short, the inevitable tendency of the disruption of the Establishment will be to increase the movement party in the country, by imparting, from causes such as we have enumerated, a deep tinge of radicalism to minds which, but for that event, would have remained under the control of the conservative influences.

Now, what, we ask, with such a state of things in prospect, will be at once the duty and the interest of the Free Church of Scotland? Here is a powerful current, that threatens to set in athwart her course. How should she steer with regard to it? Exactly as the mariner steers, who, in crossing the Atlantic, takes into account the influence of the great Gulf Stream, and directs his course a few points higher than his destined port, in order to counteract its effects and make allowance for leeway. If the Church become in all her congregations what some of our Dissenting bodies have become, — a mere congeries of political societies, — she will inevitably make shipwreck, and perish. There is no more dissipating element in existence, with regard to all that constitutes the life and strength of religion, than the political element.

Let us look steadily at the matter. The Church, we would first remark, has been removed, in the course of Providence, from all temptation of making common cause with the whigs. She has scarce more to do with them as a party than with their antagonists the tories. Her friends and her enemies are ranked equally on both sides. Lord John Russell and Sir Robert Peel make common cause against her. The Church has been removed, we repeat, from all temptation of making common cause with the whigs. She has been taught, in a manner sufficiently significant, that her cause and theirs, however assimilated by apparent analogies, is not at all identical; it is in no degree more identical with that of the radicals as a party; and in the history of her struggle for the last three years, she has had proofs in abundance that Chartism is determinedly hostile to her. It would seem as if Providence, in the course of events, was shutting her out of that political field, in the mazes of which she might otherwise lose herself. If there be a perilous current threatening to bear her away in one direction, the breath of heaven is evidently swelling her sails in the other; and we think she would do well to profit by what must be deemed more than mere warning in the case, — what must be regarded rather as the compulsory guidance extended by a wise and tender parent to a child, which, if left to itself, might, in its ignorance and its wilfulness, go grievously astray. There is a call in Providence to the Church that she dissipate not her powers in the political field.

The subject is so important that we may be permitted to indulge in an additional remark or two regarding it. If, during the last twelve years, any one lesson has been taught to the country with more point and emphasis than any other, it is the lesson that no one should trust very implicitly to any merely political party, or expect very great advantages from any merely political change. In the course of that eventful period we have seen Whiggism come into office in the character of a powerful principle, and ejected from it in the character of a weak and *effete* one; and it must have required but ordinary powers of observation to see, from the peculiar data furnished during this time, that such must be forever the fate of Liberalism in Britain, until an age arrive in which the majority of both statesmen and the people shall be pervaded by a spirit of vital Christianity. A recurrence of cycles has been often remarked in the history of states and peoples, —cycles in which long periods of despotism are followed by comparatively brief and stormy periods of liberty running wildly into license, and in which these are succeeded by long periods of despotism again. Chateaubriand has written a whole volume on the subject,—a sparkling, if not a very solid one,—in which he shows that all history is little else than a record of these cycles of alternate despotism and license. They form, if we may so speak, the gusts and pauses of the great moral storm which sin has raised in the world, and which must continue to rage until He who stilled the tempest of old shall, when the appointed time comes round, command it to be still also. Now, we have just seen one of these cycles revolve in Britain in a comparatively still atmosphere. Among a less civilized people, or in a worse balanced constitution, it would have taken the more strongly marked form of a stormy revolution, preceded and followed by a state of despotism. In Britain it has been of a quieter and more subdued character; and we may see in its workings, in consequence, some of the laws in which these ever-recurring cycles originate; just as we may see, through the unbroken eddies of a river, those irregularities of bank and bottom by which the eddies are produced; whereas, in the wilder rapids, where all is foam and uproar, we find the disturbing agents concealed by the very turmoil which they occasion.

Whiggism, out of office in this country, and purified by being much and long in a minority, addresses itself, in all its questions of real strength, to the natural consciences of men, and finds a ready response among the classes in whom no selfish interest disturbs the free exercise of the guiding power with respect to the particular points agitated. Nor is the principle to which it appeals — the native sense of right — by any means a weak one, in matters in which it does not meet, in those who entertain it, with a sense of personal advantage as an antagonistic power. The cry, "Emancipate your slaves," for instance, was just the proper voice of this natural sense of right; and it was a loud and powerful cry. It procured eventually the good which it demanded. Be it remembered, however, that it arose from men who derived none of their wealth from the thews and sinews of the slave. It was a cry in which the merchants of Liverpool or the planters of the West Indies did not join. And why? Did these men want natural conscience? or were their wives and daughters, who made common cause with them, less influenced by the sense of right than the other wives and daughters of England and the colonies? No. We are convinced it would be unjust to say so. They were persons of just the average rate of virtue; but their sense of right was controlled and overpowered by what, in the unrenewed human character, is, and always must be, an immensely more powerful principle, — the sense of personal advantage. And so the entire class — though on other questions of right and wrong that did not involve their personal interests they might and would have been sufficiently sound — struggled hard to prevent the emancipation of the slave. The illustration is pregnant with those principles which serve to unlock the problem of the political cycle. Let us but imagine the great bulk of the men who called loudest for the emancipation of the slave at one time, becoming, through some unexpected turn of fortune, slaveholder at another, — their possessory feelings, as in the case of the planters, converted into principles of greater strength than their sense of right, — and we have Whiggism before us in its character in and out of office. Its strength in the opposition is the strength of the natural conscience; it becomes weak in office, because it comes under the influence of the selfish and possessory feelings, and because, in the average human character, these invariably prevail as principles of action over the conscientious ones. And be it remarked that this character of average virtue must as certainly be that of every merely political party numerously composed, as the stature of the members that compose it must, when thrown into the aggregate, and divided by their number, be of the average height, or their longevity, when similarly treated, be of the average duration. Individuals may attain to a much higher rate of virtue, — individuals may be generous, disinterested, much influenced by the better motives, and little moved by the worse, — but bodies must continue to bear the average character; bodies must continue to be moved more strongly by the selfish than by the generous feelings, until a period arrive when, through the diffusion of a Christianity not merely nominal, but vital and real, the virtue of society shall be elevated to the high level of the converted man. And till that time come, the political cycle must continue to revolve, like the giddy and restless wheel to which the Psalmist compared the wretched *unrest* of his enemies, exciting hopes to produce only disappointment, agitating men's minds and arousing their passions, but leaving their characters unimproved, and lessening in no degree the amount of their unhappiness.

Does the remark seem rather declamatory than solid?

We are convinced it contains an important truth, which bears with no indirect effect on the true vocation of ministers of the gospel. The Free Church of Scotland has nobler and better work before her than can be found in climbing the political wheel, and in seeing it ever and anon descending to the mediocre level above, to which society cannot permanently rise so long as its average virtue is that, not of renewed, but of unregenerate nature. She will have many temptations to cast herself into the movement party. It would be well for her to know that they are, in almost every case, temptations to be resisted. There is, in particular, one specific form in which, in at least our country districts, temptation bids fair often to present itself. In almost all the rural parishes of Scotland, the great bulk of the people will be determinedly on her side, and the great bulk of the lairdocracy as determinedly opposed to her; and where the large farm system prevails, and the political franchise is enjoyed by only some five or six individuals in a parish, and these, mayhap, all Moderates, it may be deemed desirable, in order to give her weight in the political scale, that the franchise should be extended. A species of radicalism threatens to be thus induced, at one, in at least its main doctrine, with the universal suffrageism of the mere political radical and chartist; and members of the Free Church would perhaps do well to be on their guard against it. The true character of universal suffrage cannot be adequately tested by any reference to its probable style of working in a quiet Presbyterian parish, or to the moral and intellectual fitness for the franchise of our humbler classes, where best instructed, and most under the influence of religion. It must be judged with reference to its probable effects in the aggregate. The popular voice in the Scottish parish might be right; but the important question to be determined is, whether the popular voice all over the British empire would be right. We much fear it would not. Civil and religious liberty have long gone hand in hand, and their names have been so united for centuries in toasts and watchwords, that we can scarce mention the one without calling up the other. It does not seem at all unlikely, however, that there is a time coming when what will be termed civil liberty shall cease to tolerate religious liberty. The question bids fair to arise, Is a citizen to be denuded of his rights of Christian membership simply for acting in accordance with both the spirit and letter of the law of his country?—a law constitutionally enacted, be it remarked, by the people's representatives. And thus the case promises to be so stated, that the spiritual liberty of retaining in the Church's own hands the power of the keys will be deemed not only an aggression on the civil liberty of the subject, but an offence also against the representative majesty of the people. The two liberties will be brought into direct collision as antagonist powers. That liberty which constitutes the *beau ideal* of the chartist is invariably of an Erastian cast; and the class, if such there be, who may long for universal suffrage on the Church's behalf would do well to be aware of the fact. There are Voluntary spirit-dealers in Edinburgh that sell whisky on Sabbath under the protection of Mr. Home Drummond's act, and deem it a very absurd thing that their churches should have a different law on the subject. Their churches have a right to make the fourth commandment a test of communion, and in this right *their* religious liberty is involved. But it is Mr. Home Drummond's act that involves the civil liberty of the spirit-dealing members. A persecution originating among the masses on principles such as these might be a very terrible one. In her troubles hitherto, the earth has invariably helped the woman. It is not improbable that a time of trouble may yet arise in which the earth will refuse to help her.

One of our main objections, however, to a course of political agitation on the part of the Church is the dissipation of strength and spirit, if we may so speak, which such an agitation must induce. The political element in this country is rather a restless than a strong one. It acts vigorously up to a certain point, and there fails at once. The contest comes. Votes are recorded; the stronger party gains; the losers sit down under the disappointment, to console themselves as they best may; and this is just all. There are no great sacrifices demanded, and none made; and a habit comes to be formed, in consequence, by no means favorable to those larger and more serious demands which in times of trouble religion makes on her adherents. It is a fact not unworthy of notice, that the merely politico-Evangelicals of the Church soon left her. They voted, spoke, and canvassed for her reform bill, the Veto Law, regarding votes, speeches, and canvassings, as just the proper enginery of party, and then left her when a time of suffering arrived, because suffering is no word in the vocabulary of the mere partisan. The spirit of the ordinary ten-pound freeholder who records his vote in behalf of his party, and does no more, is an essentially different thing from that of the martyr; and it is the spirit of the martyr that Christianity, in times like the present, demands. We would not have indulged in these desultory remarks, were the danger to which they refer less imminent. It can scarce be necessary to add, by way of qualification, that it is one thing to become a mere political society, and quite another to perform in the right spirit political duties. Many of the members of the Free Church must possess, as members of the community, political privileges; and to these, as to privileges of every other kind, a sense of responsibility must attach. They must exercise them, and their voices in the legislature of the country must, in the aggregate, be found influential. In a constitution such as ours, the strength of parties must continue to fluctuate. There will be periods of action and reaction ever recurring. The cycles will revolve as before. In the commencement of these cycles, when the spirit of liberty remains still fresh and unweakened by the selfish influences, permanent advantages in the cause of right will continue to be gained. In the commencement of the last cycle, for instance, the slave was emancipated; and the friends of the Church would do well to possess their souls in patience, and watch, in the Church's behalf, the commencement of the next cycle. It is one thing to direct to right ends the political power of a party, and quite another to be carried away by it.

But our subject lengthens on our hands, and there are various other points on which it might be well to touch. How ought the Free Church to deal by the residuary Establishment?—how by the Voluntaries?—how by the bitterer opponents among the lairdocracy? What other dangers has she to fear besides the great danger of dissipating her power and lowering her character in the political field? How shall she best guard against the growth of a narrow and exclusive spirit? and on what objects mainly should she concentrate her energies?

PART FIFTH.

How ought the Free Church to deal by the residuary Establishment, and how by the Voluntary body? We are convinced that very great danger may be incurred by mistaking the true course with regard to either. A war of extermination waged blindly against the one, or an equally blind union formed with the other, for but the purpose of carrying on that war with greater effect, could scarce fail to be attended with disastrous consequences to the Free Church of Scotland. Her strength would leave her in the struggle, and she would sit down at its termination, whatever the result, in a lower and far less advantageous position than that which, when the disruption takes place, it will be assuredly her destiny to occupy.

Let us remark, in the first place, that nothing seems more natural, in the circumstances, than that she *should* rush headlong into such a war. It seems quite as much a thing to be expected, on the ordinary principles which govern human conduct, as that, in the hour of her extremity, she should have yielded to the encroachments of the civil power rather than forfeit her endowments, and have set herself down degraded and useless, — one of the less respectable sinecurists of the state; for it is as natural for a man to strike when he is injured, as to cry for quarter when he is overcome. In the party who will continue to harbor within the Establishment, the Church must recognize of necessity the men who have injured her most deeply; and the recent agitation of the Voluntary controversy must serve to draw her attention to the exact point, if we may so speak, at which the retributive blow might be dealt at least most readily, if not with most effect. There is a line of batteries already thrown up against the Establishment, simply in its character as such, conspicuous enough to catch every eye; a numerous and formidable body lie entrenched behind these; and all that may seem necessary in order to secure the overthrow of the beleagured institution, in its miserably undermined and exhausted condition, may be just to join forces with the besiegers, and, with numbers and artillery increased in the proportion in which those of the garrison will be diminished, attempt carrying it by storm. Independently, too, of this natural feeling of hostility, and of the circumstances which may well serve to direct it into the Voluntary channel, the Free Church must inevitably meet with an amount of provocation from the skeleton Establishment which Voluntaryism has never yet received from any Establishment whatever. There will be a struggle for the possession of the people between the Church and the endowed institution, in which the latter, conscious of its weakness in all that constitutes moral and religious character, will call to its assistance the factor and the landlord; the same coarse instruments of persecution which were employed in England in the middle of the last century against the followers of Whitefield and Wesley will be set into operation at the bidding or through the influence of the residuary Establishment in Scotland, against disestablished Evangelism; and in wide districts of country the state endowment will take, in consequence, the very repulsive form of a sort of government grant for putting down the gospel. The Establishment will be recognized as an unsightly incubus, squatted in all its leaden weight on the very bosom of religious liberty; and the feeling for its destruction bids fair, in consequence, to mount very high. A war against the Establishment seems quite as natural in the circumstances, we repeat, as it seems natural that the Church, in her hour of extremity, should have quitted her hold of her spiritual privileges, and clung fast to her endowments.

But we can trust that the Free Church of Scotland is destined to baffle the calculations of mere men of the world, however sagacious, on more questions than one. They have already seen her casting into the golden balance of the sanctuary, with its one scale visible to the material eye, and its other scale invisible save to the eye of faith, all her worldly possessions, and seen what to them must have been a mysterious and unknown *quantity* outweighing them all. And we anxiously hope that those who, calculating on data such as we have indicated, trust in a short time to see the Free Church a community of Voluntaries, are destined to be disappointed as signally. We deem it of paramount importance, at a time like the present, that she cleave to her Establishment principles. We say, at a time like the present. We would have deemed it of great importance at any time, especially in connection with that testimony which the Church of Scotland, in all her periods of trouble, has been so peculiarly called on to maintain, — her testimony for the Headship of Christ, not only over the Church, but over states and nations in their character as such; and with this testimony we deem the Establishment principle closely interwoven. But we are much mistaken if there are not peculiar circumstances, in the present time, which conspire, on other accounts, to render the maintenance of the principle more important politically than perhaps at any previous period since the Revolution.

We do not take our place among those radicals and chartists of the day who can see nothing admirable in the framework of the British constitution. We hold, on the contrary, by the old-fashioned belief so well expressed by De Lolme, and so invariably entertained by all the more philosophic intellects of the last century, that the constitution of Britain is by far the most perfect which the world has yet seen. Many a favoring providence, which human means could never have effected, and whose remote consequences lay far beyond the reach of human sagacity, have conspired to render it what it is. It would be as impossible for mere politicians to build up such a constitution by contract, as it would be for them to build up an oak, the growth of a thousand summers. We need scarce add, so obvious must the remark seem, that the man or party who stands upon confessedly constitutional ground must have a mighty advantage over the man or party who stands on some unrecognized principle which one individual may deem good, and another quite the reverse. One British subject holds, for instance, that the murderer should be put to death; another, that death is too severe a punishment for any crime, even for murder itself; and the point of difference betwixt them, regarded merely as a matter of argument, leaves much, no doubt, to be said on both sides. But, for all practical purposes, how immense the advantage derived to the former from the circumstance that his principle is a constitutional principle! In the same way, how very great the advantage which the ten-pound freeholder, deprived unjustly of his franchise, possesses over the mere chartist, prevented from voting because he wants the qualification! The freeholder can base his claim on constitutional ground; the chartist can base his on but what he deems the intrinsic justice of one of the Five Points. Now, be it remarked, that the Voluntary principle is not a constitutional principle; it is less so than some of the Five Points even. It is as little so as that of the man who contends that the murderer should not be put to death. The Establishment principle is the constitutional one; and there are battles in prospect which can be fought on this ground alone. And so signally important do these conflicts promise to be, that the integrity, nay, the very existence, of the constitution, may come to be staked upon them. Let us refer to just two of the number, — one of these a highly probable occurrence, the other at least a possible one.

It is far from improbable, as we have repeatedly shown, that the skeleton Establishment, in its time of exhaustion and peril, may call to its aid the Episcopacy of England, and barter its Presbyterial forms for that assistance without which it may find it altogether impossible to subsist. Now, on what ground, we ask, could the people of Scotland raise their protest with most effect against a transaction so utterly iniquitous in itself, and so pregnant with disastrous consequences to the country? How best fight, on this question, the battle whose result may be found to determine ultimately that of the great battle of Protestantism itself? As a Voluntary? The Voluntary has not a handbreadth of constitutional ground on which to fight it. His quarrel is with establishments in the abstract, — a quarrel in no degree less alien to the genius of the constitution than the cause of the chartist. He could assail a Scoto-Episcopal Establishment with but the arguments which he has already employed in assailing a Scoto-Presbyterian Establishment. He could but propose dealing with it as the chartist proposes dealing by the House of Lords. But in the event of an invasion such as we anticipate, how very different the ground which the assertors of the Establishment principle could occupy! The opponent of all establishments could appeal to but a sort of unembodied conviction, which he himself entertains, — a something which hovers between an opinion and a belief in his mind, and which would underlie, of necessity, the insuperable disadvantage of being denied the status of a first principle. The assertor of establishments could appeal, on the contrary, to the plain letter of the constitution. He would be placed in the circumstances, not of the chartist, alleging that he had a right to exercise the franchise in virtue of one of the Five Points, but of the ten-pound freeholder, asserting that he had a right to exercise the franchise in virtue of his ten-pound freehold. He could take his stand on the treaty of union; he could take his stand on the unequivocal pledge embodied in that solemn oath which all our monarchs have sworn at their accession, from the days of Queen Anne to the days of Queen Victoria. In raising his protest, he could remind the advisers of the Crown that high treason against the constitution is still a capital offence. He could caution ministers of the state — not in the style of a wild, bloodthirsty democrat, but with the sobriety of a British subject, aware of his rights, and determined to assert them — that they were in danger of rendering themselves amenable to the fate of Strafford. To political Churchmen, bent on the conquest of *Samaria*, and enamored of the principles of Laud, he could point, in no spirit of intolerance, to the bloody scaffold of the zealot. So long as Puseyism was in the ascendency, he could maintain against it, on constitutional ground, a war of appeals and protests; and he could occupy the hour of reaction, when that hour came, in tabling his articles of impeachment for high crimes and misdemeanors against the constitution. Surely, a vantage-ground of such mighty importance is not, at a time like the present, to be lightly abandoned.

Let us advert to just one point more. If Popery be not destined to rise in this country, and become for a time the dominant power, not a few of the country's best and most sagacious men have greatly misunderstood the mind of God as revealed in prophecy. And certainly not since the days of James VII. did its rise seem more probable, from causes in actual operation, than at the present time. It is of importance, surely, in preparing for the coming contest, that those remaining ramparts of the constitution which were reared with a direct view to it — reared to bear point-blank against Popery — should at least not be suffered to fall into a state of dilapidation and decay; and, among these, where shall we find a bulwark half so important as that which the doctrine of the Protestant Succession furnishes? Hume himself — a man not at all apt to be biased in his judgments by religious predilections — has characterized this doctrine as a leading one in the constitution; nay, as, beyond any other, the doctrine that *fixed* the constitution. He has described it as the grand expedient through which the long controversy between the prerogatives of the Crown and the rights of the people was terminated in favor of the latter. "It obtained," he says, "every advantage, as far as human skill and wisdom could extend." "It established the authority of the prince on the same bottom with the privileges of the people. By electing him in the royal line, we cut off all hopes of ambitious subjects, who might in future emergencies disturb the government by their cabals and pretensions; by rendering the crown hereditary in his family, we avoided all the inconvenience of elective monarchy; and by excluding the lineal line, we secured all our constitutional limitations, and rendered our government uniform and of a piece. The people cherish monarchy because protected by it; the monarch favors liberty because created by it; and thus every advantage is obtained by the new establishment." The philosopher remarks further — and surely his testimony on the point may be received without scruple — that "the disadvantages of recalling the abdicated family consisted chiefly in their religion, — a religion prejudicial to society, and which affords no toleration, or peace, or security, to any other communion." Now, be it remembered, that we live in a time when, by an already powerful and still rising party, this doctrine of the Protestant

Succession is covertly assailed, and the revolution through which it was secured assailed not so covertly. They already designate it as the rebellion of 1688. The conversion of the British monarch to Roman Catholicism, did no such doctrine exist, would be a glorious event in the annals of Popery. The rising apostasy would hold in the throne of the united kingdom such a post of vantage as the whole world could not equal. It has its golden dreams regarding it now, — dreams which, if destined to rise into power, it will assuredly strive hard to realize; and the only constitutional point on which Protestantism could plant itself in its war of defence would be just the point furnished by this doctrine. But could Voluntaries occupy that point? Could it be occupied by the man who asserts that religion is but the business of individuals, and that states and nations, in their character as such, should have no religion? Assuredly not. If religion be but the business of individuals, the British monarch, in his character as an individual, has a right to choose a religion for himself. If states, as such, should have no religion, on what right principle can it be held that states should determine the religion of their sovereigns? The doctrine of the Protestant Succession falls at once if dissociated from the principle of *national* religion. It is a doctrine behind which no consistent Voluntary can entrench himself.

We would fain press on every member of the Free Church the great importance of the establishment principle. To lay it down at a time like the present would be such an act of madness as if a warrior divested himself of his armor on the eve of a great battle, and then entered naked and defenceless into the fray. It furnishes the only ground on which coming contests are to be maintained, and the cause of Presbytery and of Protestantism asserted.

But it is one thing to hold resolutely by the establishment principle, and quite another to determine on the course proper to be pursued respecting some existing Establishment. The government, in its wisdom, has been pleased to endow Maynooth. It is quite possible, however, vigorously to oppose the yearly grant to that institution, without being in the least a Voluntary. A Convocationist may hold firmly, on similar grounds, by the establishment principle, and yet set himself in determined opposition to the residuary Establishment. Be it remarked that, had not the latter been converted into something which he deemed exceedingly bad, he would not have quitted it. He foregoes its temporal advantages rather than remain in connection with it. Rather than acquiesce in the revolution which has been effected in it, by yielding allegiance, in matters spiritual, to the revolutionizing power, he gives up his whole living, and, thus resembling one of those French royalists who preferred submitting to voluntary exile to taking the oaths to the Convention, what principle is there to prevent him from resembling these royalists still further, by taking up arms against it? For our own part we are utterly unable to see any. If in reality revolutionized into so bad a thing that honest men refuse to remain within its pale, even though their whole means of living, altered in character by the revolution, be held out to them as a bribe for doing so, on what grounds could they be censured for making war on it? We have but one reply to the question, — we can see none.

In this, however, as in all other things, it may be well to employ St. Paul's distinction between the expedient and the lawful. A war of the kind might be entirely just, but we are far from being convinced that it would be in any degree expedient. Unlike the Voluntary controversy in its principles, it would yet resemble it in its effects. It would scarce fail to assume in its progress the secularizing, semi-political form which would best consort with its semi-political character; and the deep-toned religious feeling which has, we trust, been strengthening in the course of the present controversy, would infallibly evaporate in the progress of a controversy in which the Free Church would have a great many more hands to assist her than now, but, we are afraid, much fewer hearts to pray for her. Nay, that very assistance would be of itself an evil. It would mix up her people, through the influence of a common object, with Destructives and mere Voluntaries,—men at one with them in their hostility to the residuary Establishment, but thoroughly at variance with them in their principle of action; and they would derive, to a certainty, no benefit from the contact. But one inevitable effect of the controversy we would deplore more than any of the others. It would surround, as with a wall, the residuary Establishment, and freeze within it—bind up, as if in ice—many a well-meaning man, infirm of resolution, and halting at present between two opinions, who, were the matter managed otherwise, might be solicited and drawn forth. Voluntary opinions were decidedly on the increase in this country some fifteen or twenty years ago. The Voluntary controversy broke out; men took their side; and from that moment Voluntaryism ceased to increase. The Free Church must deal more wisely; nor, in this respect at least, is her course a difficult one. There are strong religious sympathies operating in her behalf; she has but to throw herself full upon these by engaging heart and soul in her proper work,—the evangelizing of the country. It is a highly dangerous matter for two vessels to meet in rude collision in the open sea,—so dangerous, that there are instances not a few in which the effects have been fatal to both. But the loadstone rock of which we read in the Eastern tale, with its long flight of stairs and its tower atop, was in no danger whatever. It did not go out of its way to run down vessels; it merely exerted its attractive power, while they were yet at a distance, in drawing out their nails and fastenings, and they then fell to pieces of themselves. The Free Church would do well not to set herself to *run down* the residuary Establishment, but to employ her attractive influence in drawing out its few remaining fastenings.

If it be comparatively easy to say how the Free Church should deal by Voluntaryism, it seems a still more simple matter to say how she should deal by Voluntaries. The controversy is over for the time for all practical purposes. It divided many excellent men; it divided also many men who were by no means excellent. Never, in this respect at least, was there a more unfortunate quarrel. It found the pious Churchman linked close to the Evangelic Dissenter, and, tearing them apart, united the one to some malignant tory, — a mighty friend to establishments, but a bitter hater of the Cross; and bound the other to some miserable infidel, not more an enemy to religious establishments than to religion itself. There were strange unions effected on both sides. Of the five northern proprietors who have refused the Convocationists sites on their lands, three were such sound Establishment men that they stood contested elections on the strength of their attachment to the principle. And Voluntary journalists, who would have filled whole columns with frothy indignation had these proprietors been Irish ones and the Convocationists Papists, have given a place in their pages to their insolent and repulsive epistles, without the addition of note or comment, as if the religious liberty of the country was in no way involved in the case. The fact has thus a double bearing, and is illustrative of the rubbish on both sides. Be it remarked, that the mingled heap of grain, dust, and chaff which the controversy gathered up on the part of the Church, has been thoroughly winnowed of late; whereas the corresponding heap on the Voluntary side still remains what it was. Providence has not yet seen meet to apply the fan, — an obstacle, it may seem, in the way of union. It is probable, however, that in thus speaking of a union of Voluntaries and Establishment men we make use of wrong terms, — we make use of terms of difference, not of agreement, — and fall into some confusion of idea in consequence. With the Voluntary, simply in his character as a Voluntary, a devout Churchman can have no sympathy; with a Churchman, simply in his character as a Churchman, the devout Voluntary can have no sympathy. Voluntary and Churchman are their terms, not of agreement, but of difference, — their respective battle-cries when they fought against one another. It would be absurd to dream of a union coëxtensive with their *designations* of difference; it can be coëxtensive with but their *sentiments* of agreement. It can be but a reunion of Christian with Christian; not a heterogeneous coalition between mere Voluntaries and mere Establishment men.

PART SIXTH.

How ought the Church to deal by her bitterer opponents among the land-owners of the country? We very recently propounded the question, in one of our serial articles, as worthy of consideration. Only a few weeks have passed, and the hostility, whose scope and direction we could but anticipate then, has taken a determinate course, and become embodied in action. Events move quickly in these latter stages of the controversy, — so quickly that well-nigh half the anticipations of the "Tendencies" have been already converted into facts. We are continually reminded of the striking figure of that old poet who complained that the language was growing upon and covering up his earlier writings, as the flowing sea grows upon the sand, and obliterates and covers up all its tidal lines and all its ripple-markings. One northern baronet, who is an Episcopalian, denies the Convocationists sites on his lands because he himself is not a Convocationist; another northern baronet, who is a philosopher, denies them sites on his lands because they weakly prefer the *Assembly's Shorter Catechism* to the *Catechism of Phrenology;* a third northern baronet, who is a Presbyterian, denies them sites on his lands because he has a thorough respect for them, and agrees with them in all matters essential. The pretexts are various, but the overt acts are the same. In each and every case the rights of property are stretched to overbear the rights of conscience, and the principle virtually embodied, that the country's acres should determine the country's religion.

Now, there must be something monstrously wrong here: property can have no such rights attached to it. A sophism in argument may escape at times the detection of even acute intellects; whereas a sophism in action lies open, from its very nature, to the detection of every honest mind. The common sense of mankind is sufficient to ensure its discovery; and even were common sense to fail, common feeling would fasten upon it with the unerring precision of an instinct. The sophism in action never escapes; and the practical sophism of our northern proprietors, that the rights of property may be so stretched as legitimately to overbear the rights of conscience, has been already appreciated in its true character all over Britain. Wherever over the world the vital influences of Christianity exist, — nay, wherever there exists common sense and common honesty, associated with the tolerating principle, — policy such as theirs must be at once recognized as grossly offensive and fragrantly unjust.

There is an element of strength in the circumstance that, in order to estimate aright the policy of such men, it is not at all necessary one should hold by the principles of the Convocationists. Our readers are not Papists: they believe, on the contrary, that the conversion to Protestantism of the deluded adherents of the Man of Sin would be one of the most desirable events which could possibly take place in the Christian world. But not on that account, were the Protestant proprietors of Ireland to deal by their Papist tenants and cottars as our northern baronets are dealing by their Presbyterian ones, would they have any hesitation in making up their minds regarding the real nature of the transaction. It would at once appear to them in its true character, as an act of coarse and repulsive oppression; and as coarse and repulsive must such acts be ever held in the common sense of mankind, whether the objects on which they are brought to bear be Presbyterian or Popish.

In stretching the rights of property so far that they overlay the rights of conscience, there is a monstrous sophism involved, which all can at least feel; and the circumstance has served to originate many a curious speculation regarding the true limitations of the right of the proprietor, among a people never yet characterized by any peculiar obtuseness of intellect. And certainly the age of the Chartist and the Radical is not quite the age which a wise proprietor would choose for forcing such inquiries on the masses. The speculations which necessity imposes upon a people are generally very acute, and rarely inoperative in the end. We are told of Bunyan by Sir James Mackintosh, that "he foiled the magistrates, the clergy, the attorneys, who beset him, in every contest of argument, especially in that which relates to the independence of religion on the civil authority; for it was a subject on which his naturally vigorous mind was better educated by his habitual meditations, forced upon him by necessity, than it could have been by the most skilful instructor." There were many in the age of Bunyan to whom the despotism of Charles and his brother rendered such meditations habitual; and when these reached their degree of ultimate intensity, like those fluids that crystallize at a certain point of saturation, they solidified into the great national act, which we are now accustomed to designate as the Revolution of 1688. It is unwise, we repeat, on the part of the proprietary of the country, to force upon its people a train of inquiry regarding the rights of the proprietor, — especially unwise at a time like the present, when there are so many disturbing elements to lead to extreme conclusions. Chartism has arrived at its own characteristic findings, — findings which it embodied last year in its great petition; and were the infection to spread among the soberer and more solid classes of the community, the effects might be fatal. It is of importance, however, — for the strength of opinion always depends eventually on the breadth and soundness of the foundations on which it rests, and there are sacred rights of property against which no man, or no class of men, can safely transgress, even in speculation, — it is of importance, we say, that the people of the Free Church should entertain just sentiments on this matter, from which no insolence of insult, or no degree of oppression, should be permitted to drive them.

It was one of the enormous hardships to which the Puritans of England were subjected in the reign of Charles II. that "every Dissenting clergyman was forbidden from coming within five miles of his former congregation." Now, there are proprietors of the north of Scotland who will be able, if they but carry their threats into execution, to prevent Presbyterian clergymen from residing within twenty miles of their former congregations. But, monstrous and tyrannical as such a power may seem, has not every man a right, it may be asked, to do what he pleases with his own? and does not the power of the proprietor arise solely, in this instance, from just the legitimate exercise of this right? Nay, not so fast. It is true, there are cases in which a man may do what he pleases with his own; but it can be in only those cases in which the effects of what he does terminate with what is his own; and not even in the whole of these. He may employ the bludgeon which he has purchased in any and every way in which that bludgeon is alone concerned; but he must not employ the bludgeon which he has purchased in breaking his neighbor's head; for, though the bludgeon be his own, the head is not. Nay, further, he must not employ the bludgeon which he has bought in cruelly maltreating the horse which he has also bought. There are thus cases in which he may *not* do what he pleases with his own. The law takes into account not only the sense of suffering in the irrational animal which is his, but also the feelings of his neighbors with regard to the sufferings of that irrational animal, and fines and imprisons him for outraging them. The rule that a man may do what he pleases with his own is a rule of exceptions and limitations. Now, be it remembered that, though the acres of the north country belong to the proprietors of the north country, its religion does not belong to them. The bludgeon is theirs, but not the head; and if they *violently* employ those acres to the detriment of that religion, they do so at their imminent peril. Nay, by putting these acres to other than the recognized and legitimate use, they grievously shock and outrage the feelings of their neighbors: that they also do at their peril. If it be at all just to protect those proper feelings which sympathize in the sufferings of the brute creation, does not immutable justice decree that those higher sentiments of the soul which rest on the Son of God as their proper object, and those rights of conscience which bear reference to his law exclusively, should be at least equally shielded from violence and outrage? The rights of property can be but coëxtensive with the true ends and purposes of property. The possessor of a field tills, sows, and then, that he may reap the fruit of his labor, carefully encloses it; and the law affords him its protection by punishing the trespasser, just because the trespasser interferes with the true end and purpose for which property is held. But property is not held in order that the course of useful science may be arrested; and so, when government is employed in taking a trigonometrical survey of the kingdom, it empowers its surveyors to enter the man's field, if necessary, and fix their theodolites there. Property is not held in order that an important branch of national industry may be put down; and so, should the field be on the sea-shore, a herring-curer, if he can find no other place on which to heap up his fish, in order to get them transferred to his casks, may fence off a portion of it, and heap them up there, giving, of course, remuneration fully adequate for the produce which he may have trampled down, or the general deterioration which he may have occasioned. Property is not held in order that great and beneficial designs may be successfully thwarted; and so Parliament, if it see meet, may empower some projector or joint-stock company to cut a deep canal into the centre of the man's field, or to span it over with some vast viaduct, or to cut it asunder by some broad thoroughfare. The rights of property, we repeat, are but coëxtensive with the ends for which property is held; and he who, on any pretext, stretches these rights so as to render them subversive of the rights of conscience, is guilty of as flagrant injustice as if he had had no property on which to take his stand. He is simply a persecutor, worthy the unqualified detestation and abhorrence of mankind; and his worn-out plea, that he has a right to do what he may with his own, is but a miserable sophism, in every way worthy of the deeds of wrong and oppression of which he renders it the apology. But it can scarce be necessary to insist on points of a character so palpable as these.

It will not be enough, however, thus to remove the bars and obstacles which might otherwise prevent the current of popular opinion from dashing full against the persecuting proprietary of the country. So great is their power, and so many the means of annoyance within their reach, that, had the Church to maintain with them merely a political quarrel, she would scarce fail to be o'ermastered and borne down in the conflict, however unequivocally in the right. The tide of popular sympathy would set in too late and too feebly to avail her. She must not forget in what, under God, her strength lies, — that she has a hold of the religious feelings of the country; and that wherever she succeeds in enlightening a conscience dark before, there also does she of necessity succeed in making good a lodgment from which the power of the landlord and the factor will be utterly unable to expel her. She is strong, doubtless, in the popular character of the rights for which she *has* so resolutely and so devotedly contended, — strong on a principle somewhat similar to that through which the whigs were strong when, after carrying the Reform Bill by a bare majority in the lower House, they dissolved Parliament, and appealed to the country. But were her strength of this merely semi-political kind, — were it based on but the popularity of her principles, — it would be a strength insufficient for her. It would evaporate in the furnace. The only strength which can ultimately avail her must lie in the unchanging fealty of converted hearts. Wherever she is rendered the honored means of a conversion, there she secures an inalienable friend, fitted to abide in her behalf the day of trial. We have been often struck by the remarkable figure in the Apocalypse, in which the witnessing Church is represented as lying slain in the great city. The dead bodies of the two prophets are exposed in the street; the sounds of mirth and wassail ring loud around them; and there is rejoicing and giving of gifts because they are gone. What more hopeless than a cause sunk so low that its sole representatives are two lifeless carcasses, cruelly denied the repose and shelter of the tomb, and exposed to the heartless insults of an ungenerous enemy! They lie festering and dead; a moment passes, and, lo! "the spirit of life from God has entered into them;" they stand upon their feet; o'ermastering astonishment and terror fall upon all beholders; and in the presence of their enemies a great voice from heaven talks with them. In even her darkest day there are hopes to which the Church may continue to cling. The numbers and energy of her assertors will bear no chance proportion to the conversions of the country; and one of those seasons of wide-spread and sudden revival which are, we trust, destined to characterize and bless the latter day, would have the effect of raising her up at once, like the resuscitated bodies of the slain prophets, a terror to her enemies, and a wonder to all. Her strength must lie in the conversions of the country, and her chance of success, humanly speaking, in directing all her exertions under an abiding sense of the importance of the fact. It is, in truth, the grand secret, which her friends know, and her enemies do not.

Ere we conclude for the time, let us add one remark more. The true way of utterly ruining the cause of the Free Church, when the crisis comes, would be simply to yield to those feelings of excitement which in some districts it may well occasion, and fly in the face of the law. Let the authorities be supplied with but a single act through which a charge of outrage and *bona fide* rebellion may be fixed upon the Church, and there will be means instantly exerted to put her down, which have not been employed in Britain since the times of the persecutions of the Charleses. A few ploughmen, assisted by the *bedral's son*, in Culsalmond, smoked their pipes in the parish church, and broke some dozen or a score of panes, and straightway a detachment of the military were marched into Strathbogie, and there was a justiciary trial got up, at which an enlightened jury decided there was nothing to try. The soldiery and the Justiciary Court would be but imperfectly typical of the means which, in the result of some unhappy outbreak, would be set in instant requisition to crush the dissociated Church. The menials of Pilate and Caiaphas are coming out against her with their swords and staves; but a too zealous Peter must not be permitted to strike in her defence. It is essential to her well-being — perchance to her very existence — that all the outrages should be perpetrated by her opponents. It was O'Connell's most important lesson to the people of Ireland that they should keep their tempers and the peace. We would warn, in especial, warm-hearted friends of the Church in the Highlands, — the fighting men of Scotland, — the men who, in not a few districts, are to be separated violently from their beloved ministers, and to see miserable hirelings set in their place, — that they may do much for her by their prayers, but nothing, and less than nothing, for her by their swords; that they cannot strike a single blow in her behalf which *will* not be made to descend with tenfold effect on her own honored head.

MR. FORSYTH'S "REMARKS."

It has been made a principle in selecting these articles to omit those of a decidedly personal character. A vein of original and powerful humor entered, however, so largely into Mr. Miller's writing in defence of the Evangelical party, that it was desirable to have some manifestation of it in the present volume. The following article conveys no idea of Mr. Miller's keener irony and more refined satire. It is in his roughest style, but, so far as it goes, it is characteristic, and it is believed that its broad humor can now be enjoyed without the infliction of pain upon any. — Ed.

There has appeared within the last few weeks a very remarkable little work, on our ecclesiastical struggle, from the pen of Robert Forsyth, Esq., advocate, an Edinburgh philosopher, who settled the principles of moral science rather more than thirty years ago, and who has now very laudably come forward — impelled by patriotic feeling and a strong sense of duty — to settle the Church question. He found himself "*not entitled*," he says, "to look on in silence." The mere *capacity* of doing good suggests always to well-regulated minds the absolute *necessity* of doing it; and so, while very many individuals who have not written essays on moral science, nor acquainted themselves with the *secret causes* of the immortality of the soul, have felt that they had a right to maintain the character of silent spectators, Mr. Forsyth, finding that he had no such right, — that he was not "entitled to look on in silence," — has been, of course, precipitated into authorship; and his pamphlet, which has the merit, as we have said, of being a very remarkable one, has already attracted the favorable notice of most of our Edinburgh contemporaries. "A very excellent and seasonable treatise," says the *Edinburgh Advertiser*, and characterized by "great ability and research." Assuredly yes, says the *Evening Post;* "it exposes with equal profoundness and originality the illegal and dangerous proceedings of the democratic party in the Church." "The pamphlet of Mr. Forsyth seems to us an able one," adds the *Scotsman;* it "sets the pretensions of the non-intrusionists in a very clear light," and "we would direct attention to it, as presenting the ideas of a well-informed, experienced, and religiously-disposed man." And the *Observer* tells his readers that it is a work eminently worthy even his notice, though, from a press of occupation, he has not been able to notice it as yet.

Now, all this is certainly high praise. It has been often satisfactorily shown that the opinion of the Scottish newspaper press is just the opinion of the people of Scotland; of course, by parity of reason, the opinion of the Edinburgh press must be just the opinion of the people of Edinburgh; and here have we our intelligent and respectable citizens, whig and tory, harmoniously at one in regarding the pamphlet which Mr. Forsyth has been so happily necessitated to produce, as seasonable, excellent, able, original, profound, clear in the light which it casts, and full of research, — and in eulogizing Mr. Forsyth himself as an "experienced, well-informed, and religiously-disposed man." Now, it would be, of course, absurd on our part to risk an opinion in direct opposition to all this. We may venture to remark, however, that Mr. Forsyth's pamphlet, though much more consistent than any other production which has appeared on the same side, and though, in the main, somewhat more amusing, has the disadvantage of being not quite complete in itself. Many of its more striking passages bear tacit reference to the doctrines of his great philosophical work, — reference so direct, that, to a man unacquainted with the peculiarities of the doctrine developed in his "Principles of Moral Science," his Church principles must often appear either altogether obscure, or in a very considerable degree extreme, if not irrational. And this, we say, is decidedly a defect. We hold that

Mr. Forsyth's pamphlet on the Church question should be in every respect as independent of his great philosophical work as his great philosophical work is independent of his pamphlet on the Church question. Mr. Forsyth must be surely aware that, in this unthinking and superficial age, in which metaphysics languish, there are many men and many women deeply interested in our ecclesiastical struggle who have yet cultivated no close acquaintance with his "Principles of Moral Science."

"The truths of Butler are more worthy the name of *discovery*," says Sir James Mackintosh, "than any with which we are acquainted." We infer, from the assertion, that Sir James must have been ignorant of the ethical philosophy of Mr. Robert Forsyth. It was reserved for this man of high philosophic intellect to discover, early in the present century, after first spending several years as a licentiate of the Church of Scotland, that though there are some human souls that live forever, the great bulk of souls are as mortal as the bodies to which they are united, and perish immediately after death, like the souls of brutes. Thinking souls, such as the soul of Mr. Robert Forsyth, continue to think on forever; but the vast rabble of souls, that either do not think at all, or think to little purpose, curl, and revolve, and expand, for a very little after they are exhaled from the body, somewhat like the puff of a cigar in a quiet atmosphere, and then melt away into nothing. Of what possible use, argued the philosopher, could the souls of the mere populace be in another world? In the present they are of very considerable value. They constitute a sort of moving power to the bodies of our artisans, clerks, and manufacturers. They produce hats, and shoes, and broadcloth, and law documents; they build houses, and keep shops, and makes sausages and suits of clothes; but in the future state they would be of quite as little value as the steam or water power of a mill or engine dissociated from the cranks of the engine or the pinions of the mill, and sublimed to the dignity of a soul. Where there are neither heads nor feet there can be no demand for either hats or shoes. No attenuated tailor-soul will be required to take measure with his figured tape of the thinking part of Mr. Robert Forsyth, or to illuminate his disembodied sensorium with rows of buttons. He will be independent of broadcloth and of bend leather, and miss neither his clerk nor the butcher's shop. All must have heard of the famous argument once maintained between Corporal Trim and Uncle Toby regarding the souls of negroes, and how the honest old captain came finally to the conclusion, that if the blacks have not souls as certainly as the whites, "it is a sad setting up of one man over another." Now, a similar thought seems to have crossed the mind of the philosophic Mr. Forsyth; nor can we imagine aught more suited to render a person of a benevolent disposition uneasy; but a further discovery served at once to remove the painful feeling. He discovered, by a singularly ingenious process, that the happy few who inherit immortality achieve it for themselves. They work it out simply by dint of thinking. The ploughman's soul does not sink into annihilation simply because it is the soul of a ploughman, nor does the shoemaker's soul perish *qua* shoemaking soul. They perish just because they have not been exercised in thinking,—just because they have not been writing treatises on moral science, or pamphlets on the intrusion side in the Church question. The sensoriums of a Burns and a Bloomfield may be living yet. If souls die, it is all their own fault. They do not take exercise to render them strong and hardy, and so perish the moment they step out of doors; just as children over-delicately nurtured and kept in an over-heated nursery are killed at times simply by running out into the cold. All the hardy, well-trained souls survive. But we are doing less than justice to Mr. Forsyth in not employing his own philosophic language.

"From the capacity that is conferred upon the human mind of

advancing in perpetual improvement, we conclude that it is destined for immortality. . . . . . *But it is not to every individual that this capacity or this destiny belongs.* Some minds are too undiscerning to perceive the value of intellectual improvement. Other minds become so deeply enamored of certain pursuits peculiar to their present state, that they will be unable to burst through the fetters of habit, and to engage in the study of what is good and excellent in the works of their Maker. *These minds, having no employment in which to occupy themselves, would exist hereafter in vain;* and such is the constitution of mind, that if it is not employed, it sinks into thoughtlessness, and loses its intelligent character. But those minds that *engage in the pursuit of intellectual improvement*, or in the *study and diffusion of science*, when they remove from this world will find themselves only placed in a better situation for advancing successfully in their career. Their employment cannot come to an end, for it is infinite; and their minds will continue forever to become still more active, more discerning, and more enlarged. It is no mean prize, then, that awaits the lovers of Wisdom. She is lovely in herself, and worthy of all regard and pursuit; but she is not given to man as a bride without a dowry. *The possession of her communicates no less than immortal life.* This is the highest prize in the great lottery of existence. . . . . . Let it never be forgotten, then, for whom it is that immortality is reserved. It is appointed as the portion of those who are worthy of it; *and they shall enjoy it as a natural consequence of their worth.* This is a part of the plan according to which the Mighty Artist has formed the universe. Whatever is defective or imperfect, and has no tendency to improvement, will gradually pass away and disappear forever; but the minds that shoot vigorously towards excellence will be cherished, and endure and flourish without end. *And this is all that can be said with any tolerable degree of certainty on so obscure a subject.*" — *Principles of Moral Science*, 1805, pp. 501, 502.

But though beyond this Mr. Forsyth did not arrive at certainty (and unquestionably minds of a lower and less philosophic nature could scarce have carried demonstration so far), he was enabled, through the exercise of that fine faculty, imagination, to go a very considerable way further. In an exquisite allegory, attached, by way of appendix, to the chapter in which his great discovery is promulgated, we are presented with a view, singularly graphic and picturesque, of the expectoration of souls. The reader of the "Principles of Moral Science" is suspended in mid-air, with Mr. Forsyth, in the character of the "Angel of Instruction," beside him; and on the earth beneath he is made to see all the dying, brute and human, engaged in vomiting souls. The view somewhat resembles that which the adventurous sailor takes from the maintop of a crowded and tempest-overtaken transport, when horrible nausea occupies the laboring passengers below. We see the "souls of dying men departing from their bodies," and the "souls of dying beasts." We mark the spirits of the beasts coming creeping out, like half-suffocated wasps escaping from the fumes of the deadly sulphur, when, in the silent twilight, some reckless urchin assails with fire and brimstone their devoted citadel, and then squatting themselves down in the open air, and quietly evaporating; or, to employ Mr. Forsyth's own classic illustration, "melting away gradually, like the cloud rising from the river, which the morning sun drinks up." Not so tranquil, however, the process through which the spirits of unthinking men pass into annihilation. "The souls of dying men are more active," says Mr. Forsyth, "than the souls of dying beasts, for they spring upward, and seem to look around them, as if seeking for some work wherein to labor." They come frothing out like small beer in the dog-days, just escaped from the bottle, and wheel round and round in uneasy and short-lived activity, like drops of boiling oil sprinkled from a dipped rush-light on the colder oil of the lamp; or like vivacious lady-birds stuck fast upon pins; or like the wicked old lady in Beckford's Vathec, the rapidity of whose revolutions rendered her altogether invisible. But, soon squatting themselves down in utter exhaustion, they evaporate, "and pass away, and are forgotten, and no trace of them remains." Very different, however, is the destiny of vigorous souls of profound thought and solid acquirement, — the souls that have "engaged in the pursuit of intellectual improvement," and produced treatises on moral science. They "never lose their activity, nor fall asleep at all, like the rest." They visit "the sun, and the moon, and other worlds," expatiate at large over the whole earth and the whole sea, make their way into the recesses of Mr. Forsyth's study, and there acquaint themselves thoroughly with his opinion on the Church question, long ere his invaluable manuscripts have passed into the hands of the publisher. Well has it been remarked by this Edinburgh philosopher, that "it is no mean prize that awaits the lovers of wisdom."

Now, without some previous acquaintance with this fine philosophy, there are passages in Mr. Forsyth's Church pamphlet the force of which cannot be adequately appreciated. And hence, we urge, the incompleteness of the work, regarded as a whole. The happy few who have mastered his "Principles" must, of course, feel themselves quite qualified to enter into the deeper meanings of his "Remarks." But why write for only the happy few? Why not render his pamphlet as independent of his "Principles" as he has already rendered his "Principles" independent of his pamphlet? All interested in the Church question are not, we repeat, deeply read in the metaphysical discoveries of Mr. Forsyth. And yet, what, without a knowledge of the great discovery whose results we have just communicated to our readers, is the real force of a passage such as the one in which Mr. Forsyth sets himself to annihilate the Veto? United to his discovery, it is all-potent; dissociated from it, it is a piece of mere commonplace. We quote from his pamphlet:

"A young man," says Mr. Forsyth, "after employing his best years, and considerable expense, in a university education, and the study of the learned languages and of theology, would, according to custom, present himself for examination before the presbytery of his birth or residence. He is declared qualified to preach, and is allowed to preach for any minister employing him. Yet, on receiv-

ing a presentation from the Crown, or some other patron, he might find his prospects blasted, because a number of clowns had been pleased to say, without assigning a reason, that they dissented from his settlement, whether because they wished some other individual, or wantonly acted to show their power. Admission to the communion table affords no test of the ability of a man to decide on the qualifications necessary to a minister who is to instruct men in the history and principles of Christianity. A man may be a sincere believer in the gospel, and of the most decent life, who yet is truly an illiterate person, engaged in mechanical labor. To say that such a man shall have power to ruin the prospects of a learned man, against whom he can state no well-founded objections, is palpably absurd."

Now, if this passage be taken simply as it stands, even Mr. Forsyth's warmest friends must be forced to allow that it is by no means a striking one. Dr. Cook has said as much, and Dr. Bryce, and the Edinburgh *Advertiser*, and the gentleman who in the *Observer* writes "Columns for the Kirk." But, taken in connection with Mr. Forsyth's great discovery, even the *Witness* itself must confess that it does all it was intended to do, — that it annihilates the Veto. Let the reader mark well some of the phrases employed: "Number of clowns," — "admission to the communion table no test of ability," — "illiterate person engaged in mechanical labor." These are all phrases of deep significancy when coupled with the discovery of Mr. Forsyth. In his "Principles of Moral Science" we are expressly told that "men who spend their lives in the unremitting drudgery of such kinds of labor as require little exercise of the mind, are apt to sink into a state of indolence and stupidity." "They become incapable of thinking," it is added; "and if at any time they make an unusual exertion towards it, their attention soon wavers and fails, and they speedily relinquish an effort that is so sensibly above their strength." They are, in short, men whose souls, like the souls of brutes, perish at death. Mark, next, the antagonist class of phrases used in connection with the licensed candidate: "University education," — "learned languages," — "theology," — fitted to "instruct in the history and principles of Christianity," — "qualified preacher," — "learned man." There is an achieved immortality of soul implied in the very terms. The human souls that do not die, says Mr. Forsyth, in his "Principles," are the souls that, when on earth, are "engaged in the pursuit of intellectual improvement, or in the study and diffusion of science." Now, in how striking a light does not this place the entire question! True, it militates with much directness against the great bulk of our Scottish patrons, — men whose souls, on Mr. Forsyth's showing, could be of no manner of use in the other world, unless, indeed, the other world had its mail-coaches to drive, and its dog-kennels to superintend, and its tournaments to ride tilts at; and whose minds, as they have been doing nothing whatever to improve and strengthen them, must of necessity be thin, weak, rickety minds, disposed to evaporate in the moment of expiration. But, then, does it not make more than amends by at once clearing up the line between the rights of licentiates and the claims of the people? We can scarce imagine anything more preposterous than that plebeian clowns — poor illiterate ploughmen and mechanics — men whose spirits must wriggle in uneasy consciousness for some ten or twelve minutes after death only to give up existence forever — should be once permitted to stake their supposed spiritual interests against the well-based temporal welfare of some meritorious man of learning, who has studied his soul into immortality, and who, in following up his high destiny, may one day play somersaults in the sun's fiery atmosphere, or disport, delighted, amid glowing pumice and molten lava, in some sublime volcano of the moon. There is a flood of light cast here on the cases of Dunkeld and Auchterarder, and on the intrusions of Culsalmond and Marnoch.

We had marked several other passages for quotation in the pamphlet of Mr. Forsyth; and, from the respect which we must at all times entertain for the "ideas of a well-informed, experienced, and religiously-disposed man," may possibly again return to them. By the way, is it not a gratifying circumstance to find that the *Scotsman* is beginning to think all the better of people for their religion?—nay, that he now actually knows what religion is? There is still hope of our contemporary. He had a lugubrious article, some few weeks ago, on the damage which he has sustained in his circulation from the misrepresentations of ministers and the insinuations of ministers' wives. They have censured him as Socinian,—they have denounced him as infidel. But their hostility will now surely cease. They may be assured that he has learned to set a high value on "religiously-disposed men," and to know them wherever he finds them. With regard to the philosophic Mr. Forsyth, our reflections are more melancholy. He was at one time a licentiate of the Church of Scotland, and yet the Church lost him. There are respectable citizens of Edinburgh who have heard him preach in the West Kirk; and it is a fact, known to at least a few, that he was a candidate, on one occasion, for the parish of Liberton. But the *mortal* rabble, who have not learned to think,—the dying illiterate, born to plough and make shoes,—were unable to value him as they ought; and so, setting himself to the study of the law, and to the discovery of the true principles of moral science, the Church lost him. And, save for this untoward circumstance, this fine old Moderate of the classical model of Robertson and Blair would be now a leader in the General Assembly, on the side that lacks talent most. How tantalizing the reflection! We must add further that the perusal of his writings of remoter and more recent date has awakened in our mind a rather melancholy thought, which we scarce know how to express. "Let it never be forgotten," he says, in promulgating his discovery regarding the immortality of the great bulk of human souls,—"let it never be *forgotten*, that whatever has no tendency to improvement will gradually pass away, and disappear forever." Now, it is a solemn but not the less indisputable fact, that there has been no improvement in the writing or thinking of Robert Forsyth, Esq., advocate, for the last thirty-seven years. Nay, the reverse is very palpably the case. He writes worse, he thinks less vigorously, he has less of taste, his style is rougher, and his grammar less unexceptionable, than when he fixed the principles of moral science in the good year 1805. Alas for the inference! but we at least have determined not to draw it.

STATE CARPENTRY.

It has been remarked, that in proportion as our English dramatists sank in the genius of their profession, they made amends in some sort by becoming adepts in all the merely mechanical parts of it. If they could no longer attain to the sublime in their poetry, they at last succeeded in making unexceptionable thunder. If their dialogues were no longer easy and natural, no one could say the same of their side-scenes of painted canvas or their snow-showers of white paper. If wit no longer flashed athwart the scenes, never in any former time were their flashes of ground rosin equally vivid. If their descriptions were tame, so were not their draperies and drop-curtains. Their plots might be unskilfully managed, but their trap-doors were wrought to admiration. They were masters of costume, if not of character; and ghosts, lions, and tempests, Nahum Tates and Elkannah Settles, amply occupied the place of truth, power, and nature, William Shakspeare and Philip Massinger. The poets disappeared, but their successors, the playwrights, were ingenious after their kind.

We live in an age in which, apparently for some purpose of judgment, the more prominent actors on the political stage are but a kind of mechanists and playwrights,— men that bear the same sort of relation to true statesmen that the Shadwells and Settles of the English drama bore to its Jonsons and Fletchers of an earlier period. There is this difference, however, that whereas the playwrights were skilful after their kind, our mechanical statesmen are not. They are by no means mechanical statesmen of a high degree of skill. Their trap-doors creak in the opening; their ghosts awkwardly drop the winding-sheet in the rising; their lions betray the pasteboard; when they thunder, we detect the roll of the rusted shot in the iron kettle; and when they lighten, the rosin puffs unkindled in a cloud of white dust athwart the stage. They are statewrights of an inferior grade.

Never was there an age or country in which problems of more signal difficulty or of more awful importance rose to demand the practical solution of the true statesman than rise in Britain at the present day. The masses are sinking everywhere into perilous ignorance,— degenerating into a vast brute power, terrible of fang and claw, and more terrible still in the brute heart that is growing up within it, growling in its den in uneasy hunger, and threatening to burst out, that it may lap the blood and tear the entrails of these poor state carpenters. And lo! they are setting themselves to see whether they cannot smooth down the shag of its degenerate nature, and humanize its heart again by a scheme of Puseyite education. They are trying whether it may not be tamed into quiet and good order just by parading a few ghosts in front of it, — old, dry, bloodless ghosts of the apostolic succession, baptismal regeneration, and the real presence, — and by getting up behind these a picturesque screen of pillared aisles and transepts, crosses and choirs, organs and stained glass. They have fallen, in their wisdom, on a scheme resembling that of the ingenious breeder of live stock, who fixed bits of looking-glass in the walls of his pig-styes, immediately *behind* the feeding-troughs, that the animals within might occupy their whole minds in admiring the impalpable images, and feed, in consequence, with the quiet and profit which a state of pleasurable excitement induces. Between the two schemes, however, there obtains this mighty difference, that whereas the swine-feeder associated his bodiless images with his well-filled feeding-troughs, our less intelligent governors trust to the bodiless images alone, without taking into account in what manner the poor brute power is to be fed, or caring a farthing whether it is to feed or no. And so they strain hard in their Factory Bill to raise their obsolete images, — their old scarecrow ghosts, — things in which they themselves, with reference to themselves, have no faith whatever. But they lack the true art of the playwright; and, lo! amid the clapping of trapdoors and the creaking of hinges, the wretched design, as defective in its management as deplorable in its conception, stands palpable to all. And then, how exquisitely mean their style of dealing with the growing pauperism of the country, that frightful gangrene which is so fast eating into its very vitals! How utterly unable have they shown themselves to seize on one principle of power, — one moral element, — through which the plague might be staid! By dint of great mental exertion they have contrived to learn that sixpence of assessed money, after due deductions for the expense of collection and superintendence, is well-nigh adequate to the purchase of a threepenny loaf, and that rather fewer threepenny loaves are demanded by the hungry pauperism of the country when they are eaten in workhouses or on the treadmill than when eaten in any other way. And this is just all they know. Those great moral means of adding to the general health of the body politic, through which it might be made to absorb its pauperism, just as a sound natural body absorbs the extravasated blood and inert matter of a severe contusion, filling with life and feeling what had become dead and insensate, they altogether lack the ability of comprehending. There is no guiding moral sense within them sufficiently enlightened by revelation to lead their intellects into the right track; and so they wander blind in a perplexing labyrinth of mean and inadequate expedients.

Never, perhaps, was there a time in which the exigencies of the kingdom so enormously overtopped the capabilities of its rulers. Our own poor Scotland, in her periods of greatest difficulty hitherto, had always her great men, — rulers fitted to the time, and adequate to the work of her deliverance. She lay in a rude state when Edward I. attempted her subjugation; and it might have seemed a very small matter whether her fierce and barbarous people, our early ancestors, should have lived as the slaves of England, or have continued to enjoy the wild liberty of their half savage condition. But there were great though remote consequences involved in the preservation of her independence. She had purposes to serve in the economy of Providence which could not be effected by an enslaved province; and so, in her time of extremest peril, God called upon two great men to fight her battles, — men of that very type and mould of greatness that was best fitted for her deliverance in such an age, — iron-headed, iron-handed champions, whose very nature it was that they could neither yield nor despair. They had a long and a sore battle to maintain in her behalf; and one of the two, ere its close, fell under the axe of the headsman. But they were thoroughly fitted for the appointed work, and so the appointed work was thoroughly done. A great moral revolution drew on. The Man of Sin, red with murder and reeking with impurity, was to be struck down in Scotland. The people that had been preserved from the domination of a foreign state had now to be delivered from the thrall of a degrading superstition. The exigencies of the contest demanded quite a different kind of greatness from that of Wallace and the Bruce; and so John Knox was called forth to fight out the quarrel in behalf of the truth; and he did fight and gain it. The contest altered in its character; it had to be maintained for the rights of conscience, not with an ecclesiastical power, but with the civil magistrates. The dauntless reformer who had fought in the front of the first battle had passed to his reward, and he seemed to have left no man behind him fitted to take his place; but there was one Andrew Melville, a poor, sickly, orphan boy, attending one of our public schools at the time; and when a leader was most needed, — needed so much that the cause of civil and religious liberty seemed lost for want of one, — Andrew Melville was summoned to take the lead. And so the battle was carried on. At the second Reformation, the same want was felt as at the first; but it was necessary that the cause should prevail, and so the quiet manse of Leuchars furnished in Henderson a leader adequately fitted to grapple with every difficulty of the time, and whose extraordinary commission was at once recognized by his country. How wofully different the state of matters with regard to our governing powers of the present day! One is continually reminded of the complaint of the kelpie in the old legend, — "The hour is come, but not the man." Great exigencies have found little men to grapple with them, and in a style, of course, that exhibits the character of the men, not of the exigencies. The stratagems by which chambermaids out-manœuvre one another in the graces of their mistresses have been substituted for the large principles by which the guidance of great affairs should be invariably regulated; and questions that affect the deepest feelings, and involve the vastest consequences, — questions that can have rest on only the basis of eternal truth and justice, — have been attempted to be settled through the exercise of exactly the same kind of arts that are employed by jockeys when they sell horses at fairs. We are reminded of the text in which God represents himself as taking away, for the sins of a people, the prudent and the counsellor, the captain and the honorable, the judge and the prophet; and appointing "children to be their princes, and babes to have rule over them."

The Church question has been again brought before the House of Lords, and with just the usual result. Truly, the part taken by her Majesty's Government in these barren discussions would be eminently ludicrous were it not so pitiable. Has the reader ever seen a nervous gentleman running on tiptoe with his coat-tails tucked up under his arm, magnanimously resolved on clearing at a leap some formidable five-feet ditch, but stopping abruptly short at the edge, at once panic-struck and angry, and merely gazing across for lack of courage to do more? Has he seen him repeat and re-repeat the vast effort, and bring it in every instance to the same grave conclusion? If so, he will find it no easy matter to fall on a fitter emblem of my Lord Aberdeen and his coadjutors than the nervous gentleman. Ever and anon his lordship tucks up his coat-tails, and, taking a vast run, to clear at a bound the Church question, gets panic-struck just as he reaches its nearer edge, and, standing stock still, grins angrily across. His lordship, and his lordship's coadjutors, have not yet felt what it is they have to deal with. The steam of their ministerial Sunday dinners so obscures their dining-room panes, that they fail to see through them the religious beliefs of the country. They mark on the dimmed glass what they deem impalpable shadows stalking past, and as impalpable shadows they persist in treating them. Fools and slow of heart, who have failed utterly to know the day of their visitation! Do they not even yet see that it is not with a handful of clergymen, but with the deeply-based religion of Scotland, that they have to do?—that they have come in rude collision, in their blindness, with a principle which, in its long struggles, has been often over-borne and grievously oppressed, but never eventually over-come, and whose battles, once begun, never terminate till opposition dies?

The Church, however, should feel grateful to the Earl

of Aberdeen for the declarations of his short speech. They are not in the least equivocal. We find his lordship complaining, in his introductory sentence, of a certain existing desire "to extort from her Majesty's government, at the last moment before the meeting of the General Assembly, some declaration different from that which had been already deliberately given." And this desire, as her Majesty's government had thoroughly made up their minds on the matter, his lordship deemed, of course, a very annoying sort of thing. We find him politely adding, however, that "he had no objections AGAIN TO STATE the nature of the measure which, at a *fitting time*, her Majesty's ministers were ready to bring forward."

"AGAIN TO STATE!" These are plain English words, and they mean that what his lordship on this occasion had no objection to state was, not a new revelation of the mind of government, but a revelation which had been made on some occasion before. They unequivocally premise that his lordship's statement was but the repetition of a former statement; and obvious it is that that former statement cannot be held to mean some vague, little marked statement of some uninfluential member of the Cabinet, but just none other than the statement "deliberately given," with express reference to which his lordship had resolved not to be entrapped into any antagonist declaration. Now, where shall we find this deliberate statement? There was no allusion made in her Majesty's speech to our Scottish Church question. Her Majesty's speech was a great document, filled with quite higher matters, — matters such as her Majesty's gratitude for the Scottish lath-arches and Scottish huzzas, which arose in honor of her Majesty's last year's visit. Virtually, however, the Church question had a queen's speech of its own; and this sort of queen's speech — a public document embodying the deliberate declaration of her Majesty's government — their stereotyped scriptural canon, from which they were too good Christians to be driven, — bears the name of "*Sir James*

Graham's Letter." There exists no other "deliberately given declaration" on the part of government, to which a crown minister could refer; and our readers would do well to ponder the Earl of Aberdeen's frankly avowed resolution regarding it.

His lordship's restatement of its conditions is in a somewhat short-hand style, though not quite unmarked by the adroitness of the diplomatist. He condenses the rather tedious sophistry of the red-hair argument into a not unplausible-looking sentence, which intimates liberty of objection on the part of the people, and freedom of judgment in deciding on the grounds, on the part of the Church; with the proviso, however, that these grounds should be in every case faithfully recorded. The people may object, if they please, to the red hair of the presentee; and then the Church, should it also conscientiously dislike red hair, and so deem the objection a solid one, has straightway but to enter on its books,—"*Unsuitable presentee,—red-haired; people and we don't like red hair;*" and then—why, then, the red-haired presentee must just be content to despair of his settlement, unless, indeed, there be some hope for him in those details and modifications of the measure which the Earl of Aberdeen "abstained purposely from entering into," lest "certain persons" should misinterpret and misrepresent them. The comment of Lord Brougham on this important portion of the noble earl's speech was sufficiently emphatic. "If his noble friend's announcement was understood in one sense," he said, "it would be an utter abandonment of the claims of the civil courts, and would be calculated to excite much alarm;" but "taken in another view, it was quite consistent with sound doctrine and civil rights, and did not touch patronage." He might well have added that the Church was quite at liberty to repose as confidently as she could on the one meaning; and lawyers, such as his lordship, to seize fast hold of the other.

The Earl of Aberdeen stated further, in just accordance

with his introductory sentences, that "the broad and general principles on which the government were ready to act" were in "conformity with the declarations that had been often made by him;" and "that it remained to be seen whether the General Assembly, after what he had said, would think it necessary to secede, or to wait for the purpose of ascertaining what her Majesty's government intended to propose to the legislature." There must surely be some confusion of idea here. Had the noble earl set out by stating that her Majesty's government were at length determined to give some declaration "different from that which they had already deliberately given," — had he, instead of using the significant "*again to state*," used the equally significant "*state for the first time*," — had he said that their broad and general principles of settlement were principles not in conformity with their previously emitted declarations, but, on the contrary, principles which they had but recently taken up, — principles newly adopted by them, not the old ones, — then, on at least his lordship's showing, there might be some plausible reason for delaying the secession, just "for the purpose of ascertaining what government intended proposing to the legislature." But seeing that the principles of this prospective measure are confessedly the old principles, where, we marvel, lies the reason for delay? With measures on the old principles the Church is sufficiently acquainted already; she has seen and does not like them; they are disagreeable sights at best; and she would be but little in earnest should she lengthen out delay until the "fitting" but undeterminate time when her Majesty's government may think proper to add one more to their number. The Earl of Aberdeen's concluding remark might surely have been spared, and yet it is possible enough to find an apology for it too. "If *they*" [the Evangelical party] "did think it necessary to secede at once," said his lordship, "he imagined that they would be scarcely able at the last day to call on the God of truth to witness that they had been driven to this course by the persecution of the legislature." "When you consider," says Carlyle, in an eulogium on Cromwell, — "when you consider that Oliver believed in a God, the difference between Oliver's position and that of the subsequent governors of this country becomes, the more you reflect on it, the more immeasurable." His lordship's allusion to Deity here, charitably regarded, and taken in connection with the fact that his lordship is one of those governors, may tell, after all, to his lordship's advantage.

In shipwreck much depends on knowing the exact moment in which the wreck, fast beating to pieces on a lee shore, may be quitted with greatest chance of escape; and it requires both resolution and presence of mind to enable the seaman promptly to avail himself of it. Much depends, in battle, on knowing the exact moment in which the charge may be made with most effect. It would be well that on Thursday the Church should not linger, no not for a moment, beyond the propitious hour, within the wreck of the Erastian Establishment. It might be fatal to convert her broad, unanimous question of principle into a contracted, disputed question of time, — a question respecting an hour or a day, — a question whether the separation should take place at one instant or at another, — whether it should be an incident of the eighteenth, or of the nineteenth, or of the twentieth. It would be quite worthy of our state carpenters to exert themselves heart and soul in striving to transpose the whole matter into a question of hours and minutes, — to hold out some vague promise, to tuck up their coat-tails at the last moment, and cry out: "O, wait for one short half-week, till we have gathered way, and we shall then overleap the separating ditch, and be altogether with you." But it would be quite unworthy of the Church to suffer the state-wrights so to entrap her.

THE DISRUPTION.

The fatal die has been cast. On Thursday last the religion of Scotland was disestablished, and a principle recognized in its stead which has often served to check and modify the religious influences, but which in no age or country ever yet existed as a religion. Not but that it has performed an important part, even in Scotland. It has served hitherto to control the Christianity of the Establishment — to dilute it to such a degree, if we may so speak, as to render it bearable to statesmen without God. And now its appointed work seems over. It constituted at best but the drag-chain and the hook — things that have no vocation apart from the chariot. But the time has at length arrived in which the state will bear with but the hook and the drag, apart from that which they checked — with but the diluting pabulum, apart from that which it diluted; and so a mere negation of Christianity — an antagonist force to the religious power — has been virtually recognized as exclusively the principle which is to be entrenched in the parish churches of Scotland. The day that witnessed a transaction so momentous can be a day of no slight mark in modern history. It stands between two distinct states of things — a signal to Christendom. It holds out its sign to these latter times, that God and the world have drawn off their forces to opposite sides, and that His sore and great battle is soon to begin.

The future can alone adequately develop the more important consequences of the event. At present we shall merely attempt presenting the reader with a few brief notes of the aspect which it exhibited. The early part of Thursday had its periods of fitful cloud and sunshine, and the tall, picturesque tenements of the Old Town now lay dim and indistinct in shadow, now stood prominently out in the light. There was an unusual throng and bustle in the streets at a comparatively early hour, which increased greatly as the morning wore on towards noon. We marked, in especial, several knots of Moderate clergy hurrying along to the levee, laughing and chatting with a vivacity that reminded one rather of the French than of the Scotch character, and evidently in that state of nervous excitement which, in a certain order of minds, the near approach of some very great event, indeterminate and unappreciable in its bearings, is sure always to occasion.

As the morning wore on, the crowds thickened in the streets, and the military took their places. The principles involved in the anticipated disruption gave to many a spectator a new association with the long double line of dragoons that stretched adown the High Street, far as the eye could reach, from the venerable Church of St. Giles, famous in Scottish story, to the humbler Tron. The light flashed fitfully on their long swords and helmets, and the light scarlet of their uniforms contrasted strongly with the dingier vestments of the masses, in which they seemed as if more than half ingulfed. When the sun glanced out, the eye caught something peculiarly picturesque in the aspect of the Calton Hill, with its imposing masses of precipices overtopped by towers and monuments, and its intermingling bushes and trees now green with the soft, delicate foliage of May. Between its upper and under line of rock a dense living belt of human beings girdled it round, sweeping gradually downwards from shoulder to base, like the sash of his order on the breast of a nobleman. The Commissioner's procession passed, with sound of trumpet and drum, and marked by rather more than the usual splendor. There was much bravery and glitter, — satin and embroidery, varnish and gold lace, — no lack, in short, of that cheap and vulgar magnificence which can be got up to order by the tailor and the upholsterer for carnivals and Lord Mayors' days. But it was felt by the assembled thousands, as the pageant swept past, that the real spectacle of the day was a spectacle of a different character.

The morning levee had been marked by an incident of a somewhat extraordinary nature, and which history, though in these days little disposed to mark prodigies and omens, will scarce fail to record. The crowd in the Chamber of Presence was very great, and there was, we believe, a considerable degree of confusion and pressure in consequence. Suddenly — whether brushed by some passer by, jostled rudely aside, or merely affected by the tremor of the floor communicated to the partitioning — a large portrait of William the Third, that had held its place in Holyrood for nearly a century and a half, dropped heavily from the walls. "There," exclaimed a voice from the crowd, "there goes the revolution settlement."

For hours before the meeting of Assembly the galleries of St. Andrew's church, with the space behind, railed off for the accommodation of office-bearers not members, were crowded to suffocation, and a vast assemblage still continued to besiege the doors. The galleries from below had the "overbellying" appearance in front described by Blair, and seemed as if piled up to the roof behind. Immediately after noon the Moderate members began to drop in one by one, and to take their places on the moderator's right, while the opposite benches remained well-nigh empty. What seemed most fitted to catch the eye of a stranger was the rosy appearance of the men, and their rounded contour of face and feature. Moderatism, in the present day, is evidently not injuring its complexion by the composition of "Histories of Scotland" like that of Robertson, or by prosecuting such "Inquiries into the Human Mind" as those instituted by Reid. We were reminded, in glancover the benches, of a bed of full-blown piony-roses glistening after a shower; and, could one have but substituted among them the monk's frock for the modern dress-coat, and given to each crown the shaven tonsure, not only would they have passed admirably for a conclave of monks met to determine some weighty point of abbey-income or right of forestry, but for a conclave of one determinate age, — that easily circumstanced middle age in which, the days of vigil and maceration being over, and the disturbing doctrines of the Reformation not yet aroused from out of their long sleep, the Churchman had little else to do than just amuse himself with concerns of the chase and the cellar, the larder and the dormitory. The benches on the left began slowly to fill, and on the entrance of every more distinguished member a burst of recognition and welcome shook the gallery. Their antagonists had been all permitted to take their places in ominous silence. The music of the pageant was heard outside; the moderator[1] entered, attired in his gown; and ere the appearance of the Lord High Commissioner, preceded by his pages and mace-bearer, and attended by the Lord Provost, the Lord Advocate, and the Solicitor-General, the Evangelical benches had filled as densely as those of their opponents; and the cross benches, appropriated, in perilous times like the present, to a middle party careful always to pitch their principles below the suffering point, were also fully occupied. Never before was there seen so crowded a General Assembly. The number of members had been increased beyond all precedent by the double returns; and almost every member was in his place. The moderator opened the proceedings by a deeply impressive prayer; but though the silence within was complete, a Babel of tumultuary sounds outside, and at the closed doors, expressive of the intense anxiety of the excluded multitude, had the effect of rendering him scarcely audible in the more distant parts of the building. There stood beside the chair, though on opposite sides, the meet representatives of the belligerent parties. On the right we marked Principal M'Farlan, of Glasgow, — the man, in these altered times, when missions are not held disreputable, and even Moderates profess to believe

1 The late Rev. Dr. Welsh, Professor of Church History in the University of Edinburgh.

that the gospel may be communicated to savages without signally injuring their morals, who could recommend his students to organize themselves into political clubs, but dissuade them from forming missionary societies. On the left stood Thomas Chalmers, the man through whose indomitable energy and Christian zeal two hundred churches were added to the Establishment in little more than ten years. Science, like religion, had its representatives on the moderator's right and left. On the one side we saw *Moderate* science personified in Dr. Anderson, of Newburgh, — a dabbler in geology, who found a fish in the Old Red Sandstone, and described it as a beetle. We saw science not *Moderate*, on the other side, represented by Sir David Brewster.

The moderator rose and addressed the House in a few impressive sentences. There had been an infringement, he said, on the constitution of the Church, — an infringement so great that they could not constitute its General Assembly without a violation of the union between Church and State, as now authoritatively defined and declared. He was therefore compelled, he added, to protest against proceeding further; and, unfolding a document which he held in his hand, he read, in a slow and emphatic manner, the protest of the Church. For the first few seconds, the extreme anxiety to hear defeated its object; the universal hush, hush, occasioned considerably more noise than it allayed. But the momentary confusion was succeeded by the most unbroken silence; and the reader went on till the impressive close of the document, when he flung it down on the table of the house, and solemnly departed. He was followed, at a pace's distance, by Dr. Chalmers; Dr. Gordon and Dr. Patrick M'Farlan immediately succeeded; and then the numerous sitters on the thickly occupied benches behind filed after them, in a long, unbroken line, which for several minutes together continued to thread the passage to the eastern door, till at length only a blank space remained. As the well-known faces and forms of some of the ablest and most eminent men that ever adorned the Church of Scotland glided along in the current, to disappear from the courts of the state institution forever, there rose a cheer from the galleries, and an impatient cry of "Out, out," from the ministers and elders not members of Assembly, now engaged in sallying forth, to join with them, from the railed area behind. The cheers subsided, choked in not a few instances in tears. The occasion was by far too solemn for the commoner manifestations of either censure or approval: it excited feelings that lay too deep for expression. There was a marked peculiarity in the appearance of their opponents, — a blank, restless, pivot-like turning of head from the fast emptying benches to one another's faces; but they uttered no word, not even in whispers. At length, when the last of the withdrawing party had disappeared, there ran from bench to bench a hurried, broken whispering: "How many?" "How many?"—"A hundred and fifty?"—"No."—"Yes." "Four hundred?"—"No;" and then for a moment all was still again. The scene that followed we deemed one of the most striking of the day. The empty, vacated benches stretched away from the moderator's seat in the centre of the building to the distant wall. There suddenly glided into the front rows a small party of men whom no one knew, — obscure, mediocre, blighted-looking men, that, contrasted with the well-known forms of our Chalmerses and Gordons, Candlishes and Cunninghams, M'Farlans, Brewsters, and Dunlops, reminded one of the thin and blasted corn-ears of Pharaoh's vision, and, like them, too, seemed typical of a time of famine and destitution. Who are these? was the general query; but no one seemed to know. At length the significant whisper ran along the house, "The Forty." There was a grin of mingled contempt and compassion visible on many a broad Moderate face, and a too audible titter shook the gallery. There seemed a degree of incongruity in the sight, that partook highly of the ludicrous. For our own part, we were so carried away by a vagrant association, and so missed Ali Baba, the oil-kettle, and the forty jars, as to forget for a time that at the doors of these unfortunate men lies the ruin of the Scottish Establishment. The aspect of the Assembly sank, when it had in some degree recovered itself, into that expression of tame and flat commonplace which it must be henceforth content to bear, until roused, happily, into short-lived activity by the sharp paroxysms of approaching destruction.

A spectacle equally impressive with that exhibited by the ministers and elders of the Free Church, as they winded in long procession to their place of meeting, there to constitute their independent Assembly, Edinburgh has certainly not witnessed since those times of the Covenant when Johnston of Warriston unrolled the solemn parchment in the churchyard of the Greyfriars, and the assembled thousands, from the peer to the peasant, adhibited their names. The procession, with Dr. Chalmers, and the moderator in his robes and cap of office, at its head, extended, three in depth, for a full quarter of a mile. The Lord Provost of the city rode on before. Rather more than four hundred were ministers of the Church; all the others were elders. Be it remembered, that the number of ministers ejected from their charges at the Restoration, and who maintained the struggle in behalf of Presbytery during the long persecution of twenty-eight years, amounted in all to but three hundred and seventy-six; but then, as now, the religious principles which they maintained were those of the country. They were principles that had laid fast hold of the national mind, and the fires of persecution served only to render their impress ineradicable. We trust in a very few weeks to see the four hundred increased to five. Is it not strange how utterly the great lessons of history have failed to impress the mean and wretched rulers of our country in this the day of their visitation? Bishop Fairfoul, when urging on the act that desolated the parishes of Scotland, assured Commissioner Middleton that there would not be ten in his diocese who would not prefer sacrificing their principles to losing their stipends; and Commissioner Middleton believed him. The time of ejection came. On the last Sabbath of October, 1662, the Presbyterian ministers preached and bade farewell to their congregations; and on that day, as we find it stated by Burnet, two hundred churches were at once shut up, and abandoned equally by pastors and by people. "And never," says Kirkton, "was there such a sad Sabbath in Scotland." Great was the astonishment, and even consternation, of the government. "They had committed," says Hetherington, "the grievous error into which unprincipled men are so apt to fall, of concluding what the Presbyterian ministers would do by what they themselves would have done in similar circumstances, and saw their error when it was too late to repair it." The struggle went on for more than half an age, and terminated only when a dynasty had changed, and a discrowned king wandered in unhappiness, and begged, an exile in a foreign land.

THE CLOSE.

The Free and Residuary Assemblies have closed their sittings; the over-strung mind of the Scottish public demands its interval of rest, and thrilling excitement and incessant labor give place, for a brief period, to comparative quiescence and repose. For our own part, for at least a few months to come, we shall see the sun rise less frequently than we have done of late, and miss oftener the earliest chirp of the birds that welcome the first gray of morning from among the old trees of Heriot's and the Meadows. The chapter added to the History of the Church of Scotland has just been completed. The concluding page presents the usual blank interval; and we feel inclined to lay down the volume for a space, and ponder over its contents.

Almost all our readers must be acquainted with Hetherington's admirable History of the Church of Scotland,—our only existing ecclesiastical history that brings down its eventful narrative to times so near the present as to record in its latter pages the events which but a year or two ago were exhibited as matters of news in the public prints. The unfinished appearance of the close of this volume must have been remarked by all its readers. It reminded us always of an interesting story, with a handful of the concluding leaves torn away. It was a drama mutilated in the terminal scenes of the fifth act. The current of the narrative flowed onwards, broadening and deepening in its interest to one definite point of time, and then, like the current which Mirza saw in his vision, disappeared abruptly in the thick mists of futurity, just when the signs of some great change had increased most in number, and become most palpable in their indications. The historian may now complete his work by uniting to his concluding chain of occurrences the catastrophe in which they have terminated. The old state of things is over, and a new state has begun.

There are points of prominent interest involved in the event, which must be apparent to all. It is now exactly two hundred and eighty-three years since the General Assembly of the Church of Scotland held its first meeting, and laid down in its First Book of Discipline, and its first Confession of Faith, the truths in which it believed, and the principles by which its government was to be regulated. These embodied in all their breadth the Redeemer's rights of prerogative as sole Head and King of his Church, and, with these, all those duties and privileges of the Church's members which *his* rights necessarily involve and originate. They brought out everywhere the grand master-idea, that wherever God, as King, promulgates a law, there must there spring up on the part of man, as his subject, not merely a corresponding duty, but also a right; a duty in relation to his adorable King, a right in relation to his fellows; the duty of obedience with respect to the one, the right of being at perfect freedom to obey with regard to the others. The fogs of a dreary superstition had enveloped for ages the throne of Deity; God had been long an unknown and unrecognized Sovereign; and it was necessary, therefore, that his rights should be broadly asserted. An iron despotism had pressed upon the people. It was imperative, therefore, that their corresponding rights — *their* rights, which originate in *his* rights — should be broadly asserted also; and on this master-idea — the fundamental idea of all revelation — the Church of Scotland, in accordance with the Divine pattern, built up her Confession of Faith and her Book of Discipline. The points most prominently developed in her first General Assembly must be familiar, through these well-known works, to all our readers. Her doctrine of the Divine Headship, her doctrine of spiritual independence, her scheme of ecclesiastical discipline, and her broad anti-patronage principle, rose up in high relief. The relation, too, in which she stood to all the other Reformed Churches of the world was one of peculiar mark. Her great leader had been, only a few years before, one of the chaplains of the King of England. He had been the chosen minister, at an early period, first of a congregation at Frankfort, then of a congregation at Geneva. He had held communion with Evangelism wherever he had found it; and the Church to which he belonged, and which he led, had, like himself, her bonds of Christian communion and fellowship extended all over Europe. Wherever there existed a Church of the Reformation, there the Church of Scotland recognized a sister and ally.

Now, let the reader but compare her last General Assembly, in which Evangelism maintained its place, — the Assembly of 1842, — with her first General Assembly, — that of 1560; and we are sure he will scarce fail to be struck by the resemblance. There was not a single principle prominently maintained in the one that was not determinedly asserted in the other. It would seem as if, in completing her cycle of nearly three centuries, she had taken a few steps in advance over the identical ground from which she had at first started. Her last Assembly was just her first Assembly come back again. The doctrine of the Divine Headship asserted its prominent place, as at first, in due connection with the old master-idea that the rights of the Divine King originate, of necessity, inalienable rights of his subjects; and hence her struggle with the invading civil power, to preserve intact her spiritual independence. She asserted her discipline; and, in the due exercise of the keys, ejected and shut out of her communion the thief and the swindler, holding fast the door against the beleaguering force that would have so fain thrust them in again. She received friendly letters and deputations, as of old, from her sisters of the Reformation. She repealed the infamous act of 1799, that had placed her in a state of non-communion with the whole Christian world. And, passing upwards from the mere non-intrusion principle of her Second Book of Discipline to the free-election principle of her First Book, she solemnly avowed, with her great founders, that "it appertaineth to the people, and to every several congregation, to elect their minister." The last step completed the cycle, — it was all that was wanting to complete it; and the Church of Scotland stood once more on the identical ground from which three centuries ago her career of usefulness had begun. How exquisitely true to Goldsmith's fine simile! The beleaguered hare, when pursued by "hounds and horses," is described as "panting to the place from which at first she flew." Her course may have included many a distant track, and involved many a tortuous winding; but she dies in her form at last. Is it not a significant circumstance, that the Church disestablished by a British Parliament in 1843 should be in every respect, down to even the minutest point, the identical Church established by a Scottish Parliament in 1567? Restored in all her lineaments, she quits, just as she entered it, the asylum furnished her by the state, for the state refuses to grant her harborage any longer on the old terms; and, shaking off the dust of her feet in testimony against it, she again sets out on her pilgrimage with the same hostile world around her, and the same unchanging God above, — that world in which her Master suffered, and which he will one day thoroughly overcome, — and that God for the integrity of whose laws she has contended, and who has promised that in her hour of persecution he will be with her in the fire.

Curiously significant as this circumstance may seem, it has found in the Disruption a kind of counterpart, if we may so speak, which we deem at least equally curious and significant. Has the reader ever marked a watch-spring snapping in the centre, and the two fragments, which in their entire state formed but one circle, coiling into two independent circles, that presented to each other no point of reunion? The Disruption no sooner takes place than each, through a principle of elasticity in itself, instantaneous in its operation, is bent away in a direction diametrically opposed to that of its neighbor. And such, on an immensely extended scale, has been the effects of the Disruption in the Church. Its two parties, that for so many years formed, ostensibly at least, but one body, have no sooner drawn apart, than, moved each by its own internal principle, they have coiled up into antagonistic bodies. The residuary Assembly of 1843 has been even more remarkable than the General Assembly of 1842. It required a series of years to bring up Evangelism to the identical ground occupied by our first reformers; whereas, to throw Moderatism back to the ground which it occupied in its palmiest days — to throw it back a whole half-century — was but the work of a moment. To use the figure of Cowper, "the bow, long forced into a curve," and then suddenly released, has "flown to its first position with a spring." Is it not strange how very obviously, in these latter days, almost every form and modification of religion among us is returning to its original type? There is a resurrection everywhere of the identical bodies in which their deeds of good or of evil were wrought of old. Laudism stands erect in England, with all its rags of Rome about it, like a thief surrounded in court by the property which he has stolen. Rome herself has revived among us, and receives, in her true character, the patronage and support of the state. The Evangelism of our first reformers comes forward, disestablished and denounced, to begin among the people anew her peculiar work of reformation. And now, here is Moderatism shutting itself up from the communion of all Christendom, — recognizing the secular power as possessed of sole authority to bind and to loose, — throwing up at once the reins of discipline, — brim-full as ever of cruel pity for its erring ministers, — coarsely regardless as ever of those sacred rights of the people which originate in their duties, — true, in short, in every respect to its original type, — the identical Moderatism of the days of Robertson and of Hill. Graves are opening in these latter times, and churches are coming forth, restored to their original state and condition. What does so wonderful a resurrection portend? Is there no hour of judgment at hand, in which there is a throne to be set, and books to be opened?

How very brief a period has elapsed since the government of this country could have settled at small expense the Church question! and how entirely has it passed beyond the reach of human adjustment now! In disestablishing the religion of Scotland, there has been a breach made in the very foundations of national security, which can never be adequately filled up. The yawning chasm is crowded with phantoms of terror. There are the forms of an infidel Erastianism in front, and surplices, crosses, and treble crowns in the rear; while deep from the darkness comes a voice, as of many waters, the roar of infuriated multitudes broken loose from religion, and thirsting for blood. May God avert the omen! That man must have studied to but little purpose the events of the last twelve days who does not see that there is a Guiding Hand ordering and regulating all. The pawns in this great game do not move of themselves; the adorable Being who has "foreordained whatsoever cometh to pass" is working out his own designs in his own way. The usurpations of civil magistrates, the treachery of unfaithful ministers, the errors and mistakes of blind-hearted and incompetent statesmen, all tend to accomplish his decrees; and it would be well, surely, since in one way or other all must forward his purposes, to be made to forward them rather as his fellow-workers than as his blind, insensate tools. Let the disestablished Church take courage; there is a time of severe conflict before her; but the result of the battle is certain.

UNION AND ITS PRINCIPLES.

Some of our readers must have witnessed the singularly imposing scene at Canonmills, on the evening of Sabbath the 28th May, when Edinburgh so poured out its inhabitants to attend the ministrations of the Free Church, that the vast hall, containing with ease an assemblage of three thousand persons, could receive scarce a tithe of the whole; and when, after the building had been filled with its one huge congregation to overflowing, and many thousands had returned disappointed to their homes, such vast multitudes still continued to linger outside, that they were formed into five congregations more. Perhaps on no former occasion was Edinburgh the scene of a spectacle so extraordinary. The unbroken stream of human beings that continued to pour downwards from the city, long after a counter-current, like an eddy tide creeping along the shore, had begun to ascend, giving evidence that hundreds had been already disappointed; the vast masses that blackened the area around the building, and choked up every avenue of access; the crowds that besieged the doors; the mustering into distinct groups, as congregation after congregation was formed in the open air, under a dark and lowering sky; the voice of psalms arising from so many contiguous points, united and yet distinct, as if each of the six assemblages had been but an individual worshipper; and then, when the clouds broke and the rain descended, the perseverance manifested by each of the groups in holding its place in undiminished bulk around the preacher, like our Scottish congregations of old, faithful in times of trial, till at length the showers ceased, and the quiet of a mild though sombrous twilight settled down over the whole, — the spectacle, in short, with all its various accompaniments, formed one of those pregnant scenes which grow upon the mind, affecting the imagination more powerfully when called up in memory at an after period than even when under the eye, and that, from this quality of increasing instead of diminishing in bulk as months and years intervene, are once witnessed never to be forgotten.

Imposing and unprecedented, however, as the spectacle must have seemed, the present age bids fair to witness many such. They seem destined to form one of the characteristic marks of these latter times, in which religious questions are so fast assuming their old place and importance. The spectacle described took place, as we have said, on the 28th May. Only four days passed, and the capital of the sister kingdom became, in turn, the scene of a spectacle which, if less picturesque in its details, was almost identical in its character. Exeter Hall — a building which accommodates with comparative comfort, in its one huge apartment, fully five thousand persons — was crowded by at least six thousand; and out of the surplus multitudes that could not gain access, two other large meetings were formed. What object could have drawn together such immense crowds, — an object, says one of the speakers who addressed the larger meeting, in an explanatory letter to the editor of the *Patriot*, altogether new to the religious public? They assembled to lay the foundations of an expansive scheme of Christian union among all the various Evangelistic Churches of the empire; and there met on the same platform, for the purpose of cordial coöperation in this good cause, Baptists and Moravians, Presbyterians and Episcopalians, Wesleyans, Independents, and Lutherans. Every Evangelistic Church sent its representatives; and the absence of all representation on the part of the others served but to indicate their character. The Papist was not there, nor the Puseyite, nor the High Churchman, nor the Socinian, nor the Unitarian, nor the *Residuary*. The two extremes were wanting, — Erastianism and semi-infidelity were absent on the one hand, and superstition and priestly domination on the other.

It cannot, we think, be doubted that, in the religious world, the current has at length fairly set in in favor of union and coöperation. The Evangelistic Churches are at length yielding to the emergencies of time. During a long period of external quiet they existed as a congeries of independent states, rather more at peace, we are afraid, with the world without than with one another. Each had its own disputed rights and by-laws, — its own municipal and burghal privileges, — for which it stood up quite often enough against its fellows; and they forgot at times, in the heat of controversy, the great federal union by which they had been bound together. They differed as near neighbors sometimes differ when there is no common enemy to annoy them. But the exigencies of the time demand a wiser and more expansive course of policy. Persia is on the march, and so Athens and Lacedemon must resign their private quarrels, and arm, not in front of one another, but side by side. Hitherto the confederated states have held but their own local parliaments; we hail in the Exeter Hall meeting on Thursday the rudiments of a general congress. The armies of the rising apostasy are mustering on every side of us. A decrepit Erastianism holds the temporalities of the Scottish Establishment, not so much on its own behalf as on behalf of Puseyite Episcopacy, in the way that a guardian holds property for a minor; of the temporalities of the English Establishment, Rome, under a false name, has already entered on possession. The invading power has seized, either in its own proper character or by proxy, on the strongholds and fortalices of the country; and it is high time, therefore, and more than time, that Protestantism should be calling her war councils, and laying down her lines of defence.

The bond of union in such councils — the *constitution*, if we may so speak, of such general congresses — does not threaten to involve, if a spirit of wisdom and charity be present, any very formidable difficulty. It was moved at the great Exeter meeting, by the Hon. and Rev. Baptist Noel, that the meeting had assembled on the grounds furnished by truths common to all the Evangelistic Churches, especially on that first principle of the Reformation, "the sufficiency and authority of the holy Scriptures as the sole rule of Christian faith, and the right of private judgment," — that "it recognized as the bond of union the great doctrines unanimously received by all Evangelical Christians, such as the doctrine of the holy Trinity, of the infinite love of the Father, of the perfect atonement of the Lord Jesus Christ, of the sanctifying grace of the Holy Spirit, of justification by faith alone, and of the necessity of regeneration to a Christian life and character;" and, further, that the meeting held "the agreement in these fundamental truths among Evangelical Christians to be so unanimous in substance and spirit as to form a firm foundation for concord and union." To somewhat similar effect were the remarks of Dr. Candlish in our Free Assembly, on the bicentenary commemoration of the Assembly of Westminster, — a meeting well suited, we trust, to forward and mature the scheme of general coöperation. Though the committee appointed in reference to the commemoration contemplated, he said, a meeting of churches holding the

Westminster standards, they by no means wished it to be understood that they included in their design no other churches. Were it of a character so restricted, some of their best friends would be excluded,—such a body, for instance, as the Wesleyan Methodists. Their scheme embraced, he repeated, the whole Evangelistic Churches of Christendom.

As forming the true pale of these churches, we recognize just two barriers. There are two walls, if we may so speak, which shut in the Evangelistic bodies on opposite sides from all those churches with which they must not and cannot associate. The one, where Christianity abuts on the antagonist superstition, is the wall of baptismal regeneration; the other, where Christianity abuts on the antagonist infidelity, is the wall of Christ's mere humanity. These are impassable barriers. We cannot scale the rampart above; we cannot ford the moat below; we cannot join hands with the parties that lie entrenched behind. Does the Socinian and the Unitarian long for union on the one hand?—then let them unite with their proper congener the Deist. Does the High Churchman and the Puseyite long for union on the other?—then let them unite with their proper congener the Roman Catholic. Between these and the Evangelistic Churches there can be no union. From the one wall there stretches away a dolorous region of ice and darkness, under the polar night and polar winter of Popery, in which no plant of grace can thrive, or where, if the true seed falls, carried as if by the winds, it produces, amid the chills and the gloom, merely a stinted and colorless verdure, that speaks of but the lack of the cheering light and the absence of the genial warmth. From the other wall there spreads an arid and burning waste of fluctuating sand,—the howling desert of infidelity,—watered by no refreshing rain or by no living spring, and where, if the seed falls, it lies inoperative and dead forever. Of the *temperate* and well-watered region between, it is one's proper part, at a time like the present, to look rather to the spiritual produce than to the phenomena, if we may so speak, of its various climates. All the churches of this zone, in which conversion from sin to God takes place as the legitimate end and object of their ministrations, are to be regarded as sister churches. What, for instance, constitutes the chief bond of union between the Free Church and that body to which Dr. Candlish so directly alluded, — the Wesleyan Methodists? The fact mainly that, notwithstanding certain doctrinal differences, our common Father recognizes both bodies, by sending down upon them his Spirit, and thus appropriating in both, through conversion, a seed to Himself. God owns Wesleyanism, and therefore we own it. He owns, after a similar manner, the Presbyterianism of Scotland, and therefore Wesleyanism owns *it* in turn. And this we hold to be a simple and perfectly intelligible bond of union. It is a bond which furnishes us with the principle on which Wesleyanism, and the other Evangelistic bodies similarly circumstanced, may well join with us in commemorating the bicentenary of our Westminster Assembly. Our standards are not theirs in every respect; but if they recognize them in the main as great boons to the world, — works through which, by the blessing of God, many conversions have been effected and the beliefs in great truths kept alive, — if they look upon them, in connection with the Presbyterianism of Christendom, in the same light in which we look upon the labors of the earlier Methodists in connection with its Methodism, — then most certainly may they join us with all cordiality in our bicentenary commemoration.

The reader will perhaps forgive us should we illustrate our views on this subject by a simple story. We remember telling it once before, in a rather widely-circulated periodical; but our object on that occasion was somewhat different from the present, and we addressed a very different circle of readers. We may perhaps be permitted to urge, by way of apology, that if we somewhat exceed the conventional limits of the article-writer of the present day, we keep far within those of the article-writer of the days of Queen Anne, when Whiggism was at once elaborate and happy in the *Freeholder*, and Toryism in the *Examiner* and the *Craftsman.*

Need we point out the *rationale* of the story, or the moral which it carries? Willie had quitted the north country a respectable Presbyterian, but it was not until after meeting in the south with some pious Baptists that he had become vitally religious. The peculiarities of Baptist belief had no connection whatever with his conversion; higher and more generally entertained doctrines had been rendered efficient to that end; but, as is exceedingly common in such cases, he had closed with the entire theological code of the men who had been instrumental in the work; and so, to the place which he had left an unconverted Presbyterian, he returned a converted Baptist. Certain it was, however, — though until after his death his townsmen failed to apprehend it, — that Willie was better fitted for Christian union with the truly religious portion of them in the later than in the earlier stages of his career. Willie the Presbyterian was beyond comparison less their Christian brother than Willie the Baptist, maugre their diversity of opinion on one important point. And in course of time they all lived to see it. We may add that, of all the many arguments promulgated in favor of toleration and Christian union in this northern town, there were none that told with better effect than the arguments furnished by the life and death of Willie Watson, the "poor lost lad."

It is now fifty years since Willie Watson returned, after an absence of nearly a quarter of a century, to his native place, a seaport town in the north of Scotland. He had been employed as a ladies' shoemaker in some of the districts of the south. No one at home had heard of Willie in the interval; and there was little known regarding him on his return, except that, when he had quitted town many years before, he had been a neat-handed, excellent workman, and what the elderly people called a quiet, decent lad. And he was now, though somewhat in the wane of life, a more thorough master of his trade than before. He was quiet and unobtrusive, too, as ever, and a great reader of serious books. And so the better sort of the people were beginning to draw to Willie by a kind of natural sympathy. Some of them had learned to saunter into his workshop in the long evenings, and some had grown bold enough to engage him in serious conversation when they met with him in his solitary walks; when out came the astounding fact, — and, important as it may seem, the simple-minded mechanic had taken no pains to conceal it, — that during his residence in the south country he had left the Kirk and gone over to the Baptists. There was a sudden revulsion of feeling towards him, and all the people of the town began to speak of Willie Watson as "a poor lost lad."

The "poor lost lad," however, was unquestionably a very excellent workman; and as he made neater shoes than anybody else, the ladies of the place could see no great harm in wearing them. He was singularly industrious, too, and indulged in no expense, except when he now and then bought a good book, or a few flower-seeds for his garden. He was, withal, a single man, with only an elderly sister, who lived with him, and himself, to provide for; and what between the regularity of his gains on the one hand, and the moderation of his desires on the other, Willie, for a person in his sphere of life, was in easy circumstances. It was found that all the children in the neighborhood had taken a wonderful fancy to his shop. He was fond of telling them good little stories out of the Bible, and of explaining to them the prints which he had pasted on the walls. Above all, he was anxiously bent on teaching them to read. Some of their parents were poor, and some of them were careless; and he saw that, unless they learned their letters from him, there was little chance of their ever learning them at all. Willie, in a small way, and to a very small congregation, was a kind of *missionary*; and, what between his stories, and his pictures, and his flowers, and his apples, his labors were wonderfully successful. Never yet was school or church half so delightful to the little men and women of the place as the shop of Willie Watson, "the poor lost lad."

Years of scarcity came on; taxes were high, and crops not abundant; and the soldiery abroad, whom the country had employed to fight in the great revolutionary war, had got an appetite at their work, and were consuming a great deal of meat and corn. The price of the boll rose tremendously; and many of the townspeople, who were working for very little, were not in every case secure of their little when the work was done. Willie's small congregation began to find that the times were exceedingly bad. There were no more morning *pieces* among them, and the porridge was always less than enough. It was observed, however, that, in the midst of their distresses, Willie got in a large stock of meal, and that his sister had begun to bake as if she were making ready for a wedding. The children were wonderfully interested in the work, and watched it to the end, — when lo! to their great and joyous surprise, Willie began and divided the whole baking amongst them. Every member of his congregation got a cake. There were some who had little brothers and sisters at home who got two; and from that day forward, till times got better, none of Willie's young people lacked their morning *piece*. The neighbors marvelled at Willie. To be sure, much of his goodness was a kind of natural goodness; but certain it was, that, independently of what it did, it took an inexplicable delight in the Bible and in religious meditation; and all agreed that there was something strangely puzzling in the character of "the poor lost lad."

We have alluded to Willie's garden. Never was there a little bit of ground better occupied. It looked like a piece of rich needlework. He had got wonderful flowers, too, — flesh-colored carnations streaked with red, and roses of a rich, golden yellow. Even the commoner varieties — auriculas and anemones, and the party-colored polyanthus

— grew better with Willie than with anybody else. A Dutchman might have envied him his tulips, as they stood, row above row, on their elevated beds, like so many soldiers on a redoubt; and there was one mild, dropping season in which two of these beautiful flowers, each perfect in its kind, and of different colors, too, sprung apparently from the same stem. The neighbors talked of them as they would have talked of the Siamese twins; but Willie, though it lessened the wonder, was at pains to show them that the flowers sprung from different roots, and that what seemed their common stem was in reality but a green, hollow sheath, formed by one of the leaves. Proud as Willie was of his flowers, — and, with all his humility, he could not help being somewhat proud of them, — he was yet conscientiously determined to have no miracle among them, unless, indeed, the miracle should chance to be a true one. It was no fault of Willie's that all his neighbors had not as fine gardens as himself. He gave them slips of his best flowers — flesh-colored carnation, yellow rose, and all. He graffed their trees for them, too, and taught them the exact time for raising their tulip-roots, and the best mode of preserving them. Nay, more than all this, he devoted whole hours at times to give the finishing touches to their parterres and borders, just in the way a drawing-master lays in the last shadings and imparts the finer touches to the landscapes of a favorite pupil. All seemed impressed with the unselfish kindliness of his disposition; and all agreed that there could not be a warmer-hearted man or a more obliging neighbor than Willie Watson, "the poor lost lad."

Everything earthly must have its last day. Willie was rather an elderly than an old man, and the childlike simplicity of his tastes and habits made people think of him as younger than he really was. But his constitution, never a strong one, was gradually failing; he lost strength and appetite; and at length there came a morning on which he could no longer open his shop. He continued to creep out at noon, however, for a few days after, to enjoy himself among his flowers, with only the Bible for his companion; but in a few days more he had declined so much lower, that the effort proved too much for him, and he took to his bed. The neighbors came flocking in. All had begun to take an interest in poor Willie; and now they had learned that he was dying, and the feeling had deepened immensely with the intelligence. They found him lying in his neat little room, with a table, bearing the one beloved volume, drawn in beside his bed. He was the same quiet, placid creature he had ever been, — grateful for the slightest kindness, and with a heart full of love for all, — full to overflowing. He said nothing of the Kirk, and nothing of the Baptists; but earnestly did he urge on his visitors the one master truth of revelation. O, to be secure of an interest in Christ! There was nothing else, he assured them, that would stand them in the least stead, when, like him, they came to die. As for himself, he had not a single anxiety. God, for Christ's sake, had been kind to him during all the long time he had been in the world; and He was now kindly calling him out of it. Whatever He did to him was good, and for his good; and why, then, should he be anxious or afraid? The hearts of Willie's visitors were touched, and they could no longer speak or think of him as "the poor lost lad."

A few short weeks went by, and Willie had gone the way of all flesh. There was silence in his shop; and his flowers opened their breasts to the sun, and bent their heads to the bee and the butterfly, with no one to take note of their beauty, or to sympathize in the delight of the little winged creatures that seemed so happy among them. There was many a wistful eye cast at the closed door and melancholy shutters, by the members of Willie's congregation; and they could all point out his grave.

APPENDIX.

THE Free Church of Scotland originated in a struggle for spiritual independence. Its constituent members refused to recognize the right of civil courts to supervise its spiritual sentences. The Court of Session in Scotland decided that, as the church was supported by the state, it was under the jurisdiction of the state, in spiritual as well as temporal concerns. The courts of appeal in England confirmed this decision, after long and patient deliberation. The advocates of spiritual independence found themselves, therefore, shut up to one of two alternatives: either to bow to the decision and yield to the authority of the state, or to sever themselves from the Established Church at the sacrifice of their stipends and parsonages and houses of worship. They did not hesitate; and their exodus in a body from the General Assembly, and the organization of a new church, filled all Scotland with wonder or admiration.

They exulted in having attained spiritual freedom, though at great cost, and supposed that, by the sacrifice of support from the state, they were released from its jurisdiction. But their freedom was subjected to new perils. The Court of Session again laid claim to the right of supervision over the spiritual discipline of the Free Church. The following statement of the Cardross case, which has given rise to a new struggle between the Free Church and the civil courts, is taken from the Appendix to the English edition of this volume:—

"Mr. M'Millan, while Free Church minister of Cardross, was, under two separate counts, charged by the Presbytery of Dumbarton, of which he was a member, with drunkenness, or with being 'the worse of drink;' and also, under a third count, of immodest conduct towards a married female, with certain aggravations. The Presbytery, after hearing evidence, found, by a majority, the first count in the libel not proven; the second count, by a majority, proven, with the exception of indistinctness of articulation; and with respect to the third count, they set aside the aggravating circumstances, and by a majority found a part of it proven.

"Against this judgment Mr. M'Millan appealed to the Synod, the next highest court, who, after hearing parties, unanimously discharged the first count of the libel, and by a majority found the second and third counts not proven.

"An appeal against this decision was taken by certain members of the Synod, and the matter accordingly came before the General Assembly, the supreme court of the church. After the case had been debated at great length on both sides, the General Assembly, on the motion of Dr. Candlish, seconded by George Dalziel, Esq., W. S., by a large majority delivered the following judgment 'That on the first count of the minor proposition of the libel, the Assembly allow the judgment of the Synod to stand; on the second count of the minor proposition of the libel, sustain the dissent and complaint and appeal, reverse the judgment of the Synod, and affirm the judgment of the Presbytery finding the charge in said count proven; and on the third count of the minor proposition of libel, sustain the dissent and complaint, reverse the judgment of the Synod, and find the whole of the charge in said count, as framed originally in the libel, proven.'

"In consequence of this decision, Mr. M'Millan was suspended *sine die* from the office of the holy ministry, and the pastoral tie between him and the congregation of Cardross was dissolved.

"Mr. M'Millan hereupon raised an action in the civil court to prohibit the General Assembly from carrying out their sentence; and on an interdict being served upon that body, he was cited to appear at their bar to answer for his conduct. Having appeared at the time appointed, and admitted that he had raised the action in question, the Assembly at once unanimously passed sentence of deposition upon him. Mr. M'Millan now raised other two actions in the civil court against the General Assembly, and individual members of it, for a reduction of their sentences, and claiming damages."

In these suits the Free Church at first refused to appear as a party, putting in the pleas that in spiritual matters it is independent of civil jurisdiction; and that by the Constitution of the Church it is made a duty to depose from the ministry, by a summary process, any clergyman who applies to the civil court for redress against its discipline.

These pleas were overruled by Lord Jerviswoode, of the Court of Session, and the Free Church was enjoined to produce its Constitution in court, that the court might decide whether in this act of discipline it had conformed to the Constitution. In announcing this decision, the learned judge virtually denied the distinctions between things spiritual and things civil, and between the church as under the authority of Christ and an association of individuals formed by mutual consent. He distinctly claimed that the Free Church in its dealings with its members is amenable to the civil courts, like any voluntary association; and that even in cases of suspension or deposition for spiritual offences. The committee of the Free Church, though denying utterly the authority of the court, thought it expedient to yield to the decision, so far at least as to submit the Constitution of the Church to its inspection.

Here the matter rests for the present; but, as may readily be seen, the gravest issues are involved. If the court overrules the sentences of the church, it will virtually restore Mr. M'Millan to the ministry from which he has been deposed, and reinstate him in the pastoral connection which has been dissolved. In short, it will nullify the spiritual power of the church, and make it completely subordinate to the state. All other churches will be shorn of independence by the same decision, and the most odious form of state absolutism will be asserted. A struggle must ensue in Scotland which will convulse its social order, and array the spiritual forces in solid phalanx against the civil power; for the spiritual freedom won by the Reformation will not be surrendered by those who have been taught by their own history, no less than by the Bible, to give unto Cæsar the things that are Cæsar's, and unto God the things that are God's.

The previous paragraphs were written more than two years ago. Since that time the Court of Session, with a full bench, has dismissed the appeal of Mr. M'Millan, on certain technical grounds, but without renouncing the jurisdiction claimed by Judge Jerviswoode. Mr. M'Millan, with a pertinacity worthy of a better cause, has commenced suits against the Moderator of the Assembly which deposed him, and many of its prominent members; but none of them have come to trial, and the spiritual authority of the Free Church is, therefore, still held in suspense.

The End.

CPSIA information can be obtained
at www.ICGtesting.com
Printed in the USA
LVHW022018120422
716028LV00006B/175